New Medieval Literatures 24

New Medieval Literatures

ISSN 1465-3737

Editors
Prof. Laura Ashe, University of Oxford
Dr Philip Knox, University of Cambridge
Prof. Wendy Scase, University of Birmingham

New Medieval Literatures is an annual of work on medieval textual cultures. Its scope is inclusive of work across the theoretical, archival, philological, and historicist methodologies associated with medieval literary studies. The title announces an interest both in new writing about medieval culture and in new academic writing. The editors aim to engage with intellectual and cultural pluralism in the Middle Ages and now. Within this generous brief, they recognize only two criteria: excellence and originality.

Founding Editors
Prof. Rita Copeland, University of Pennsylvania
Prof. David Lawton, Washington University, St Louis
Prof. Wendy Scase, University of Birmingham

Advisory Board
Hans Ulrich Gumbrecht, Stanford University
Jeffrey Hamburger, Harvard University
Christiane Klapisch-Zuber, École des Hautes Études en Sciences Sociales, Paris
Alastair Minnis, Yale University
Margaret Clunies Ross, University of Sydney
Miri Rubin, Queen Mary, University of London
Paul Strohm, Columbia University
Jocelyn Wogan-Browne, Fordham University

Submissions are invited for future issues. Please write to the editors:

Laura Ashe (laura.ashe@ell.ox.ac.uk)
Philip Knox (pk453@cam.ac.uk)
Wendy Scase (w.l.scase@bham.ac.uk)

For submission guidelines and further information please visit
http://www.english.ox.ac.uk/new-medieval-literatures

New Medieval Literatures 24

Edited by Wendy Scase, Laura Ashe, and Philip Knox

D. S. BREWER

© Contributors 2024

All Rights Reserved. Except as permitted under current legislation no part of this work may be photocopied, stored in a retrieval system, published, performed in public, adapted, broadcast, transmitted, recorded or reproduced in any form or by any means, without the prior permission of the copyright owner

First published 2024
D. S. Brewer, Cambridge

ISBN 978 1 84384 688 8

D. S. Brewer is an imprint of Boydell & Brewer Ltd
PO Box 9, Woodbridge, Suffolk IP12 3DF, UK
and of Boydell & Brewer Inc.
668 Mount Hope Avenue, Rochester, NY 14620–2731, USA
website: www.boydellandbrewer.com

A catalogue record for this book is available
from the British Library

The publisher has no responsibility for the continued existence or accuracy of URLs for external or third-party internet websites referred to in this book, and does not guarantee that any content on such websites is, or will remain, accurate or appropriate

This publication is printed on acid-free paper

Contents

	List of Illustrations	vi
	Editors' Note	viii
	List of Abbreviations	ix
1	Feeling Thinking in the Old English *Boethius* *Jennifer A. Lorden*	1
2	Arthurian Worldbuilding around the Round Table: Wace's *History*, Chrétien's Fictions, and Continental Romance *Michael Lysander Angerer*	32
3	Gautier de Coinci's *Miracles de Nostre Dame* and the Powers of Olfaction *Henry Ravenhall*	60
4	Obscured by Smoke: Occluded Sight as Epistemological Crisis in Eyewitness Narratives of the 1241–2 Mongol Invasions *Misho Ishikawa*	101
5	Richard de Bury's *Philobiblon*, *Translatio Studii et Imperii*, and the Anglo-French Cultural Politics of the Fourteenth Century *Emma-Catherine Wilson*	133
6	Margery Kempe's Penitential Credit *Nancy Haijing Jiang*	168
7	Books, Translation, and Multilingualism in Late Medieval Calais *J.R. Mattison*	199

Illustrations

Gautier de Coinci's *Miracles de Nostre Dame* and the Powers of Olfaction, Henry Ravenhall

3.1 The opening of Saint Leocadia's fragrant tomb (1 Mir. 11). Paris, BnF, MS fr. 22928, fol. 57v (c. 1300). Source: <Gallica.bnf.fr>/BnF. Reproduced with permission from the Bibliothèque nationale de France. 79

3.2 Opening page of 1 Mir. 44 in Besançon, Bibliothèque municipale, MS 551, fol. 82r (c. 1275–1300). Source: <memoirevive.besancon.fr>. Reproduced with permission from the Bibliothèque municipale de Besançon. 81

3.3 An intercolumnar thief points to the O of *Odor*. Besançon, Bibliothèque municipale, MS 551, fol. 82r (c. 1275–1300), detail. Source: <memoirevive.besancon.fr>. Reproduced with permission from the Bibliothèque municipale de Besançon. 82

3.4 The loss, recovery, and celebration of Saint Leocadia's relics (1 Mir. 44). Paris, BnF, MS fr. 22928, fol. 147v (c. 1300). Source: <Gallica.bnf.fr>/BnF. Reproduced with permission from the Bibliothèque nationale de France. 87

3.5 The cured sacristan. Paris, BnF, MS fr. 25532, fol. 66r (c. 1270–80). Reproduced with permission from the Bibliothèque nationale de France. 91

Obscured by Smoke: Occluded Sight as Epistemological Crisis in Eyewitness Narratives of the 1241–2 Mongol Invasions, Misho Ishikawa

4.1 A Mongol rider spearing two fallen, unarmed figures. The Parker Library, Corpus Christi College, Cambridge, MS 16ii, fol. 145r, reproduced by kind permission. 128

ILLUSTRATIONS vii

4.2 Mongol figures roasting and eating human flesh. The Parker Library, Corpus Christi College, Cambridge, MS 16ii, fol. 167r, reproduced by kind permission. 130

Books, Translation, and Multilingualism in Late Medieval Calais, J.R. Mattison

7.1 The opening page of a Middle English *Secretum secretorum* with a rebus for the Whetehill family of Calais. Oxford, University College, MS 85, p. 70. Reproduced by kind permission of The Master and Fellows of University College Oxford. 201

7.2 An unusual full-page initial with an aphoristic saying in a manuscript of *Ponthus et Sidoine*. Cambridge, University Library, MS Ff.3.31, fol. 88r. Reproduced by kind permission of the Syndics of Cambridge University Library. 215

7.3 The opening page of a Middle English translation of Alain Chartier's *Quadriologue invectif* with the wheat hill design and the motto 'oublier ne doy'. Oxford, University College, MS 85, p. 1. Reproduced by kind permission of The Master and Fellows of University College Oxford. 220

7.4 A page from *Le Livre des histoires du miroer du monde* with wheat hill design accompanied by a ragged staff. Paris, BnF, MS fr. 328, fol. 8r. Source: <gallica.bnf.fr>/BnF. Reproduced with permission from the Bibliothèque nationale de France. 240

The editors, contributors, and publisher are grateful to all the institutions and persons listed for permission to reproduce the materials in which they hold copyright. Every effort has been made to trace the copyright holders; apologies are offered for any omission, and the publisher will be pleased to add any necessary acknowledgement in subsequent editions.

Editors' Note

This volume includes the second of two joint winners of the inaugural *New Medieval Literatures* (*NML*) Scholars of Colour Essay Prize: 'Obscured by Smoke: Occluded Sight as Epistemological Crisis in Eyewitness Narratives of the 1241–2 Mongol Invasions', by Misho Ishikawa. The other winning essay, by Bernardo S. Hinojosa, was published in *NML* 23. The Prize is designed to recognise work that contributes to a more inclusive discipline of Medieval Studies and is specifically intended to highlight the work of early career scholars of colour who are working in the fields of premodern literature, history, art, and culture. The Prize will be awarded biennially. The closing date for the second iteration of the Prize was 6 January 2024.

Entries are now welcomed for the third iteration of the Prize, for which the closing date is 6 January 2026. The Prize-winner will receive either £150 in cash or £300 of Boydell & Brewer books, in addition to publication in *NML* 27 or a subsequent volume, as appropriate. It is a condition of the Prize that the essay be submitted for exclusive publication in *NML*.

Entrants should submit their essays to the editors in the usual way, by email to the current volume editor, with an accompanying statement that they wish to be considered for the *NML* Scholars of Colour Essay Prize and agree to the terms of the Prize competition. All entries will be considered for publication in *NML*, whether or not they win the Prize. The entries will be judged by a selection committee composed of members of the *NML* editorial board and with external review as necessary; their decision will be final, and no correspondence will be entered into. The board reserves the right not to make an award should no essay of sufficient quality be entered in a given year.

All submissions will undergo the usual *NML* peer-review process, and all successful submissions will be published, whatever the outcome of the Prize.

Abbreviations

AND	*Anglo-Norman Dictionary (AND2 Online Edition)* <https://anglo-norman.net>
BL	British Library, London
BnF	Bibliothèque nationale de France, Paris
BodL	Bodleian Library, Oxford
CCCC	Corpus Christi College, Cambridge
CUL	Cambridge University Library
DOE	*Dictionary of Old English: A to I Online* <https://doe.utoronto.ca>
EETS	Early English Text Society (e.s. – Extra Series; o.s. – Original Series; s.s. – Supplementary Series)
MED	*Middle English Dictionary* <https://quod.lib.umich.edu/m/middle-english-dictionary/dictionary>
NML	*New Medieval Literatures*
STC	*Short-Title Catalogue*: A.W. Pollard and G.W. Redgrave, *A Short-Title Catalogue of Books printed in England, Scotland, & Ireland and of English Books Printed Abroad: 1475–1640* (2nd edn, rev. W.A. Jackson, F.S. Ferguson and Katharine F. Pantzer (1976–86)
TNA	The National Archives, Kew

1

Feeling Thinking in the Old English *Boethius*[1]

JENNIFER A. LORDEN

In book III of Boethius's Latin *Consolatio philosophiae* (*Consolation of Philosophy*), Philosophia tells Boethius that her remaining teaching will cause pain when first tasted yet grow sweet when ingested.[2] When the Old English *Boethius* translates this section, however, Wisdom (Philosophia's vernacular counterpart) adds the further specification that this medicine will be 'swiðe swete to belcettan' – very sweet to belch.[3] The metaphor of digestion extends a consideration of affective apprehension and contemplation that the text develops at some length, acknowledging that her previous, simpler teaching had been ingested *swa lustlice* (so eagerly) when her pupil wanted 'mid inneweardan mode hi ongiton and smeagean' (to perceive and examine it with the inward

---

1 I am grateful to Nicole Guenther Discenza, Spencer Strub, Katherine O'Brien O'Keeffe, and Emily Thornbury for comments on earlier drafts of this essay, and to the organizers of the conference 'Between the Lines: Discerning Affect and Emotion in Pre-Modern Texts' at Columbia University, where I presented part of this work.
2 *Anicii Manlii Severini Boethii* Philosophiae Consolatio, ed. Ludwig Bieler, Corpus Christianorum Series Latina 94 (Turnhout, 1957), book III, prose 1, section 3. Hereafter cited as *Consolatio* by book, prose or meter, and line or section number. The text reverses a biblical image from the book of Revelation, when John is told to eat a book that will be sweet to taste but grow bitter in his stomach (Rev. 10:9–10). The text puns on *mordeant* – the image is of being bitten by the very thing that one eats.
3 *Consolatio*, IIIp1.3; Boethius, *The Old English* Boethius: *An Edition of the Old English Versions of Boethius's* De Consolatione Philosophiae, ed. Malcolm Godden and Susan Irvine, 2 vols (Oxford, 2009), B-Text, cap. 22, line 26. Hereafter cited as *OEB* by text version, section, and line number. All translations my own unless otherwise indicated.

mind).[4] But where the Latin warns, strikingly, that he will not be able to perceive the true felicity while his sight remains 'occupato ad imagines' (occupied with images), the Old English names the problem not as images themselves but only 'ansine ðissa *leasena* gesælða' (the likeness of these *false* felicities).[5] In both the Latin text and the Old English translation, we meet metaphors for the affective reception of instruction as well as instruction by means of such metaphors and images, and in both, sweetness is more than a mere coating on a bitter pill – rather, bitter experience must first be borne in order for lasting sweetness to come about. Elaborate, affectively engaged metaphors and narrative exempla can thus guide the weak from error, yet as Wisdom warns, their influence over the emotions has the power to lead one astray. The digestive metaphor anticipates later figures of belching that will appear in, for example, Bernard of Clairvaux. But in context, the Old English elaboration of the image suggests that both the sweetness, and certain kinds of similitude, must persist, as the Latin text increasingly leaves both of these things behind in favor of increasingly abstract philosophy. As Mary Carruthers has argued, *sweetness* as a medieval aesthetic category denotes not an abstract concept of beauty but a 'definable sensory phenomenon', a bodily one, and one that did not necessarily entail a preconceived moral judgment.[6] This characteristic of embodied sensory experience and not abstracted, conceptual goodness made such sweetness particularly salient for the English translator of the *Boethius*. In the context of early English understanding of embodied psychology and affective apprehension, such sweetness, and the bodily metaphors that evoke it, cannot be so readily abandoned in favor of abstract philosophical attainment as in the Latin *Consolatio*. The Old English *Boethius* adds both a bodily specificity to the metaphor and a further step: the bitter will not only sweeten but transform by means of digestion, producing further sweetness.

In this essay, I seek to demonstrate that the Old English translation of Boethius's *Consolatio philosophiae* negotiates two historically specific phenomena as it adapts and extends the material of its source text: first, early English understandings of the embodied mind, and second, the role of embodied affect in devotion. The figure of belching, found nowhere in the Latin *Consolatio*, furnishes one example of the

4   *OEB*, B-Text, cap. 22, lines 18–19.
5   *Consolatio*, IIIp1.3; *OEB*, B-Text, cap. 22, lines 35–6; emphasis added.
6   Mary Carruthers, 'Sweetness', *Speculum* 81.4 (2006), 999–1013 (999–1000).

commitments of the Old English translation more broadly: the Old English *Boethius* brings Late Antique philosophy into conversation with concepts of theological and devotional thought closer to home in late ninth- to tenth-century England. Extrapolating on a digestive metaphor, it actually continues an even earlier one: when Wisdom first approaches the lamenting Boethius, she asks, 'Hu ne eart ðu se mon þe on minre scole wære afed and gelæred?' (How are you not the man who was fed and taught in my school?)[7] What he supposedly has digested defines whom he should have become and should now be. And even in this early moment, Wisdom expects what he produces from his mouth to reflect that digestion, and the song of bitter grief he has sung instead lets Wisdom down.

The figure of belching as affective response to devotional understanding itself reflects the broader devotional trope of rumination, recalling sentiments like that found in Psalm 44, 'Eructavit cor meum verbum bonum', glossed in Old English: 'Belcette heorte min word god' (My heart belches [or, simply, utters] a good word).[8] In this psalter gloss and elsewhere, the verb *bealcettan* should be understood to mean not strictly to belch, but to utter, as its secondary definition in the *Dictionary of Old English* indicates.[9] But the framing metaphor of digestion in the *Consolatio*, taken to its logical bodily conclusion in the Old English *Boethius*, makes perfectly clear that the figure of belching and not mere utterance is intended there. Rumination upon the Psalms themselves was a central practice in Benedictine monasticism: '[T]he monk was called on to feel what the psalmist felt, to learn to fear, desire, and love God in and through the words of the Psalms.'[10] While the term *ruminatio* already evokes associations with chewing and eating, the connection between its cultivated devotional affect and the very digestively specific metaphor of belching

7 OEB, B-Text, cap. 3, lines 3–4.
8 Psalms 44:2, quoted from the Vulgate; for the Old English gloss, see Fred Harsley, ed., *Eadwine's Canterbury Psalter*, EETS, o.s. 92 (Oxford, 1889), 77.
9 DOE, s.v. bealcettan, 2.
10 Amy Hollywood, 'Song, Experience, and Book', in *The Cambridge Companion to Christian Mysticism*, ed. Amy Hollywood and Patricia Z. Beckman (Cambridge, UK, 2012), 59–79 (66). For the importance of this practice in pre-Conquest England specifically, see George Hardin Brown, 'The Psalms as the Foundation of Anglo-Saxon Learning', in *The Place of the Psalms in the Intellectual Culture of the Middle Ages*, ed. Nancy Van Deusen (Albany, 1999), 1–24.

may be more readily associated with Bernard of Clairvaux in the twelfth century, whose Sermon 67 on the Song of Songs declares:

> DILECTUS MEUS MIHI, ET EGO ILLI. Nil consequentiae habet, deest orationi. Quid inde? Ructus est. Quid in ructu quaeris orationum iuncturas, solemnia dictionum? Quas tu tuo ructui leges imponis vel regulas? Non recipit tuam moderationem, non a te compositionem exspectat, non commoditatem, non opportunitatem requirit. Per se ex intimis, non modo cum non vis, sed et cum nescis, erumpit, evulsus potius quam emissus. Tamen odorem portat ructus, quandoque bonum, quandoque malum, pro vasorum, e quibus ascendit, contrariis qualitatibus. Denique BONUS HOMO DE BONO THESAURO SUO PROFERT BONUM, ET MALUS MALUM. Bonum vas sponsa Domini mei, et bonus mihi odor ex illa.[11]

> (My beloved is mine, and I am his. This has no consequence, there is no prayer. What comes of it? It is a belch. Why do you seek associated prayers or solemn speech in a belch? What laws or rules do you impose upon your own belch? It does not accept your moderation, nor does it await your composition, nor convenience, nor does it seek opportuneness. They burst forth themselves from within, without your will but when you do not know it, powerfully torn out and not uttered. Nevertheless the belch bears an odor, sometimes good and sometimes bad, according to the qualities of the vessels from which it arises. Finally a good man from his good treasure brings forth good things, and a bad man bad things. The bride of my lord is a good vessel, and a good odor comes from her.)

From there, Bernard goes on to describe the sweet belches of biblical figures: Moses, Isaiah, David, Jeremiah.[12] The Latin verb *eructare*, meaning both to belch and to utter, invites some of this play on words. In his sermons, Bernard 'undertakes to recover the *experientia* – the immediacy of God – in the reading of Scripture'.[13] Belching, for him,

---

11 Bernard of Clairvaux, *Sermons on the Song of Songs*, Sermon 67, section III, in *Sancti Bernardi Opera*, ed. Jean LeClercq, C.H. Talbot, and H.M. Rochais, 7 vols (Rome, 1957–74), 2:190–1. Philip Liston-Kraft discusses the figure of belching in this sermon at length; see Liston-Kraft, 'Bernard's Belching Bride: The *Affectus* that Words Cannot Express', *Medieval Mystical Theology* 26.1 (2017), 54–72 (58–67).
12 Bernard, *Sermons*, 191.
13 Duncan Robertson, 'The Experience of Reading: Bernard of Clairvaux's "Sermons on the Song of Songs", I', *Religion & Literature* 19.1 (1987), 1–20 (2).

evokes just the sort of immediacy as this affective experience of God. Yet much the same concern with the affective experience of philosophical and devotional teaching guides the Old English *Boethius*. But Bernard wrote in the twelfth century; the Old English translation of the *Boethius* was made in the late ninth or early tenth. Moreover, the Old English *Boethius* would be read and studied in later centuries, becoming a source for Nicholas Trevet's Latin commentary on the *Consolatio* in the late thirteenth or early fourteenth century.[14] Monastic tradition in England well before Bernard already drew upon the *ruminatio* tradition, reaching back to the desert fathers and particularly to the *Institutes* of Cassian: English writers translated and versified the Psalms in the vernacular, and monks were enjoined not only to memorize the Psalms but to reflect upon them affectively.[15] Medieval writers long after Bernard, drawing upon the desert fathers, further embraced metaphors of belching and regurgitation.[16] As Carruthers observes, even Latin *sapientia*, knowledge or intelligence, comes from *sapio, sapere*, to taste – *tasting* figuratively standing in for *perceiving* in general, when perceiving is the necessary means of all knowing.[17] But Carruthers further distinguishes 'the cerebral senses – vision, hearing, and smell, all of which operate out of the brain' from 'touch and taste [which] both connect directly to the heart […] or somewhere close to it'.[18] But for the *Boethius* translator, the mind and heart are not so clearly distinguished. Situated between the desert fathers on the one hand and Bernard and his belching successors on the other, the Old English

14 On the provenance and influence of the Old English *Boethius*, see Rohini Jayatilaka, 'Old English Manuscripts and Readers', in *A Companion to Medieval Poetry*, ed. Corinne Saunders (Oxford, 2010), 51–64 (56–7); Ian Cornelius, 'Boethius' *De consolatione philosophiae*', in *The Oxford History of Classical Reception in English Literature, Volume I: 800–1558*, ed. Rita Copeland (Oxford, 2016), 269–98.

15 M. Jane Toswell, 'Psalters', in *The Cambridge History of the Book in Britain, Volume I: c. 400–1100*, ed. Richard Gameson (Cambridge, UK, 2012), 468–81 (468–70); Brown, 'The Psalms', 1–24; Francis Leneghan, 'Making the Psalter Sing: The Old English Metrical Psalms, Rhythm, and *Ruminatio*', in *The Psalms and Medieval English Literature: From Conversion to the Reformation*, ed. Tamara Atkin and Francis Leneghan (Cambridge, UK, 2017), 173–97 (193–7).

16 Eric L. Saak, '"Ex vita patrem formatur vita fratrum": The Appropriation of the Desert Fathers in the Augustinian Monasticism of the Later Middle Ages', *Church History and Religious Culture* 86 (2006), 191–228 (213).

17 Carruthers, 'Sweetness', 1003–4.

18 Carruthers, 'Sweetness', 1004.

Boethius heightens the devotional implications of its Latin source by taking part in this broader tradition of conceiving and affectively internalizing the experience of devotional matter, concretizing the figurative tradition in the context of a literal understanding of affect as a bodily state. The metaphor of teaching that only grows sweet in time associatively evokes such topoi of affective digestion for the *Boethius* translator, prompting this elaboration on the digestive metaphor as an eructation all its own.

The elaboration of embodied metaphor in the *Boethius* derives from these older traditions, read into the metaphors of the Latin *Consolatio* itself. The translation negotiates the trajectory of the Latin in light of the vernacular understanding of the embodied mind, and thus the embodied nature of both thinking and feeling. For the late ninth-century translator of the *Boethius*, affect is not, as it is in the Latin *Consolatio*, something that can be improved in order to be finally transcended; it is an ongoing and integral part of both intellectual and devotional apprehension. Many of the major changes to the Old English text can be explained by the confluence of the early English vernacular understandings of embodied psychology and the ongoing development of affective piety, a term I use here for the variously defined practices of deep emotional engagement with devotional objects as a means of more profound devotional understanding and experience. These changes include an increase rather than relinquishing of concrete exempla, extended discussions of the nature of will and the soul, and the abbreviated treatment of book V of the *Consolatio*. As we shall see, concepts drawn from affective piety and the embodied mind shape the Old English *Boethius* as it navigates its Latin source. In making these concerns newly central as they had not been in the Latin *Consolatio*, the translation displays a curious – but explicable – preference for the verse and concrete exempla the Latin leaves behind.[19]

The Old English *Boethius* helps to inform pre-Conquest devotional and philosophical thinking, and in its adaptation of Late Antique Neoplatonist Christian philosophy, it reflects early English forms of affective devotion that are in turn inflected by early English understandings of how mind, body, and soul work together. 'Affective piety' or 'affective devotion' are terms of art that predate most contemporary literary affect theory, yet they do concern the habitual yet spontaneous

---

19   Amy Faulkner has argued that the meters in particular offer 'a truly original model of the mind, in which introspection is foregrounded'; see, 'Seeking within the Self in *The Metres of Boethius*', *Anglo-Saxon England* 48 (2019), 43–62 (46).

responses to phenomena that contemporary discussions of *affect* might entail.[20] While the Latin text declares that its illustrative exempla must be superseded by higher-level philosophical thinking, the Old English apparently has more trouble with those exempla to begin with. But having struggled to digest them, it also has more trouble giving them up, or thinking they ought to be. In what follows, I consider how the *Boethius* negotiates the turn from things lower to higher across the *Consolatio*, incorporating concepts of the mind and soul current to its English audience to reconcile the different understandings of psychology and corporeality in its source. I further consider how the very figures of rumination and digestion associated with later affective piety already occur in early form in this translation. Finally, I will show how the Old English translator innovates upon the Latin original in supplying further affective figures where the Latin had left them behind, ostensibly to achieve the same philosophical and literary ends. Thus while the Latin text engages in an affective project whose culmination transcends the need for stories and exempla as it ascends to the highest realms of philosophy and knowledge of the divine, the Old English *Boethius* retains a commitment to these figures and their implications for embodied affective experience. Nor is this commitment a turn *away* from intellect – too often modern scholarship assumes dichotomies of body and mind, and of feeling and thought, that would have been unintelligible to premodern thinkers like the translator of the *Boethius*.[21]

20 The prevalent narrative of the rise of affective devotion in the twelfth century was first advanced by R.W. Southern, *The Making of the Middle Ages* (New Haven, 1953). Other accounts of this shift include Caroline Walker Bynum, *Holy Feast and Holy Fast: The Religious Significance of Food to Medieval Women* (Berkeley, 1987); and Sarah McNamer, *Affective Meditation and the Invention of Medieval Compassion* (Philadelphia, 2010). For arguments for a pre-Conquest English affective devotion, see, among others, Thomas Bestul, 'St. Anselm and the Continuity of Anglo-Saxon Devotional Traditions', *Annuale Mediaevale* 18 (1997), 20–41; Bestul, 'St Anselm, the Monastic Community at Canterbury, and Devotional Writing in Late Anglo-Saxon England', *Anselm Studies* 1 (1983), 185–98; and Scott DeGregorio, 'Affective Spirituality: Theory and Practice in Bede and Alfred the Great', *Essays in Medieval Studies* 22 (2005), 129–39. For the increasing attention to affect and emotion before the Conquest, see the essays in Alice Jorgensen, Frances McCormack, and Jonathan Wilcox, eds, *Anglo-Saxon Emotions: Reading the Heart in Old English Language, Literature and Culture* (Farnham, UK, 2015); and Irina Dumitrescu, *The Experience of Education in Anglo-Saxon Literature* (Cambridge, UK, 2018), 35–51.
21 Leslie Lockett, *Anglo-Saxon Psychologies in the Vernacular and Latin*

Rather, we see a manifestation of early English conceptions of thought that reflexively integrate, rather than exclude, affective experience as indispensable to intellectual work. This integration of affect and intellect asks us to reconsider a commonplace of religious history, by which affective devotion, evocations of deep feeling in religious experience, only arises in the twelfth century and later. The Old English *Boethius* represents a sophisticated process of adapting Christian philosophy particularly concerned with the workings of the embodied mind – which means, for its author, the workings of the affects as well.

The Old English Boethius *within the History of Affective Devotion*

The very notion of Christian *consolatio* conveys the Latin text's investment in the affective development of its protagonist. Yet while the Latin source depicts its protagonist moving beyond his emotional suffering into higher philosophical understanding, the Old English *Boethius* maintains a greater interest in the affective psychology of learning itself. The power of the Old English *Boethius* depends upon appealing to the same potentially unruly affects it seeks to direct and control. From its first pages, the Latin *Consolatio* presents a story of affective transformation toward the highest good. Although Boethius has been imprisoned by an external power, his true suffering is described in terms of his mental state: Philosophia recognizes that Boethius has turned from her teaching because of his extreme sadness, which is both cause and symptom of his trouble. The protagonist of the Old English translation similarly bemoans, 'Me þios siccetung hafað / agæled' (This sighing has oppressed me).[22] To this end, the Latin Philosophia and her Old English counterpart, Wisdom, both use concrete exempla, song, and myth as instruments to encourage the mind of the Boethius figure toward contemplation of the *soðe gesælð* (true prosperity) that will offer his only relief from suffering. In this conceit, the protagonist's affective

---

Traditions (Toronto, 2011), esp. 11–13 and 19–43. Lockett explores further influences that began to change this vernacular understanding in her later essay, 'Prudentius's *Apotheosis* and *Hamartigenia* in Early Medieval England', in *Textual Identities in Early Medieval England: Essays in Honour of Katherine O'Brien O'Keeffe*, ed. Rebecca Stephenson, Jacqueline Fay, and Renée R. Trilling (Cambridge, UK, 2022), 44–71.

22 *OEB*, C-Text, Meter 2, line 5.

state, his despairing response to his circumstance, is both true cause and symptom of his trouble.

The Old English *Boethius* is not novel in its affective investments – indeed, the Scriptures themselves already demanded devotion from the heart, and this strain of devotional thinking was developed through the writings of the desert fathers. The Old English *Boethius* represents, however, a distinctive confluence of early affective devotional tradition, early English vernacular understandings of psychology and epistemology, and a developing medieval understanding of the *Consolatio*. The translation's meditation upon the role of affect in education reveals the importance of affective devotion where we might not have expected it.

Boethius's Latin *Consolatio philosophiae* is an early sixth-century philosophical treatise written as a dialogue between its author, an imprisoned late Roman consul, and the personified Philosophia herself. The late ninth- or early tenth-century Old English translation follows that dialogue, to a point. But it also adds new verses reflexively considering itself as a translated book, introduces new metaphors, replaces much material, and ends abruptly.[23] The Latin *Consolatio* is prosimetrical, alternating prose and verse, but exists in two forms in Old English: an earlier prose text (known as the B-Text), and a second prosimetrical text (the C-Text) whose form mimics that of the original. Yet the two versions remain so similar that they may be thought of as a single project; as Malcolm Godden and Susan Irvine observe, '[t]he close verbal correspondence between the prose *metra* and the verse *Metres of Boethius* [...] demonstrates that the one is the source of the other'.[24] For this reason, I will consider the translation as a single work in what follows,

---

23 The prefaces claim authorship of the translation by Alfred the Great. Nicole Guenther Discenza argues that the explicit claim to Alfredian authorship in both extant versions invokes a specific devotional framework and cultural authority; see *The King's English: Strategies of Translation in the Old English Boethius* (Albany, 2005); and Malcolm Godden, 'Prologues and Epilogues in the Old English *Pastoral Care*, and Their Carolingian Models', *Journal of English and Germanic Philology* 110.4 (2011), 441–73; Godden has cast doubt upon the notion that the historical Alfred himself translated the Old English *Boethius* or much of anything else; see Godden, 'Did King Alfred Write Anything?', *Medium Ævum* 76.1 (2007), 1–23 (12–16); but also Janet Bately, 'Did King Alfred Actually Translate Anything?: The Integrity of the Alfredian Canon Revisited', *Medium Ævum* 78.2 (2009), 189–215 (190–9); and Malcolm Godden, 'Alfredian Prose: Myth and Reality', *Filologia Germanica – Germanic Philology* 5 (2013), 131–58.
24 Godden and Irvine, *OEB*, 1:80.

except when a significant difference arises between them. Godden, Haruko Momma, and Paul Szarmach have considered the ways that the Old English *Boethius* elaborates upon its source and freely develops its own concepts, attempting 'the first English works of philosophy'.[25] In this vein, its philosophy and approach to philosophical teaching are not quite those of the Latin original. Among other departures, the Old English translation moves from the Christian Neoplatonist paradigm of its source to more explicitly announce itself as a devotional meditation.

First, the translation recasts Boethius himself as a Christian martyr, offering a history that the Latin text itself could not have anticipated in which Boethius suffers, and will eventually die, at the hands of Theodric. While the Latin begins in the middle of Boethius's sorrow, the first chapter of the Old English B-Text explains how the Goths overcame Rome, and how their leader Theodric, a Christian but a heretical one, promised peace to the Romans only to deliver hostility culminating in his execution of Pope John I.[26] Boethius, *se rihtwisesta* (the most righteous), perceives Theodric's actions as 'þa manigfealdan yfel þe se cyning Ðeodric wið þam cristenandome and wið þam Romaniscum witum dyde' (the manifold evils that the king Theodric did against Christianity and against the Roman counsellors).[27] The metrical version of this passage in the C-Text dials up the holy drama considerably, casting Theodric's dedication to Christianity and baptism as a more recent event, at which 'Fægnodon ealle / Romwara bearn' (All the children of the Romans rejoiced).[28] He promises peace to the Romans, but 'He þæt eall aleag. / Wæs þæm æþelinge Arrianes / gedwola leofre þonne drihtnes æ' (He lied about all of that. The heresy of Arian was dearer to that nobleman than God's law).[29] The C-Text verses go so far as to assert, without basis in

---

25 Malcolm Godden, 'The Alfredian Project and Its Aftermath: Rethinking the Literary History of the Ninth and Tenth Centuries', *Proceedings of the British Academy* 162 (2009), 93–122 (122); Haruko Momma, '*Purgatoria clementia*: Philosophy and Principles of Pain in the Old English *Boethius*', in *The Legacy of Boethius in Medieval England*, ed. A. Joseph McMullen and Erica Weaver (Tempe, AZ, 2018), 53–69 (esp. 65–9); and Paul E. Szarmach, 'The Old English *Boethius* and Speculative Thought', in *The Legacy of Boethius in Medieval England*, ed. McMullen and Weaver, 35–52.
26 *OEB*, B-Text, cap. 1, lines 6–11.
27 *OEB*, B-Text, cap. 1, lines 13–15.
28 *OEB*, C-Text, Meter 1, lines 33–4.
29 *OEB*, C-Text, Meter 1, lines 39–41.

the prose version, that Theodric in fact had the pope decapitated.[30] Both versions of the Old English *Boethius* cast Boethius's struggle against and imprisonment by Theodric as a righteous, Christian cause, in a way never expressed by the Latin. The C-Text takes this further, suggesting even more overtly that Theodric's Christianity was not just heretical but recent and possibly deceptive, as his promise of peace was, with his loyalty to Arianism explicitly opposed to God's law. The added material casts Boethius, or the *mod* who suffers as a result of these events, as not merely one wise in philosophy but in Christian faith. His ongoing grief is the grief of an orthodox and devout Christian, one with proper as opposed to heretical understanding, but one whose inner thoughts have nonetheless not fully aligned with the implications of that Christian understanding. Furthermore, while both the Latin and the Old English conclude with a brief exhortation to prayer, the B-Text of the Old English in fact continues with an original prayer, representing the affective devotional assent of at least one early English reader, whether translator or scribe.[31] As Wisdom teaches, intellectual understanding alone does not suffice; only affective apprehension of teaching can lead the mind to the highest good it should have had all along.

The affective apprehension so crucial to the *Boethius*, and the *Consolatio* before it, nonetheless sits awkwardly with the lingering influence of narratives of the rise of affective piety. Mid-twentieth-century scholars like R.W. Southern and Frederic Raby located an emphasis on affect in the era after Anselm, after the rise of Franciscan and Cistercian monasticism, or after the advent of mandatory confession.[32] And although that narrative was challenged by studies of earlier devotional affect as early as the 1970s in the work of Thomas Bestul,[33] in the decades since, scholars

30 OEB, C-Text, Meter 1, line 43.
31 The prayer is included in Sedgefield's edition but not that of Godden and Irvine; see *King Alfred's Version of Boethius: De consolatione philosophiae*, ed. Walter John Sedgefield (Darmstadt, 1968), 149. I am grateful to Nicole Guenther Discenza for this observation.
32 R.W. Southern, *The Making of the Middle Ages* (New Haven, 1953), esp. 223. See also F.J.E. Raby, *A History of Christian Latin Poetry* (Oxford, 1953), 419, discussed in Carruthers, 'Sweetness', 1007.
33 On affect in devotion before the twelfth century, see Bestul, 'St. Anselm and the Continuity of Anglo-Saxon Devotional Traditions' and 'St Anselm, the Monastic Community at Canterbury, and Devotional Writing in Late Anglo-Saxon England'; DeGregorio, 'Affective Spirituality'; James M. Palmer, '*Compunctio* and the Heart in the Old English Poem *The Wanderer*',

have differed on just how much affect characterizes earlier devotional literature – Frances McCormack argues that poems like *The Dream of the Rood* evince deep sadness over the crucifixion, while Daniel Anlezark argues that the emotion of Middle English devotional lyrics is 'alien to the Anglo-Saxon elegy', and Helen Foxhall Forbes acknowledges a 'developing' strand of affective writing in eleventh-century penitentials.[34] Yet contemporary histories of compassion tend to begin with the shifts of the twelfth century. These studies document crucial changes in the audiences and aims of devotional literature, and the new devotional contexts to which it answered.[35] Yet in tracking the influence of figures like Bernard of Clairvaux, Anselm, or the institution of mandatory confession and the taking of the Eucharist for all Christians after the 1215 Fourth Lateran Council, such work has given less attention not only to the ways that these phenomena carried on monastic traditions of managing devotional affect and digestive figures for conceiving of devotional affect, but how those figures operated dynamically in earlier contexts. In the Old English *Boethius*, such figures of thought take on additional duties as they both concretize the abstract philosophical

---

Neophilologus 88 (2004), 447–60; Helen Foxhall Forbes, 'Affective Piety and the Practice of Penance in Late-Eleventh-Century Worcester: The Address to the Penitent in Oxford, Bodleian Library, Junius 121', *Anglo-Saxon England* 44 (2015), 309–45; Frances McCormack, 'Those Bloody Trees: The Affectivity of Christ', in *Anglo-Saxon Emotions: Reading the Heart in Old English Language, Literature, and Culture*, ed. Alice Jorgensen, Frances McCormack, and Jonathan Wilcox (London, 2016), 143–61; Daria Izdebska, 'Repenting in Their Own Words: Old English Vocabulary for Compunction, Contrition, and Penitence', in *Cultures of Compunction in the Medieval World*, ed. Graham Williams and Charlotte Steenbrugge (London, 2021), 27–59; and Jennifer A. Lorden, *Forms of Devotion in Early English Poetry: The Poetics of Feeling* (Cambridge, UK, 2023), among others.

34 McCormack, 'Those Bloody Trees', 160; Daniel Anlezark, 'From Elegy to Lyric: Changing Emotion in Early English Poetry', in *Understanding Emotions in Early Europe*, ed. Michael Champion and Andrew Lynch (Turnhout, 2015), 73–98 (96); Forbes, 'Affective Piety', 330.

35 See among others Caroline Walker Bynum, *Holy Feast and Holy Fast: The Religious Significance of Food to Medieval Women* (Berkeley, 1987), esp. 50–69; Sarah McNamer, *Affective Meditation and the Invention of Medieval Compassion* (Philadelphia, 2010); and Sarah Beckwith, *Christ's Body: Identity, Culture and Society in Late Medieval Writings* (London, 1993). On the importance of new orders of monasticism, see Lauren Mancia, *Emotional Monasticism: Affective Piety in the Eleventh-Century Monastery of John of Fécamp* (Manchester, 2019).

and metaphysical discourse of the Latin source, and help the translator negotiate an understanding of psychology, affect, and will foreign to the English vernacular understanding.

The text's goals are set forth in a verse preface added to the later, prosimetrical Old English *Boethius*. Emily Thornbury has argued that by rendering Wisdom's 'singing' into actual verse, the prosimetrical C-Text avoids marking itself as translation in the way that the prose had and provides for the vernacular audience an experience like that of reading a real Latin text.[36] The translator curates this experience of affectively engaged reading, offering, in the verse prologue, a justification for the verses to follow. This verse prologue explains that the verse sections of this translation will help the 'selflic secg' (self-interested man), who would otherwise be too bored or overwhelmed to attend to lengthy prose filled with abstract philosophical dialogue.[37] In other words, lack of proper affective response would hinder perception of truth, while the deployment of moving verse would make one receptive. However fictive or conventional this purported audience may be, the portrayal introduces a parallel with the conceit of the Latin *Consolatio*: that of a hopelessly terrestrial learner whose mind will be better able to tackle more abstract philosophical lessons if they are dressed up in affectively appealing verse. In this way, the verse preface emphasizes the parallel between the translation's audience and its protagonist. The preface's final half-line, 'Hliste se þe wille' (let him hear who will), echoes the biblical injunction frequently appended to Christ's parables: he who

---

36 Emily V. Thornbury, *Becoming a Poet in Anglo-Saxon England* (Cambridge, UK, 2014), 233–4. Erica Weaver suggests the two versions of the *Boethius* were received as an *opus geminatum*, or a work comprising a prose and a metrical form of the same material; see 'Hybrid Forms: Translating Boethius in Anglo-Saxon England', *Anglo-Saxon England* 45 (2016), 213–38; see also Susan Irvine, 'The Protean Form of the Old English *Boethius*', in *The Legacy of Boethius in Medieval England: The* Consolation *and Its Afterlives*, ed. McMullen and Weaver, 1–18.

37 C-Text, prose 1, lines 5–9. On the narrative voice of this preface, see Katherine O'Brien O'Keeffe, 'Listening to the Scenes of Reading: King Alfred's Talking Prefaces', in *Orality and Literacy in the Middle Ages: Essays on a Conjunction of Consequences in Honour of D.H. Green*, ed. Mark Chinca and Christopher Young (Turnhout, 2005), 17–36. On the prefaces to the translations more generally, see Susan Irvine, 'The Alfredian Prefaces and Epilogues', in *A Companion to Alfred the Great*, ed. Nicole Guenther Discenza and Paul E. Szarmach (Leiden, 2014), 143–70.

has ears to hear, let him hear.[38] For the English author, for whom the mind itself was understood as embodied rather than part of an incorporeal soul, the added bodily metaphor of hearing takes on particular resonance. The uncultivated minds in which the seeds of wisdom must be sown invoke the devotional associations of the biblical allusion and offer a devotional framework for Wisdom's work with the mind itself – the protagonist must be prepared through prerequisite exempla and exhortation before tackling more difficult philosophical questions. He must learn what he is, even though by this process he will necessarily become something else.

Yet this preface belies the subsequent text. Initially, of course, the protagonist himself appears as a *selflic secg*, too caught up in his suffering to remember lessons he already knows. Moreover, the use of poetry is not an innovation of the C-Text but a feature of the Latin source itself. Most importantly, however, throughout the translation, the Old English interlocutor, Wisdom, often departs sharply from this view of verse as bearing largely instrumental value. Throughout, the text develops an argument for the enduring value of his songs and tales in instruction, and the bodily affective state of those who receive this instruction is a constant concern. Poetry and affecting exempla seem to persist in the English adaptation because their associated affect is just as important as their effect, so to speak. At the same time, their very affective quality makes their effects unpredictable and requires they be presented to a listener who has been appropriately prepared. Such conventions are thus introduced with varying degrees of caution or ambivalence over the course of the work, yet through its increased emphasis on the devotional framework of *consolatio* and its different, vernacular understanding of embodied psychology, the translation never follows its source in fully renouncing such textual strategies or their affective power.

Thinking about the Mind in the Old English Boethius

The Old English *Boethius*, in fact, rarely refers to its protagonist as *Boetius* (sic) at all; more often, the character is referred to simply as *þæt mod*, the mind, itself.[39] Since the protagonist is usually not identified

---

38 *OEB*, C-Text, Verse Preface, line 10b. Compare Matt. 11:15, 13:9, 13:43; Mark 4:9; Luke 8:8, 14:35; and Rev. 2:29.
39 The meaning of *mod* is far more capacious than Modern English *mind*; see Joseph Bosworth, *An Anglo-Saxon Dictionary*, ed. T. Northcote Toller (Oxford,

as Boethius but as a speaking abstraction, not unlike Wisdom himself, their dialogue becomes one between Wisdom and the mind.[40] The dramatic conflict of the text, then, is one for control of this *mod*. As Wisdom puts it in the Old English,

> Ac forþon þe þe is swa micel unrotnes nu get getenge ge of þinum irre ge of þinre gnornunga, ic þe ne mæg nu giet geandwyrdan ær þon ðæs tiid wyrð, forðon eall þæt mon untiidlice ongynð næfð hit no æltæwne ende.[41]

(But because you have such a great sadness now troubling you both from your anger and from your mourning, I may not yet answer you now before the time comes, because all that is begun at the wrong time has no perfect ending.)

Wisdom first recognizes that the mind has departed from his teaching because of the latter's *unrotnes*, his extreme sadness. The mind will only be returned to proper understanding when his affective state is improved. Thus the mind's problem is not merely intellectual, and its restoration will have to proceed by stages as it is gradually prepared for increasingly difficult doctrine. For this reason, the Old English *Boethius* cannot restrict itself to explications of knowledge or tests of logic; it is deeply invested in affective persuasion as a means to higher understanding. At the same time, the ways that the text enjoins higher understanding never fully transcend the sweet stories, songs, allusions, and illustrations the Latin had considered only means to a better end, including those with no basis in its Latin source. Although in Old English *bealcettan* may mean 'to utter' as well as 'to belch', the elaboration of the affective metaphor remains clear: the image of the sweet belch envisions affective excess as productive; its sweetness is the point.[42]

1898; repr., 1972), *s.v. mod*; and see discussion of this and other terms for 'mind' in Lockett, *Anglo-Saxon Psychologies*, esp. 33, 38–9; and Malcolm Godden, 'Anglo-Saxons on the Mind', in *Learning and Literature in Anglo-Saxon England: Studies Presented to Peter Clemoes*, ed. Michael Lapidge (Cambridge, UK, 1985), 271–98.

40 Britton Brooks argues that the abstraction of the *mod* takes part in the translation's shift from a 'Socratic' dialogue to an interior one; see Brooks, 'Intimacy, Interdependence, and Interiority in the Old English Prose *Boethius*', *Neophilologus* 102 (2018), 525–42.

41 OEB, C-Text, prose 4, lines 33–6.

42 DOE, *s.v. bealcettan*, 2.

Again, in the earliest English vernacular tradition, intellectual and affective apprehension – knowing in the mind, but feeling in the heart – were not yet distinguished as they commonly are in post-Enlightenment thought.[43] As a result, the affectively engaged progress of the mind from despair to Christian consolation is digested and transformed through devotional tropes and affective associations that come with those tropes.

A major hurdle faced by the translator of the Old English *Boethius* is the concept of the mind itself as set forth in the Latin *Consolatio*. As Leslie Lockett has argued, the earliest English vernacular tradition held that the mind was corporeal, located in the chest cavity and thus indistinct from the heart as the seat of the emotions, but certainly distinct from the incorporeal immortal soul. Since it was embodied, the mind's emotional fluctuations involved physical processes of heating and cooling.[44] Lockett further argues that the Old English *Boethius* represents a disruption of this vernacular tradition, as both the Alfredian-era translations of the *Boethius* and Augustine's *Soliloquies* 'were the first texts to broadcast the concept of the unitary soul in OE'.[45] At the same time, the *Boethius* reflects an ongoing negotiation with vernacular tradition, which Godden recognizes as one that 'preserved the ancient distinction of soul and mind, while associating the mind at least as much with passion as with intellect'.[46] As Godden points out, the translator draws on Alcuin to negotiate the explanation of the unitary soul, but also mixes terminology at times, 'frequently substitut[ing] *sawl* for Boethius's *mens* or *cor* in reference to the inner self, and seem[ing] to treat mind (*mod*) and soul (*sawl*) as very closely related concepts'.[47] Following Godden, Rūta Šileikytė traces words for cognition in the *Boethius*, albeit without considering directly how affect might relate to cognition, or whether cognition takes place in body or soul.[48] Godden had noted that the Old English *Boethius* raises the status of the mind 'further' than Boethius, although the role of mind and soul were at times conflated.[49] Although Godden had considered the *Boethius* as representative of the classical

43 Lockett, *Anglo-Saxon Psychologies*, 9–16.
44 Lockett, *Anglo-Saxon Psychologies*, 33–41; 54–178.
45 Lockett, *Anglo-Saxon Psychologies*, 222.
46 Godden, 'Anglo-Saxons on the Mind', 271.
47 Godden, 'Anglo-Saxons on the Mind', 274–5.
48 Rūta Šileikytė, 'In Search of the Inner Mind: Old English *Gescead* and Other Lexemes for Human Cognition in King Alfred's *Boethius*', *Kalbotyra* 54.3 (2004), 94–102 (98–9).
49 Godden, 'Anglo-Saxons on the Mind', 276–7.

rather than the vernacular tradition, Elan Justice Pavlinich has argued that the *Boethius* adopts a 'depiction of an embodied consciousness' that 'rehabilitates [the] mind–body dualism' of the Latin source.[50] Yet the distinctions never resolve because the struggle between the classical or patristic and vernacular tradition remains ongoing in the pages of the *Boethius*, and the course of affective transformation poses a particular problem. The *Boethius* strives to reconcile the disparate classical and vernacular traditions by incorporating further bodily metaphor on the one hand and careful explanation of the workings of the soul on the other, apparently requiring the body as the site of affective transformation while never fully disentangling the body from the appetitive and rational functions of the soul. To whatever extent the translation manages to integrate or distinguish these concepts, along the way it strives to find language for the concepts of the Latin *Consolatio* without departing entirely from more ingrained and familiar English conventions of embodied psychology.

The Latin *Consolatio* offers a source already deeply invested in the affective experience of knowledge; as Eleanor Johnson has argued, the *Consolatio* 'carefully teaches its readers how it should be read and experienced'.[51] The goals of Philosophia in cultivating Boethius's self-understanding parallel the goals of the *Consolatio* as a philosophical text. Those goals and their process are aesthetic in the original sense of the Greek *aisthesis*, in that they are emphatically concerned with perception and with affective response as it relates to perception: 'Sentisne, inquit, haec atque animo illabuntur tuo? [...] Quid fles, quid lacrimis manas?' ('Do you perceive', she said, 'these things, and do they enter into your soul? [...] For what do you weep, for what do you flow with tears?')[52] Philosophia uses the verb *sentire*, entailing not only perceiving but perceiving by the senses, rather than any of a number of verbs like *cognoscere*, to know or understand. The choice emphasizes the importance not merely of rational understanding or agreement but of affective experience of the thing perceived. Boethius must *feel* that her teaching is right for it to enter his soul and, as a result, stop his flow of

---

50 Elan Justice Pavilinich, 'Into the Embodied *inneweard mod* of the Old English Boethius', *Neophilologus* 100.4 (2016), 649–62 (649–56; 658–61).
51 Eleanor Johnson, *Practicing Literary Theory in the Middle Ages: Ethics and the Mixed Form in Chaucer, Gower, Usk, and Hoccleve* (Chicago, 2013), 19.
52 *Consolatio* Ip4.1. See discussion of this passage in Johnson, *Practicing Literary Theory*, 20.

tears. Philosophia perceives through Boethius's continued weeping that his current affective state prevents his receiving her instruction fully. When Boethius has begun to improve in book III, he eagerly affirms that he has not merely received knowledge but has been deeply changed: 'Me interius animaduertisse cognoscas' (You know me to have understood from within).[53] From the opening sections of the *Consolatio*, we begin to apprehend that proper perceiving is not the passive reception of external stimuli, but an active engagement. The protagonist has simply perceived his situation incorrectly, as demonstrated by his incorrect affective state, and he may come to perceive it correctly through an appropriate exercise of his will as well as his intellect. Both teacher and pupil are active agents in this process of perceiving and shaping perception and affect in concert. Boethius, in his initial state, cannot achieve the right affective response without guidance. Thus Philosophia must work by aesthetic as well as intellectual appeals, relying on various literary devices and conventions to shape Boethius's (and his audience's) perceptions until he has advanced beyond the need for them. Affect, understanding, and the exercise of the will must work in concert.

One model enlisted to help reconcile these concepts in the Old English *Boethius* is that of the tripartite soul, in which will, reason, and affect interact with one another in the soul. The Old English *Boethius* invokes this concept more frequently and at greater length than the Latin *Consolatio* does. The translator makes extensive use of the so-called Remigian glosses that were often transmitted in *Consolatio* manuscripts, copied from one manuscript of the Latin text to another. The translator uses these glosses on the Latin text, directly incorporating some of them into the text of the translation.[54] While these gloss commentaries do cite Cassian on the tripartite soul, Alcuin's *De ratione animae* provides another readily available source for the concept from an English author.[55]

53   *Consolatio* IIIp9.27.
54   On the tradition of the *Consolatio* glosses, see Rosalind Love, 'The Latin Commentaries on Boethius's *De consolatione philosophiae* from the Ninth to the Eleventh Centuries', in *A Companion to Boethius in the Middle Ages*, ed. Noel Harold Kaylor Jr and Philip Edward Phillips (Leiden, 2012), 75–133; and Love, 'Latin Commentaries on Boethius's *Consolation of Philosophy*', in *A Companion to Alfred the Great*, ed. Discenza and Szarmach, 82–109.
55   Lockett, *Anglo-Saxon Psychologies*, 222–3. *Flacci Albini seu Alcuini, Opera omnia*, Patrologiae cursus completus, series Latina, ed. Jacques-Paul Migne, 100–1 (Paris, 1863), 101:639–50. For extended discussion of this concept and its sources in the *Boethius*, see Paul E. Szarmach, 'Alfred, Alcuin, and the Soul', in

If the *Boethius* translator struggles to reconcile the *Consolatio* with vernacular conceptions of the mind, more frequent evocations of the tripartite soul with its conflicted faculties help to yoke the Old English *Boethius* to familiar traditions of early medieval English thought.

The first invocation of the tripartite soul occurs relatively early, in the rendering of *Consolatio* IIp5.1, which opens with Philosophia's observation that her initial endeavors have begun to have an effect and stronger medicines are now called for.[56] This moment invites Philosophia to emphasize the worthlessness of insensible worldly objects relative to the inherent worth of the rational human, which the Old English takes as excuse to expand upon the specific faculties of the rational soul – 'andgit and gemynd and se gesceadwislica willa þæt hine þara twega lyste' (the understanding, and memory, and the rational will that desires each of those two).[57] The expansion emphasizes the rational faculty's role in governing the will and properly apprehending things that give pleasure. The next line calls this tripartite state a likeness of God, alluding to the Trinity and underscoring the devotional orientation of the concept.

The Old English *Boethius* offers both a second invocation of the tripartite soul and a further concrete metaphor to explain the soul in the translation of *Consolatio* IIIm9, which extols God as the creator and uncaused mover of the universe. As Paul Szarmach has observed, this section in the Old English passes over the challenging concept of the Platonic world-soul featured in the Latin, shifting instead to the marvels of the more familiar human soul as created in God's image.[58] Instead of the metaphysical focus, the focus on the human rather than the world-soul also turns the passage toward affect and contemplation, using concrete bodily metaphors to do so. Here again, the rational faculty must control the animal faculties that persist alongside it. But the passage continues to explain how the soul turns as if upon a wheel, able to contemplate things above and beneath it, and we see increasingly how the necessities of governing the soul form the crux of the protagonist's difficulty.[59] The metaphor of the wheel may have been suggested by

---

Manuscript, Narrative, Lexicon: Essays on Literary and Cultural Transmission in Honor of Whitney F. Bolton, ed. Robert Boenig and Kathleen Davis (Lewisburg, PA, 2000), 127–48.

56   *OEB*, B-Text, cap. 14, lines 76–80; C-Text, prose 7, 125–9.
57   *Consolatio* IIp5.25; *OEB*, B-Text, cap. 14, lines 77–8. See Szarmach, 'Alfred, Alcuin, and the Soul', 128–9.
58   *OEB*, B-Text, cap. 33, 215–51; C-Text, Meter 20, 176–281.
59   On the importance of sensory perception to devotional practice more

an explanatory gloss on one of the Latin manuscripts, but whether the translator innovates or follows an existing reading, we see a shift in the affective concerns and psychological understanding of the translation.[60] Rather than the cosmic world-soul that moves all things within itself, the wheel offers a concrete way of thinking of the incorporeal human soul moved by God, the sort of image or physical metaphor that the Boethius of the Latin would no longer need. God shapes the human soul

> þæt hio sceolde ealne weg hwearfian on hire selfre, swa swa eall þes rodor hwerfð oððe swa swa hweol onhwerfð, smeagende ymb hire sceoppend oððe ymbe hi selfe oððe ymbe þas eorðlican gesceafta. Þonne hio þonne ymbe hire scippend smeað, þonne bið hio ofer hire selfre. Ac þonne hio ymbe hi selfe smeað, þonne bið hio on hire selfre. And under hire selfre hio bið þonne ðonne hio lufað þas eorðlican þing and þara wundrað.[61]

(that it should always turn on itself, just as all this heaven turns or just as a wheel turns, contemplating its creator or itself or on this earthly substance. When it contemplates its creator, then it is above itself. But when it contemplates itself, then it is within itself. And it is under itself when it loves this earthly matter and marvels at it.)

The metaphor is somewhat freewheeling itself: it seems that the wheel must turn up toward heaven and then down toward the earth, although if the soul turns around itself we might imagine the soul looking inward toward its own hub or outward away from itself. But the affective orientation of the metaphor – it contemplates its creator rather than loves (*lufað*) worldly things – remains clear. And lest this metaphor has not sufficiently embodied the soul in the form of a wheel, the opening of the passage adds, without prompting in the Latin source, that 'ðære sawle þy læsse ne bið on ðam læstan fingre ðe on eallum þam lichoman' (the soul is no less in the little finger than in the whole body).[62] Although the soul does not have the bodily location that the mind does, to contemplate the soul here requires the translation to locate the soul in the body, before offering a prayer found nowhere in the Latin, for 'hale eagan ures modes'

---

broadly, see Caroline Walker Bynum, *Christian Materiality: An Essay on Religion in Late Medieval Europe* (New York, 2011).
60 On similar images in manuscript glosses, see Godden and Irvine, *OEB*, 2:385.
61 *OEB*, B-Text, cap. 33, lines 225–32.
62 *OEB*, B-Text, cap. 33, lines 216–17.

(healthy eyes of our mind) with which to contemplate the divine.[63] The soul's struggle in leaving the sublunary behind belongs to the Latin original, but the struggle to formulate the faculties as they interact in the human soul, the relation of soul to mind, and the concretizing metaphors and bodily meditations, belong to the Old English *Boethius*.

One differing invocation of the tripartite soul frames the narrative illustration of the Orpheus story, in which we are told that animals, like humans, possess the faculties of desire, *willnung*, and rage, *irsung*, but only humans also possess the rational faculty, *gesceadwisnes* (reason).[64] Reason, presumably, is meant to win out over desire and rage. But the emphasis on reason does not constitute a rejection of feeling. Again, in the pre-Conquest English vernacular tradition, in which the mind would have been understood as embodied and located in the chest cavity, the figurative division between the mind that thinks and the heart that feels simply does not exist.[65] The concept of the tripartite soul helps to reconcile the disconnect between Boethius's understanding of epistemology and the Old English text's own: while the rational faculty must rule, it does not work alone. The tripartite soul allows for conflicted feeling even in a mind with serious devotional commitments.

The invocation of the tripartite soul often accompanies further invocation or extension of likenesses, concrete metaphors to illustrate affective concepts. An added, simple illustration provoking reflection upon the concerted workings of affect, perception, and the will occurs in chapter 24 of the B-Text, which adds an analogy whereby all natural things seeking the ultimate good are likened to all streams seeking the sea.[66] Mortals who attempt to seek the good through worldly vanities are amusingly compared to a drunken man who fully desires to return to his home but cannot figure out how to get there.[67] Here, the intent

---

63 *OEB*, B-Text, cap. 33, line 244. On this metaphor, see Miranda Wilcox, 'Alfred's Epistemological Metaphors: "Eagan Modes" and "Scip Modes"', *Anglo-Saxon England* 35 (2006), 179–217.

64 *OEB*, B-Text, cap. 33, 215–23. These explanations also appear to lean heavily on the glosses, see discussion in *OEB*, 2:384–5.

65 Leslie Lockett, 'The Limited Role of the Brain in Mental and Emotional Activity according to Anglo-Saxon Medical Learning', in *Anglo-Saxon Emotions: Reading the Heart in Old English Language, Literature, and Culture*, ed. Alice Jorgensen, Frances McCormack, and Jonathan Wilcox (Farnham, UK, 2015), 35–51 (36–7).

66 *OEB*, B-Text, cap. 24, 19–23.

67 *OEB*, B-Text, cap. 24, lines 89–93. Compare *Consolatio* IIIp2.13.

of one's *ingeþanc*, the state of the interior mind, is a more important metric of the good or evil of one's pursuits than proper knowledge. The 'hehste god' (highest good) pursued earnestly thus represents a crucial way in which the Old English links the rational and affective elements of perception, and, in some cases, prioritizes correct affective disposition even above correct knowledge in a way that its source does not.

The Old English *Boethius*'s explanation of this apparently simple illustration leads to a complicated theorization of how such illustrations work upon the will and how the will itself works. The translation places enduring, insistent emphasis on the primacy of the will:

> Ðe þe wille fullice anweald agan, he sceal tiligan ærest þæt he hæbbe anweald his agenes modes, and ne sie to ungerisenlice underðeod his unþeawum, and ado of his mode ungerisenlice ymbhogan, and forlæte þa seofunga his eormþa.[68]

(He that would fully possess power, he shall first strive that he may have power over his own mind, and not be dishonorably enthralled to his sins, and banish dishonorable cares from his mind, and leave off sighing for his miseries.)

Not only does fully possessing *anweald* (power) entail possessing control over the mind, but that control over the mind – and the resistance to sin thereby entailed – form a prerequisite to truly possessing other kinds of power. Although the emphasis on affective orientation comes first, this section makes explicit a connection that has been hinted at throughout the Old English *Boethius* – that while power in itself offers no freedom from suffering, it is not entirely to be despised, although it requires an affective state free of 'sighing' for present miseries. Such affective dynamics become more, and not less, important as the Old English *Boethius* moves to far more complicated teachings concerning the operation of the will. In chapter 36, in the context of a discourse on the problem of evil, Wisdom declares that not only is goodness its own reward and evil its own punishment, but that evil does not, as it often appears to do, ever succeed over the good:

> Ic nat nu þeah ðu wille cweþan þæt ða godan onginnon hwilum þæt hi ne magon forðbringan ac ic cweðe þæt hi hit bringað simle forð. Þeah hi þæt weorc ne mægen fulfremman, hi habbað þeah fullne willan,

---

68   *OEB*, B-Text, cap. 29, lines 78–81.

and se untweofealda willa bioð to tellenne for fullfremod weorc [...]. Ðeah willað þa yfelan wyrcan þæt þæt hi lyst, þeah hit nu ne sie nyt; ne forleosað hi eac þone willan ac habbað his wite [...]. Forþy hi ne magon begitan þæt god þæt hi willniað, forþy hi hit þurh þone willan secað, nallas þurh rihtne weg.[69]

(I do not know whether you wish to say that the good at times begin what they may not bring forth, but I would say that they always bring it forth. Though they may not fully perform that work, they nevertheless have complete will, and the undivided will is to be accounted for a fully performed work. [...] Though the evil desire to accomplish what they desire, nevertheless it now may not be any use, nor do they lose also that [evil] will but have punishment for it [...]. Therefore they may not receive the good that they desire, because they seek it through that will, and not at all through the right way.)

The Latin argues at this point that since everyone desires the good, only the good may obtain the good – therefore whatever the evil obtain can never be the good, and the evil thus never obtain what they seek and are weaker than the good. But the Old English extrapolates upon this, shifting from obtaining the good to committing good acts, while further arguing that the necessity of actually accomplishing a good act falls away: the orientation of the will alone suffices. Proper affect and orientation render the desired effect merely redundant. The equal and opposite holds true as well: it is not, as in the Latin, that the evil are weaker because they cannot obtain the good, but that the evil deserve punishment for their evil will whether or not they are able to carry it out. Momma argues that added material in this section of the Old English *Boethius* 'not only gives an internally cohesive argument but also presents the author's own view on the ethics of punishment, man and his fate, and the pursuit of philosophy'.[70] Even foolishness, here, is due to the evil volition of the wicked, who do not merely have foolishness thrust upon them but apparently have agency in retaining that state: 'Hwi geþafiað hi þæt hi bioð dysige? Hwy nyllað hi spyrigan æfter cræftum and æfter wisdome?' (Why do they consent to be foolish? Why will they not seek after virtues and after wisdom?)[71] The Old English *Boethius* in taking a more drastic turn inward, to the practical implications of

---

69 *OEB*, B-Text, cap. 29, lines 210–22; *Consolatio* IVp2.
70 Momma, 'Purgatoria clementia', 55; see also 58–62.
71 *OEB*, B-Text, cap. 29, lines 155–7.

inward thought and desire, also takes a logical next step from the Latin source, continuing the translation's elaboration upon psychology and affect as it moves into ever more abstract philosophical arguments. We glimpse the primacy of affective orientation in the discussion of will in prose 32, in which willing a good behavior is just as good as carrying it out. The understanding of will suggests not merely the intellectual decision to take an action, but an affective assent that it should be carried out, whatever the practical effect may be. This dynamic interaction between affect and will recalls Godden's observation that mental states are expressed in Old English with the verb *niman*, to take, rather than any verb meaning 'to feel' or 'to perceive' as in modern English.[72] Controlling one's affective orientation, then, would be one manifestation of controlling one's behavior. As Katherine O'Brien O'Keeffe has described, early medieval writers understood the obedient operation of the will not merely as a matter of action undertaken but one of internal disposition.[73] As mental states are conceived of as active rather than passive phenomena, a corresponding understanding emerges that control of one's affective state attends the control of the will, and that such affective control matters as much as control of one's actions.

The Bitter and the Sweet

Metaphor usefully illustrates abstract concepts in the Old English *Boethius*, but an intellectual understanding will not be sufficient to the mind's restoration, which requires its affective embrace. Abstract philosophy works with the stories and verse to prepare the mind for further abstraction, but the latter are not mere illustrations or glosses of difficult ideas. Wisdom's true obstacle is not the mind's misunderstanding, but its despair, and the mind's affective orientation toward teaching motivates his project. Over much of their dialogue, then, Wisdom thus uses stories, songs, and narrative exempla to encourage the mind's identification with lasting goodness and to justify – and thereby soften – present sorrows, which are themselves instrumental to the mind's perceiving true goodness.

The Boethius of the Latin *Consolatio*, however, possesses a greater suspicion of sweet words than his Old English counterpart. Beginning

---

72 Godden, 'Anglo-Saxons on the Mind', 286.
73 Katherine O'Brien O'Keeffe, *Stealing Obedience: Narratives of Agency and Identity in Later Anglo-Saxon England* (Toronto, 2012), 18–21.

in *Consolatio* IIp2, for example, Philosophia presents Boethius with hypothetical arguments that Fortune might use to defend herself against Boethius's claims of her ill use of him. Famously, the personified *Fortuna* describes the wheel upon which she raises men up and returns them right back down to earth again, pointing out that nothing Boethius has lost was really his but was properly hers to give and take; further, she invokes the rise and fall of kings to remind him that he should have known already how Fortune works. When asked how he might reply to such reasonable defenses, Boethius, in the Latin, replies that her argument has not altered his suffering:

> Speciosa quidem ista sunt, inquam, oblitaque rhetoricae ac musicae melle dulcedinis tum tantum cum audiuntur oblectant, sed miseris malorum altior sensus est; itaque cum haec auribus insonare desierint insitus animum maeror praegrauat.

> (Those are specious indeed, I said, and smeared in the sweet honey of rhetoric and music they please so greatly while they are heard, but for the wretched there is a deeper sense of his troubles, such that when these things cease to sound in the ears, deep sadness oppresses the soul.)

And Philosophia replies:

> Ita est, inquit; haec enim nondum morbi tui remedia, sed adhuc contumacis adversum curationem doloris fomenta quaedam sunt.[74]

> (It is thus, she said, for these in fact are not yet the remedy for your sickness, but certain poultices for your pain that is yet unyielding to its cure.)

Philosophia here acknowledges Boethius's suspicions of her producing sweet specious arguments but rebukes him for ever having mistaken them for the true *remedia* for his affliction, rather than a poultice to prepare him for more intensive treatment. While the lingering deep sadness, *insitus maeror*, usefully tells him that he has not been cured yet, this turns out to be the lingering of the previous pain that had obscured his understanding and delayed her ability to apply the true remedy. In this case, negative affect bears limited usefulness because it still obscures his understanding, but simply eliminating it will not be the *remedia* that will ultimately free Boethius from suffering.

---

74 *Consolatio* IIp3.2–3.

By contrast, the mind in the Old English translation offers no critique whatsoever of Wisdom's sweet rhetorical questions or narrative exempla, and more readily attributes its poor affective state to its own mistakes:

> Þa cwæð þæt mod. Ic me ongite æghwonan scyldigne, ac ic eom mid þæs laþes sare swa swiðe ofðrycced þæt ic inc geandwyrdan ne mæg. Ða cwæð se wisdom eft. Þæt is nu git þinre unrihtwisnesse þæt þu eart fullneah forþoht. Ac ic nolde þæt þu þe forþohtest. Ac ic wolde þæt þe sceamode swelces gedwolan, forðam se se ðe hine forþencð se bið ormod, ac se se þe hine sceamað se bið on hreowsunga.[75]

(Then that mind said, 'I perceive myself to be guilty in every way, but I am so greatly oppressed by the pain of the injury that I may not answer you.' Then Wisdom said in turn, 'That is still part of your iniquity that you are almost totally despairing. But I did not want you to despair. But I wished that you should be ashamed of such error, because he who despairs is hopeless, but he who is ashamed of himself is penitent.')

Gone entirely from the Old English translation are the interrogation of artful rhetoric and the similarly artful critique of honeyed sweetness, not to mention Boethius's assertion that such sweetness might fade shortly after it has been taken in. *Hreowsung* (repentance) relates to the verb *hreowsian* (to grieve or bewail), and the shift in affective state from sorrow for worldly circumstance to grief at the mind's iniquity signals the shift toward the next stage of instruction, rather than the impatience with honeyed rhetoric in the Latin.[76] As Godden and Irvine point out, the Old English here seems to simply echo material from the previous chapter to avoid confusing the argument.[77] But the Old English also acquires overt devotional connotations, and Wisdom's rhetoric is acknowledged as *effective* with its accordingly *affective* potency in this regard – the mind feels pain at the apprehension of its errors, and Wisdom begins working to turn this pain to something more useful.

And just as the artful sweetness of Wisdom's rhetoric persists unquestioned, the affective dramas of sorrow and joy are never so fully transcended in the Old English as they are purported to be in the Latin. Chapter 20 of the B-Text renders the beginning of *Consolatio* IIp8, a section in which it is somewhat ambiguous as to whether Fortune

---

75 *OEB*, B-Text, cap. 8, 1–7.
76 *DOE, s.v. hreowsian*.
77 Godden and Irvine, *OEB*, 2:285.

FEELING THINKING IN THE OLD ENGLISH *BOETHIUS* 27

is being criticized or not. In the Old English, Wisdom breaks off his singing to protest that he can barely express what he truly wishes to say:

> Ic wene þeah þæt ðu ne forstande nu git hwæt ic þe to cweðe, forþam hit is wundorlic þæt ic secgan wille and ic hit mæg uneaðe mid wordum gereccan swa swa ic wolde. Þæt is þæt seo wiðerwearde wyrd byð ælcum men nytwyrðre þonne seo orsorge, forþam seo orsorge simle lihð and licet þæt mon scyle wenan þæt heo seo sio soðe gesælð, ac sio wiðerwearde is sio soðe gesælþ.[78]

(I expect that you do not yet understand what I say to you, because what I wish to say is wondrous, and I may not easily express it with words as I would. That is, that the adverse fate is more useful to every man than the cheerful, because the cheerful always lies and flatters such that one shall consider that it is the true prosperity, but the adverse is the true prosperity.)

Many of the implications of this passage resound throughout the entirety of the text: that the mind has not yet achieved the ability to comprehend difficult doctrine, that what Wisdom seeks to express is beyond what may be literally expressed in words because of its affective power, and that bitter experience is necessary to both this affective training and to the psychological state it will ultimately produce. Paradoxically, the very thing that is *wundorlic* (wondrous) involves the apparently *wiðerwearde* (adverse) – since the cheerful fate deceives, the experience of suffering must precede the true prosperity. The Old English departs from the sense of the Latin, which simply states that adverse fate is always true – *semper uera est* – unlike prosperous fortune, which lies.[79] The Old English appears to interpret the *wiðerwearde* fate in two ways: in the first instance, the *wiðerwearde* or adverse fate is not identical to true prosperity but *nytwrðre* (more useful) in achieving that end. Yet later in the same sentence, as Wisdom explains that cheerful fortune is not the true prosperity, he states more finally, 'sio wiðerwearde *is* sio soðe gesælþ' (the adverse *is* the true prosperity).[80] As Godden and Irvine note, this interpretation has no precedent in the extant glosses, and the Old English must justify it by oddly asserting that fate is stable, as long as it is adverse. Even in this difficult passage, however, the

---

78 *OEB*, B-Text, cap. 20, 7–13.
79 *Consolatio*, IIp8, 3–4.
80 *OEB*, B-Text, cap. 20, 13; emphasis mine.

Old English hesitates to make the affective experience of fate merely instrumental. The negative must be not only endured but embraced; understood not simply as useful to prosperity, but integral to it. And so it is with the remarkable metaphor of belching with which we began. Midway through the Old English *Boethius*, Wisdom assures the protagonist that, just as honey is sweeter after the taste of bitterness, so true prosperity (*soðe gesælð*) shall be sweeter to those who suffer in life.[81] The Old English continues to expand its emphasis on how positive affect must characterize the mind's psychological transformation, as it matures and comes to embrace the more difficult doctrines promised from the beginning of the text. As the mind declares, 'ða hæfde he me gebunden mid þære wynnsumnesse his sanges þæt ic his wæs swiðe wafiende and swiðe lustbære hine to gehiranne mid inneweardum mode' (then he had bound me with the pleasure of his song, so that I was greatly astonished by him and very desirous to hear him with my innermost mind).[82] Even at this intermediate stage, the text affirms both that aesthetic perception is pleasurable and that pleasure is good for the mind, priming his innermost thought to eagerly receive instruction that he would have rejected before. Since his perceptive abilities have been strengthened, the mind no longer fears the bitter, trusting in the sweetness that Wisdom has offered to him.

This brings us to the moment in the Latin when Philosophia affirms Boethius's progress, promising that the remedies she offers next will sweeten when ingested – 'interius [...] recepta dulcescant' (grow sweet received [...] internally) – although they will at first sting when tasted – 'degustata [...] mordeant' (grow bitter [...] having been tasted).[83] In the Old English, Wisdom promises further sweetness, saying that the medicine he will administer next seems bitter at first and then sweetens (*weorodian*, to grow sweet) and becomes 'swiðe swete to belcettan' (very sweet to belch).[84] There is no precedent for this detail in the Latin, and likewise no obvious parallel in any of the extant glosses. The metaphor of a sweet affect that bursts forth also suggests the potential danger of the eruption as a loss of control, an unrestrained utterance of the kind Bernard would celebrate in later centuries.[85] Yet the remarkable

---

81 OEB, C-Text, Meter 12, 8–11a, 18–28.
82 OEB, B-Text, cap. 22, 1–3.
83 *Consolatio*, IIIp1.3.
84 OEB, B-Text, cap. 22, line 26.
85 As Spencer Strub has written, a long-standing convention of literary and

gustatory detail of sweet belching suggests a special relish in Wisdom's metaphor of teaching as a type of nourishment that may also be savored. The sweetness does not produce intelligible content; it is 'something beyond knowledge',[86] a concrete metaphor for felt experience. This is no sugared coating on a bitter pill. The sweetness does not precede digestion of nourishing doctrine, because, again, the adverse experience must be embraced in the hard truths before any sweetness may arise from them. Yet the sweetness is what remains in the Old English translation and its image of gustatory belching, exceeding its didactic requirements as lingering aesthetic pleasure with no instrumental end beyond the capacity for sweetness.

Placed in the context of the larger work of the Old English *Boethius*, the additional sensual detail, strange as it may seem, extends the positive identification with perceptual pleasure in the Old English *Boethius*. It recalls monastic traditions of *ruminatio* – principles properly ingested are not merely understood but embraced affectively, with the will and the intellect and the passions in concert. Properly directed and controlled, *wynnsumness*, joy, has improved the mind's perceptive powers – previously unable to see true goodness at all, it is now ready for higher-level teachings. But the possibility of *wynnsumness* has also been among that teaching's goals. The persistent concern with sweetness and joy acknowledges that the operation of reason, the highest part of the soul, must govern but also attend to the soul's other faculties of appetite and desire. These faculties become an indispensable asset to the mind's progression.

Sweet Endings

In the end, as the Latin *Consolatio* moves from the gentler salves of the earlier books to more difficult, more abstract philosophy, the Old English *Boethius* only partially follows. Changes made to the Old English *Boethius* reflect, of course, its broader engagement with the intellectual tradition surrounding the *Consolatio* in the centuries since

---

philosophical moral reflection 'depends on the clash between the swelling pressure of feeling and the restraint of the will'; see 'Hoccleve, Swelling and Bursting', in *Thomas Hoccleve: New Approaches*, ed. Jenni Nuttall and David Watt (Cambridge, UK, 2022), 124–41 (128).
86 As Robertson says of Bernard's *Sermons on the Song of Songs*; see 'The Experience of Reading', 12.

its composition, but they also reflect an extended engagement with vernacular understanding of the affective and embodied nature of readers' experience of learning. The figure of belching at once evinces a commitment to the lessons of instructive illustration: embodied metaphor for an also-embodied affective savoring of the sweetness they produce. The translator thus incorporates marginal glosses on the source text into its translation and supplements the source's narrative exempla, developing novel vocabulary and theorizations of what the text's embedded stories, verse, and classical references are and must do.[87] It thereby offers an interpretive translation of the *Consolatio* and reflects on the practice of reading more broadly. It does not merely translate but transforms the text, considering how its audience must affectively and intellectually respond to the philosophical matter ingested over the course of the *Consolatio*. And its conception of, and practice of, reading the *Consolatio* insist on the sweetness of the experience.

In later chapters, the Old English *Boethius* includes several illustrations absent from the Latin original – in one later chapter, the translation offers the example of children and old men who both seek worldly honor as the child plays at imitating the older man as soon as it is able to walk, as well as an example of wooden dishes being prized above gold and silver to illustrate that evil should not be prized more highly than good.[88] Even at this late stage, the Old English *Boethius* displays a desire for material illustration as its source seems increasingly willing to leave such devices behind. The translation of book V does not simply alter its sense or add additional commentary; it freely omits three of the five meters and much of several prose sections, vastly simplifying the Latin's discussion of free will and dismissing the existence of chance.[89] These thorny philosophical questions are apparently not what the Old English translation has in mind.

Instead, while the affective response to aesthetic experience proves instrumental to the mind's spiritual training, positive affect is also validated as an end in itself. The Old English *Boethius* makes persistent use of concrete, affecting songs to provide instruction that may be affectively experienced and to inspire further affective response. The Old English *Boethius* as such speaks to esteem for story and song and literary

---

87 Jennifer A. Lorden, 'Tale and Parable: Theorizing Fictions in the Old English *Boethius*', *PMLA* 136.3 (2021), 340–55 (343–52).
88 *OEB*, B-Text, cap. 36, lines 132–5; cap. 36, lines 22–4.
89 Godden and Irvine, *OEB*, 2:481–3.

form, and so too do the prose sections and the exempla they contain. The end of the Old English *Boethius* does not entail a disavowal of affecting aesthetic delights in favor of abstract intellectual understanding, but an integration of faculties that cannot, for the English text, be separated from one another. What it requires instead is a refinement of taste such that affective experience engages the higher faculties as well as the lower, in concert. Once this transformation takes place, the concrete forms of story and song become not merely instrumental as they purported to be for the *selflic secg* of the verse preface. Instead, the aesthetic plays upon the senses to provoke the affects, and this affective experience of more-than-didactic material becomes a new entry into sweetness and joy. A merely intellectual understanding will not be sufficient to the mind's restoration, which requires affective assent as well. The prose and verse of the *Boethius* are linked in their role in preparing the mind for harder concepts, but the premise underlying the dialogue is not just that Boethius needs to brush up his Plato, but that he is in despair and needs to alter his affective responses to the world around him. In other words, in this text, affect is as important as effect – in fact, indistinguishable from it. In the Old English *Boethius*, sweetness and positive affect are not merely instrumental to instruction; rather, instruction must have sweetness as its proper end. Instruction and sweetness in this conception are neither exclusive nor even fully distinct. The Old English translation hesitates to renounce the affective qualities that the Latin portrays as largely instrumental, because it understands affect to be an integral part of the working of mind and soul, and because it understands the sweetness of the belch as not mere byproduct but the experiential end of digesting wisdom. Thus when the Latin *Consolatio* departs from appeals to affect and bodily sense, the Old English *Boethius* departs from the Latin *Consolatio*.

2

Arthurian Worldbuilding around the Round Table: Wace's History, Chrétien's Fictions, and Continental Romance[1]

MICHAEL LYSANDER ANGERER

The Round Table is often described as Wace's 'most important' addition to his Norman translation of the *Historia regum Britanniae*.[2] While its origins remain unclear, it is certainly one of the most important links between the Arthurian section of Wace's *Roman de Brut* and Arthurian romance. From its first mention by Wace in 1155, the Round Table became much more than a physical object: metonymically, the term also designates the fellowship of Arthur's knights, briefly served as the namesake of a chivalric order founded by King Edward III, and ultimately came to symbolise the entire Arthurian corpus.[3] Its very ubiquitousness and polysemy complicate more detailed study. This may be why the Round Table's presence in early Arthurian romances is frequently taken for granted. Yet a comparative narratological

[1] This essay was initially written during my tenure of the Jeremy Griffiths Memorial Studentship at St Hilda's College, Oxford. I am most grateful to Laura Ashe for her advice and support, as well as to the two anonymous readers for *New Medieval Literatures* for their helpful comments. Any remaining errors are, of course, my own.
[2] Judith Weiss, 'Introduction', in Wace, *Roman de Brut: A History of the British*, ed./trans. Judith Weiss, rev. edn (Exeter, 2002), i–xxix (xxi); Norris J. Lacy, 'The Arthurian Legend before Chrétien de Troyes', in *A Companion to Chrétien de Troyes*, ed. Norris J. Lacy and Joan Tasker Grimbert (Cambridge, UK, 2005), 43–51 (49); John V. Fleming, 'The Round Table in Literature and Legend', in *King Arthur's Round Table: An Archaeological Investigation*, ed. Martin Biddle (Woodbridge, 2000), 5–30 (9).
[3] See Fleming, 'Round Table in Literature and Legend'; Juliet Vale, 'Arthur in English Society', in *The Arthur of the English: The Arthurian Legend in Medieval English Life and Literature*, ed. W.R.J. Barron (Cardiff, 1999), 185–96.

examination of its earliest appearances in Old French, Middle English, and Middle High German verse shows the Round Table's central role in the development of Continental Arthurian verse romance between the late twelfth and the early thirteenth century. Beginning with the romances of Chrétien de Troyes, the Round Table supports the creation of an ever-expanding fictional romance world, safely removed from more historical narratives focused on King Arthur himself.

In a seminal 1982 article, Beate Schmolke-Hasselmann demonstrated the usefulness of Wace's Round Table as a political symbol for King Henry II's authority. As she noted, King Arthur does not originally sit at the Round Table himself, which thus sets the king apart from his barons, rendered equal among themselves but emphatically subordinate to the king.[4] Beyond its political significance, however, this original design also makes the Round Table a potent and fundamentally ambiguous narrative device. As we shall see, Wace uses it to isolate Arthur, emphasise royal power and provide a clear historical focus. Yet by initially remaining separate from the (pseudo-)historical Arthur, the Round Table simultaneously provides a stable and effectively ahistorical point of reference for Chrétien's romances. Arthur is sidelined, and the Knights of the Round Table become protagonists instead. In Continental romance, the Round Table's narrative potential can therefore be described in terms of what Marie-Laure Ryan calls the 'aesthetics of proliferation'.[5] As a 'worldbuilding' device, the Round Table serves to locate stories in a limitlessly expandable 'storyworld', that is to say an imaginary world,[6] distinct from Arthurian history. Since several narratives can be set in the same storyworld, the Round Table can effectively be used as a narrative docking device. New narratives can then attach themselves to this

---

4   Beate Schmolke-Hasselmann, 'The Round Table: Ideal, Fiction, Reality', *Arthurian Literature* 2 (1982), 41–75 (66).
5   Marie-Laure Ryan, 'The Aesthetics of Proliferation', in *World Building: Transmedia, Fans, Industries*, ed. Marta Boni (Amsterdam, 2017), 31–46.
6   See Mark J.P. Wolf, *Building Imaginary Worlds: The Theory and History of Subcreation* (New York, 2012), 29. On the concept of storyworlds, see David Herman, 'Storyworld', in *The Routledge Encyclopedia of Narrative Theory*, ed. David Herman, Manfred Jahn, and Marie-Laure Ryan (Abingdon, 2005), 569–70; Marie-Laure Ryan, 'From Possible Worlds to Storyworlds: On the Worldness of Narrative Representation', in *Possible Worlds Theory and Contemporary Narratology*, ed. Alice Bell and Marie-Laure Ryan (Lincoln, NE, 2019), 62–87.

fictional Arthurian storyworld through the mechanics of what Richard Saint-Gelais terms 'transfictionality'.[7]

In this way, the Round Table also becomes a symbol of the processes of fictionalisation, traced notably by D.H. Green,[8] that shaped the development of Arthurian romance in Continental Europe in the twelfth and thirteenth centuries. This begins with Chrétien's appropriation of the Round Table as a worldbuilding device in *Erec and Enide*, setting up an Arthurian storyworld that has shifted away from Wace's Arthurian history – although the ahistoricity of Chrétien's storyworld is also problematised in his much less straightforward *Conte del Graal*. In stark contrast to this, the Insular tradition resolves the ambiguity of Wace's Round Table in a very different way. Laȝamon's Middle English *Brut* and, following Laȝamon, the *Alliterative Morte Arthure* place Arthur at the Round Table as a powerful historical king, and their storyworld remains firmly historical. On the Continent, however, it is from Chrétien's fictional storyworld, featuring a weak romance king, that later romances spring. This is the world expanded by Hartmann von Aue's Middle High German translations of Chrétien and problematised once again in Wolfram von Eschenbach's *Parzival*. The Round Table as a worldbuilding device is consequently central to the gradual detachment from history that creates an 'interfictive' storyworld,[9] from which European Arthurian romances can develop and proliferate.

Wace: Historical Truth against the Round Table

We begin with the Round Table's first appearance as an essentially ambiguous motif in Wace's *Roman de Brut*, composed in 1155. Although Wace claims that the Table is known from British or Breton fables,

---

7   See Richard Saint-Gelais, *Fictions transfuges: La transfictionnalité et ses enjeux* (Paris, 2011); for an English definition of transfictionality, see Richard Saint-Gelais, 'Transfictionality', in *The Routledge Encyclopedia of Narrative Theory*, ed. Herman, Jahn, and Ryan, 612–13.

8   D.H. Green, *The Beginnings of Medieval Romance: Fact and Fiction, 1150–1220* (Cambridge, UK, 2002), hereafter cited as Green. Fictionality in Continental romance was first theorised by Walter Haug in *Literaturtheorie im deutschen Mittelalter: Von den Anfängen bis zum Ende des 13. Jahrhunderts; Eine Einführung* (Darmstadt, 1985); for a viewpoint opposing Green's notion of gradual fictionalisation, see Fritz Peter Knapp, *Historie und Fiktion in der mittelalterlichen Gattungspoetik*, 2 vols (Heidelberg, 1997–2005).

9   Green, 55.

and there have been numerous but unconvincing attempts to trace its origins in various Celtic or Christian traditions,[10] there is no record of its appearance in any Arthurian stories before Wace. This strongly indicates that, as Schmolke-Hasselmann argues, the Table was introduced into the Arthurian corpus by Wace himself.[11] Maurice Delbouille even compellingly suggests it originated in a misreading of Geoffrey of Monmouth's *Historia*:[12] Wace may have misunderstood a manuscript variant of the description of Arthur's court causing 'aemulationem longe manentibus populis',[13] the envy of far-away peoples, as the envy of people seated far away from the king. Indeed, Wace's Table is designed to resolve the problematic rivalry of Arthur's vassals, with each believing himself superior to the others, during the twelve years of peace of Arthur's reign:

> Pur les nobles baruns qu'il out
> Dunt chescuns mieldre estre quidout,
> Chescuns se teneit al meillur,
> Ne nuls n'en saveit le peiur,
> Fist Artur la Runde Table
> Dunt Bretun dient mainte fable
> (lines 9747–52)[14]

---

10   A Celtic origin was posited by A.C.L. Brown, 'The Round Table before Wace', *Studies and Notes in Philology and Literature* 7 (1900), 183–205; for a more specific attribution to the legends of Brittany, see J.E. Caerwyn Williams, 'Brittany and the Arthurian Legend', in *The Arthur of the Welsh: The Arthurian Legend in Medieval Welsh Literature*, ed. Rachel Bromwich, A.O.J. Harman, and Brynley F. Roberts, 2nd edn (Cardiff, 2008), 249–72 (263). For the theory of Christian origins, see Laura Hibbard Loomis, 'Arthur's Round Table', *PMLA* 41.4 (1926), 771–84. Lori J. Walters argues that Wace's introduction of the Table was instead inspired by Charlemagne: 'Re-examining Wace's Round Table', in *Courtly Arts and the Art of Courtliness: Selected Papers from the Eleventh Triennial Congress of the International Courtly Literature Society, University of Wisconsin-Madison, 29 July–4 August 2004*, ed. Keith Busby and Christopher Kleinhenz (Cambridge, UK, 2006), 721–44.
11   Schmolke-Hasselmann, 'Round Table', 43–4.
12   Maurice Delbouille, 'Le témoignage de Wace sur la légende arthurienne', *Romania* 74 (1953), 172–99 (191).
13   Geoffrey of Monmouth, *The History of the Kings of Britain: An Edition and Translation of the De Gestis Britonum* [Historia regum Britanniae], ed. Michael D. Reeve, trans. Neil Wright (Woodbridge, 2007), 205.
14   Wace, *Roman de Brut: A History of the British*, ed./trans. Judith Weiss, rev. edn (Exeter, 2002); all further references are to this edition. All translations are my own.

(For the noble barons that he had
Of whom each felt superior,
Each held himself to be the best,
And no one knew who was the worst,
Arthur made the Round Table
Of which the Britons/Bretons tell many stories.)

The rhymes accompanying the Round Table's introduction are suggestive. The juxtaposition of *meillur* and *peiur* highlights both the rivalries inherent in the chivalric setting of Arthur's court and the new egalitarian spirit the Table is meant to represent. The second pairing, *table* and *fable*, appears to anchor the Table in British or Breton legend while seeming to prefigure the later proliferation of Arthurian romances. Both these assumptions, however, are deceptive.

First, as Schmolke-Hasselmann has shown, the supposed equality of the Round Table is a potent instrument of political domination, despite the courtly 'depoliticization' of Wace's history identified by Jean Blacker-Knight.[15] Unlike later representations, Wace never actually places Arthur himself at the Table. Contemporaneous seating arrangements would have had the king sit separately, and Arthur is on another occasion explicitly described as sitting 'al deis' (line 10459, at the high table), a rectangular high table.[16] The equality of the Table, which is never physically described, is only ever said to extend to 'li vassal / Tuit chevalment e tuit egal' (lines 9753-4, the vassals, all as knights and all as equals), who are rendered equal and indistinguishable in chivalric fellowship. Schmolke-Hasselmann sees this as political propaganda tailored to King Henry II's court, asserting control over the king's vassals: 'Far from blurring the fundamental distinction between monarch and vassals, the new order is apt to emphasize it.'[17] This use of chivalry as an instrument of power is striking, especially given how notoriously Henry II's predecessor King Stephen was hampered by his own chivalry during the Anarchy.[18] But

---

15 See Jean Blacker-Knight, 'Transformations of a Theme: The Depoliticization of the Arthurian World in the *Roman de Brut*', in *The Arthurian Tradition: Essays in Convergence*, ed. Mary Flowers Braswell and John Bugge (Tuscaloosa, 1988), 54-74.
16 Schmolke-Hasselmann, 'Round Table', 51-2; see *AND*, s.v. *deis*, 1.
17 Schmolke-Hasselmann, 'Round Table', 49.
18 See John Gillingham, '1066 and the Introduction of Chivalry into England', in *The English in the Twelfth Century: Imperialism, National Identity, and Political Values* (Woodbridge, 2000), 209-31 (209).

there is also a wider narrative implication to the Table's original design, with a significance reaching beyond Schmolke-Hasselmann's political reading, that we will have to keep in mind: fundamentally, the twelfth-century Round Table separates Arthur from the Knights of the Round Table – which for Wace, at least, still serves to elevate the king.

Secondly, Wace only introduces the *fables* allegedly associated with the Table as a way of setting himself apart and asserting his own authority as a historian. In this case, Wace's Table is as much a narrative device as a political symbol. The Table's introduction is followed by further comments on the stories surrounding the twelve-year peace:

> En cele grant pais ke jo di,
> Ne sai si vus l'avez oï,
> Furent les merveilles pruvees
> E les aventures truvees
> Ki d'Artur sunt tant recuntees
> Ke a fable sunt aturnees:
> Ne tut mençunge, ne tut veir,
> Ne tut folie ne tut saveir.
>
> (lines 9787–94)

> (During this long peace of which I have told,
> I do not know if you have heard,
> The marvels appeared
> And the adventures were sought out
> Which are so often told about Arthur
> That they have become legendary:
> Neither all lies nor all truth,
> Neither all foolishness nor all wisdom.)

The confusion between truth and lies generated by the repetitively antithetical last two lines seems to support Green's argument that Wace here already identifies a space for narrative fiction, to which the absolute dichotomy between historical truth and untruth does not apply.[19] Yet creating this confusion is also in keeping with Wace's strategy as a historian whose authority, according to Peter Damian-Grint, is generated by 'very explicit and self-conscious judgement as to the value of different sources'.[20] In fact, Wace seems to be echoing William

---

19   Green, 17.
20   Peter Damian-Grint, *The New Historians of the Twelfth-Century Renaissance: Inventing Vernacular Authority* (Woodbridge, 1999), 58.

of Malmesbury's anxieties about the distinction between *historia* and *fabula* in his early twelfth-century *Gesta regum Anglorum*, stating that Arthur should not be remembered in 'fallaces [...] fabulae sed ueraces [...] historiae' (fictitious [...] stories but true [...] histories).[21] Thus, the mention of the *fable* in fact allows Wace to reassert his own authoritative voice and his narrative's historicity.[22] In the next mention of the Table, the rhyme with *fable* accordingly carries a distinctly negative value: 'Ki sunt de la Roünde Table, / Ne vuil jo mie faire fable' (lines 10285–6, who are of the Round Table, I do not wish to tell any lies). Wace uses the Round Table to sideline fictional stories, just as he does with Arthur's vassals, in favour of his historical account of King Arthur.

And yet, the narrative device Wace uses to highlight both the king's importance and his *roman*'s historicity can also be reversed to become part of the foundation of Arthurian romance. The birth of fictional romance has repeatedly been traced to Wace's *Roman de Brut*, albeit so far without specific reference to the Round Table. Laura Ashe notably locates it in another episode concerning the twelve-year peace, when Gawain defends peacetime in response to Cador's eagerness for war: 'Pur amistié e pur amies / Funt chevaliers chevaleries' (lines 10771–2, for love and lovers do knights do knightly deeds). She sees this idea of chivalric self-fulfilment as emblematic of the 'move from "epic" to "romance"'.[23] More generally, Ad Putter notes that subsequent Arthurian romances make use of Wace's twelve-year peace to create an 'autonomous realm

21 William of Malmesbury, *Gesta regum Anglorum*, ed./trans. R.A.B. Mynors, R.M. Thomson, and M. Winterbottom, 2 vols (Oxford, 1998–9), 1:26; see Green, 17.

22 Susanne Friede, 'Die Stimme(n) der Chronik: Zur Konstruktion von Autorität in Waces Roman de Brut', in *Autorschaft und Autorität in den romanischen Literaturen des Mittelalters*, ed. Susanne Friede and Michael Schwarze (Berlin, 2015), 147–67 (151); see also Fritz Peter Knapp, 'Historiographisches und fiktionales Erzählen in der zweiten Hälfte des 12. Jahrhunderts', in *Erzählstrukturen der Artusliteratur: Forschungsgeschichte und neue Ansätze*, ed. Friedrich Wolfzettel with Peter Ihring (Tübingen, 1999), 3–22 (13–15).

23 Laura Ashe, *The Oxford English Literary History, Volume 1: 1000–1350: Conquest and Transformation* (Oxford, 2017), 245; see also Ashe, '1155 and the Beginnings of Fiction', *History Today* 65.1 (2015), 41–6 (45). For a similar conception of romance as the triumph of individual adventure over history, see Friedrich Wolfzettel, 'Temps et histoire dans la littérature arthurienne', in *Temps et Histoire dans le roman arthurien*, ed. Jean-Claude Faucon (Toulouse, 1999), 9–31.

of fiction' in which these knightly adventures can play out.[24] But on a basic narrative level, this realm is in fact already created *in potentia* by the Round Table as a freely available worldbuilding device. In separating Arthur from his vassals, the Round Table can serve to establish a storyworld that is unmistakably Arthurian but nevertheless distinct from epic history, which the *Roman de Brut* envisages as essentially dynastic. After all, in his prologue Wace primarily proposes to tell the history of a dynasty:

> De rei en rei e d'eir en eir
> Ki cil furent et dunt il vindrent
> Ki Engleterre primes tindrent.
> (lines 2–4)
>
> (From king to king and heir to heir,
> Who they were and whence they came
> Who first held England.)

Provided Arthur remains apart, the Round Table thus leaves an opening for romance within Wace's dynastic history, even though this is not exploited by Wace himself. By shifting the narrative focus from Arthur, imbricated in the historical line of kings, to his many knights, it becomes possible to destabilise Wace's hierarchy of truth and *fable*. This is also an important narrative factor in Arthur's rapid transformation from Wace's active conqueror into the passive *roi fainéant* of Arthurian romance:[25] suspending the king is necessary to remove romance from the demands of history. As Green remarks with a revealing, if presumably inadvertent, metonymy, 'the fictionality of the Arthurian romances attaches not to Arthur, whose historicity was accepted, but to the exploits of his Round Table'.[26]

Within a few decades of its appearance in Wace, the Table becomes a central device for what Ryan terms 'textual proliferation': this can be described as a process through which, across multiple texts, 'multiple stories are told about the same world, so that passing from one story to

---

24 Ad Putter, 'Finding Time for Romance: Mediaeval Arthurian Literary History', *Medium Ævum* 63.1 (1994), 1–16 (5).
25 See Barbara N. Sargent-Baur, '*Dux Bellorum/Rex Militum/Roi fainéant*: The Transformation of Arthur in the Twelfth Century', in *King Arthur: A Casebook*, ed. Edward Donald Kennedy (New York, 2002), 29–43.
26 Green, 52.

another does not require ontological relocation'.[27] As a worldbuilding device, the Table can easily attach new stories to the Arthurian storyworld without burdening them with historicity. In Béroul's late twelfth-century *Tristan*, the Table is the first visible sign of Arthur's court:

> 'Sire', fait-il, 'il sit au dois.
> Ja verroiz la Table Reonde,
> Qui tornoie conme le monde.
> Sa mesnie sit environ.'
> (lines 3378–81)[28]

('Sir', says he, 'he sits at the high table.
You will soon see the Round Table,
Which turns like the world.
His household sits around it.')

The distinction between *dois* and *table*, king and *mesnie*, is maintained, while the Table's comparison with the world signals its importance in establishing the Arthurian literary universe. The same rhyme between *reonde* and *monde* is also found in Marie de France's contemporary *Lanval*: 'A ceus de la Table Roünde – / N'ot tant de teus en tut le munde' (lines 15–16, to those of the Round Table – there are none such in all the world).[29] Although the second line in this couplet is highly conventional, the recurrence of the rhyme is significant. Emmanuèle Baumgartner notes the general predominance of *reonde-monde* rhymes over *table-fable* in Arthurian verse. While the latter rhyme largely disappears after Wace, the former becomes a commonplace, marking, as she argues, the Round Table as 'le référent le plus sûr, le plus stable, d'un univers qu'elle a fortement contribué à installer' (the most accurate, the most stable referent of a universe that it has strongly helped to establish).[30] The Table acts as the referent of a stable storyworld whose ahistoricity encourages

---

27 Ryan, 'Aesthetics of Proliferation', 34; 37–8.
28 Béroul, *Le Roman de Tristan: Poème du XIIe siècle*, ed. Ernest Muret, rev. L.M. Defourques, 4th edn (Paris, 1974).
29 Marie de France, *Lanval*, in *Lais bretons (XIIe–XIIIe siècles): Marie de France et ses contemporains*, ed./trans. Nathalie Koble and Mireille Séguy, 2nd edn (Paris, 2018), 334–87.
30 Emmanuèle Baumgartner, 'Jeux de rimes et roman Arthurien', *Romania* 103 (1982), 550–60 (553). For a reading of this rhyme scheme in relation to the Round Table's status as a cosmic table or *Weltentisch*, see Schmolke-Hasselmann, 'Round Table', 60–1.

textual proliferation in the form of 'transfictionality' as theorised by Saint-Gelais: essentially the addition of sequels, prequels, and 'midquels' (an inelegant but surprisingly useful term) into existing narratives.[31] The most important such addition, as we will now see, consists of the works of Chrétien de Troyes.

Chrétien: The Fictional World of the Round Table

The Round Table and Ryan's 'aesthetics of proliferation' thus provide a key to the world of Chrétien's romances. Their storyworld, which Green describes as 'the "interfictive world" of the Arthurian romances',[32] can equally be described in terms of Saint-Gelais' transfictionality. Chrétien's romances are essentially 'midquels' to Wace's *Roman de Brut*, inserted into the Arthurian timeline in a place left open by Wace: the ahistorical storyworld represented by the Round Table, in which the protagonist is not Arthur but one of his knights. That, at least, is the arrangement reflected in one thirteenth-century manuscript: Paris, BnF, MS fr. 1450, which inserts four romances after the description of the twelve-year peace. While this is often taken to mean that Chrétien's romances are integrated into the historical discourse of *translatio studii et imperii*,[33] the scribe made sure to preserve the distinction between Wace's and Chrétien's narrative voices by announcing that the romances are 'ce que crestiens tesmogne' (that which Chrétien testifies).[34] We might then see the compilation as allowing audiences to shift between two modes of reading, Wace's dynastic history and Chrétien's fictional romance, that are both encoded in the Round Table motif. The manuscript highlights the collaborative, intertextual origins of Arthurian fiction: on the one hand, Chrétien's authorial exploitation of a 'parenthèse romanesque [...]

---

31 See Saint-Gelais, *Fictions transfuges*; Wolf, *Building Imaginary Worlds*, 205–10.
32 Green, 55.
33 See for instance Lori J. Walters, 'Manuscript Compilations of Verse Romances', in *The Arthur of the French: The Arthurian Legend in Medieval French and Occitan Literature*, ed. Glyn Burgess and Karen Pratt (Cardiff, 2006), 461–87 (470); Keith Busby, 'The Manuscripts of Chrétien's Romances', in *A Companion to Chrétien de Troyes*, ed. Lacy and Grimbert, 64–75 (66).
34 BnF fr. 1450, fol. 139v; see Lori J. Walters, 'Le rôle du scribe dans l'organisation des manuscrits des romans de Chrétien de Troyes', *Romania* 106 (1985), 303–25 (304, note 1).

dans le texte épique de Wace' (romance parenthesis in the epic text of Wace);[35] and on the other, Wace's own creation of this potential romance storyworld inherent in his ambiguous Round Table. In Chrétien's first Arthurian romance, *Erec and Enide*, composed c. 1170, the Round Table accordingly plays a key role for narrative worldbuilding. It is no more given a physical description than in Wace but serves as a central idea of chivalric fellowship, underlying the romance's 'attenuated background of Arthurian pseudo-history'.[36] In fact, Fritz Peter Knapp notes that the Table remains the only defining element of Arthur's court in Chrétien's work.[37] Schmolke-Hasselmann, for her part, dismisses the Table's importance in Chrétien's work, noting that he only refers to it three times and that it 'evidently holds no important place in the poet's narrative plan'.[38] Yet the first thing Chrétien's audiences are told about his protagonist Erec is: 'De la Table Reonde estoit, / An la cort mout grant los avoit' (lines 83–4, he was of the Round Table and had much honour at court).[39] This immediately locates Chrétien's narrative in the romance storyworld made available by Wace, and it establishes Erec's chivalric credentials without in any way historically predetermining the narrative's further development. When Arthur's court is later described, it is primarily characterised by the assembled Knights of the Round Table, a fellowship that does not include Arthur himself:

Mes d'auques des meillors barons
Vos sai bien a dire les nons,
De ces de la Table Reonde,
Qui furent li meillor del monde.
(lines 1675–8)

35   Daniel Poirion, 'Introduction', in Chrétien de Troyes, *Œuvres complètes*, ed./ trans. Daniel Poirion et al. (Paris, 1994), ix–xliii (xix); on Chrétien's knowledge and adaptation of Wace, see Margaret Pelan, *L'influence du Brut de Wace sur les romanciers français de son temps* (Paris, 1931).
36   Donald Maddox and Sara Sturm-Maddox, '*Erec and Enide*: The First Arthurian Romance', in *A Companion to Chrétien de Troyes*, ed. Lacy and Grimbert, 103–19 (103).
37   Fritz Peter Knapp, 'Der Artushof als Raumkulisse bei Wace, Chrétien de Troyes und dessen deutschen Nachfolgern', in *Artushof und Artusliteratur*, ed. Matthias Däumer, Cora Dietl, and Friedrich Wolfzettel (Berlin, 2010), 21–41 (24).
38   Schmolke-Hasselmann, 'Round Table', 45.
39   Works by Chrétien de Troyes are cited from *Œuvres complètes*, ed./trans. Poirion et al.; all further references are to this edition.

(But of some of the best barons
I can indeed tell you the names,
Of those of the Round Table,
Who were the best in the world.)

The *reonde-monde* rhyme recurs, highlighting the Table's worldbuilding function. Conversely, its symbolic equality has by now been abandoned. The list of knights begins in a way that is explicitly hierarchical: 'Devant toz les boens chevaliers / Doit estre Gauvains li premiers' (lines 1679–80, before all the good knights, Gawain must be the first).

This first hierarchical list is followed by a second list of unranked knights (lines 1693–714 in the edition used here), which merits closer attention, since it is a site of major textual instability. Its length varies from eighteen lines in BnF fr. 1450, and twenty-two lines in BnF, MS fr. 794, to forty-six lines in BnF, MS fr. 1376, all manuscripts from the thirteenth century.[40] It is still not clear if this was originally a long list by Chrétien shortened by scribes or partly a later addition.[41] In any case, Carleton W. Carroll notes that even though some of the knights introduced here later emerge as romance protagonists in their own right, names are seemingly included or omitted irrespective of later importance.[42] What this suggests is that the names are not important in themselves – it is the fact that they can be so readily added by way of the Round Table that is significant. This illustrates one of the fundamental advantages of the Round Table as a narrative device identified by Schmolke-Hasselmann: its 'membership can be extended *ad infinitum*'.[43] Consequently, it allows for practically endless textual proliferation. Notably, the two lists in *Erec* also introduce 'Lancelot del Lac' (line 1682, Lancelot of the Lake) and 'Yvains li preuz' (line 1693,

---

40 See Carleton W. Carroll, 'The Knights of the Round Table in the Manuscripts of *Erec et Enide*', in '*Por le soie amisté*': *Essays in Honor of Norris J. Lacy*, ed. Keith Busby and Catherine M. Jones (Amsterdam, 2000), 117–27 (126–7); hereafter cited as Carroll. See also Keith Busby, 'Erec, le Fiz Lac (British Library, Harley 4971)', in *People and Texts: Relationships in Medieval Literature*, ed. Thea Summerfield and Keith Busby (Amsterdam, 2007), 43–50.
41 For the argument in favour of an original long list, see Carroll, 124; for a view of it as a list later expanded by scribes, see Busby, 'Erec, le Fiz Lac', 50.
42 Carroll, 122.
43 Beate Schmolke-Hasselmann, *The Evolution of Arthurian Romance: The Verse Tradition from Chrétien to Froissart*, trans. Margaret and Roger Middleton (Cambridge, UK, 1998), 60.

Yvain the valiant). Each of them is inserted into an ontologically stable Arthurian storyworld and primed to become the protagonist of his own adventure. This narrative mechanism might even be said to govern the centripetal impulse of Arthurian romances, by which defeated knights are compelled to join Arthur's court themselves, beginning with Ydier in *Erec* (lines 1234–5). The court, organised around the Round Table, acts as the central locus of chivalric identity. Indeed, one of the axioms Stephen G. Nichols establishes in his theorisation of the romance genre is a lack of 'indigenous identity': 'The Knights of the Round Table come from the Celtic marches of Britain and France [...] but their life and identity is with Arthur's court',[44] a court that can accordingly incorporate anyone. In addition to being ahistorical, Arthurian romance becomes ageographical: the romances' storyworld is fully identified with the fictional community of the Knights of the Round Table.

This is not to say that the Round Table's narrative function remains unproblematised in Chrétien's romances. The unfinished *Conte del Graal* offers a perspective on the Round Table that demonstrates Chrétien's awareness of the artificiality of his fictional romance world. On a broad narrative level, this is apparent when we consider Perceval. His quest is, as Geneviève Young argues, tied to the 'troublesome nature of his ancestry', and her genealogical reading highlights the resulting complexity of competing familial, chivalric and spiritual dimensions.[45] This presents an obvious problem to a storyworld divorced from dynastic history. But the Round Table is also explicitly addressed during Gauvain's stay with, unbeknownst to him, King Arthur's mother, his own mother, and his sister, yet another genealogical intrusion into an ahistorical space. This uneasy coexistence of different modes of understanding dominates the exchange concerning the Table, whose role in the storyworld becomes once more unstable and ambiguous. Ygerne, Arthur's mother and Gauvain's own grandmother, asks Gauvain on his arrival:

> Et estes vos, dites le moi,
> De ces de la Table Reonde,
> Des meillors chevaliers del monde?
>   (lines 8124–6)

[44] Stephen G. Nichols, 'Counter-figural Topics: Theorizing Romance with Eugene Vinaver and Eugene Vance', *MLN* 127.5 (2012), S174–S216 (S208).
[45] Geneviève Young, '"Chevaliers estre deüsiez": Genealogy and Historical Sense in Chrétien de Troyes's *Conte du Graal*', *New Medieval Literatures* 21 (2021), 1–28 (9, 22).

(And are you, tell me,
Of those of the Round Table,
The best knights in the world?)

His affirmative answer then confirms his chivalric status while ironically completely failing to give away his identity. In this case, the Table as the focus of chivalric identity obstructs familial identification, even when Gauvain is specifically asked about his father King Lot and his sons (lines 8135-47), causing a breakdown of language that parallels Perceval's own failure to put the crucial question to the Fisher King.[46] The text further highlights the Table's artificiality when Gauvain continues: 'Ne me faz mie des meillors / Ne ne cuit estre des peiors' (lines 8129-30, I do not put myself among the best, nor do I think I am among the worst). The demands of courtliness require Gauvain to place himself in the middle, with the *meillors-peiors* rhyme echoing the equality originally invoked by Wace. This, however, completely contradicts Gauvain's otherwise consistent placing at the top of Chrétien's Round Table hierarchy. The complexity of the *Conte del Graal*'s storyworld in general is acknowledged by Irit Ruth Kleinman when she argues that 'Chrétien's fiction cannot hold at bay the temporality and violence of the history Wace recounts.'[47] But this is equally apparent in those instances when the Round Table's ahistorical chivalric storyworld, in its conspicuous artificiality, fails to contain the story of the Grail.

In fact, another remark in this passage also problematises the ahistoricity of Chrétien's Arthurian universe. As the conversation moves to King Arthur himself, Ygerne says: 'Il est anfes, li rois Artus. / S'il a cent anz, il n'a pas plus' (lines 8169-70, he is a youth, this King Arthur. If he is a hundred years old, he is not a year older). This paradoxical statement has rather needlessly puzzled editors,[48] or has alternatively been explained as just 'displaying her wit in clever language.'[49] It may instead well represent Chrétien's self-conscious reflection on the ahistorical nature of his

---

46 Young, 'Genealogy and Historical Sense', 25. On the doubling of Perceval and Gauvain, see Matilda Tomaryn Bruckner, 'The Poetics of Continuation in Medieval French Romance: From Chrétien's *Conte du Graal* to the *Perceval* Continuations', French Forum 18.2 (1993), 133-49.
47 Irit Ruth Kleinman, 'Chrétien's *Conte du Graal* between Myth and History', Arthurian Literature 31 (2014), 1-34 (29).
48 See Chrétien de Troyes, *Œuvres complètes*, 1384-5, note 3.
49 Rupert T. Pickens, 'Arthurian Time and Space: Chrétien's *Conte del Graal* and Wace's *Brut*', Medium Ævum 75.2 (2006), 219-46 (237).

Arthurian romances, in which even over the decades narrated in *Cligès* Arthur neither changes nor ages. Set aside from the narrative action by the Round Table's Arthurian storyworld, Arthur is no more touched by romance temporality than the romances participate in Arthurian history. This way of exaggerating the king's age to remove him from historical action additionally recalls a passage in the twelfth-century Oxford version of the *Chanson de Roland*, a distinctly historical *chanson de geste*: King Marsile insults Charlemagne by declaring that 'Il est mult vielz, si ad sun tens usét: / Men escïent, dous cenz anz ad passét' (lines 523–4, he is very old, his time is at an end: I think he has passed two hundred years).[50] Yet Marsile's hopes are frustrated when Charlemagne returns to Spain to defeat the Saracens in an act of definitive history-making. Conversely, despite the problematisation of King Arthur's position in the *Conte del Graal*, Chrétien's fragmentary romance is not yet reintegrated into Arthurian history, and the problem of Arthur's age remains unresolved. Although Sara Sturm-Maddox comments on Chrétien's efforts to 'reinscribe his King Arthur into the legendary history whence he came',[51] the unfinished text cannot complete such a manoeuvre. While ancestry and lineage provide unsettling impulses, the storyworld remains the ahistorical world of the Round Table.

Chrétien's use of the Round Table thus provides a key to the fictionality of the French Arthurian romances. It is often suggested that the emergence of fictional Arthurian romance is simply 'possible because in France that story was not part of national history as it was in England'.[52] Yet in view of the above, we must add: it is also possible because Wace, while following Geoffrey in indelibly imbricating Arthur in a historical sequence, also provided Chrétien with a narrative device to separate Arthurian romance from dynastic history *altogether*. After all, dynastic history is the narrative mode employed not only by Wace's national history but also by the French *chansons de geste*. As Joseph J. Duggan has it, the Old French epic 'organizes history in genealogical fashion', and indeed the word *geste* can also mean 'lineage'.[53] In contrast, Chrétien's

---

50   *La Chanson de Roland*, ed./trans. Ian Short, 2nd edn (Paris, 1990).
51   Sara Sturm-Maddox, '"Tenir sa terre en païs": Social Order in the *Brut* and in the *Conte del Graal*', *Studies in Philology* 81.1 (1984), 28–41 (39).
52   Felicity Riddy, *Sir Thomas Malory* (Leiden, 1987), 41; see also Robert W. Hanning, *The Individual in Twelfth-Century Romance* (New Haven, 1977), 59.
53   Joseph J. Duggan, 'Social Functions of the Medieval Epic in the Romance Literatures', *Oral Tradition* 1.3 (1986), 728–66 (741); see *AND*, s.v. geste, 1.

romances become fictional because the Round Table allows them not to be part of any national history at all. As long as the Round Table continues to provide a space distinct from King Arthur and Arthurian history, it can harbour a fictional storyworld that can absorb knights from anywhere. This also offers another way to explain Jehan Bodel's famous assessment of the three *matières* in the prologue to his late twelfth-century *Chanson des Saisnes*:

> Li conte de Bretaigne si sont vain et plaisant,
> Et cil de Ronme sage et de sens aprendant,
> Cil de France sont voir chascun jour aparant.
> Et de ces trois materes tieng la plus voir disant.
> (lines 9–12)[54]

(The stories of Britain are then empty and pleasant,
And those of Rome wise and instructive in meaning,
Those of France are true, as is evident every day.
And of these three matters I keep to the most truthful.)

Green may be right to argue that Bodel is 'clearly speaking *pro domo*' on behalf of Carolingian epics and French history.[55] Yet this perception of the Matter of Britain as empty of historical meaning is also quite justified as far as Chrétien's reworkings of the Matter of Britain, within the opening left by Wace, are concerned. As romances of the Round Table, their storyworld exists outside the dynastic progression of history embodied by King Arthur.

Eventually, of course, King Arthur will gradually be integrated back into the Round Table. Under the influence of Robert de Boron, the Round Table is merged with the Grail Table and transformed into a Christian fellowship, of which Arthur is a part,[56] and with quite different historical and narrative implications. As part of the Grail narrative, both king and Table are subordinated to a larger Christian teleology that overrides the ahistorical stagnation of Chrétien's romances. At the same time, the thirteenth century also sees the emergence of a different

---

54 Jehan Bodel, *La Chanson des Saisnes*, ed. Anne Brasseur, 2 vols (Geneva, 1989).
55 Green, 138.
56 Schmolke-Hasselmann, 'Round Table', 58; see also Gina L. Greco, 'From the Last Supper to the Arthurian Feast: *Translatio* and the Round Table', *Modern Philology* 96.1 (1998), 42–7.

source of textual proliferation in Arthurian romances – the Grail itself. It is the mysterious nature of the Grail, coupled with the fragmentary state of the *Conte del Graal*, that seems to drive the multiple continuations that seek to supplement Chrétien's last, unfinished romance. As Matilda Tomaryn Bruckner writes, across its many continuations, the Grail story is 'a tale more interested in middles than ends, a story in which there is always something more to sandwich in before reaching the end'.[57] This protean Grail story encourages the proliferation of its own 'midquels', reshaping the Round Table along with the storyworld built around it. But initially at least, it is the world of the Round Table that is shared by most Arthurian verse romances of the twelfth and early thirteenth centuries and that encourages their rapid spread across Europe.

Historical Round Tables in the Insular Arthurian Tradition

The developments that accompany the emergence of the French Arthurian romances are all the more remarkable because they stand in stark contrast to adaptations of Wace's Arthurian history in England. Ashe notes the different nature of Insular romance compared to Continental romance, identifying a development towards 'historical' Anglo-Norman romance from the twelfth century.[58] Of course, Chrétien's Arthurian storyworld ultimately also underlies later fictional English romances. But while Continental Arthurian romances were certainly available in England, no Arthurian romances from England survive from before the end of the thirteenth century.[59] The more historical trend, however, does include Insular adaptations of Arthurian material, which noticeably tend to maintain Arthur's place among his knights at the Round Table and often assign him a far more active role than the Continental *roi fainéant*. Ashe attributes this 'absence of the *romance* King Arthur' to 'the strength of the Insular ideal of kingship'.[60] In practical narrative

57 Matilda Tomaryn Bruckner, *Chrétien Continued: A Study of the Conte du Graal and Its Verse Continuations* (Oxford, 2009), 188.
58 Laura Ashe, *Fiction and History in England, 1066-1200* (Cambridge, UK, 2007), 158.
59 See Catherine Batt and Rosalind Field, 'The Romance Tradition', in *The Arthur of the English*, ed. Barron, 59-70 (69).
60 Laura Ashe, 'The Anomalous King of Conquered England', in *Every Inch a King: Comparative Studies on Kings and Kingship in the Ancient and Medieval Worlds*, ed. Lynette Mitchell and Charles Melville (Leiden, 2013), 173-93 (189);

terms, however, it is conditioned by an approach to the ambiguous potential of Wace's Round Table that in many ways is the opposite of Chrétien's. Beginning with Wace's Middle English translator Laʒamon and his early thirteenth-century *Brut*, the potential split between history and fiction encoded in Wace's Table is resolved not by constructing a fictional storyworld, but by immediately reintegrating Arthur into the Round Table fellowship. As a result, this tradition allows for no distinction between Arthurian romance and Arthurian history. This is of course a pattern already laid out in Wace's *Roman de Brut*, in which the Round Table is inevitably tied into the progression of dynastic history: on his return from the Roman expedition, Arthur dies together with 'cil de la Table Roünde' (line 13269, those of the Round Table). Here we can detect the roots of the later tradition that has been subsumed under the designation of 'dynastic romance'.[61]

Laʒamon's account of the Round Table is notable for its significant expansion of the brief episode in Wace, for which Welsh or Cornish sources have been suggested.[62] Remarkably, however, the *Brut* does not use the term 'round table': the word used throughout is *bord*, which elides the distinction between *table* and *deis*, as it can mean both 'table' and 'high table'.[63] Additionally, unlike Wace's tale of baronial jealousy, Laʒamon's *Brut* presents the Table as the solution to the fact that 'Þat folc wes of feole londe; þer wes muchel onde' (line 11355, those people were from many countries, there was great enmity).[64] It is designed to resolve violent international rivalries, inscribed in the rhyme between *feole londe* and *muchel onde*. After Arthur's equally violent suppression of unrest, which pre-emptively banishes any notion of a weak or ineffectual king, the Cornish carpenter who fashions the Table insists on its portability, so that it can follow Arthur wherever he goes: 'Whenne þu wult riden; wið þe þu miht hit leden' (line 11437, when you

---

on Arthur's place in English history, see also James P. Carley, 'Arthur in English History', in *The Arthur of the English*, ed. Barron, 47–57.
61 See Karen Hodder et al., 'Dynastic Romance', in *The Arthur of the English*, ed. Barron, 71–111.
62 Françoise Le Saux, *Laʒamon's Brut: The Poem and Its Sources* (Cambridge, UK, 1989), 143.
63 See *MED*, s.v. *bōrd*, n.
64 Laʒamon, *Brut*, ed. G.L. Brook and R.F. Leslie, 2 vols, EETS, o.s. 250, 277 (London, 1963–78); all further references are to this edition. The version of the text quoted is that found in BL, Cotton MS Caligula A.ix, but concerning the Round Table this largely agrees with the version in BL, Cotton MS Otho C.xiii.

wish to ride out, you may take it with you). From the beginning, the Table is tied to Arthur as an active and mobile head of a multinational community, in which capacity he shares the Table with his men: 'Þa þe king wes isete; mid alle his duʒeðe. to his mete. / eorles and beornes; at borde þas kinges' (lines 12267–8, there the king was seated, with all his retainers, for his meal: noblemen and knights, at the king's table). Arthur chiasmically frames both earls and barons of his retinue; this is an inclusive Table, but nevertheless a Table firmly dominated by its king. It is therefore notable that Françoise Le Saux still sees Laʒamon's transformed Table as an 'indication of the king's firm hand'.[65] This is the result of a purposeful political reframing of Wace's Table – quite possibly in response to King John's ineffectual kingship – which also eliminates its narrative potential to sideline the king.

Laʒamon thus shapes a distinctly historical Insular tradition that leaves no space for romance. He is particularly careful not to suggest the existence of Arthurian stories not tied to Arthur himself. Where Wace speaks of stories told about the Round Table, Laʒamon writes: 'Þis wes þat ilke bord; þæt Bruttes of ʒelpeð. / And sugeð feole cunne lesinge; bi Arðure þan kinge' (lines 11454–5, this was that same table of which the Britons/Bretons boast and say many kinds of lies about Arthur the King). With the last phrase, he ensures that even the Britons' lies are understood to be about his historical King Arthur rather than any ahistorical storyworld. Although Elizabeth Bryan describes Laʒamon's attitude towards these untruthful stories as a careful negotiation of 'the very multivocality that Wace blames',[66] it is not so different from either Wace's or William of Malmesbury's anxieties about the production of true history. The assertion 'Ne al soh ne al les; þat leod-scopes singeð. / ah þis is þat soððe; bi Arðure þan kinge' (lines 11465–6, neither all truth nor all lies, which song-wrights sing, but this is the truth about Arthur the King) is mainly notable for repeating the earlier phrase emphasising Arthur's role as the focus of both story and history. Laʒamon's Arthurian history grows out of stories about King Arthur, closing the narrative gap in Wace's *Roman de Brut* in which the ahistorical storyworld of Arthurian romance could be situated.

65   W.R.J. Barron, Françoise Le Saux, and Lesley Johnson, 'Dynastic Chronicles', in *The Arthur of the English*, ed. Barron, 11–46 (26).
66   Elizabeth J. Bryan, 'Truth and the Round Table in Lawman's *Brut*', *Quondam et Futurus* 2.4 (1992), 27–35 (32).

The fact that Laȝamon does not stand alone, but rather as the representative of a distinct Insular tradition, is visible in the traces of his Round Table that we still find in the much later *Alliterative Morte Arthure*. The question of its generic classification is vexed enough for it to be broadly categorised as a 'dynastic romance'.[67] Although it is dated to c. 1400, it draws at least some of its material from Laȝamon's *Brut*,[68] and unlike the *Stanzaic Morte Arthur*, it shows no influence from the Grail tradition. Of particular interest is the prologue announcing: 'And I shall tell you a tale that trew is and noble / Of the real renkes of the Round Table' (lines 15–16).[69] The Table as a focus for historical truth would seem jarring in the context of the Continental romance tradition, but it soon becomes clear that Arthur himself is among the 'real renkes' and the protagonist of this narrative. (Interestingly, while *real* primarily means 'royal' here, it is around 1400 that it additionally acquires its modern meaning of 'actual'.)[70] Compared with Laȝamon, the emphasis lies on Arthur as member rather than ruler of the Round Table. As Rosalind Field notes, the Table seems to serve baronial interests in depicting Arthur and his knights on an even footing.[71] Consequently, however, the Table also binds Arthur's knights to him in his struggle with Rome: 'There shall thou give reckoning for all thy Round Table, / Why thou art rebel to Rome and rentes them with-holdes' (lines 101–2). Once more, this Insular Round Table eliminates any possibility of Arthurian romance branching off from dynastic history. The narrative it shapes is far removed from the fictional Arthurian storyworld first established by Chrétien – a storyworld that, as we shall now see, also drives Arthurian textual proliferation in Middle High German romances of the twelfth and thirteenth centuries.

---

67 Hodder et al., 'Dynastic Romance'; see also K.S. Whetter, 'Genre as Context in the Alliterative *Morte Arthure*', *Arthuriana* 20.2 (2010), 45–65.
68 See James I. McNelis III, 'Laȝamon as Auctor', in *The Text and Tradition of Layamon's Brut*, ed. Françoise Le Saux (Cambridge, UK, 1994), 253–72 (259–60).
69 *Alliterative Morte Arthure*, in *King Arthur's Death: The Middle English Stanzaic Morte Arthur and Alliterative Morte Arthure*, ed. Larry D. Benson, rev. Edward E. Foster (Kalamazoo, 1994), 131–284; all further references are to this edition.
70 *MED*, s.v. *rēal*, adj., 2.
71 Rosalind Field, 'The Anglo-Norman Background to Alliterative Romance', in *Middle English Alliterative Poetry and Its Literary Background*, ed. David Lawton (Cambridge, UK, 1982), 54–69 (68–9).

The Round Table and the Proliferation of Continental Arthurian Romance

Although the Round Table's role in German romance has largely been studied from a historical perspective,[72] it provides useful insights on the further proliferation of Continental Arthurian romance. Hartmann von Aue first introduced the Arthurian world into Middle High German around 1185 with his translations of Chrétien's *Erec* and, later, *Yvain*.[73] From the beginning, Hartmann's *Erec* and *Iwein* thus draw on Chrétien's fictional storyworld, and his Round Table works very similarly to Chrétien's by enlarging the Arthurian romance universe. In *Erec*, Hartmann significantly expands the list of knights of the Round Table (lines 1630–97), far beyond the length found in any manuscripts of Chrétien's romance, and gives the total number of knights as 140. Notably, the list now reaches back to the work of Marie de France by including 'Lanfal' (line 1678), while also introducing several characters that subsequently reappear in Wolfram von Eschenbach's *Parzival* (see lines 1672–3; 1679). While it is possible that these names derive from oral traditions, Christoph J. Steppich argues that Hartmann in part actively draws on an expanded catalogue of knights compiled from the work of Geoffrey and Wace.[74] As in the work of Chrétien, the Table therefore seems to serve as a nexus of intertextual references that anchors the Arthurian storyworld. Its intertextual function parallels that of a more explicit example in *Iwein*, in which Gawein warns Iwein against neglecting knighthood for love 'als dem hern Êrecke geschach' (line 2792, as happened to Sir Erec). Green argues that this intertextual reference creates the impression of 'a wider narrative world in which both romances are located';[75] the same can be said, on a much larger scale, of the Round Table.

There is, however, one significant difference in the Round Table's depiction in the works of Hartmann when compared to Chrétien's

---

72 See Jan Mohr, 'Agon, Elite und Egalität: Zu einem Strukturproblem höfischer Selbstkonzepte im Medium des Artusromans', *Deutsche Vierteljahrsschrift für Literaturwissenschaft und Geistesgeschichte* 91.4 (2017), 351–77 (355).
73 See Silvia Ranawake, 'The Emergence of German Arthurian Romance: Hartmann von Aue and Ulrich von Zatzikhofen', in *The Arthur of the Germans: The Arthurian Legend in Medieval German and Dutch Literature*, ed. W.H. Jackson and Silvia Ranawake (Cardiff, 2000), 38–53 (38–45).
74 Christoph J. Steppich, 'Geoffrey's *Historia regum Britanniae* and Wace's *Brut*: Secondary Sources for Hartmann's *Erec*?', *Monatshefte* 94.2 (2002), 165–88.
75 Green, 56.

romances. Like Laȝamon's *Brut* and the *Alliterative Morte Arthure*, German romances generally place Arthur at the Round Table, albeit with very different implications. In Hartmann's *Erec*, we see Arthur sit 'mit manegem guoten knehte / dâ zuo der tavelrunde (lines 1615–16, with many a good knight, there at the Round Table).[76] Similarly, in *Iwein*, the knights of the Round Table sit 'umbe den künec' (line 4535, around the king).[77] While Schmolke-Hasselmann attributes this to 'fundamental differences between the political systems of England and France on the one side, and Germany on the other',[78] this distinction cannot hold in view of the Insular approach to the Round Table after Wace. It has perhaps more to do with the fact that Hartmann's translation of Chrétien's *Erec* did not have to deal directly with the ambiguity of Wace's Round Table. For Hartmann, the Arthurian storyworld was already firmly established in the works of Chrétien: a fictional storyworld built around the Round Table, in which Arthur only figures as a *roi fainéant*, 'a necessary but static figurehead'.[79] Under these circumstances, Arthur's presence at the Table as a weak romance king does not seriously threaten the ahistoricity of the fictional romance world, and as a result Arthur's exact place at the Table becomes incidental.

When this storyworld does come under threat in Wolfram von Eschenbach's early thirteenth-century *Parzival*, following the complexity of Chrétien's *Conte del Graal*, the threat is of a rather different nature. Initially, Wolfram's Round Table seems to act as a narrative device very similar to that of Chrétien and Hartmann. Parzival is first properly introduced into the Arthurian world when he is told 'ich pringe dich durch wunder / für des künges tavelrunder' (143, lines 13–14, I bring you, for marvelling, before the king's Round Table).[80] This is equivalent to entering the storyworld of Arthurian romance, as becomes clear through the authorial address that immediately follows:

---

76 Hartmann von Aue, *Erec*, ed. Albert Leitzmann and Ludwig Wolff, 7th edn rev. Kurt Gärtner, Altdeutsche Textbibliothek 39 (Tübingen, 2006); all references are to this edition.
77 Hartmann von Aue, *Iwein*, ed. G.F. Benecke and K. Lachmann, 7th edn rev. Ludwig Wolff, 2 vols (Berlin, 1968); all references are to this edition.
78 Schmolke-Hasselmann, 'Round Table', 70.
79 Ashe, 'Anomalous King', 188.
80 Wolfram von Eschenbach, *Parzival: Studienausgabe*, ed. Karl Lachmann, trans. Peter Knecht, with an introduction by Bernd Schirok, 2nd edn (Berlin, 2003); all references are to this edition.

mîn hêr Hartman von Ouwe,
frou Ginovêr iwer frouwe
und iwer hêrre der künc Artûs,
den kumt ein mîn gast ze hûs.
(143, lines 21–4)

(My lord Hartmann von Aue,
Lady Guinevere, your lady,
And your lord, King Arthur,
Receive a guest of mine in their home.)

As Green argues, by invoking characters that Hartmann 'introduced […] in the first Arthurian romance in German', Wolfram identifies both his and Hartmann's world as fictional products.[81]

Wolfram explicitly acknowledges Hartmann as the German originator of the Arthurian storyworld, into which he brings Parzival as his own protagonist, perfectly following the established pattern of transfictional textual proliferation. At the same time, however, this explicit address also highlights the artificiality of this Arthurian world, which is also reflected in Wolfram's choice of rhyme words for the Round Table. Remarkably, there are only two possible rhymes for *tavelrunder* (Round Table) when it is in the rhyming position: either *wunder* (marvel) or *(be)sunder* (specially, apart). This stands in stark contrast to Hartmann's much more varied usage, but also to the French *reonde-monde* rhymes; instead of emphasising the Table's worldbuilding potential, Wolfram's rhymes primarily point to its exceptional artificiality.

The depiction of the Round Table itself later makes this particularly apparent. So far, Wolfram's Round Table has received comparatively little attention, with the notable exception of Konstantin Pratelidis and Bruno Quast, who both see it as a ceremonial centre of the Arthurian world that parallels the world of the Grail.[82] Yet the Table's depiction is more complicated than this. Most importantly, in the two *Parzival* episodes in which the Table features prominently, it is not even physically

---

81 Green, 66.
82 Konstantin Pratelidis, *Tafelrunde und Gral: Die Artuswelt und ihr Verhältnis zur Gralswelt im 'Parzival' Wolframs von Eschenbach* (Würzburg, 1994), 105–20; Bruno Quast, 'Dingpolitik: Gesellschaftstheoretische Überlegungen zu Rundtafel und Gral in Wolframs von Eschenbach *Parzival*', in *Dingkulturen: Objekte in Literatur, Kunst und Gesellschaft der Vormoderne*, ed. Anna Mühlherr, Heike Sahm, Monika Schausten, and Bruno Quast (Berlin, 2016), 171–84 (174).

present. When Arthur sets up his tent camp at the Plimizœl, the Table is noticeably absent: 'swie si wær ze Nantes lân, / man sprach ir reht ûf bluomen velt' (309, lines 12–13, although it had remained in Nantes, its rights were applied on a flower-meadow). Instead, it is represented by a piece of costly silk:

> Niht breit, sinewel gesniten,
> al nâch tavelrunder siten;
> wande in ir zuht des verjach:
> nâch gegenstuol dâ niemen sprach,
> diu gesitz wârn al gelîche hêr.
>
> (309, lines 21–5)

(Not broad, cut into a circle,
All according to the custom of the Round Table;
For its conventions forbade this:
No one asked for the seat of honour,
The seats were all equally noble.)

Eberhard Nellmann remarks that this invocation of equality recalls Wace's introduction of the Round Table.[83] As happens with Chrétien's echo of Wace in the *Conte del Graal*, however, this is also strongly undercut by the fact that the Table itself is deferred and remains unavailable. Additionally, this is made all the more remarkable by the fact that Chrétien does not mention the physical Round Table at all in the *Conte del Graal*. Yet when departing from his main source in choosing to include it, Wolfram does so by conspicuously marking its absence. Consequently, the storyworld built around it loses much of its power to contain the *Parzival* narrative.

The Table's problematic nature is only emphasised by its second appearance, during the climactic scene at Joflanze that confirms Parzival's and his half-brother Feirefiz's (re-)admission to the Round Table and thus the Arthurian world.[84] In this scene, the Table is certainly not, as Quast has it, 'buchstäblich ins Zentrum gestellt' (literally placed at the centre).[85] Not only does Arthur once again rely on 'ein tavelrunder rîche / ûz eime drîanthasmê' (775, lines 4–5, a splendid Round Table out

---

83 Eberhard Nellmann, 'Zu Wolframs Bildung und zum Literaturkonzept des *Parzival*', *Poetica* 28.3–4 (1996), 327–44 (339).
84 See Pratelidis, *Tafelrunde und Gral*, 117–18.
85 Quast, 'Dingpolitik', 174.

of a piece of *drîanthasmê* [a type of silk]); it is not even modelled after the real Table. Instead, Wolfram refers back to the representation of the Round Table at the Plimizœl: 'nâch der disiu wart gesniten' (775, line 9, this one was cut following the example of that one). We are then left with a representation of a representation, whose practical use is completely disavowed when the knights sit

> daz wol ein poynder landes was
> vome sedel an tavelrunder:
> diu stuont dâ mitten sunder,
> niht durch den nutz, et durh den namn.
> (775, lines 14–17)

> (so that there was half a list field's space
> Between the seats and the Round Table:
> That stood apart there in the middle,
> Not for its use, but for its name.)

On this occasion, the Table is diminished to a small symbolic central point.[86] It is there to provide a notional focus for the fictional Arthurian storyworld but is only tenuously connected to the larger world of Wolfram's *Parzival*.

The Round Table as the anchor of the fictional Arthurian storyworld is thus present and absent at the same time, once more becoming an ambiguous motif. In a way that recalls Wace's *Roman de Brut*, it both establishes the world of Arthurian romance and fails to completely tie Wolfram's *Parzival* to it. Of course, Parzival himself is ultimately called away as 'Gahmuretes suon' (781, line 3, son of Gahmuret) to join his wife Condwiramurs and his son Lohengrin to reign as Grail King, leaving the world of the Round Table behind. The romance's genealogical ending, in which Wolfram makes sure to refer to 'sîniu kint, sîn hôch geslehte' (827, line 15, his children, his noble line), could be seen as a conscious departure from the ahistorical storyworld, separate from Wace's dynastic history, established by Chrétien. As Timothy McFarland argues, by placing Parzival's story between that of his parents and that of his children, Wolfram appears to frame his story as 'a family history of the fictional dynasty of Anjou'.[87] It is therefore interesting to note that it

---

86 Knapp, 'Artushof als Raumkulisse', 32.
87 Timothy McFarland, 'The Emergence of the German Grail Romance: Wolfram von Eschenbach, *Parzival*', in *The Arthur of the Germans*, ed. Jackson

is now the genealogical history of one of Arthur's knights that threatens the ahistorical romance world of King Arthur and his Round Table. Nellmann even suggests that Wolfram may have known both Wace's *Roman de Brut* and Chrétien's romances from a manuscript compilation like BnF fr. 1450,[88] which would provide a precedent for this kind of oscillation between genealogical history and fictional romance. In any case, the instability of the Round Table in *Parzival* can only add to the multivalent reception posited by both Green and Nellmann, who argue that Wolfram's heterogeneous audiences could have understood his narrative as either fiction or history.[89]

Beyond Wolfram's ambiguous depiction, however, the Round Table certainly retained its importance for facilitating textual proliferation in Continental romance, usually by adding new protagonists to the Arthurian storyworld. This includes the early thirteenth-century *Wigalois* by Wirnt von Grafenberg, which is thought to have been at least partly influenced by Wolfram's *Parzival*.[90] Although the plot of *Wigalois* is largely based on French romances, it introduces a protagonist who, in this form, is most likely original.[91] The Round Table then serves as a benchmark of chivalric honour, which gives Wigalois legitimacy as an Arthurian protagonist. In the beginning, it is announced that a knight who has done remarkable deeds 'daz er der taveln reht besaz, / den hêt man immer deste baz' (lines 161–2, so that he had the right to sit at the Table, he was always better regarded for it).[92] Accordingly, the first

---

and Ranawake, 54–68 (64); see also Adrian Stevens, 'Wolfram von Eschenbach, Gottfried von Strassburg, and the Politics of Literary Adaptation: The Grail and Tristan Romances and the Court of Otto IV (1198–1218)', in *Medieval Francophone Literary Culture outside France: Studies in the Moving Word*, ed. Nicola Morato and Dirk Schoenaers (Turnhout, 2019), 213–40.

88 Nellmann, 'Zu Wolframs Bildung', 338.
89 Green, 69; see also Nellmann, 'Zu Wolframs Bildung', 343.
90 The prevalent theory is that Wirnt only knew books I–VI of Wolfram's *Parzival*, which includes the first but not the second Round Table scene; see particularly Eberhard Nellmann, '"Parzival" (Buch I–VI) und "Wigalois": Zur Frage der Teilveröffentlichung von Wolframs Roman', *Zeitschrift für deutsches Altertum und deutsche Literatur* 139.2 (2010), 135–52; see also Gesine Mierke, 'Genealogie und Intertextualität: Zu Wolframs von Eschenbach *Parzival* und Wirnts von Grafenberg *Wigalois*', *Amsterdamer Beiträge zur älteren Germanistik* 74 (2015), 180–200.
91 See Christoph Fasbender, *Der 'Wigalois' Wirnts von Grafenberg: Eine Einführung* (Berlin, 2010), 8–12.
92 Wirnt von Grafenberg, *Wigalois*, ed./trans. Sabine Seelbach and Ulrich

narrative climax is then marked by Wigalois's ceremonial addition to the fellowship of the Round Table:

> Der milte künic vuorte in sâ
> zuo der tavelrunde
> und gap im an der stunde
> der taveln reht unde stat
>   (lines 1670–3)
>
> (The gracious king thus led him
> To the Round Table
> And gave him at the same time
> The right and dignity to sit at the Table.)

Wigalois is thus added to the storyworld built around the Round Table, and Wirnt's romance can initially draw on its transfictional romance world.[93] In this way, textual proliferation facilitated by the Round Table continues to shape Continental Arthurian romance.

*

In short, we see that the Round Table as a narrative device plays a central role in the development of Continental romance following the trend summarised by Green as 'the liberation of the author from being tied to history'.[94] Wace creates an essentially ambiguous motif, setting up a separation between, on the one hand, King Arthur and historical truth and, on the other, the Knights of the Round Table and fictitious tales. His prioritisation of king and history, however, is easily reversible. In the terms of the aesthetics of proliferation, Chrétien then simply had to use the ontologically stable yet ahistorical storyworld offered by the Round Table to situate his transfictional Arthurian romances. This artificial world can only subsist in twelfth- and early thirteenth-century verse romance by sidelining the dynastic history King Arthur represents. Yet, as we have also seen in the case of Middle High German Arthurian romances, it comes to characterise the early Continental romance tradition. Conversely, the historical Insular tradition represented by

---

Seelbach, 2nd rev. edn (Berlin, 2014); all references are to this edition.
93 On Wirnt's own complex engagement with fictional and historical traditions, see Annegret Oehme, *The Knight without Boundaries: Yiddish and German Arthurian* Wigalois *Adaptations* (Leiden, 2021), 47–72.
94 Green, 195.

Laȝamon resolves the ambiguity of Wace's Round Table by maintaining King Arthur as a historical king and giving him a seat at the Table, allowing no space for romance to branch off from history. Of course, the Round Table's importance is not restricted to fictional narratives: it also powerfully shaped the political imagination throughout Europe in the Middle Ages.[95] As a worldbuilding device, however, it provides a key to the processes of transfictional textual proliferation that can be retraced in both Old French and Middle High German verse romances. The same may be possible in other medieval European literatures: as Lori J. Walters suggests, for instance, the motif of the Round Table may also play a significant role in the emergence of Middle Dutch verse romance.[96] For now, however, this survey of the importance of the Round Table in the development of Arthurian romances clearly demonstrates its crucial role for fictional worldbuilding. The Round Table facilitates the creation of the storyworld in which fictional Arthurian romances can be set, and it furthermore encourages the proliferation of these romances throughout Europe in the late twelfth and early thirteenth centuries. We may then agree all the more emphatically with Baumgartner's incidental comment that Chrétien's Arthurian romances, as well as the works derived from them, are 'more accurately categorised as "Romances of the Round Table"'.[97]

95 See particularly Paul Töbelmann, 'Imaginationen und Fiktionen des Adels im Mittelalter: Eine Annäherung am Beispiel von König Artus' Tafelrunde', *Archiv für Kulturgeschichte* 94 (2012), 261–91; see also Vale, 'Arthur in English Society'.
96 See Lori J. Walters, 'Reconfiguring Wace's Round Table: Walewein and the Rise of the National Vernaculars', *Arthuriana* 15.2 (2005), 39–58.
97 Emmanuèle Baumgartner, 'Chrétien's Medieval Influence: From the Grail Quest to the Joy of the Court', trans. Véronique Zara, in *A Companion to Chrétien de Troyes*, ed. Lacy and Grimbert, 214–27 (214, note 2).

3

Gautier de Coinci's *Miracles de Nostre Dame* and the Powers of Olfaction[1]

Henry Ravenhall

> Smell is the mute sense, the one without words. Lacking a vocabulary, we are left tongue-tied, groping for words in a sea of inarticulate pleasure and exaltation.[2]

Smell is hard to represent in text or image. Describing the difference between two pleasant or unpleasant fragrances – in English at least – pushes us into comparative structures that can only point outside representational limits to the world of real experience (it smells *of*, it smells *like* …). What tends to be registered primarily in our descriptions is a value judgment or an affective response, normally pleasure or disgust. Aroma acts on us, activating memories and emotions, past and present. Spaces may be coterminous with scents, which makes olfactory perception a way of navigating and understanding our environment. Because smell can be so visceral, it is a site onto which ethical and social values are projected. Bigoted distinctions in class and race may be expressed along olfactory lines. Discernment for truth may be conceived as an act of sniffing (Nietzsche located his genius in his nostrils), and suspicious activity may give off a 'fishy' smell.[3] Olfactory scientist Avery Gilbert states that while smell is in the animal world predominantly a

---

1 I thank Giulia Boitani, Miranda Griffin, Johannes Junge Ruhland, Lucy MacGregor, and William Tullett for their advice and feedback on this essay. This research was funded by a British Academy Postdoctoral Fellowship held at the University of Cambridge from 2021 to 2023.
2 Diane Ackerman, *A Natural History of the Senses* (New York, 1990), 6.
3 On Nietzsche's nose, see Chantal Jacquet, *Philosophie de l'odorat* (Paris, 2010), 410–25. For the roots of the metaphor in medieval and early modern discernment of the freshness of produce, see William Tullett, *Smell in Eighteenth-Century England: A Social Sense* (Oxford, 2019), 45–7.

call to action, 'human cognitive abilities turn smells into symbols'.[4] As an object of cultural inquiry, smell sits therefore at a suggestive intersection of actual sense-experience, affect, and symbolization. All the while, the serious challenge of disentangling these three aspects from one another makes smell of potential methodological and theoretical importance for new lines of research in sensory history, affect theory, and aesthetics as a branch of philosophy.[5]

This essay takes as its focus the poetic output of Gautier de Coinci, a monastic author writing in Old French between 1214 and 1233 at the Abbey of Vic-sur-Aisne in northeastern France. Gautier composed what is now called the *Miracles de Nostre Dame* (Miracles of Our Lady), a compilation made of two 'books' (*livres*) that follow a carefully designed structure.[6] Each book opens and ends with a series of lyric songs and chants, while the main bulk of the text is taken up by miracle narratives of various lengths written in octosyllabic rhyming couplets, a standard French narrative form of the twelfth and early thirteenth centuries. These miracle stories have a strong moralistic bent, and what Gautier calls the 'tail' (*queue*) of the tale ends on an ethical or religious truth. Gautier is one of the most widely transmitted French-writing authors of the century, as his narratives survive in over a hundred manuscripts.[7] The *Miracles* in their manuscript context are sometimes accompanied by biographical texts about the historical Virgin.[8] Gautier is rightly seen as a key figure in the rapid spread of the cult of the Virgin in the 1200s, and

---

[4] Avery Gilbert, *What the Nose Knows: The Science of Scent in Everyday Life* (New York, 2008), 65–6.

[5] There is an emerging field of 'smell studies' that cuts across history, literature, theory, and museum/heritage studies. See, for instance, William Tullett et al., 'Smell, History, and Heritage', *The American Historical Review* 127.1 (2022), 261–309. For a philosophy of aesthetics that addresses the stakes of 'olfactory art', see Larry Shiner, *Art Scents: Exploring the Aesthetics of Smell and the Olfactory Arts* (Oxford, 2020).

[6] On the careful design and chronology of the *Miracles*, see Masami Okubo, 'La Formation de la collection des *Miracles* de Gautier de Coinci I', *Romania* 123 (2005), 141–212, and 'La Formation de la collection des *Miracles* de Gautier de Coinci II', *Romania* 123 (2005), 406–58.

[7] Roughly 60 per cent of which are from the thirteenth century. For the list of manuscripts divided chronologically, see Alison Stones's appendix to *Gautier de Coinci: Miracles, Music, and Manuscripts*, ed. Kathy M. Krause and Alison Stones (Turnhout, 2006), 353–7.

[8] On these genealogical texts within their literary and manuscript contexts, see Maureen Barry McCann Boulton, *Sacred Fictions of Medieval France:*

to this end scholars are quick to point out his ingenious appropriation of the courtly register.[9] The Virgin becomes the idealized female beloved of secular lyric. Highly interesting from a musicological perspective is his use of contrafacture for the lyric portion of the *Miracles*.[10] Gautier takes well-known melodies from secular trouvères and repurposes them as vehicles through which to praise the mother of God. The effect of such a layering points to the associative, and to an extent indeterminate, powers of music. In addition to sound, sight and touch have been recognized as crucial to Gautier's project in its material forms, that is, as performance and/or book.[11] The Virgin's miraculous apparitions, often arising out of a believer's interaction with a representation of the Virgin within the narrative frame, are reflected in manuscript illuminations that become themselves *loci* of divine potential.[12] Relatedly, 'tactile devotion', a set of practices placed under the umbrella term 'affective piety', through which believers acted out their faith by touching objects, is also considered central to the manuscripts' use across their many illuminated copies.[13]

Narrative Theology in the Lives of Christ and the Virgin, 1150–1500 (Cambridge, UK, 2015), 21–79.

9   Tony Hunt, *Miraculous Rhymes: The Writing of Gautier de Coinci* (Cambridge, UK, 2007), 49: 'His aim is to appropriate the language, themes and characters of courtly literature with the intention of transcending that world in a vision of Mariocentric love to which his audience will find themselves subtly transported.'

10 See, for example, Ardis Butterfield, 'Introduction: Gautier de Coinci, *Miracles de Nostre Dame*: Texts and Manuscripts', in *Gautier de Coinci*, ed. Krause and Stones, 1–18 (8–13); and Meghan Quinlan, 'Repetition as Rebirth: A Sung Epitaph for Gautier de Coinci', *Music & Letters* 101.4 (2020), 623–56 (625–6).

11 Brigitte Roux and Marion Uhlig, 'L'*Invention* de Léocade: Reliques et figures d'auteur dans les *Miracles de Nostre Dame* de Gautier de Coinci', *Cahiers de civilisation médiévale* 249.1 (2020), 19–40 (21): 'Une œuvre d'art totale, où texte, chant et peinture concourent à un seul et même édifice artistique' (A total work of art, where text, song, and painting contribute to one and the same artistic edifice). All translations are my own unless otherwise indicated.

12 See, for instance, Anna Russakoff, *Imagining the Miraculous: Miraculous Images of the Virgin Mary in French Illuminated Manuscripts, ca. 1250–ca. 1450* (Toronto, 2019), 21–49.

13 See Jane Sinnett-Smith, 'Blood, Bones, and Gold: Rewriting Relics in Medieval French Verse Saints' Lives 1150–1300' (unpublished PhD thesis, University of Warwick, 2019), 289–305 (305): 'Engaging with Mary's open, transmissible materiality in this tactile way suggests that the reader's presence also has the capacity to be extended and transmitted beyond the boundaries of his or her ordinary body.' Manuscripts of the *Miracles*, and the haptic interactions they

Multisensory perception, as it relates to aesthetic experience, is thus an important part of the *Miracles*' design and reception. Gautier's treatment of the sense of smell, however, has been overlooked. Olfactory references punctuate the *Miracles* and function in a variety of ways. In this essay, I will first argue that odors in the *Miracles* are a site onto which values are projected, but where smell's viscerality – its apparent short-circuiting of linguistic mediation – is mobilized to connect dogma with affect. Next, I will examine the miracle regarding the theft and recovery of Saint Leocadia's relics, which is considered Gautier's most personal and emotional miracle, and in which the topic of smell recurs at several points. I will suggest that smell's associative and memorial power – the way it joins up affect, memory, and an experience of space – works to bind Gautier's community of listeners together in their shared relation to local spaces of devotion and the materiality of prior miraculous activity. The potential of odors to move between the human and more-than-human is shown to be a key affordance in this regard. An issue of broader methodological and theoretical concern, the relationship between olfaction (a term I use to focus more on *how* smell is processed), form, and aesthetics is considered in my essay's final section. I argue that smell's modal specificity – its ontological doubling into both odor-source and odor-proper – gives it a special place in Gautier's devotional and aesthetic framework. Drawing on lines of inquiry in cognitive linguistics and olfactory aesthetics, and reacting against a latent tendency among modern scholars to 'deodorize' premodernity, I propose that we consider textual smell a fundamental part of the multisensory experience imparted by the *Miracles*.[14]

---

have elicited, are a case study in my British Academy Postdoctoral Fellowship project, 'Tactile Communities: Emotion and the Experience of Medieval French Literature'.

14 Alain Corbin, *Le Miasme et la jonquille: L'odorat et l'imaginaire social XVIIIe–XIXe siècles* (Paris, 1982), popularized the (highly Eurocentric) idea that modernity and the 'deodorization' of society co-evolved. Constance Classen has suggested that 'no sense has suffered such a reversal of cultural fortune as smell', *Worlds of Sense: Exploring the Senses in History and across Cultures* (New York, 1993), 15.

The Values of Smell

For Gautier, smell is a labile site of accessible meaning that lends itself to a mode of direct, homiletic communication. At the same time, as we will see later, smell resists linguistic equivalence, and its ineffability is mobilized in service of the devotional and mystical aspects of Gautier's project. Throughout the *Miracles*, 'good' and 'bad' scents become representative of 'good' and 'bad' qualities and behaviors. Smell marks a level of consonance between inner worth and outer perception.[15] Virtue manifests itself in a sweet odor. Sin, like disease (a materialization of sin), is stench. These motifs have biblical and patristic precedents. As Susan Ashbrook Harvey puts it in her discussion of early Christianity: 'To be mortal was to reek of sin. Rottenness and putrefaction were mortality's nature, revolting stink its unmistakable mark.'[16] The *Song of Songs* contains many allusions to sweet fragrances (1:2–3, 1:14, 4:11–16, etc.).[17] In the *Miracles*, the fragrant flower represents at once Gautier's lyric compositions (1 Pr. 2, 1:21, 33–5), the Virgin they laud (e.g., 2 Mir. 29, 4:340, 2–4), and the virginity she embodies (2 Chast. 10, 3:472, 325–7).[18] The senses may be gateways to bodily temptation, but they are also paths to spiritual regeneration. A holy aroma remakes body and soul (1 Mir. 44, 3:216, 65–7), as does the taste of the word *Maria* when chanted, felt on the tongue, and thereby savored in the mouth (2 Mir. 30, 4:406, 754–65 and 4:408–9, 817–25).[19] In narratives of healing, the transformative ethical power of the Virgin's intervention is reflected in a change in olfactory state: stench becomes fragrance as sin becomes virtue.

15   The proverb 'Ki de boins est, souef flaire' (He who is good smells sweet) is expounded in the opening lines of the second part of the so-called *Chronique de Tournai*, as transmitted, for instance, by Paris, BnF, fr. 24430, fol. 151r.
16   Susan Ashbrook Harvey, *Scenting Salvation: Ancient Christianity and the Olfactory Imagination* (Berkeley, 2006), 202.
17   Le Mans, Bibliothèque municipale, MS 173, contains a French verse paraphrase of the *Song of Songs* that is followed by *Du vilain asnier*, a very short fabliau about a low-born man who faints upon smelling the sublime scent of an electuary and is only revived through the stench of manure. See Philippe Ménard, *Fabliaux français du Moyen Âge* (Geneva, 1998), 1:199–200.
18   Quotations are taken from *Les Miracles de Nostre Dame par Gautier de Coinci*, ed. V. Frederic Koenig, 4 vols (Geneva, 1955–70). References appear in-line as follows: (shorthand poem name, volume number: page number, line numbers).
19   The Virgin's name also smells sweeter than any electuary ('Tes doz nons ieult souef plus de nul laituaire', 2 Sal. 35, 4:550, 124).

Any discussion of smell in the *Miracles* must be related to the language of sin, waste, and pollution that pervades the text. Terms like *ordure* (filth), *pullent* (stinking/sinful), and *puïr* (reek) signal the abjection of moral decay.[20] Gautier employs the standard homiletic register to warn his audience to take care of their souls, for instance:

Tant puans est l'orde pullente
L'ame envenime et enpullente,
Le cors esnerve et amaigrist
Et l'ame torne et enaigrist.
(1 Mir. 42, 3:189, 609–12)

(The polluting filth is so smelly that it poisons and pollutes the soul, weakens and wastes the body away, and the soul turns and grows sour.)

This rhetoric centers on an awareness of the body as organic life and of the processes of decomposition to which it is subject. The stench of decay haunts human embodiment and marks its mortality and sin.

Gautier frequently draws on the language of purity, cleanliness, and virginity as a direct counterpoint to this rhetoric of decomposition. In his laudatory poem addressed to the nuns of the Abbey of Notre-Dame in Soissons, Gautier encourages his female audience to aspire to the sweet smell of chastity:[21]

Virginitez par est si nete
Que flors de lis ne vïolete
N'iout si soëf come ele fait.
(2 Chast. 10, 3:467, 190–2)

(Virginity is so very clean that neither lily nor violet smells as sweet as it does.)

Gautier is keen to emphasize the social dimensions of such a rejection of carnal pleasure. The sisters of Notre-Dame-de-Soissons embody the virtues of virginity and chastity, which are

---

20 The importance to Gautier of the lexical cluster around *pullent/enpullenter* is suggested by its appearance as an *annominatio* in 1 Mir. 21, 2:203, 158–62.
21 On smell and virginity for medieval thinkers, see Katelynn Robinson, *The Sense of Smell in the Middle Ages: A Source of Certainty* (New York, 2020), 186–90. Robinson discusses Jacobus de Voragine (c. 1230–98/99), the author of the *Legenda aurea*, who in his sermons on the Virgin and on Lent makes many references to odors.

deus fleurs si enflorees
Que qui les a bien odorees,
Plaisanz li sont sour toute chose.
(2 Chast. 10, 3:476, 409-11)

(two flowers that have blossomed so much that for whoever has smelled them well, they are more pleasing to him/her than anything else.)

Here, the ethical example that the nuns set for the community at large is represented in smell's status as being 'for' others as much 'for' the self. In other words, its transmissibility compels the wider public body to partake of the same 'fragrant' behavior. The Old French verbs *odorer* and *flairer* refer both to the emission and reception of scents. An ethics of 'give and take' among the social body is reflected in the idea of contributing positively to, and benefiting from, the shared olfactory space.

Smell, then, reflects one's moral state, but it can also have corporeal or spiritual effects. Its jointly indexical and agential capacities are what give smell specificity as a metaphor. Gautier notes how the Virgin *qua* scent revives those in desolation, like the Empress of Rome, who in smelling Mary is 'saoulee' (soothed), 'confortee' (comforted), and 'releesciee' (returned to joy, 2 Ch. 9, 3:385, 2076-82). Yet, while the Virgin as restorative fragrance is understood as a metaphor for the consolation to be found in piety, Gautier is always insistent that these are real olfactory experiences. Towards the end of his *Miracles*, he describes how his own migraines, which he associates with diabolic intervention, were cured by the Virgin's scent (2 Dout. 34, 4:497-8, 1470-94).[22] He approaches her, finds the air around her pleasing, and lingers there:

Je croi n'arai gaires esté
Delez la blanche fleur d'esté,
Delez la precïeuse rose
Ou Diex meïsmes se repose,
Quant recrïee iert ma cervele.
Tout mal assomme et escervele

22 Gautier's migraines – if they are to be identified as actual medical experiences – could have caused hypersensitivity to strong sensory encounters. A recent study, for instance, found that of the migraine-sufferers surveyed, 55.1 per cent had 'osmophobia', an aversion to potent odors (Keisuke Suzuki et al, 'Investigating the Relationships between the Burden of Multiple Sensory Hypersensitivity Symptoms and Headache-Related Disability in Patients with Migraine', *The Journal of Headache and Pain* 22, article no. 77 (2021)).

> Et tout diable evanuïst
> La sainte oudeurs qui de li ist.
> Vie et santez de li nous vient.
> De vos amez s'il vos souvient,
> Oudourez la sanz nul delai
> De cuer et d'ame, clerc et lai.
> La sainte oudeurs de Nostre Dame
> Saoule toute et refait l'ame.
>
> (2 Dout. 34, 4:497–8, 1479–91)

(I think I'd barely been beside the white summer flower, beside the precious rose, in which God Himself rests, when my mind was created anew. The holy odor she emits hammers and batters all pain and lays low any demon. Life and health come to us from it. As such it reminds you of your souls, fragrance them without any delay, both body and soul, cleric and layperson. The holy smell of Our Lady satisfies and remakes any soul.)

The Virgin's 'holy smell' ('sainte oudeurs') is figured here as a material force that physically beats away illness, whose moral and corporeal dimensions are co-constitutive in their relation to the sin that is its condition. Smell as an aerial element, like breath, affords a way of thinking about the physical movement from exterior body to interior soul. The act of olfaction prompts introspection, care for the health of the soul, and a desire for devotion.

The Virgin's scent is thus figured as anathema to diabolic influence in the material world. Demons are everywhere in the *Miracles*. Carrying out Satan's will, they try to take their victims to Hell and, in most cases, are only thwarted by the Virgin's intercession. They are the very embodiments of evil and temptation, and they move physically in the world. These infernal agents represent the corruptibility of flesh and the carnal sin that is a moral condition of humanity's existence on earth. No human is safe from their wickedness, and, as such, humanity must rely on the redemptive power of the Virgin. As Brigitte Cazelles has argued, a state of weakness, and hence of vulnerability to the diabolic, is what unites the characters of the *Miracles* and justifies Gautier's whole poetic operation.[23] These demons are often represented in illustrations of *Miracles* manuscripts, and, in many instances, have been aggressively smudged by readers who, intent on countering their nefarious force, express their

---

23 Brigitte Cazelles, *La Faiblesse chez Gautier de Coinci* (Saratoga, 1978).

own ethical allegiance to the side of good.[24] Far from being metaphysical or abstract beings, these demons require a corporeal response.

The notion of sweet odor as a physical force that counters stench in the air, therefore, mirrors the Manichean opposition between Virgin and Satan in the ethical landscape. Smell's medicinal capacities are used to represent, and thus render more immediate, a set of conflicting values. These medicinal capacities are noted by the Reclus (or 'Recluse') de Molliens, a monastic author with whom Gautier is often compared and who was also writing didactic-moralistic vernacular poetry in the 1220s:[25]

> D'odour de lis, d'odour rosine,
> D'odour d'espeche et rachine
> Est au nes bons congiés donés
> Por santé et por medechine
> Et por oster le puasine
> Del enferm tant k'il soit sanés.[26]

(The smell of the lily, the rosy smell, the smell of spice and root give good relief to the nose for health and for medicine, and to get rid of the stench of the ill person so that he may be cured.)

When it comes to the materiality of smell, the distinction between the medicinal and the spiritual did not exist as it does now.[27] Cutting across

24 For example: Besançon, Bibliothèque municipale, MS 551, fol. 51r; Paris, BnF, fr. 1533, fol. 39r; Paris, BnF, fr. 19166, fol. 145v; Paris, BnF, fr. 22928, fol. 103r; Paris, BnF, fr. 25532, fol. 45v. Michael Camille, *The Gothic Idol: Ideology and Image-Making in Medieval Art* (Cambridge, UK, 1989), 63: 'To understand the power of representations in demonic form, we must rid ourselves of the modern notion of evil as immaterial action of the will or embodied in historical character. Evil was not an idea to medieval people. It was real and had bodies. These bodies were devils, which were as "real" in pictorial terms as a king or calendar scene in medieval art.'
25 On the popularity and material context of the Reclus, whose works survive in forty-four manuscripts, often alongside Gautier's *Miracles*, see Ariane Bottex-Ferragne, 'De la Production à la réception: Le Reclus de Molliens en morceaux dans les recueils de fabliaux', in *Les Centres de production des manuscrits vernaculaires au Moyen Âge*, ed. Gabriele Giannini and Francis Gingras (Paris, 2015), 139–60.
26 Li romans de carité et miserere *du Renclus de Moiliens*, ed. A.-G. van Hamel, 2 vols (Paris, 1885), 1:208–9, CXL, 7–12.
27 In a study of eighth- and ninth-century recipes, Claire Burridge has emphasized the medical application of incense, which shares many ingredients

the scientific and ethical registers, the Reclus stresses how smell, like the other senses, can lead to temptation as much as redemption. Humans, he writes, smell simply for pleasure, so where there is no need:

> Mout est li nes desordenés;
> A mainte odour est enclinés
> Ou besoigne pas ne l'encline.[28]

(The nose is greatly disordered; it is inclined to many odors where necessity does not require it.)

He moralizes on the danger of being misled by the nose, that is, of following animal impulses rather than listening to reason. Using the *exemplum* of the Wildman Merlin, who is captured in the forest through a bait of cooking food (as narrated, for instance, in the *Roman de Silence*), the Reclus warns of abiding by 'espiehaste le narine' (the spit-seeking nostril).[29] The target of his moralization is both those who, lacking restraint and self-control, follow their noses, and those who, also lacking restraint, tempt others to do so. In this regard, perfume is especially dangerous:

> Ki mist en robe odour ambrine
> Ou autre espeche alexandrine
> Mout fu de flairier deffrenés.[30]

(He/she who doused his/her clothes in amber scent, or any other Alexandrian spice, lost all control over his/her sense of smell.)

The view that enticing scents impede reflection was a theological commonplace, as expressed for instance by Bernard of Clairvaux ('odoratus impedit cogitationem', smell impedes reflection) and Ambrose

---

with remedies. See 'Incense in Medicine: An Early Medieval Perspective', *Early Medieval Europe* 28.2 (2020), 219–55.
28 *Miserere*, ed. van Hamel, 1:208–9, CXL, 4–6.
29 *Miserere*, ed. van Hamel, 1:209, CXLI, 6–12. *Silence: A Thirteenth-Century French Romance*, ed./trans. Sarah Roche-Mahdi (East Lansing, 1992), lines 5953–8: 'Et quant Merlins le flaërra, / A la car lués repaiërra. / S'il a humanité en lui, / Il i venra, si com jo cui, / Par la fumiere et par le flair / Del rost qu'il sentira en l'air.' (Roche-Mahdi's translation: 'As soon as Merlin smells the scent and smoke, he'll come running. If there is any human nature left in him, he will come here, I'm certain, attracted by the smoke and the scent of the roasting meat in the air.')
30 *Miserere*, ed. van Hamel, 1:209, CXLI, 1–3.

of Milan ('inhalavit odor, et cogitationem impedivit', he who inhales odor impedes reflection).[31] Counterbalancing redemption and temptation throughout the *Miracles*, Gautier is equally cautious of fragrance as a sign of artifice, excess, and depravity. In a vituperative, thirty-line diatribe, he rails against the 'pullentes', that is, impure or fallen women, who wear cosmetics to attract sexual attention. Gautier's gendered engagement with smell here hinges on the contrast between the Virgin as the pinnacle of non-artificial womanhood and a lower class of mortal, ageing, and sexually active women. The olfactory dimensions of cosmetics, reflecting moral pollution, are conveyed in two related images: the use of saffron as a beauty product, and the metaphor of crocodile excrement for make-up (derived from the Latin *croceus*, the adjectival form of the word for 'saffron', and, by analogy, the association of *crocodilus* with falseness in the bestiary tradition).[32] Gautier attempts to show the abject reality beneath the artifice, all the while drawing awareness to the abjection *within* the artifice:

> N'i a si vielle ne si grille
> N'ait do merdier do cocodrille.
> Fame bien doit, c'en est la some,
> Puïr et a Dieu et a home
> Qui vis a paint, taint et doré
> *Cocodrilli de stercore.*
>
> (1 Mir. 42, 3:184, 481–6)

(There isn't a woman so old or so gaunt who isn't made up in crocodile shit. A woman who has her face painted, tinged, and shimmering with

---

31 Bernard of Clairvaux, *De cognitione humanae conditionis*, in *Opera omnia*, ed. Jean Mabillon, 2 vols (Paris, 1839), 2:685; Ambrose, *De fuga saeculi*, in *S. Ambrosii Opera*, ed. Karl Schenkl, 2 vols (Prague, 1897), 2:164 (1.3.15–16). Ambrose's declarations of olfactory renunciation still leave space for sensual delight in the liturgy, as Harvey acknowledges in *Scenting Salvation*, 161: 'Here, the barest trace of a scent threatens to sabotage the soul's entire discipline; to the catechumen in the liturgy, however, sweet scents guide the soul through the ritual processes and even through the revelatory capacities of the occasion.'

32 Guillaume le Clerc's *Bestiaire divin* (c. 1210) refers to old women who wear a crocodile-derived *onguent* (*oignement*, ointment) on their faces. *Le Bestiaire, das Thierbuch des normannischen Dichters Guillaume le Clerc*, ed. Robert Reinsch (Leipzig, 1890), 295, lines 1679–82. On medieval saffron, see Paul Freedman, *Out of the East: Spices and the Medieval Imagination* (New Haven, 2008), 10.

crocodile faeces (*cocodrilli de stercore*) truly will, that is the fact of the matter, stink both to God and to man.)

The repetition of the conjunction *et a ... et a ...* (both to ... and to ...) hints at the double-meaning of *puïr* (stink), one metaphorical and the other literal, that lies at the heart of Gautier's rhetoric of sin and sensuality. As C.M. Woolgar notes, medieval cultures had 'standard repertoires of bad smells to associate with prostitutes and old and ugly women'.[33] Seeking to trigger a disgust-response through the association of excrement with sex, Gautier goes on to equate this excessive sight-smell with nausea and revulsion:

> Ausi sont mais ensafrenees
> Con s'estoient en safren nees.
> Si se florissent, si se perent
> Pasque florie de loins perent,
> Mais a un mot vos en di tout:
> De loins 'enhen!' et de pres 'tprout!'
> (1 Mir. 42, 3:184, 487–92)

(They are so stained/perfumed in saffron (cosmetically enhanced) it's as if they were born in saffron. They are so floral and so dressed-up that from afar they seem like Palm Sunday, but in a word I'll tell you it all: from afar '*enhen!*' and up close '*tprout!*')

The floral and fragrant motifs that are associated with the Virgin and the virtues she embodies are turned on their head. The *rime équivoque* of 'ensafrenees' (lit. 'stained/perfumed with saffron' = cosmetically enhanced) and 'en safren nees' (born in saffron) humorously splices the excessive artifice and its opposite, a natural attribute from birth. The ostensibly positive imagery of Palm Sunday is tempered with a verb of semblance (*perent*) and a prepositional adverb marking distance (*de loins*). Gautier models what he considers an appropriate affective reaction when encountering these women in the urban space. The precise meaning of the interjections 'enhen!' and 'tprout!' – something like 'phwoar!' and 'yuck!' – would have depended on their use within the social sphere, as well as their sounding and gestural accompaniment in performance. The moralistic force of these interjections relies on

---

33 C.M. Woolgar, 'Medieval Smellscapes', in *Smell and History: A Reader*, ed. Mark M. Smith (Morgantown, 2018), 50–75 (61).

their actual use in response to sensory stimuli and their reference to the phenomena of daily life, and then their contrastive force within the same line. Gautier circles back to make an equivalence between moral turpitude and the wearing of cosmetics:

> N'i a torchepot ne giffarde,
> Tant ait desous povre fardel,
> N'ait cuevrechief, manche ou hardiel
> Et qui ne weille estre fardee
> Por plus sovent estre esgardee.
> Assez ont merde en lor fardiaus.
> (1 Mir. 42, 3:184, 494–9)

(There isn't a kitchen- or servant-girl, whatever she is like beneath her wretched appearance, and whatever her headscarf, coat, or fashion piece, who doesn't want to be made-up so she can be looked at more often. They have a fair bit of shit in their make-up.)

The characteristic wordplay that runs through this passage, and that can only partially be translated in how 'make-up' in English refers both to the cosmetic product and one's bodily constitution, depends on a suggestive indeterminacy between *fart* – *farder* (make-up – to wear make-up) and *fardel* (figuratively a body, or load/burden, especially of a moral kind).[34] The tricky line 'tant ait desous povre fardel', as Olivier Collet suggests, could mean both 'whatever she is like beneath her wretched appearance', or, if *fardel* is understood as diminutive of *fart*, 'whatever she is like beneath her cheap slap.'[35] In the same way, the final line can be read as referring to the moral failing, symbolized in excrement as filth ('merde'), that is carried in the body, while presenting the ostensibly 'factual' (though still symbolic) truth of having feces ('merde') as a constitutive ingredient for make-up.[36] The truth of smell, as opposed to sight, which can be deceived by appearance, is what

---

34 See *fardel (-iaus)*, in Olivier Collet, *Glossaire et index critiques des œuvres d'attribution certaine de Gautier de Coinci (Vie de sainte Cristine et Miracles de Nostre Dame)*, établis d'après les éditions d'Olivier Collet et V. Frederic Koenig (Geneva, 2000), 244–5.
35 Collet, *Glossaire*, 245, translates as: 'La dernière des filles, quelle qu'elle soit sous sa pauvre apparence (i.e., "aussi misérables que soient ses dehors", sous-entendus: "trompeurs") ne songe qu'à s'attifer et à se peinturlurer pour attirer les regards.'
36 Woolgar, 'Medieval Smellscapes', 57: 'A formula used by the Dominicans for

betrays these women as morally inferior, even if the visual qualities of 'shit' are used to make them more attractive.[37] In a style of qualification that we find in other instances of clerical misogyny, Gautier proceeds to differentiate the 'good' and 'foolish' women through their smell:[38]

> Por Dieu, por Dieu, vos bonnes dames,
> Ne vos griet pas se foles fames
> Un petit ai ici blasmees.
> Vos bonnes dames enbasmees
> Estes de basme et de toz biens.
> Bonne fame, n'en dout de riens,
> Est si tres sainte et si tres nete
> Qu'ieut plus soef que vïolete,
> Que flor de lis ne fresche rose,
> Et Diex en li maint et repose.
> (1 Mir. 42, 3:185–6, 523–32)

(By God, by God, you good women, don't become aggrieved over the foolish women I have blamed here a little. You good women are embalmed with balm and with all good things. A good woman – don't doubt this at all – is so very holy and so very clean that she smells sweeter than violet, lily, and fresh rose, and God dwells and rests in her.)

If lower-class prostitutes or temptresses, the 'foles fames' evoked here, are *ensafrenees*, then the 'bonnes dames' are *enbasmees*. The ethical contrast in feminine behavior is thus also an olfactory one (enticing saffron to soothing balm), as well as a visual one (eye-catching color to earnest transparency).[39] At a literal level, balm, as opposed to saffron,

---

secular confession from the mid-thirteenth century inquired whether musk or other perfume had been worn by women with a view to its odor attracting men.'
37 On smell's relationship to truth and certainty for medieval theologians before Gautier, see Robinson, *Sense of Smell*, 157–73.
38 See, for example, the apologetic interpellation of the 'bone feme' at the end of the *Roman de Silence* (ed. Roche-Mahdi, line 6696), on which see Roberta L. Krueger, *Women Readers and the Ideology of Gender in Old French Verse Romance* (Cambridge, UK, 1993), 124–7.
39 This moralizing distinction between the *bonne* and *fole* woman is epitomized by Gautier in the clerical commonplace of contrasting the Virgin with Eve, which notably intensifies towards the end of the *Miracles* (2 Sal. 35, 2 Ch. 36, 2 Pr. 39). Here, Gautier moves from the olfactory to gustatory register: if uttering *Ave* is sweet, its anagram *Eva* tastes sour (2 Sal. 35, 4:545, 29–30).

is more firmly located within a religious ecology and value-system of smell. Mary Magdalene, a reformed prostitute and, for Gautier, the symbol of repentant sinners (e.g., 1 Mir. 18, 2:147, 469; 2 Mir. 9, 3:452, 3800; 2 Chast. 10, 3:472, 312), is often represented in medieval visual traditions with a receptacle containing balm. As Holly Dugan puts it, 'The ointment bottle containing scented oil or balm works as a hinge between these two aspects of her legend [promiscuousness and repentance] and thus is critical to understanding (and staging) both Mary Magdalene's descent into cupidity and her penitent submission at the feet of Christ.'[40] The 'bonnes dames', whom Gautier addresses in his audience, are 'embalmed', literally with 'balm' and figuratively with 'all good things', but which in Gautier's syntax function as a synonymic pair.

For Gautier, then, the sense of smell is thus of rich symbolic potential, especially with regard to sexual morals. Scents are powerful metaphors because they enfold the world of ordinary experience into language, connecting affective response to ethical judgment. Real-world odors and their metaphorical referents become indissociable within Gautier's poetic creation: the smell of flowers is connected to virginity, just as excrement is connected to the sexual promiscuity implied by cosmetics (and metonymically the morally suspect women who apply them). At the same time, smell is a redemptive and ethical force located within the social sphere. If a Manichean opposition between Satan and the Virgin, and their respective mediators, has as its arena the material world, often the towns of northern France, this arena is one where contrasting scents fill the air. The olfactory space gives sensory form to the variegated ethical landscape that justifies the moralistic-didactic speech act itself.

Smell, Memory, and the Local

The symbolic potential of textual odors, then, relies in some way on the real world of odors, on the local spaces in which certain scents are encountered. Odors shaped the perception of, and thus delimited, spaces. The 'smellscapes' of thirteenth-century northern France interacted with the representation of both space and smell in the *Miracles*.[41]

40   Holly Dugan, 'Scent of a Woman: Performing the Politics of Smell in Late Medieval and Early Modern England', *Journal of Medieval and Early Modern Studies* 38.2 (2008), 229–52 (235).
41   This concept, which has been widely picked up in the social sciences, was

In this section, I turn to how the local spaces of devotion, situated within a broader topography of smell, are invested with olfactory meaning.[42] It is first important to point out that actual scents would have accompanied the reading, listening, or manuscript viewing experience. David A. Flory suggests that the liturgy may have preceded oral delivery of Gautier's *Miracles*, in which case scents would have been present in the performance space.[43] If the *Miracles* were read aloud in front of a mixed clerical–lay audience in the monastic church, then the visual and olfactory markers of Marian presence – representations of the Virgin and accompanying scents, like incense, flowers, or beeswax – would have prompted listeners to look inwards and to feel her consolatory, remedial, and ecstatic power (especially if other 'outside', and less pleasant, scents were brought in by listeners).[44] The association of incense with these performance spaces is perhaps suggested by the miniatures opening *Miracles* manuscripts that show angels swinging censers (for instance, the full-page illustration of BnF, fr. 2163, fol. 1v, or the small opening miniatures of BnF, fr. 1533, fol. 1r and BnF, fr. 22928, fol. 1r).[45] As Peggy McCracken observes, Gautier's

---

developed by J. Douglas Porteous, *Landscapes of the Mind: Worlds of Sense and Metaphor* (Toronto, 1990), 21–46. As Porteous notes, 'the perceived smellscape will be non-continuous, fragmentary in space and episodic in time' and thus not a straightforwardly smell-oriented version of a landscape (25).

42 On devotion, smellscapes, and material culture, see Wendy Wauters, 'Smelling Disease and Death in the Antwerp Church of Our Lady, c. 1450–1559', *Early Modern Low Countries* 5.1 (2021), 17–39. For the importance of smellscapes in late medieval drama, see Rory G. Critten and Annette Kern-Stähler, 'Smell in the York Corpus Christi Plays', in *The Five Senses in Medieval and Early Modern England*, ed. Annette Kern-Stähler, Beatrix Busse, and Wietse de Boer (Leiden, 2016), 237–68.

43 David A. Flory, 'The Social Uses of Religious Literature: Challenging Authority in the Thirteenth-Century Marian Miracle Tale', *Essays in Medieval Studies* 13 (1996), 61–9.

44 See Herbert L. Kessler, *Experiencing Medieval Art* (Toronto, 2019), 221–2, and Wauters, 'Smelling Disease', 33–5.

45 Cynthia Hahn, 'Theatricality, Materiality, Relics: Reliquary Forms and the Sensational in Mosan Art', in *Sensory Reflections: Traces of Experience in Medieval Artefacts*, ed. Fiona Griffiths and Kathryn Starkey (Berlin, 2019), 142–62, draws on the example Saint Remaclus's reliquary, which was experienced in processions of multisensory delight, and where the smell of candles and incense would have featured prominently. Brussels, Royal Library of Belgium (KBR), MS 9229–9230, also sometimes represents the Virgin alongside angels swinging censers (e.g., fol. 30r).

text locates the Virgin's power in the material forms through which it is mediated.[46] Sculptures (*ymages*) and icons of the Virgin populate the *Miracles*, and they function as conduits through which her presence is felt and that mediate her miraculous power. When Gautier describes his close, transformative encounter with the Virgin's sacred scent (quoted above, 2 Dout. 34, 4:497–8, 1470–94), he may have been referring to, or imagining, an encounter with a scented representation of the Virgin. The *Miracles*' insistence that such scents originate from, or grow in intensity around, the Virgin's presence would have complemented a use of fragrance and sculpture in the performance space.

References to olfaction would have attuned audiences to their own smellscapes. As we saw in the previous section, the *Miracles* depict scents in terms of both what they *show* and what they *do*. The contrast between the odors of devotion and those of the outside world consolidates the importance of miraculous Marian intervention. Many of the miracles deal with disease, and specifically touch upon the plague of the 'mal des ardents' or Saint Anthony's Fire (a type of ergotism) that struck the region in the twelfth century. The smell of disease and infection must have been a reality of town life, so the capacity of fragrance to combat disgusting odors would have been appreciated as a positive social force.[47] One narrative recounts how a low-born man, Robert, had such a rotten foot that, even when covered in cloth, 'si fort puoit / Que de pueur la gent tuoit' (2 Mir. 25, 4:247, 67–8, it stank so badly that it would lay people low with the stench). Gautier plays on the viscerality of smell through a hyperbolic description of churchgoers' reactions to Robert's foot in a textual *mise en abyme* of the performance space:

Une si puanz puasine
Que trestout cil dou mostier crïent
Et as gardes em plorant prïent
Qu'aucuns d'aus fors, pour Dieu, le mete,
Car il put plus que nule sete.

Nes la pueurs tolt tout le cuer
As dames qui chantent en cuer.
Chascuns crie pour la grieté:
'Boutez la hors cel espieté!'
(2 Mir. 25, 4:247, 78-86)

(Such a stinky stench [comes from his foot] that everyone in the church shouts out and, crying, beseech the wardens that one of them, for God's sake, put him outside, as he stinks more than any latrine. The stench knocks the heart out of the ladies who are singing in the choir. Because of the discomfort, everyone cries: 'Get this footless man out of here!')

The transition from indirect, to free indirect, and then to direct speech communicates a sense of the church as polyphonic space, filled with local, intolerant voices. Thrown out of the place of worship, Robert repeatedly prays to the Virgin, begging for deliverance. His wife and children stay away, and total isolation leads him to desire his own death (2 Mir. 25, 4:254, 256-60). Smell here has an obvious narrative function in allowing an emotionally stirring reversal of fortune. After the Virgin cures him, which she does better than any earthly surgeon or physician (2 Mir. 25, 4:255, 279-80), he re-emerges, ecstatic, into the social sphere, and his healed foot is celebrated through song and bellringing (2 Mir. 25, 4:262, 447-8). Gautier proceeds to moralize on the need to treat the sick and not to fear their smell or bodily contact:

La mere Dieu par est si tenre,
Si piteuse, si debonnaire
Que ne li put ne ne li flaire
Enfers, tant soit plains d'emposture,
Puis qu'ait pensee nete et pure.
(2 Mir. 25, 4:256, 304-8)

(The mother of God is so very tender, so compassionate, so noble, that Hell would not stink or smell to her, however full it is of dirtiness, because she would be of clean and pure mind.)

Piety results in a selective asnomia that, in circular fashion, facilitates charitable behavior. The target of Gautier's moralization are those

qui leurs nez mout en estoupassent
Et qui tout porrir le laissassent
Ainz qu'i daignassent atouchier.
(2 Mir. 25, 4:257, 328-30)

(who would greatly block their noses, and would let him completely rot, rather than deign to touch him.)

The lesson is one of transcending a disgust-response to partake of ethical action, and it is this ethical action that should eliminate the cause of the disgust-response. The power of the Virgin's miracle, and her example to others, hinges on smell, in terms of how it evidences the transformation (the body no longer reeks), how it functions as an obstacle to be overcome, and how it restores a unity to the community. The contrasts and crossovers between aromatic and malodorous spaces reflect an idealized vision of religious and lay interaction in the social sphere: just as the laity enter pious spaces like the church and encounter holy scents, the pious enter lay spaces and, with clean and pure mind, remove bad odors by ministering care and displaying moral exemplarity.[49]

Holy scents thus represented the potential of the divine latent within the world of ordinary experience. The 'odor of sanctity' is a hagiographical trope in which saints' bodies, miraculously defying putrefaction, were believed to maintain a sweet smell long after death. The second and the last miracles of Gautier's first book (1 Mir. 11 and 1 Mir. 44) are symmetrically connected by their focus on Saint Leocadia (died c. 304), whose tomb in Toledo remained miraculously fragrant when reopened:

> Une odeurs vint tant odorans
> Dou sepucre, quant il ovri,
> Que li doz Diex bien descovri
> Que mout ert sainte et glorïeuse,
> Nete, esmeree et precïeuse
> La sainte fleurs, la sainte rose
> Qui la dedens estoit enclose.
> (1 Mir. 11, 2:9, 102–8)

(An odor came from the tomb, when he opened it up, uncovered by the sweet Almighty, that smelled so strongly, because so very holy and glorious, clean, pure, and precious was the holy flower, the holy rose, that was contained inside.)

The affective pull of this miracle would no doubt have been heightened in an urban context where the olfactory fate of the body was of particular

---

49 The capacity of incense to linger on clothing may have olfactorily marked those entering and leaving religious spaces, as noted by Wauters, 'Smelling Disease', 23.

Figure 3.1 The opening of Saint Leocadia's fragrant tomb (1 Mir. 11). Paris, BnF, MS fr. 22928, fol. 57v (c. 1300). Source: <Gallica.bnf.fr>/BnF. Reproduced with permission from the Bibliothèque nationale de France.

concern (especially at times of disease on which many of the miracles center).[50] Manuscripts often illustrate this miracle with the dramatic moment of opening the tomb.[51] In the case of BnF fr. 22928 (see Fig. 3.1), sewing holes above this illumination indicate the erstwhile presence

---

50 Woolgar, 'Medieval Smellscapes', 62: 'The embalming of the bodies of the upper classes may have been designed not only to preserve them from putrefaction until burial but also to imbue them with an odor that might reflect the virtue of their lives.' See also Carole Rawcliffe, *Urban Bodies: Communal Health in Late Medieval English Towns and Cities* (Woodbridge, 2013), 54–71.
51 For instance: BnF, fr. 25532, fol. 22r; Besançon, Bibliothèque municipale, MS 551, fol. 19v and 20r; St Petersburg, National Library of Russia, Fr.f.v.XIV 9, fol. 58r; Brussels, Royal Library of Belgium (KBR), MS 10747, fol. 20r; and Paris, BnF, nouvelles acquisitions françaises 24541, fol. 21r.

of a textile curtain used to veil and protect the image.[52] Here lifting the curtain would have replicated the act of uncovering Leocadia's fragrant body in the tomb, thus extending the fragrant air into the air surrounding the book.[53] Drawing on the faculties of touch, sight, and now smell, the manuscript creates a space that elicits a sensory imagination.

Leocadia's odor of sanctity is picked up again and amplified in the final miracle of Gautier's first book, where it becomes a dominant theme that binds together Gautier, his readers and listeners, and the spaces of local devotion. Leocadia was of high local and personal significance to Gautier and his audience. Her relics were translated first from Toledo Cathedral to the Abbey of Saint-Médard in Soissons in the Carolingian period, before being taken in the twelfth century from Soissons to the Abbey at Vic-sur-Aisne, where Gautier composed his *Miracles*. The final narrative of his first book recounts the theft, loss, and recovery of Leocadia's relics – along with a statue of the Virgin that Gautier himself painted – in 1219. Scholars agree that this miracle story is Gautier's most emotional and subjective.[54] Three songs about the miracle follow, further highlighting their devotional importance.[55] While the relics are stolen from Vic Abbey by three thieves, Gautier frames the events as his own personal torture at the hands of a hideous demon, who had threatened to kill him if he did not abandon his project. He spends considerable space describing his pain, even comparing his outpouring of grief to that of a young child (1 Mir. 44, 3:222–3, 201–29). He also takes the opportunity to mourn the death of his close friend Abbot Milo of Saint-Médard in the same year (1 Mir. 44, 3:238–9, 621–46). The joy of being reunited with Leocadia's relics and the Virgin's statue prompts him to employ the only evocation across the *Miracles* of the otherwise widely referenced

---

52   For an example of a surviving curtain in a thirteenth-century *Miracles* manuscript, see Paris, Bibliothèque de l'Arsenal, 3517, fol. 148r.
53   See Henry Ravenhall, 'Veiled Reading, Reading Veils: Textile Curtains and the Experiences of Medieval French Manuscripts, 1200–1325', *Digital Philology* 12.1 (2023), 155–94.
54   See Roux and Uhlig, 'L'*Invention* de Léocade', 27, for how Besançon, Bibliothèque municipale, MS 551 (see Fig. 3.2) – a richly illuminated copy of the *Miracles* – places emphasis visually on the autobiographical elements of 1 Mir. 44.
55   On these songs and their six manuscripts, see Claire Chamiyé Couderc, 'L'Interprétation musicale du *Cycle de Sainte Léocade*', in *Gautier de Coinci*, ed. Krause and Stones, 149–66. 1 Ch. 45 laments the loss of the relics and statue, 1 Ch. 46 celebrates their retrieval, and 1 Ch. 47 praises the saint.

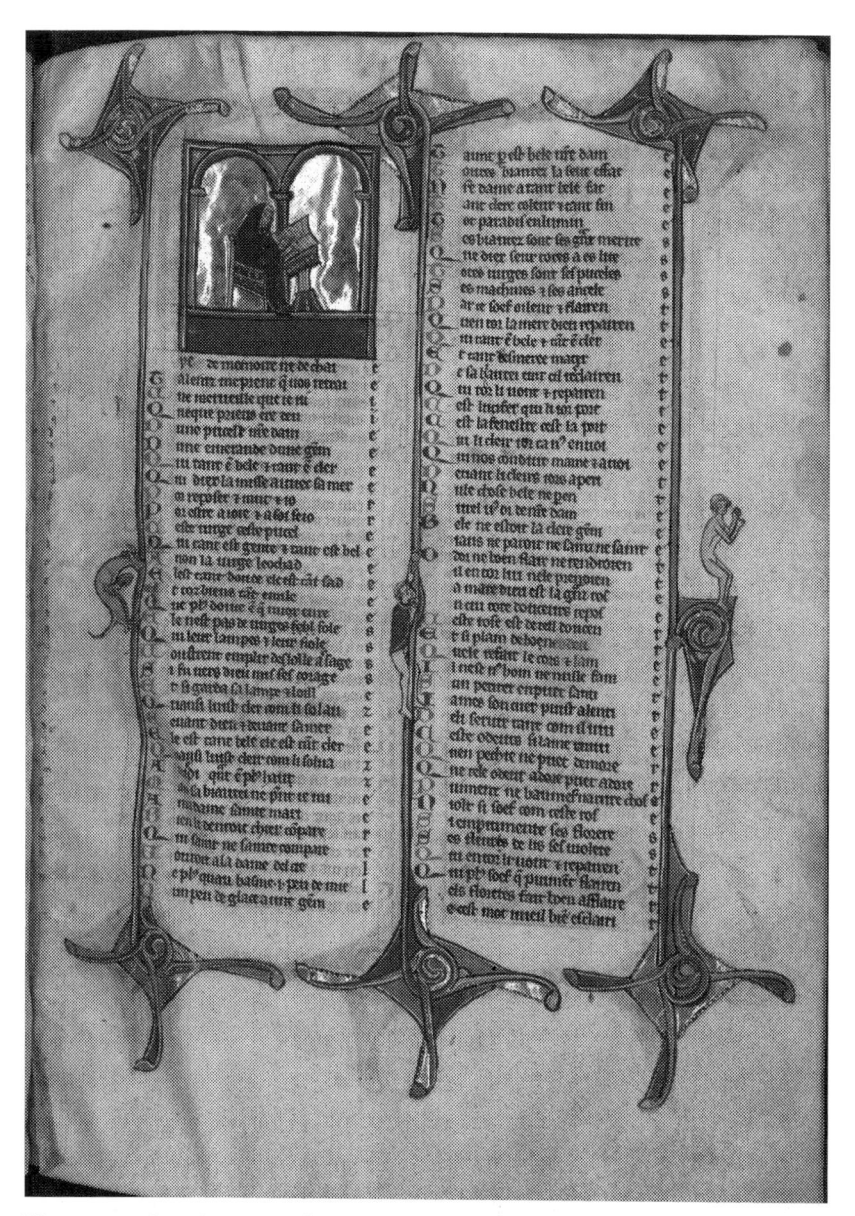

Figure 3.2   Opening page of 1 Mir. 44 in Besançon, Bibliothèque municipale, MS 551, fol. 82r (c. 1275–1300). Source: <memoirevive.besancon.fr>. Reproduced with permission from the Bibliothèque municipale de Besançon.

Figure 3.3 An intercolumnar thief points to the O of *Odor*. Besançon, Bibliothèque municipale, MS 551, fol. 82r (c. 1275–1300), detail. Source: <memoirevive.besancon.fr>. Reproduced with permission from the Bibliothèque municipale de Besançon.

Trojan story, as he embraces her more lovingly than Paris ever did Helen (1 Mir. 44, 3:225, 298–9). Beside the high affective charge of the miracle, it is significant also because it is technically the only miracle that Gautier himself witnessed and that is not drawn from the Latin book at Saint-Médard (now lost) that he names as his main source.

From a purely quantitative perspective, this miracle is the one most concerned with smell. Nine per cent of the total lines are related to the theme of olfaction.[56] Latin marginal glosses accompanying the miracle

56 The lines include: 41–4, 65–87, 354–60, 473–6, 798–801, 806–21, 827–46.

in some of the manuscripts pick up on this topic.[57] The illumination of Besançon, Bibliothèque municipale, MS 551 (see Figs. 3.2 and 3.3) playfully hints at the importance of the theme to the miracle. On the miracle's opening page (fol. 82r), there is a half-naked thief figure, who climbs the intercolumnar decoration to steal a golden orb. The result is to point towards another O-shape in the text beside it, the O initial for *Odor*. This is the only miracle, too, in which Gautier's trademark closing passage of *annominatio* centers on an olfactory experience (the Virgin's 'musk', *mugue*). Smell here works in continuity with descriptors of Marian presence evoked in previous miracles. Both the Virgin (*dame*, Mary) and the virgin (*damoisele*, Leocadia) are defined by their floral scent, which reflects their shared virginity and which can be transmitted to other chaste women in the community (1 Mir. 44, 3:216–17, 65–87).[58] Amplifying the reference to Leocadia's odor of sanctity from the early miracle, and thus to an extent mirroring in the compilation itself a *translatio* of relics, Gautier stresses the transmissibility of the Virgin's power – mediated through the saintly virgin Leocadia – in the water of the river Aisne:

> De ses os ist uns flairs si sades
> Qu'encor en est plus odorans
> Et plus souez l'iaue corans
> La ou baignié furent si os.
>
> (1 Mir. 44, 3:244–5, 798–801)

(Her [Leocadia's] bones released a scent so delicious that the running water in which they were bathed is even more fragrant and smells more sweetly.)

Submerged in the Aisne and later recovered from its banks, Leocadia's relics not only retain their sweet fragrance; they also transfer it, with even more potency, to the river water that they touched. While the Aisne is shaded elsewhere in the *Miracles* as a site of death or loss, and

---

57 See Veikko Väänänen, *Gloses marginales des* Miracles *de Gautier de Coinci* (Helsinki, 1945), 43 (line 26), 49 (line 856), 53 (line 848), 78 (lines 46, 63, and 350), and 79 (line 865).
58 'Leochade est des violetes / Et des flouretes Nostre Dame' (3:230–1, 432–3, Leocadia is among the violets and little flowers of Our Lady). The feminine diminutive plural *flouretes* opens up this assignation to other women, perhaps referring explicitly to the nuns of the Abbey of Notre-Dame in Soissons.

its rapid current is frequently mentioned (e.g., 'mout est rade', 1 Mir. 44, 3:223, 238), here the river is life-giving as its waters start to heal the sick. A major waterway in the region, the Aisne flows through the monastic center of Compiègne, Gautier's place of work and worship Vic, and then Soissons, where several of the miracles take place. Reference to the Aisne's fragrance defies a common-sense logic of dilution and attunes audiences to the entangled relations between the human and more-than-human.[59] Water's visibility and tangibility, compared to air's invisibility and intangibility, are thus mobilized to provide a material reminder of the miraculous potential in the urban and rural landscape. Transmissible across different elements (from solid to air, from solid to liquid), smell affirms the community's togetherness by moving between objects, bodies, and their environment.

While this poem operates on several temporal levels, recounting in non-linear fashion the loss, recovery, miracles, and subsequent celebration of the relics, smell is a leitmotif running through the text that functions to bind together these different events spatially. In other words, smell is evoked in this miracle because of its associative potential to unify people around common experience and the spaces of that experience. The yearly celebration of Leocadia's relics is signaled in the songs that follow the narrative (1 Ch. 46, 3:254, 2; 3:256, 55), a celebration that demands lay participation ('et clerc et lai', 1 Ch. 45, 3:253, 94; 1 Ch. 46, 3:254, 7). Leocadia's relics are recovered from the Aisne the night before Pentecost and subsequently celebrated the day following Pentecost:

> Mais de sens fus si aornee
> Et tant fus saige et bien aprise
> Qu'oïr volsis tot ton service
> La vegile de Pentecouste.
> C'est une feste qui moute couste,
> Mais ceste gaires ne cousta,
> Car Sains Espirs nos ajousta
> Une tel feste avec la siue,
> Qui tant fu douce et tant fu piue
> Tout en fumes empiumenté.

[59] Anna Lowenhaupt Tsing, *The Mushroom at the End of the World: On the Possibility of Life in Capitalist Ruins* (Princeton, 2015), 52, notes the 'intriguing nature-culture knot' in the smell of the matsutake mushroom: 'It seems impossible to describe the smell of matsutake without telling all the cultural-and-natural histories condensed together in it.'

Mout i ovra Diex piument. E!
Com ou cuer a peu de piument
Qui le piu Dieu ne sert piument!
Le jour si nous enpiumenta
Li rois qui tout le piument a
Et conroia d'un tel conroi
Que conreé fumes con roi.

(1 Mir. 44, 3:227-8, 346-62)

(But you [Leocadia] were so replete with good sense and you were so wise and well-raised that you wished to hear all of your mass on the Vigil of Pentecost. It's a feast that costs a lot, but this one hardly cost anything, for the Holy Spirit added for us such a celebration alongside its own, which was so gentle and sweet [*piue*] that we were all fragranced [*enpiumenté*] by it. God worked on it very sweetly/piously [*piument*]. Oh! Whoever does not serve sweet/pious [*piu*] God sweetly/piously [*piument*] has little spice [*piument*] in the heart! The king [Christ] who has all the spice [*piument*] fragranced [*enpiumenta*] us over the day and supplied [*conroia*] us with such supplies [*conroi*] that we were supplied [*conreé*] like kings [*con roi*].)

As a Christian feast strongly connotative of gathering and union (observing when the disciples are filled with the Holy Spirit), Pentecost is particularly appropriate for the celebration of a given community's relics.[60] Gautier's text reminisces over the liturgical procession, which would have spanned the major landmarks in the area around Vic, including the Abbey, the town itself, the castle, the banks of the Aisne, and the Herbot meadow (now Berny-Rivière):[61]

L'endemain de la Pentecouste,
Ce sai je bien, je fui dejouste,
Portee en fu en pre Erbout,
Ou bele place et bele herbe out,

---

60 As pointed out by Hunt, *Miraculous Rhymes*, 151, there is perhaps a playful allusion to the rhyme associating Arthur's Pentecost feast with 'costly' expenditure found in the opening of Chrétien de Troyes's *Le Chevalier au lion* (c. 1176–81).

61 'La vile rit de sa venue, / Quar d'ordure et de vilenie / Le chastel et la vie nie' (3:232, 462–4, The town smiles upon her arrival, for she denies filth and villainy from the castle and town). For the identification of place names in 1 Mir. 44, see Jacques Chaurand, 'Les Noms de lieux dans l'œuvre de Gautier de Coinci', *Actes des colloques de la Société française d'onomastique* 13 (2007), 79–105 (90–1).

A grant joie la damoisele.
Processïon i ot si bele
Et si biau tanz fist Nostre Sire
Que qui la fu il puet bien dire
Qu'aprés doleur si dolereuse
Ne vit nus joie si joieuse.
Tant i ot gent, si con moy samble,
C'onques mais tant n'en vi ensamble.

(1 Mir. 44, 3:239, 647–58)

(The day after Pentecost, this I know well, I was right there, the maiden [Leocadia] to great joy was carried to Herbot meadow, where there was a nice spot and nice grass. There was such a beautiful procession, and Our Lord made such fine weather, that whoever was there can indeed say that no one had seen such joyful joy after such painful pain. There were so many people, so it seems to me, that I've never since seen so many together.)

Manuscript images for this miracle, such as that of Figure 3.4, foreground the processional nature of the poem itself: the relics move forward from compartment to compartment in agreement with narrative time.[62] The poem thus weaves together historical events (local, biblical, and martyrological), devotional interpretation, and shared perceptual experience of the procession. If scents were included as part of the liturgy, or were present on the processional route (such as the 'bele herbe' of Herbot meadow on an early June day), then olfactory – in tandem with kinetic and auditory – sensation grounded historical depth in the cyclical, devotional present.

Although not mutually exclusive, two ways of reading Gautier's miracle story, and its preoccupation with smell, emerge. The first is through the lens of involuntary memory. The well-established nexus between smell, memory, and emotion is exemplified in Proust's 'madeleine' moment, in which the scent of something can plunge us into a memory whether we like it or not.[63] Perhaps olfactory references punctuate this poem because smell was bound up in how Gautier, who stresses his eyewitness status throughout, remembered the events and the emotional responses they elicited at the time. Of course, such an interpretation buys into the

---

62 This manuscript is closely based on St Petersburg, National Library of Russia, Fr.f.v.XIV 9 (c. 1250–75), whose corresponding image opening 1 Mir. 44 (fol. 131r) arranges the six compartments across three rows rather than two.
63 Marcel Proust, *A la recherche du temps perdu*, 3 vols (Paris, 1954), 1:44–8.

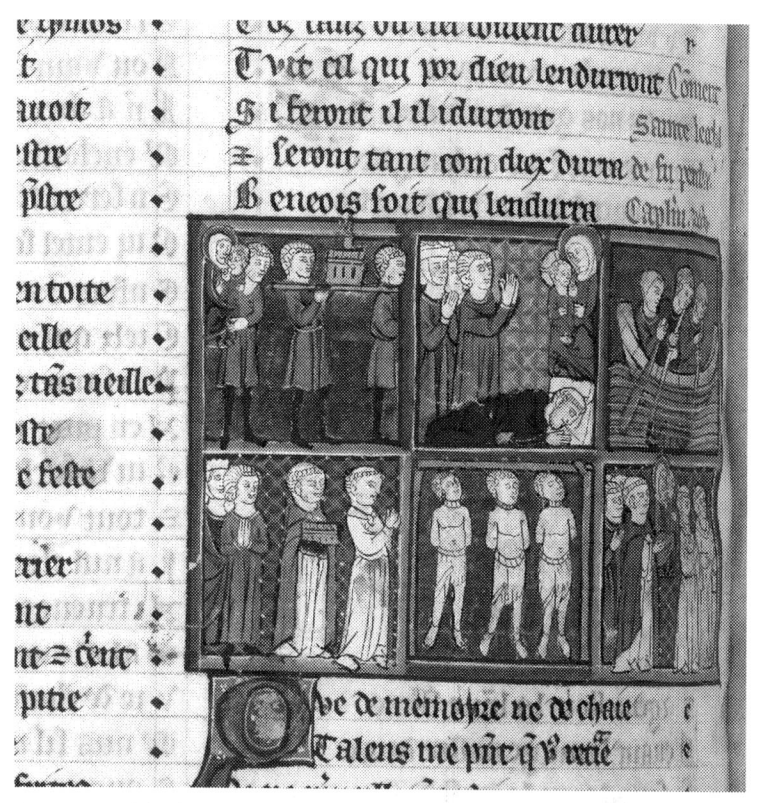

Figure 3.4   The loss, recovery, and celebration of Saint Leocadia's relics (1 Mir. 44). Paris, BnF, MS fr. 22928, fol. 147v (c. 1300). Source: <Gallica.bnf.fr>/ BnF. Reproduced with permission from the Bibliothèque nationale de France.

authorial construction of a highly personal, emotional voice speaking through Gautier's *je*. The second way, however, is to foreground the conscious strategies of memory-making employed by Gautier.[64] Indeed, Gautier begins by declaring that the poem's function is to resist oblivion: 'Que de memoyre ne dechaie' (1 Mir. 44, 3:214, 1, So that it does not disappear from memory). Moreover, the third song following the poem uses the collocation 'faire feste et memoire' (1 Ch. 47, 3:258, 6) to refer to

[64] On Gautier's practices of memory-making, with special reference to 1 Mir. 44, see Michelle K. Bolduc, 'Faire Mémoire, composer de la poésie: La dévotion de Gautier de Coinci au culte de Sainte Léocadie', in *Faire Mémoire: Les arts sacrés face au temps; Actes du colloque de Chartres (3–5 octobre 2013)*, ed. Françoise Michaud-Fréjaville (Châtillon-sur-Indre, 2016), 72–83.

the jointly celebratory and memorial functions of the devotional artefact. Seen in this light, Gautier may have intertwined references to smell with events of communal significance to aid their memorialization. After all, as anthropologist and sensory theorist David Howes has noted, while the Proustian madeleine is mostly held up – often sentimentally – as proof of smell's affective potential, it also risks being read as merely affective.[65] In the case of Proust's novel, the intellectual dimension of Proust writing about, and his readership relating to, a sensory experience is crucial. This is not to deny that the immediacy of olfaction is at stake in the scene. It is to emphasize the mediated nature of Proust's description. Articulating a past olfactory experience or reliving it, in other words, connects us to others through shared perceptual memories.

Gautier thereby associates the *realia* of the local setting with the sites and scents of miraculous intervention. This, his most fragrant miracle-story can perhaps be read as a kind of topography of smell. Perception of the Aisne, with its infused presence both of the saint's relics and the Virgin's intercession on earth, becomes a mnemonic cue for Marian compassion and devotion, as well as a site of shared experience around which the community can coalesce.

Olfaction, Form, Aesthetics

Odor can therefore mark spaces, circulating between people and their environment. The devotional poem attunes audiences to these circuits of smell, space, and communal values. In this section, my attention turns to two concerns prompted by discussions taking place in the fields of 'olfactory aesthetics' and cognitive linguistics. The first concern is the relationship between olfaction and form. As Hsuan L. Hsu puts it, 'Smell's subjectively variable, flitting, immersive, spatially dispersed, and hybrid (mixed with other smells or atmospheric conditions) qualities seem to defy the very concept of form – a concept that, even in literary studies, is frequently modeled on the visual arts (figured in terms of shapes, diagrams, and well-wrought urns).'[66] Here I wish to propose that the aesthetic-devotional form – or, for that matter, the formlessness

---

65 David Howes, 'Introduction', in *Designing with Smell: Practices, Techniques and Challenges*, ed. Victoria Henshaw et al. (New York, 2018), 5–8.
66 Hsuan L. Hsu, *The Smell of Risk: Environmental Disparities and Olfactory Aesthetics* (New York, 2020), 21.

– of the *Miracles* might be conceived in terms of the olfactory. The second concern is the relationship between the representation and the experience of olfaction. It seems logical that reading or hearing about a smell is not the same as perceiving that smell. Yet, research in cognitive linguistics has pointed to the activation of parts of the brain that process sense-experience in response to sensory language. While the sensation of olfaction is not needed to understand olfactory terms and images, the conscious mental simulation of olfactory metaphors and scenarios can produce an experience that – at the cognitive level at least – can be assimilated to the act of smelling. If, following Gautier himself, we think about textual smells as *actual smells* rather than only as metaphors, we may get closer to understanding the devotional and aesthetic components of Gautier's broader project in the *Miracles*.

An odor's intangibility and invisibility, but strong material presence, offer a way of thinking about divine transcendence and mediation. Smell is special within a framework of the senses because it is said to have two 'intentional objects', the odor itself and the source of the odor.[67] Aristotle placed smell in the middle of his sensory hierarchy: below the noble, distant faculties of sight and hearing but above the base, proximal faculties of taste and touch.[68] Smell is proximal insofar as the air that carries it is transmitted materially to the body, and distant insofar as the object that releases the odor may be far away or even out of sight. It is the detachability of the odor-source from the odor-proper (and the olfactory experience it induces) that contribute to smell's specificity as a metaphor.[69] Towards the end of his compilation, Gautier compares the Virgin's miracles – as they are mediated by his poetic output – to the diffusion of a sweet odor:

> Si myracle par tout s'esclairent,
> Par tout souef oelent et flairent:
> L'oudeurs s'espant et ça et la,
> Par deça mer et par dela.
> (2 Dout. 34, 4:528, 2249–52)

---

67 On the discussion of smell's 'object', see Shiner, *Art Scents*, 25–6.
68 On Aristotle's schema in relation to Aquinas and Plato, see Shiner, *Art Scents*, 20.
69 It has dramatic potential too. Woolgar, 'Medieval Smellscapes', 51: 'The martyrdom of Becket was likened to the breaking of a perfume box, suddenly filling Christ Church, Canterbury, with the fragrance of ointment.'

(Her miracles shine through everywhere, become fragrant and smell sweet everywhere: the odor spreads here and there, on this and that side of the sea.)

Her miracles are both the source of smell and its resultant experience, where the former is proximal but the latter can be distant. This duality of objecthood is crucial to Gautier's devotional project: the Virgin's miracles are local acts of divine intercession as much as they are transmittable ('supralocal') stories that involve ethical transformation and aesthetic appreciation.[70] Moreover, the historical origins of the Virgin in the East – *Outremer*, or the other side of the sea – are reflected in the smell of exotic spices, a point reinforced when she is described as the 'spice merchant' (*espiciere*) who provides zedoary, cinnamon, and cloves (1 Mir. 44, 3:232, 473-7).[71] The *translatio* of the Virgin is thus figured in olfactory terms as the movement of fragrant material from East to West. Smell, like devotion itself, not only speaks to how the 'immaterial' experience derived from the odor-source is as important as its 'material' origin, but how they are inextricably intertwined.

Smell, like the devotional poem, becomes a means of perceiving the Virgin, whose reality is indicated by her scent but which is both intangible and separate from the Virgin *qua* source of the scent. Those she heals take notice of her holy odor. In the story of the sacristan she cures, for instance:

> Avis li est qu'il encor sente
> La sainte oudeur de la sainte ente
> Qui aporta la sainte fleur
> Qui paist les angeles de s'oudeur.
> De la roÿne glorïeuse
> Sent une oudeur si savoreuse
> Qu'il i met si s'ame et son cuer
> Qu'il n'entent riens c'on die en cuer.
>   (1 Mir. 31, 3:19, 201-8)

(It seems to him that he can still smell the holy odor of the holy stem that bears the holy flower that feeds the angels with its odor. He smells such a

---

70 Gautier compares those who fail to appreciate the beauty of his miracle stories to toads who cannot stand the sweet smell of a flowering vine (2 Mir. 29, 4:341, 22-9).
71 'La riche dame, l'espiciere / Qui a en sa riche aumosniere / Tante espece fresche et novele, / Aprés chitoal et canelé / Nos departi clos de gynoffle.' See Freedman, *Out of the East*, 76-103, especially 88-9.

Figure 3.5 The cured sacristan. Paris, BnF, MS fr. 25532, fol. 66r (c. 1270–80). Reproduced with permission from the Bibliothèque nationale de France.

delicious odor from the glorious queen that he invests her with his soul and heart and he no longer has anything on his mind.)

The encounter with the mother of God here induces a devotional ecstasy, a letting-go. Feeling the Virgin's continued presence is figured as an act of olfaction. The miracle may be a visionary experience, but it is also an olfactory one.[72] Manuscript illuminations depicting this miracle, such as BnF fr. 25532, fol. 66r (see Fig. 3.5), and BnF fr. 22928, fol. 111r, emphasize

---

72 In healing-narratives where Marian milk is drunk, it is a gustatory one too (e.g., 1 Mir. 17, 2:127, 140–5; 1 Mir. 40, 3:138–9, 124–9).

the proximity between the sacristan and Our Lady: the text relates how the Virgin instructs her visitee, addressing him, like a courtly *domna*, as her 'biaus doz amis' (fair sweet friend), to kiss her on the mouth (1 Mir. 31, 3:17, 167–8). Such images may be seen as representing an act of smelling as much as kissing (which lies at the intersection of taste and touch). Paired with textual reference to imagining the persistent scent of the Virgin ('il encor sente'), the image may have stimulated viewers to smell the air around the manuscript and thus to imagine the smell of the Virgin.[73]

The language and imagery of smell in the *Miracles*, both as word and as image, prompted readers and listeners to feel the presence of the divine, to be attuned to the potentiality of the divine in the spaces around them. Gautier's stylistic and rhetorical flourishes partake of this sense of sharing in the presence of the divine. His 'miraculous rhymes', as Tony Hunt shows, work by transcending the world of courtly literature and showing the spiritual potential that lies within its language, motifs, and characters. Hunt pays special attention to Gautier's favored technique of *annominatio* (or *paronomasia*), which is the concentrated repetition of a word-stem either through homophones or related etymological forms.[74] While this technique, Hunt demonstrates, was used to satirical ends, it also embodied 'passion or devotion', and this 'is nowhere more reverberantly displayed than in his account of the disappearance from Vic of the relics of Saint Leocadia (1 Mir. 44)', which I discussed in the previous section.[75] Near the end of this miracle, Gautier composes an *annominatio* based on the very rare term *mugue* (musk):[76]

> Plus soef ieut de nul piument.
> La mere Dieu ieut plus piument
> De basme et de **muguelias**.
> Diex, tant donné **mugue li as**
> Qu'ausi est **enmuguelïee**
> Con s'ert toute **en mugue lïee**.

---

73 On medieval illuminators and 'sensorimotor literacy', see Guillemette Bolens, 'Inventive Embodiment and Sensorial Imagination in Medieval Drawings: The Marginalia of the Walters Book of Hours MS W.102', *Cogent Arts & Humanities* 9 (2022), DOI: 10.1080/23311983.2022.2065763.
74 Hunt, *Miraculous Rhymes*, 123–60.
75 Hunt, *Miraculous Rhymes*, 151.
76 For *mugue*, see Collet, *Glossaire*, 340–1. On this passage, see also Hunt, *Miraculous Rhymes*, 152–3, who notes how it perplexed subsequent scribes.

Qui ne **s'enmugue** de **son mugue**
Enmuguiez est de mugué mugue,
Mais tuit cil bien **s'enmuguelïent**
Qui entor aus **son mugue lïent**.
Diex doinst toz nos **enmuguelit**
Et qu'entor nos **son mugue lit**. Amen.

(1 Mir. 44, 3:246, 836–46)

(She smells more than any spice [*piument*]. The mother of God smells more sweetly [*piument*] of balm and of musk fragrance [*muguelias*]. God, you have given her so much musk [*mugue*] that she is so musky [*enmugueliee*] it's as if she were completely bound in musk [*en mugue liee*]. Whoever does not get musky [*ne s'enmugue*] from her musk [*son mugue*] is made musky [*enmuguiez*] by musty musk [*mugué mugue*], but all those people who come together around her musk [*son mugue lient*] get fragranced with musk [*s'enmuguelïent*]. May God fragrance us all in musk [*enmuguelit*] and bind [*lit*] us together around her musk [*mugue*]. Amen.)

The high concentration of *rimes équivoques* (in bold) establishes here a semantic association between scenting musk and binding together the Virgin's devotees. Musk, one of the world's most expensive animal-derived products (from the male musk deer), is particularly associated with paradise in Islamic cultures, where its rarity and origin further in Asia marked it as exotic.[77] In medieval Europe, it had medicinal uses for women's reproductive health, as described in the widely transmitted medical treatises known as the *Trotula*.[78] Highly potent and heavy, one of musk's perceived qualities was to become more fragrant among fetid smells and less fragrant among sweet smells.[79] This mutability in valence may lie behind the negative meaning of the adjective *mugué* (lit.

---

77   See Anya H. King, *Scent from the Garden of Paradise: Musk and the Medieval Islamic World* (Leiden, 2017), 3: 'Musk was considered the best of aromatics and used in perfumes by men and women. It was present in the highest echelons of society, at the caliphal court. As a drug, musk appeared in a striking range of medical applications and prescriptions.'
78   See Robinson, *Sense of Smell*, 98–9.
79   Robinson, *Sense of Smell*, 85. Corbin, *Le Miasme*, 78–82, traces the reconceptualization of musk as intolerably animalistic, excremental, potent, and feminine in the eighteenth century. Holly Dugan, *The Ephemeral History of Perfume: Scent and Sense in Early Modern England* (Baltimore, 2011), 10, points out that modern 'musk' is a synthetic substance and therefore different from earlier animal-based musk.

'musked') to modify *mugue*. Musk, with its possibly Edenic overtones, caps off an aromatic crescendo as Gautier's first book of miracles comes to a close, drawing together the spiritual, medicinal, and community-making capacities of fragrance. If equivocality locates semantic multiplicity and diversity within sensory singularity and repetition, smell's associative power operates in a similar way. But equally, as the passage progresses and meaning-making operations come under strain, the sheer repetition of homophonous words brings their sonic, rather than semantic, resonance to the fore.[80] *Annominatio*, like smell, directs its audience's attention to the materiality of bodies gathered with the same goal of rejoicing in worship.[81]

Smell's ineffability and mode of transmission provide a way of understanding Gautier's aesthetic and devotional project. It offers an olfactory form that centers an equivocal doubleness within sensory experience, where divine presence is there and not there, where meaning intensifies just as, or because, it threatens to disappear. In terms of temporality, smell evokes the past within the present, giving an imprecisely historical depth to a moment of perceptual experience. As Jonathan Gil Harris notes in his historical phenomenology of Shakespeare's *Macbeth*, 'the centrifugal nature of smell – its propensity to smell *like* something else, and hence to evoke the past by metonymic association – locates its polychronicity ambivalently inside and outside the object'.[82] Gautier's *Miracles* are 'historical' at the same time as being sensuously brought into the here and now, where the devotional present dissolves into a set of past experiences across time and space that reaffirms the importance of worship to the community.[83] Smell, as what Hsu calls 'an inchoate medium "in between" subject and object',

80 As Robert L.A. Clark, 'Gautier's Wordplay as Devotional Ecstasy', in *Gautier de Coinci*, ed. Krause and Stones, 113–25, puts it, 'the sonorous aura of Gautier's language in these passages draws us into a deep mystical space' (118).

81 For Cazelles, *La Faiblesse*, 104, what is at stake in *annominatio* is 'le réseau de correspondances entre le matériel et l'immatériel, entre la chose visible et sa vérité intangible, entre ce que perçoivent les sens et ce qui demeure imperceptible à l'entendement humain' (the network of correspondences between the material and immaterial, between the visible thing and its intangible truth, between what the senses perceive and what remains imperceptible to human understanding).

82 Jonathan Gil Harris, *Untimely Matter in the Time of Shakespeare* (Philadelphia, 2008), 124.

83 On the temporalities of olfaction, especially the notion of smell as 'pastness',

troubles the ontological solidity of divisions that otherwise structure a visual perception of reality.[84] Its affective, memorial, and associative power – its tendency to point us always elsewhere and to another time within a moment of sensory intensity – represents the broader aesthetic experience of the *Miracles*.

However, the argument that smell's modal specificity provides a way of formally approaching Gautier's *Miracles* should not imply that we are dealing only in abstract meaning.[85] The first section of this essay demonstrated that while Gautier's use of olfactory language and imagery corresponded to a value-system connected to virtue and sin, it was nevertheless dependent on the world of ordinary experience. Similarly, the second section showed how the spaces of local devotion, as sites of prior miraculous activity, were associated with olfaction, where real and imagined smellscapes attuned audiences to the divine latent within their environment. At play in both instances is a complex relationship between the sensorium, aesthetic-devotional experience, and the symbolic superstructure. The point is precisely not to disentangle these components (and thus to isolate 'meaning' from one's embodied existence), but to consider how physical sensation – often taking shape reiteratively as a memory of prior sensation – is always imbricated into the experience and interpretation of the *Miracles*. In other words, textual or visual representation of smell may have prompted a reader, listener, or viewer towards something akin to a perception of smell.[86]

Although Roland Barthes once famously stated that 'écrite, la merde ne sent pas' (when written, shit doesn't smell), twenty-first-century findings in cognitive science seem to suggest that the parts of the brain involved in processing sensation are activated when processing imagined sensation.[87] As G. Gabrielle Starr writes, 'investigations of imagery began to produce very good evidence [from functional brain imaging] that across

---

see William Tullett, *Smell and the Past: Noses, Archives, Narratives* (London, 2023), 77–81.
84 Hsu, *The Smell of Risk*, 21.
85 On smell and metaphor, see Dugan, *Ephemeral History*, 4–5.
86 I am inspired here partly by the work of Terence Cave and others on the '"ghost" feelings' elicited by literary kinesis, which is 'the transmission (usually from one body to another) of motor activation which the observer of some salient action or physical sensation feels as a neural readiness to perform the same action'. See Cave, *Thinking with Literature: Towards a Cognitive Criticism* (Oxford, 2016), 36.
87 Roland Barthes, *Sade, Fourier, Loyola* (Paris, 1971), 141.

sensory modes, when people experience perceptual imagery, areas of the brain involved in actual perception are active, and function in similar patterns for imagined sensation as during actual perception'.[88] More recently, Laura J. Speed and Asifa Majid have assessed the neurolinguistic evidence for a 'grounded theory of language' for touch, taste, and smell.[89] While the sensorimotor system (perception of movement and action) is involved in the processing of movement and action language, it seems that smell, like taste, is not automatically triggered – at least not in a specific or 'fine-grained' way – in the understanding of words and images related to olfaction. Consistent with the fact that odors are comparably difficult to imagine, this leads to the conclusion that word meaning is far less 'grounded' in smell (and in taste and touch) than in vision, audition, and action.[90] Nevertheless, there is solid evidence that 'low-level olfactory representations can be deliberately activated in the absence of odour stimuli, but not necessarily automatically during language comprehension'.[91] Conscious deliberation on a smell – whose level of cognitive engagement is heightened in the presence of an actual odor – can activate odor perception processing, but only in an abstract and non-specific way (one can try to imagine a floral smell but it would not be perceived with the valences of an actual floral smell). In one respect, the idea that mental simulation of odor language is perhaps more abstract or schematic reflects the *Miracles'* association of smell with divinity, ineffability, and non-localizable presence. In another, the hypothesis that olfactory-related concepts may be 'mentally simulated close to the body, possibly reflecting the act of sniffing or inhaling odours' complements Gautier's reference to the Virgin's fragrance when insisting on her proximity.[92]

One upshot of the neuroscientific literature is that 'odor and language are weakly connected in the brain for comprehension, as well as production', and for this reason, associated modalities may scaffold

88 G. Gabrielle Starr, *Feeling Beauty: The Neuroscience of Aesthetic Experience* (Cambridge, MA, 2013), 75.
89 Laura J. Speed and Asifa Majid, 'Grounding Language in the Neglected Senses of Touch, Taste, and Smell', *Cognitive Neuropsychology* 37.5-6 (2020), 363–92.
90 Speed and Majid, 'Grounding Language', 364–6. An important caveat here is that this conclusion applies to 'English and related languages' (366).
91 Speed and Majid, 'Grounding Language', 377.
92 Speed and Majid, 'Grounding Language', 380.

or compensate for olfaction when mental simulation is difficult.[93] Studies have shown that colors, especially, are crossmodally associated with odors: thinking of the color of odor-related nouns, like coffee, mint, or roses, may aid in their linguistic processing in an olfactory context.[94] The pervasive use of the image of the rose in the *Miracles* may be related conventionally to ideas of ornament and beauty, but a crucial part of this is its role as a color-word that visually conveys its perceived olfactory quality. The cluster 'fragrance–flower–pink' works synesthetically to produce an effect that seems to sit outside the narrow confines of individual sensory modalities. Manuscript illuminations of the *Miracles* may have contributed yet further to this effect with liberal use of pinkish pigments, often representing background spaces. The semantic condensation of *rose* may have attuned audiences to otherwise invisible, or undescribed, scents within the represented scene, making 'background' color an integral component in one's sensory engagement with the narrative. The scene of opening Leocadia's tomb is one example where rosy pigment may have sensorially augmented reference to the odor of sanctity in the accompanying text.[95]

Michael Camille makes a similar argument when he calls on art historians working on illuminated manuscripts not to read painted flowers as symbols – which would then become reduced to simulacra and thus 'deodorized' – but as sites of sensational play and meaning:

> Parchment books really do 'smell' of animal, as anyone who has visited a manuscript reading room and a tannery can tell you, but they also have a strong metaphorical olfactory dimension. Is this increasing importance of good smells (which were thought to ward off sickness and the plague) why the borders of medieval manuscripts from the thirteenth century onward tend to become more and more pharmacopoeias filled with vegetal and floral growth? While art historians have explored the symbolic meaning of flowers – their medicinal and magical properties,

---

93 Speed and Majid, 'Grounding Language', 378–9.
94 Speed and Majid, 'Grounding Language', 380.
95 See manuscripts listed in note 51 above. The orthographical variant in the richly illuminated BnF, nouvelles acquisitions françaises 24541, fol. 110r, 'pigment' instead of 'piument' (both < *pigmentum*) draws attention to the olfactory potential of the book's paints, especially for artists in manuscript workshops.

for example – their being associated with the page as objects of pleasure and vivid sensation is far more fundamental.[96]

These comments speak to the notion that medieval aesthetic principles are rooted in synesthetic experience by contrast to, in Mary Carruthers's words, a 'modern western sensibility that favours "pure" forms and ascetic simplicity'.[97] The extent to which an image may induce an olfactory or multisensory experience, however abstract, is currently a subject of debate. When visualized, 'odor situations', like holding something up to or covering one's nose, may prompt viewers to imagine that scent, if only in relation to a prior experience. Larry Shiner provides a number of examples where olfaction is implicated into the artistic object, such as Louise Bourgeois's drypoint *The Smell of the Feet* (1999), the New Testament scene of Lazarus raised from the dead (John 11:1–44) by Giotto in Padua's Scrovegni Chapel (c. 1305), or Adriaen Brouwer's *Interior of a Tavern* (c. 1630), the latter of which 'almost gives one a sick headache', according to essayist William Hazlitt.[98] Of course, viewing these images is not the same as actually smelling the represented scent. But if odor imagery aids a visual decoding of, or triggers a memory of, the representation, at the same time as playing on corporeal reactions and affect, these representations may act on audiences with the effects of an actual odor.

Reodorizing the Miracles

In the conclusion to her study of the *Miracles*, Cazelles makes the point that to subject Gautier to literary criticism risks sacrificing the sensible and devotional aspects of his project to the intelligible.[99] What Hans Ulrich Gumbrecht calls the 'presence effects' of literature, as opposed to 'meaning effects', may encompass Gautier's evocations of smell: they always act on bodies, they alert audiences to sensory perception

---

96 Michael Camille, 'Sensations of the Page: Imaging Technologies and Medieval Illuminated Manuscripts', in *The Iconic Page in Manuscript, Print, and Digital Culture*, ed. George Bornstein and Theresa Tinkle (Ann Arbor, 1998), 33–53 (40).
97 Mary Carruthers, *The Experience of Beauty in the Middle Ages* (Oxford, 2013), 48.
98 Shiner, *Art Scents*, 152–3.
99 Cazelles, *La Faiblesse*, 161.

in a here and now, and they point them to that which resists representation.[100] In Gautier's verses, presence effects inscribe the Virgin as physical force in the performance space and the diegetic world of the *Miracles*. All the senses are enlivened, and even when his language becomes dense, complex, and playful (so full of 'meaning effects'), the sonic quality of repetition produces a strong presence effect. If, as my essay's epigraph intimates, smell is the 'mute sense', and immerses us in a 'sea of inarticulate pleasure and exaltation', then this resistance to the substitutionary logic of language is what, paradoxically, may make it such a powerful tool *for* literature.

The modal specificities of smell, I have suggested, provide a way of reading the *Miracles*, where the 'miracle' is understood as both historical event and its aesthetic-devotional mediation. We rarely use olfactory metaphors to describe literary form, production, and consumption, but smell's ineffability, spatial entanglements, and associative affordances perhaps represent Gautier's broader project in the *Miracles*.[101] The power of odor to draw us into the present of perception at the same time as pointing us elsewhere to an indeterminate past, to a system of meaning that cannot quite be articulated, reflects how equivocal rhymes and *annominatio* foreground the act of listening at the expense of, but not at all eliminating, semantic complexity and doubleness. While similar arguments may be made about sound, smell's mode of transmission in empty space, where 'good' and 'bad' scents (en)counter each other, connect ethical to aesthetic considerations. Its metonymic reliance on the world of ordinary objects and experience makes smell a site of homiletic possibility, especially as performance or reading spaces would entail their own specific smellscapes.

We should, then, be cautious of a tendency to deodorize, to read smell out of texts, manuscripts, and performances. In other respects, we overly odorize the medieval past in order to other or distance it, as exemplified by the scratch-and-sniff book *Medieval Muck* in the 'Smelly Old History' series.[102] As Dolly Jørgensen points out, popular representations of

---

100 Hans Ulrich Gumbrecht, *Production of Presence: What Meaning Cannot Convey* (Stanford, 2003).
101 For a reading that engages with Hegel's analogy between poetic meter and scent, see Rowan Boyson, 'Shelley's Republic of Odours: Aesthetic and Political Dimensions of Scent in "The Sensitive-Plant"', *The Keats-Shelley Review* 27.2 (2013), 105–20.
102 Mary Dobson, *Medieval Muck* (Oxford, 1998).

medieval cities and their waste management reflect modern anxieties about cleanliness rather than past realities.[103] Similarly, Norbert Elias's sociological model of the 'civilizing process' is sustained by an othering of the Middle Ages that includes assigning an olfactory animality to the period.[104] On the one hand, 'reodorizing' the *Miracles* would entail a greater awareness of smell's significance to issues of performance, ethics, devotion, and aesthetics. And, on the other, it would necessitate a more critical treatment of the theoretical genealogies that have led to olfaction's muted presence in historical, literary, and cultural studies.[105]

103 Dolly Jørgensen, 'Modernity and Medieval Muck', *Nature and Culture* 9.3 (2014), 225–37.
104 See Norbert Elias, *The Civilizing Process*, trans. Edmund Jephcott, 2 vols (Oxford, 1977–82), 2:297–8, 1:203, cited in Mark S.R. Jenner, 'Follow Your Nose? Smell, Smelling, and Their Histories', *The American Historical Review* 116.2 (2011), 335–51 (343).
105 David Howes, *Sensual Relations: Engaging the Senses in Culture and Social Theory* (Ann Arbor, 2003), 201–2, notes that Freud's 'animalization of the sense of smell pushed it beyond the pale of culture', and thus contributed to 'the destruction of the elaborate semiotics of premodernity'.

4

Obscured by Smoke: Occluded Sight as Epistemological Crisis in Eyewitness Narratives of the 1241–2 Mongol Invasions[1]

MISHO ISHIKAWA[2]

In the spring of 1242, after nearly a year of occupying the Danubian plains, Batu Khan abruptly withdrew his forces from central Europe. Latin chronicles from the period express both horror and dismay around the Mongols' mysterious departure. Ivo of Narbonne relates how the sudden retreat caused even 'more fear for all those who witnessed it' than the initial attacks;[3] while a German annalist bluntly concludes that 'only God himself knows' the reason for it.[4] Amidst this backdrop of fear and uncertainty, Pope Innocent IV appointed John of Plano Carpini to lead a diplomatic mission to the court of the Great Khan with the hope of finding some 'remedy against the Tartars'.[5] John

---

1 Joint Winner of the Inaugural *New Medieval Literatures* Scholars of Colour Essay Prize.
2 I would like to thank Christine Chism for her feedback throughout the writing process for this essay. In addition, I would also like to thank the reviewers and editors at *NML* for their helpful suggestions and insights. Special thanks to the Parker Library, Corpus Christi College, Cambridge for use of CCCC MS 16ii.
3 Ivo's letter to the archbishop of Bordeaux is recorded in Matthew Paris's *Chronica majora*, under the year 1243: 'Qui ut subito aderant, sic et aberant repentini; unde magis omnes hoc videntes reddunt formidantes' (*Matthaei Parisiensis, Monachi Sancti Albani*, Chronica majora, ed. Henry Richards Luard, 7 vols, Rolls Series 57 (London, 1872–83), 4:270–7 (273–4)). My translation.
4 'Sed qualiter a finibus christianorum recesserint, ipse solus Deus arbiter novit', *Annales Scheftlarienses maiores (1092–1248)*, ed. Ph. Jaffé, Monumenta Germaniae Historica (Hanover, 1861), SS 17:335–43 (341). My translation.
5 'inveniri remedium contra Tartaros', from Innocent IV's letter to the archbishop of Sens (archiepiscopo Senonensi) dated 3 January 1245 (*Monumenta*

embarked on the journey in 1245, passing first through the conquered Kyivan Rus' principalities before reaching Güyük Khan's court near Karakorum. When John returned to Lyon in 1247, his advice to the pope was unequivocal: the Mongols intended 'to bring the whole world into subjection' and Latin Europe must prepare.[6] The *Ystoria Mongalorum* compiles John's observations into a lengthy ethnographic report that covers a range of topics, including Mongol funeral rites, clothing construction, and a historiographic account of Chinggis Khan's unification of the Mongolian steppe. But because John concludes that 'the Tartars never make peace except with those who submit to them', the *Ystoria* most closely attends to Mongol military tactics.[7] Throughout his minute depictions of Mongol warfare, John of Plano Carpini twice repeats how the Mongol military is divided 'into groups under captains of a thousand, a hundred, and ten, and "darkness" – that is, ten thousand'.[8] This description is, for the most part, accurate. While the Mongol army was indeed arranged by decimalization, John's description seems to confuse the Old Turkic and Mongolian word *tumen* (ten thousand) for *duman* (obscured by

---

Germaniae Historica, Epistolae saeculi XIII selectae e regestis pontificum romanorum, 3 vols, ed. C. Rodenburg (Berlin, 1883–94), 2:57). This was the phrase used for Innocent IV's agenda at the First Council of Lyon in June of 1245. The Tatars were not Mongols but rather were incorporated into the Mongolian empire when Chinggis Khan formally unified the tribal steppe confederations in 1206. The terms *Tartar* and *Tartary*, however, were frequently used by medieval European writers to describe both the Mongols and the Mongol empire. The shift from *Tatar* to *Tartar* likely alludes to Tartarus, a part of the Greek underworld.

6   Christopher Dawson, ed., *The Mongol Mission: Narratives and Letters of the Franciscan Missionaries in Mongolia and China in the Thirteenth and Fourteenth Century*, trans. a nun of Stanbrook Abbey (New York, 1955), 43. English translations of the *Ystoria* are taken from Dawson's edition unless otherwise noted. John of Plano Carpini, cap. 8: 'Intentio Tartarorum est sibi subicere totum mundum si possunt' (Anastasius van den Wyngaert, ed., *Sinica Franciscana, Volume 1: Itinera et Relationes Fratrum Minorum saec. XIII et XIV* (Florence, 1929), 93). All Latin citations of the *Ystoria* are taken from Wyngaert's edition.

7   Dawson, *The Mongol Mission*, 38. John of Plano Carpini, cap. 7: 'Sciendum quod cum nullis hominibus faciunt pacem nisi subdantur eis, quia, it dictum est supra, a Chingischan habent mandatum ut cunctas sibi si possunt subiciant nationes' (Wyngaert, *Sinica Franciscana*, 84).

8   Dawson, *The Mongol Mission*, 32. John of Plano Carpini, cap. 5: 'Statuit etiam quod per millenarios et centarios et decanos et tenebras, id est decem milia, debeat eorum exercitus ordinari' (Wyngaert, *Sinica Franciscana*, 92).

smoke). The error is a telling one. Each time John discusses the Mongol decimalization system, he is careful to translate *tumen/duman* twice; once as 'darkness', using the Latin *tenebrae*, and once as 'ten thousand'. By providing two translations for the same word, the text insists that both meanings are significant. A ten-thousand strong troop unit, then, is always *also* a 'darkness'. Given in the accusative case, *tenebras* further evokes the transitive verb *tenebrare* to which it is related. All these semantic slides test the limit of ethnographic 'sight'. A group of ten thousand is a darkness that darkens, it actively obscures the ability to see. John's mistranslation also carries a material resonance. Following the Battle of Legnica (the first of the 1241–2 invasions), eyewitness reports describe an unfamiliar – and confounding – tactic of Mongol warfare, the deployment of noxious black smoke to incapacitate enemy combatants and mask troop movement. Polish chronicles remark with horror how the Mongols hid within this 'witchcraft' to enclose the Christian troops within their ranks while remaining unseen.[9] John's use of 'darkness' evokes real battle experience that attests to how Mongol warfare disrupts modes of perception. Thus, the *Ystoria* articulates a growing fear within the Latin West: the peculiar invisibility of the Mongol threat.

Within the Latin tradition, medieval discourses of the senses typically correlate sight with *illumination* – a form of enlightenment associated with both physical and mental processes (lighting up and knowing). Although theories of vision vary throughout the European Middle Ages, most maintain a central thematic link between sight and knowing; namely that sight has the capacity to apprehend both natural and spiritual meaning. Sight thus functions as an element of anthroposemiosis, a world-building mechanism that knits the biosphere to cultural understandings. But if sight is constitutive to the known world, what happens when vision fails? The present study approaches this question in relation to a 'world-ending' event, the 1241–2 Mongol invasions of central Europe.[10] Through a reading of Roger Bacon's

---

9 See Jan Długosz, *The Annals of Jan Długosz: An English Abridgement*, trans. Maurice Michael (Chichester, 1997), 180.
10 Having identified the Danubian plain as a strategic entry-point into central Europe, Batu Khan led his forces into Poland and Hungary in 1241. One wing of Batu's army defeated the Polish forces at Legnica on 9 April 1241; two days later, the other wing defeated the Hungarian army at Mohi. The Hungarian king, Béla IV, was forced to flee the region, leaving Batu with full control of the plain.

theory of optics, I trace how formations of self and world are (de)constructed in two eyewitness narratives: an epistle from Roger of Torre Maggiore and a compiled history of the attacks by Thomas of Split. Written in the years following Batu Khan's withdrawal from central Europe, the two texts narrate the experience of violent contact with the Mongol invaders from the perspective of those within the Hungarian kingdom. Here, shock and violence trigger epistemological crisis; vision repeatedly fails within these narratives just at the moment when the Mongol forces should be apprehended.

Roger Bacon's Optical Theory: World-Building by 'Rational Sight'

The English Franciscan friar Roger Bacon (c. 1219–92) is an important interlocutor for understanding why disordered sight emerges as a persistent leitmotif in Latin accounts of Mongol warfare. Bacon's *Opus majus*, presented to Pope Clement IV in 1267, uses natural philosophy to affirm a Christian cosmology. Moments of failed vision in the Mongol invasion narratives are thereby indicative of more universal disturbances; indeed, as I discuss toward the end of this essay, Bacon himself interprets the Mongols as harbingers of Antichrist. Bacon's optical science gives proof to the Christian worldview through a practice of *translation studii* that unifies extramissive and intromissive theories into a single model for vision. As Holly Crocker explains, the primary difference between the two theories pertains to how power is distributed across the field of visual relations. Extramission invests the viewer with active agency, whereas intromission – stemming from Aristotelian natural philosophy – considers the viewer to be passively impressed upon by the emitted species (causal forces) of a sighted object.[11] Bacon's theory of sight maintains the intromissive idea that every point on a visible object emits species in all directions, forming a pyramid of radiation that reaches its apex across the surface of the eye.[12] Drawing from Christian extramission, Bacon then adds that vision is not solely a receptive power. Vision exerts its own agential force, for the species of

---

However, Batu – perhaps anticipating issues of succession – issued a general withdrawal of his forces in March 1242, following Ögödei Khan's death.
11   Holly Crocker, *Chaucer's Visions of Manhood* (New York, 2007), 18–19.
12   David C. Lindberg, *Theories of Vision from Al-Kindi to Kepler* (Chicago, 1976), 109.

the eye 'changes the medium and ennobles it, and renders it analogous to vision, and so prepares the passage of the species itself of the visible object'.[13] The species generated by visible objects – for example, species of light and species of color – can only be *seen* through the transformative emanations of the eye. Thus, Bacon acculturates intromission to a Christian context. The following section traces how Bacon knits the visual power to exertions of the will, forming what I term *rational sight*.

According to Bacon, sight is unique among the senses because it requires distance from the perceived object to function. Real objects are not seen by coming into direct contact with the eyes; rather, 'vision must perform the act of seeing by its own force' (2:471).[14] Sight is active, it is performed by force, creating a dynamic relationship between viewer and object.[15] The viewer's force of sight renders the object 'analogous to vision', it transforms the object into a *sight*. Making objects legible to sight, or rather making them *known* to sight, is a vulnerable process. Once transformed, the sighted object can then alter vision by overworking the eyes. Eyestrain – caused by the quality of a sight's impression – interrupts the performance of seeing.[16] Vision has the power to make objects into sights, and once transformed, these sighted objects have the power to unmake vision. The effects of seeing (sights) threaten sight itself. Of course, excessive sound can destroy hearing, just as excessive heat can destroy any feeling in the skin. Sight differs because it is not a passive form of perception. If not for the eyelids, the eyes would indeed 'work continuously', but the eyelids can always close. Sight can always be stopped. The viewer, therefore, has choice: the eyelids can

13   Roger Bacon, *The* Opus majus *of Roger Bacon*, trans. Robert Belle Burke, 2 vols (New York, 1962), 2:471. English translations are from Burke unless otherwise noted. Subsequent citations from this translation will appear in text for ease of reference. Roger Bacon, *Opus majus*, 'Unde oportet quod juventur et excitentur per speciem oculi, quae incedat in loco pyramidis visualis, et alteret medium ac nobilitet, et reddat ipsum proportionale visui, et sic praeparet incessum specie ipsius rei visibilis, et insuper eam nobilitet, ut omnino sit conformis et proportionalis nobilitati corporis animati, quod est oculus' (Roger Bacon, *Opus majus*, ed. John Henry Bridges, 2 vols (London, 1897), 2:52). All subsequent references to the Latin text come from this edition.
14   'Et ideo oportet quod visus faciat operationem videndi per suam virtutem' (Bacon, *Opus majus*, 2:52).
15   For a general overview of the topic, see David C. Lindberg, 'Roger Bacon on Light, Vision, and the Universal Emanation of Force', in *Roger Bacon and the Sciences: Commemorative Essays*, ed. Jeremiah Hackett (Leiden, 1997), 243–75.
16   Cf. Bacon, *Opus majus*, trans. Burke, 2:540–1.

remain open, or they can close. Keeping one's eyelids open, choosing to see, thus resembles an act of will.

Bacon contextualizes optical science in relation to its 'ineffable usefulness in regard to divine truth' (2:576).[17] Here Bacon offers his clearest articulation of the will as a cause for human sight, claiming that spiritual 'vision' requires 'the exercise and agreement of our free will [...] together with the grace of God to the end that we may see and secure the state of salvation' (2:578).[18] Natural and spiritual sight are analogous – they are both conscious exertions of force and will that strive toward knowledge production. Indeed, Bacon states that any observations about sight as a natural phenomenon 'must be serviceable' to both 'natural and spiritual meaning' (2:576).[19] Divine truth orders the world; therefore, knowledge of the world is a means for apprehending knowledge of God. As a natural phenomenon, vision can – or rather, must – be studied in the pursuit for spiritual meaning. Structurally then, the study of any natural phenomenon should similarly result in the dual elucidation of worldly and divine truths. But for Bacon 'nothing is more necessary for the natural and spiritual meaning than definite knowledge of [optical] science' (2:576),[20] precisely because human sight actively coordinates between the rational soul and the material world. George Molland thus concludes that Bacon's optical science provides 'a paradigm case of the communication of action'.[21] Purposive human sight – in other words, *rational* sight – is an action that communicates between forces of mind, world, and God.

Rational sight is an action that narrativizes experience within the intersecting spheres of natural and spiritual truths.[22] This understanding

17 'Volo nunc in fine innuere quomodo hace scientia habet ineffabilem utilitatem respectu sapientiae divinae' (Bacon, *Opus majus*, 2:159).
18 'Nam motus liberi arbitrii et consensus requiritur cum gratia Dei ad hoc ut videamus et consequamar statum salutis' (Bacon, *Opus majus*, 2:161).
19 'Et primo considerandum est, quod cum haec scientia res naturales certificat, ut planum est per ea quae dicta sunt, et per consequens liquet quod caeteras scientias elucidat et declarat, necesse est quod haec scientia sit utilis divinae veritati, propter hoc quod illa requirit notitiam scientiarum et rerum hujus mundi' (Bacon, *Opus majus*, 2:159).
20 'nihil magis necessarium est sensui naturali et spirituali, sicut hujus scientiae certitudo' (Bacon, *Opus majus*, 2:160).
21 George Molland, 'Roger Bacon and the Hermetic Tradition in Medieval Science', *Vivarium* 31.1 (1993), 140–60 (155).
22 Here I follow Peter Goldie, in whose view narrative 'is more than just a

of human sight aligns with what John Deely calls a semiotic web, a network of relations that constitute 'the reality of all that is experienced, but suchwise as to ensure that that reality cannot be divided in a final way into what is and what is not independent of cognition'.[23] Reality is a narrative shaped by purposive entanglements of body, mind, and physical environment. And because Bacon imagines this reality as species-specific (uniquely formed by the human rational soul), it can be understood as an Umwelt, a 'model world' organized around specific interests and needs.[24] The term *Umwelt* is helpful in exposing how culture becomes caught up in the narrativization of experience.[25] Deely argues that human Umwelten develop through social interactions mediated by language, which opens the possibility for worlds that are not tied to the immediacy of physical stimuli.[26] Extrapolating from Deely, I posit that rational sight functions precisely as this kind of world-building system within the *Opus majus*. The 'rational' component of rational sight extends the physical environment into a realm of socio-cultural signification. Attuned to both natural and spiritual truth, Bacon's understanding of human sight articulates an Umwelt that is coextensive with religious doctrine. As an act of communication, rational sight organizes different types of information into a unified and coherent narrative about the world. Rational sight is constitutive to the Umwelt of thirteenth-century Christendom; therefore, any sight that challenged the narrative unity of this world should be recognized as a potential rent in the very fabric of reality. By 1240, this much was clear: the Mongol empire was one such 'sight'.

---

bare annal or chronicle or list of a sequence of events, but a representation of those events which is shaped, organized, and coloured, presenting those events, and the people involved in them, from a certain perspective or perspectives, and thereby giving narrative structure – coherence, meaningfulness, and evaluative and emotional import – to what is related' (Peter Goldie, *The Mess Inside: Narrative, Emotion, and the Mind* (Oxford, 2012), 2).

23 John Deely, *The Human Use of Signs, or: Elements of Anthroposemiosis* (Lanham, MD, 1994), 7.

24 Deely, *The Human Use of Signs*, 42.

25 The term *Umwelt* comes from biologist Jakob von Uexküll's theory of animal life-worlds as distinct perceived realities. For example: the tick is eyeless but has skin that is sensitive to light. Light stimuli *are* tactile stimuli, which means that visual and tactile sites coincide within the tick's environment. See Jakob von Uexküll, *A Foray into the Worlds of Animals and Humans: With a Theory of Meaning*, trans. Joseph D. O'Neil (Minneapolis, 2010).

26 Deely, *The Human Use of Signs*, 44.

Inverted Ethnographic Sight: Roger of Torre Maggiore's Epistola in miserabile carmen

At the time of the Mongol invasions, the Italian-born Roger of Torre Maggiore was archdeacon of Nagyvárad (Oradea) in the eastern part of the Hungarian kingdom. Following Batu Khan's victory against King Béla IV at Mohi (11 April 1241), the Mongol armies focused on sacking Hungary's eastern cities before moving westward. Most of these cities, particularly east of the Danube, were protected only by earthen walls – not stone fortresses – that did little to stop the onslaught of Mongol attacks.[27] Nagyvárad quickly fell; but Roger survived the attack by fleeing into the nearby woods. Like many Hungarian refugees, he was then forced to keep moving in order to evade Mongol roving parties. Eventually Roger was captured by a Hungarian who joined the Mongols and 'had already become a Tatar in deeds'.[28] As a prisoner, Roger traveled with the main part of the Mongol army until 1242, when the confusion of Batu's withdrawal presented an opportunity for him to escape. Sometime before 1244, Roger composed an epistle that has since come to be known as the *Epistola in miserabile carmen*.[29] Likely intended for wide circulation, the *Epistola* promises to record 'the truth about [the Mongols'] life, behavior and battling' through the narration of Roger's firsthand experience.[30] The *Epistola* attempts to circumscribe the Mongol invaders as objects for study by establishing an ethnographic framework for the text. However, this project is repeatedly thwarted by the fact that the

---

27   Peter Jackson, *The Mongols and the West: 1241–1410*, 2nd edn (New York, 2014), 64.

28   Master Roger, *Epistola in miserabile carmen super destructione regni Hungarie per Tartaros facta/Epistle to the Sorrowful Lament upon the Destruction of the Kingdom of Hungary by the Tatars*, ed./trans. János M. Bak, Martyn C. Rady, and László Veszprémy (Budapest, 2010), 211 (English); 'ditioni cuiusdam Hungari facti, ut dixi, operibus Tartari me submisi' (210, Latin). All citations (both English and Latin) come from this edition unless otherwise noted. While little documentary evidence remains regarding Hungarians who decided to join with the Mongols, John of Plano Carpini notes that some were present at the court of the Great Khan as translators.

29   The letter is extant only in a 1488 print edition, where it is erroneously addressed to 'Bishop John of Pest'. János Bak and Martyn Rady explain that the manuscript exemplar likely used the initials *I* and *P* for the addressee, as Pest had no bishopric. See the introduction in Master Roger, *Epistola in miserabile carmen*, ed./trans. Bak, Martyn, and Veszprémy, xlii.

30   Master Roger, *Epistola in miserabile carmen*, 135.

Hungarian–Mongol contact zone was by no means a neutral one. As a result, the *Epistola* is often in conflict with its purported aims: instead of recording observations, it ultimately narrates the experience of being observed.

The *Epistola* opens with a justification of the text. Anticipating that his narrative will be met with disbelief, Roger stresses that many of the events detailed in the letter happened beneath his gaze ('meo subiacuerunt aspectui').[31] By linking veracity to the gaze (*aspectus*), the letter immediately establishes the eyewitness as a crucial interlocutor of truth. Roger's emphasis on eyewitness truth frames the letter as an empirical record undisturbed by authorial intervention; hence, his disclaimer that the matter has not been taken up 'in order to denounce or dishonor anyone', but simply to 'instruct' (135).[32] To present 'the truth' about the Mongols, Roger must inform his audience through a kind of mimesis. For the audience to see that which occurred 'beneath my gaze' – to see *as* Roger saw – is crucial, '*so they that read may understand*, who understand believe, who believe observe, and who observe perceive that the days of perdition are near, and that the times are running towards the end' (135, emphasis in original).[33] To understand (*intelligere*), to believe (*credere*), to hold (*tenere*), to perceive (*percipere*); the letter strings together verbs associated with both mind and body to underscore how the text ultimately facilitates comprehension through the senses. The millenarian rhetoric of the passage is uncharacteristic of the rest of the *Epistola* but works here to articulate the stakes of 'truthfully' signifying the Mongols. As the letter later details, the Hungarians – to their own great detriment – disregarded similar information about the Mongols coming from the Rus' principalities in the months leading up to the invasion.[34]

The *Epistola* begins by affirming a paradigm that inextricably binds conceptual understanding to empirical observation.[35] Sight – specifi-

31 Master Roger, *Epistola in miserabile carmen*, 132.
32 'Quia non ad deprehensionem cuiquam vel derogationem, sed ad instructionem id potius examinavi' (Master Roger, *Epistola in miserabile carmen*, 134).
33 'ut *legentes intelligant* et intelligentes credant, credentes teneant et tenentes percipiant, quod prope sunt dies perditionis et tempora properant ad non esse' (Master Roger, *Epistola in miserabile carmen*, 134, emphasis in original).
34 Master Roger, *Epistola in miserabile carmen*, 157.
35 This is a paradigm that is also characteristic of late medieval ethnographic writing. As Shirin Khanmohamadi explains, late medieval ethnographic texts are identifiable through a shared language of intent: a text's stated interest in

cally *Roger's* sight – thereby takes on a new function within the text. The letter primarily figures sight, to borrow a phrase from Zrinka Stahuljak, as a technology of transmission.[36] By sharing Roger's experiences, the *Epistola* transmits encounters with the Mongols to a network that extends beyond the immediate zone of conflict. The impetus to transmit experience beyond the conflict zone holds real-world urgency. Referencing again the initial dismissive attitude adopted by the Hungarians toward a Mongol attack, Roger describes how most of the nobility thought that 'any such calamity would only hit some in particular and not all in general' (181).[37] The invasion and subsequent occupation of the kingdom quickly proved otherwise. The urgency of the *Carmen miserabile* is echoed in John of Plano Carpini's mission report, as it is 'the intention of the Tartars to bring the whole world into subjugation if they can'.[38] Both the *Epistola* and John of Plano Carpini's report consider it likely, if not inevitable, that the Mongols will once again return to Europe. Composed amidst the looming threat of a future invasion, Roger's epistle transmits experience to a potentially skeptical audience so that they too may know the realities of Mongol warfare. The *Epistola* disseminates experience in order to safely multiply the contact zone as a warning across Christendom. In this sense, the epistle shares much in common with the aims of travel writing in the later Middle Ages.[39]

---

observing the manners and customs of an observed people (*In Light of Another's Word: European Ethnography in the Middle Ages* (Philadelphia, 2014)). The *Epistola* explicitly uses such language, promising to describe the Mongols' way of life as well as their customs (*vita et ipsorum moribus*, Master Roger, *Epistola in miserabile carmen*, 134). For more on medieval ethnography and empiricism, see: Felipe Fernández-Armesto, 'Medieval Ethnography', *Journal of the Anthropological Society of Oxford* 13.3 (1982), 275–86; and Joan-Pau Rubiés, ed., *Medieval Ethnographies: European Perceptions of the World Beyond* (Farnham, UK, 2009); Khanmohamadi, *In Light of Another's Word*.

36 Zrinka Stahuljak, 'Medieval Fixers: Politics of Interpreting in Western Historiography', in *Rethinking Medieval Translation: Ethics, Politics, Theory*, ed. Emma Campbell and Robert Mills (Cambridge, UK, 2012), 147–63 (149).

37 'credentes plagam huiusmodi particularem quibusdem et non omnibus generalem' (Master Roger, *Epistola in miserabile carmen*, 180).

38 Dawson, *The Mongol Mission*, 43; 'Intentio Tartarorum est sibi subicere totum mundum si possunt' (Wyngaert, *Sinica Franciscana*, 93).

39 The *Epistola* predates many of the ethnographically inflected medieval travel narratives. Scholars of medieval ethnographic writing typically attribute the mission report of John of Plano Carpini as one of the earliest examples of this

OBSCURED BY SMOKE

Geraldine Heng has shown how medieval travel narratives work to inscribe the world within familiar frameworks of home; thus, 'an external reality – huge and amorphous, disorderly, chaotic, in motion – is brought home and managed by being rendered internal, and possessed internally, first within the manuscript environment of a purported travelogue, and then within the mind of a listening, reading audience'.[40] The utility and pleasures of such texts, however, depend on a process of retrieval that maintains cultural difference and geographic distance even as they become internally inscribed. Travel narratives partially operate by drawing attention to the contrast 'between the sedentary audience at home and the roving eye of the narrative as it travels around the world at large'.[41] Heng's optical metaphors allude to the empirical paradigms of late medieval travel writing and ethnography: to see is to know. Modeling Bacon's optics at a macro scale, medieval travel writing is empowered by distance. The 'roving eye' of a travelogue transmits the sedentary gaze of its audience, so that the world 'is returned more fitted to the sense'.[42] The *Epistola*, however, inverts the directionality of travel narrative's intromissive sight. The foreign Mongols have not been 'brought home' by a personified traveler's reassuring narrative circumscription but have entered by means of their own volition – their own 'advance and progress' (133, 'ingressus et processus').[43] The effect is one of disorientation: home is made strange through the transformative 'extramissions' of the outside world. Instead of envisioning the external world, the *Epistola* makes home a site/sight for foreign eyes.[44]

According to Heng, travel narratives allow for the 'inspection close-up' of the wider world 'from a vantage point of domestic fixity',[45] but, for Roger and his fellow refugees, the invasions upend the very idea

---

form of travel narratives. I draw the comparison between Roger's text and these later writings only to reveal a shared understanding of the relationship between Latin Christendom and the rest of the world.
40   Geraldine Heng, *Empire of Magic: Medieval Romance and the Politics of Cultural Fantasy* (New York, 2003), 247.
41   Heng, *Empire of Magic*, 247.
42   Bacon, *Opus majus*, 2:474.
43   Master Roger, *Epistola in miserabile carmen*, 132.
44   Khanmohamadi makes a similar point, broadly arguing that early European ethnographic writers develop an aesthetic multifocality – a 'dialogic poetics' that repeatedly imagines the perspective of those they mean to describe; see Khanmohamadi, *In Light of Another's Word*, 4–5.
45   Heng, *Empire of Magic*, 247.

of domestic fixity. Roger describes how he was forced to 'seek caves, excavate pits, or find hollow trees to have shelter, while the Tatars, like hounds tracking rabbits and boars, rushed through the thick of the thorn bushes, the shadows of the groves, the depths of the waters and the heart of the wasteland'.[46] After this period of flight, Roger narrates how the Mongols remade Hungarian life in reflection of their own laws and customs. He describes how the plains villages began to repopulate when the Mongols sent out word that those who submitted to their rule would come to no harm. Once 'every village chose its king from among the Tatars at its will', the Mongols sent bailiffs to 'render justice and supply [the people] with useful horses, animals, weapons, presents and clothing' (209).[47] Roger bitterly enumerates that this system of 'justice and supply' only functioned by forcibly dismantling pre-existing social bonds. These seemingly fixed bonds were remade into disposable commodities through the compulsory exchange of Hungarian women for the lives of their fathers, husbands, brothers, and for animal livestock. According to Roger, the Mongols – and their Cuman allies – took pleasure in *seeing* Hungarian men forced to barter their female family members:

> The Tatars and Cumans stood alongside us, saw those being killed and were glad insofar that fathers by means of their daughters, husbands by means of their wives, and brothers by means of their pretty sisters purchased their own life. Those [women], according to the [Tatars'] pleasure, were spared and became compensation to them; for they would debauch the wife or daughter in sight of the husband or father.[48]

Here the active Mongol gaze draws pleasure from watching how the structures foundational to Hungarian domestic life (family ties and

---

46 'Oportebat me invenire cavernas vel foveas facere vel arbores querere perforatas, in quibus me possem recipere, cum illi densitatem veprium, opaca nemorum, aquarum profunda, intima solitudinum tanquam canes lepores et apros investigantes percurrere videbantur' (Master Roger, *Epistola in miserabile carmen*, 206).

47 'et qualibet villa elegit sibi regem de Tartaris, quem optavit [...] balimos, qui iustitiam facerent et eis equos, animalia, arma, exennia et vestimenta utilia procurarent' (Master Roger, *Epistola in miserabile carmen*, 208).

48 'Stabant nobiscum Tartari et Comani simul, videbant quamplurimi et gaudebant, letabantur quod patres per filias, mariti per uxores, fratres per sorores pulcras vitam redimebant illas ad libitum eorum conservantes et pro qudam [sic] illis fiebat solatio, ut in conspectu patris vel mariti uxor vel filia stuprabatur' (207). Translation my own.

marriage) are violently reshaped under occupation. The watching Mongols are only glad *insofar* as the Hungarians are forced to break their social bonds. Furthermore, the Mongols seem to take pleasure in then *showing* the Hungarians the sight of their own domestic unmaking. In other words, they force the Hungarians to see what they themselves see: Hungarian society broken and remade to reflect their own foreign interests. I do not mean to imply that the Mongols used sight to exert control over the people they conquered; nor do I wish to minimize the realities[49] of Mongol warfare. Instead, I hope only to note how the *Epistola* links exertions of power with exertions of sight. In terms of narrative representation, Roger expresses the horrifying conditions of conquest as the horror of being seen for the pleasure of foreign eyes – the horror of being made into an object of sight.

Heng's treatment of medieval travel narratives also helps clarify a curious feature of the *Epistola*, the fact that the Mongols themselves are *unseeable* within the text. Despite his clear declaration of intent, Roger does not record much ethnographic detail. The text is graphic and visceral in its depictions of violence, and yet it offers no description of the people committing the violence. In stark contrast with other contemporary reports of the Mongols' 'life, behavior and battling', the *Epistola* makes no effort to represent them in relation to sensory experience. The epistle offers no account of their dress, their weaponry, their language – and it offers no account of their bodies at all. Nor does it attempt to individuate the Mongols from one another. Throughout the *Epistola*, Roger almost exclusively refers to the invaders as an undifferentiated whole (the *Tartari*). Even when captured and imprisoned, the only 'Tatar' that speaks is Roger's Hungarian captor. No single body is responsible for any particular action; rather, discrete actions are always performed by the 'Tatars' as a mass. As a result, the Mongols are strangely disembodied in the text, a 'darkness' observable only in the devastation

---

49 Although extant European sources consistently describe the 1241–2 invasions in terms of massacre, historians have questioned the scope of Mongol violence. However, the massacres described in the *Epistola* have recently been substantiated by archaeological evidence from Orosháza-Bónum, a village located in the southwest of the Great Hungarian Plain. Human skeletal remains – diverse in both sex and age – indicate a Mongol surprise attack on the community, resulting in the mass slaughter of civilians. See Attila Gyucha, Wayne Lee, and Zoltán Rósza, 'The Mongol Campaign in Hungary, 1241–1242: The Archaeology and History of Nomadic Conquest and Massacre', *The Journal of Military History* 83 (2019), 1021–66.

they wreak. For instance, when Roger learns that the Mongols have taken the village of Tămașda, he writes that 'all those whom they did not keep alive were beheaded by the sword with horrendous cruelty' (204).[50] Although Roger marks the Mongols as the subjects of the sentence (using the nominative plural *Tartari*), the syntax emphasizes a singular sword ('gladio') as an acting agent of violence. The sword is more materially present than the bodies that wield it. The Mongols are only visible in the text by their effects.

If (ethnographic) sight requires distance, it would seem that the Mongols have come too close. The space necessary for travelogue's world-inscribing power has been collapsed. Indeed, proximity seems to destroy the normal functions of Roger's vision. Once captured and forced to travel alongside the Mongol army, Roger declares that from then on 'death was always before the eyes of my body and mind' (210).[51] After his capture, Roger witnesses acts of massacre (physical death) that work to diminish his capacity for rational sight, sight motivated by acts of his own will. With his own death a seeming inevitability, Roger sees what he imagines the Mongols see: the subjugated Hungarians as objects to meet their own interests. The Mongols see the Hungarians as reflections of their will, which Roger can only explain as a kind of madness for destruction: 'Oh the pain, oh the immense cruelty and madness of this savage nation!' (210).[52] Although the Mongols *willfully* see the Hungarians as objects to satisfy their passions, the epistle describes this will as 'madness' ('rabies'). The will of the Mongols, by Roger's estimation, is not rational, but mad; therefore, such willful sight appears as another inversion/perversion of the structures that make up the Latin Umwelt. Rather than employ rational sight in the service of better knowing the divine, the Mongols use irrational sight as justification to pursue their blasphemous pleasures. Kept in extreme proximity, Roger is unable to see the Mongols. With his vision disrupted, he sees as the Mongols do – his own death; the death of domestic fixity; the death of Hungary. For this reason, then, the *Epistola* implores its audience to do

50 'Post hec statim invaluere rumores, quod dictum pontem Thome Theutonicorum villam in aurora Tartari occupaverunt et, quos tenere noluerant, horrenda crudelitas acerbitatis gladio dire iugulavit' (Master Roger, *Epistola in miserabile carmen*, 203).
51 'mortem semper pre corde preque oculis habebant' (Master Roger, *Epistola in miserabile carmen*, 209).
52 'O dolor, o crudelitas et rabies immanis populi immensa!' (Master Roger, *Epistola in miserabile carmen*, 211).

what its narrator cannot: to understand (*intelligere*), to believe (*credere*), to observe (*tenere*), and to perceive (*percipere*).

Irrational Sight: Thomas of Split's Historia

Like Roger of Torre Maggiore, Thomas of Split (c. 1200–68) recorded a narrative history of the 1241–2 Mongol invasions in central Europe within a few years of Batu Khan's withdrawal. Thomas, however, was spared from the violence that Roger experienced firsthand. At the time of the invasions, the Croatian city of Split was a nominal vassal state of the Hungarian kingdom. Split, located along the Croatian coast, sits beyond the plains-region that occupied the primary strategic interests of Batu Khan; and as a result, the city was not made subject to a Mongol siege. Still, offshoots of the Mongol army ravaged the Croatian countryside in pursuit of Béla IV following his retreat from the battlefield at Mohi. In March of 1242, Mongol forces arrived outside Split; however, they quickly traveled northward toward the island city of Traù where Béla was rumored to be hiding. As a result, the city of Split was largely spared from any direct attack.[53] With the city preserved, displaced Hungarian survivors arrived in droves, including Queen Maria and a host of noblewomen widowed after the Mongols' initial attack against the kingdom. James Ross Sweeney has shown that Thomas, serving as the city's archdeacon at the time, likely came into direct contact with some of these refugees[54] – contact that would inform his narrative of the invasions in his longer history of the Church organizations in Salona and Split, the *Historia Salonitanorum atque Spalatinorum Pontificum*.

The *Historia* is unique among contemporaneous European accounts of the Mongol invasions for its compilation of eyewitness testimony, as opposed to written report. Thomas *hears* ('audire potui') about the nature and habits ('natura et habitu') of the Mongols directly from 'those who have more diligently sought out the matter'.[55] Sweeney distinguishes

---

53   James Ross Sweeney, 'Thomas of Spalato and the Mongols: A Thirteenth-Century Dalmatian View of Mongol Customs', *Florilegium* 4 (1982), 156–83 (163).
54   Sweeney, 'Thomas of Spalato and the Mongols', 160.
55   Archdeacon Thomas of Split, *Historia Salonitanorum atque Spalatinorum Pontificum/History of the Bishops of Salona and Split*, ed./trans. Olga Perić, Damir Karbić, Mirjana Matijević Sokol, and James Ross Sweeney (Budapest, 2006), 280; 'prout ab his audire potui, qui rem curiosius indagarunt, pauca narrabo' (279). All citations (both English and Latin) come from this edition

Thomas's oral sources from textual borrowings 'in order to support a claim about factual reliability'; ultimately, he concludes that 'the general attitude Thomas displays toward the Mongols must have been shared by his informants and contemporaries'.[56] Sweeney's attention to mood (the 'general attitude' expressed in the text) suggests that the *Historia*, like the *Epistola*, garners textual authority by linking knowledge with direct experience, with feeling. The *Historia* still privileges the eyewitness only in aggregate. Whereas the *Epistola* stresses both the intimacy and the immediacy of Roger's firsthand experience, the *Historia* presents the feeling of encounter as a constitutive part of historiographic writing. And yet, the *Historia* does not adopt a millenarian approach to the invasions. Much like the *Epistola*, the *Historia* strives to suppress the appearance of the Mongols within its narrative of the invasions. Rendered only notionally visible, the Mongols are a nonentity within the text, their absence rebounding the feeling of encounter inward. The *Historia* resists depicting the Mongols as anti-Christian agents and by doing so reveals that the true threat to Christendom is an insular one.

The *Historia*, like the *Epistola*, attempts to picture the Mongols as part of an aesthetic pattern of erasure. Thomas, somewhat paradoxically, uses physical description to confine and limit the Mongols within his narrative. Thus, he produces the following caricature: 'Their appearance presents an intensely terrifying sight: their legs are short, but their chests are huge; their faces are broad, and their skin white; their cheeks are beardless, and their noses hooked; and their small eyes are set far apart' (282).[57] Before he even begins, Thomas immediately qualifies their appearance as 'intensely terrifying', thereby casting otherwise neutral physical characteristics as legible social signs. In medieval Europe, the practice of 'reading' bodies gained momentum in the thirteenth century, a trend facilitated by expanded access to the pseudo-Aristotelian *Secreta secretorum* and its physiognomic treatise.[58] Debra Higgs Strickland, in

---

unless otherwise noted; further references to the English translation are included in-text.
56 Sweeney, 'Thomas of Spalato and the Mongols', 160.
57 'Terrificum valde exhibent faciei aspectum, breves habent tibias, sed vasta pectora, lata est facies et cutis alba, imberbis gena et naris adunca, breves oculi spatio longiori disiuncti' (Thomas of Split, *Historia*, 281).
58 The *Secreta secretorum* is (erroneously) styled as a series of letters written by Aristotle to Alexander the Great. The text offers advice on topics primarily related to governance and medicine but also includes a short a treatise on the pseudo-science of physiognomy. Alongside many of Aristotle's genuine works,

her work on depictions of monstrosity in medieval art, has argued that physiognomy is a semiotic system through which concepts of moral disposition are knit to the human body as physical signs.[59] Thomas paints a 'terrifying sight' by deploying recognizable signs of evil. In particular, the hooked nose ('naris adunca') characterization registers as a strong sign of the Mongols' 'terrifying' difference. Strickland notes how the hooked nose, even before becoming a Jewish caricature, held potent associations with demonic faces throughout the Middle Ages, consistently functioning as a general sign of evil.[60] Similarly, the exaggerated contrast between the Mongols' reportedly short legs and huge chests registers as a distortion of the idealized human form, which, as outlined in the *Secreta secretorum*, equates bodily 'evenness' with mental 'goodness'.[61] Various versions of the *Secreta secretorum* also specifically equate short legs with lechery; broad chests with both hardiness and dull wittedness; white faces (as opposed to red, yellow, or black) with lust; and small eyes with smallness of heart.[62] The composite sketch Thomas offers – small eyes, hooked noses, broad chests, short legs – visualizes a symbolic field, a network of ideas, *about* the Mongols.[63] Thomas, therefore, produces a body that is only notionally visible. By deploying physiognomic stereotypes, Thomas occludes 'seeing' the Mongols outside of his conceptual framework. Furthermore, the ready

---

the *Secreta secretorum* was first translated into Latin in the twelfth century. The text, extant in numerous vernacular manuscripts, was both widely transmitted and seriously studied as part of Aristotelian natural philosophy and experimental science. Notably, Roger Bacon completed his own edition of the book sometime before 1257.
59 Debra Higgs Strickland, *Saracens, Demons, and Jews: Making Monsters in Medieval Art* (Princeton, 2003), 38.
60 Strickland, *Saracens, Demons, and Jews*, 77–8. See also Ruth Mellinkoff, *Outcasts: Signs of Otherness in Northern European Art of the Late Middle Ages* (Berkeley, 1993); and Sara Lipton, *Dark Mirror: The Medieval Origins of Anti-Jewish Iconography* (New York, 2014).
61 *Three Prose Versions of the* Secreta secretorum, ed. Robert Steele, EETS, e.s. 74 (London, 1898), 117.
62 *Three Prose Versions of the* Secreta secretorum, 226 (legs); 116 (chest); 225 (white); 229 (eyes).
63 The process of giving body to a concept is illuminated by contemporary theories of racial formation as described in Sierra Lomuto's work on the Middle English *King of Tars*. See Sierra Lomuto, 'The Mongol Princess of Tars: Global Relations and Racial Formation in *The King of Tars* (c. 1330)', *Exemplaria* 31.3 (2019), 171–92.

availability of these physiognomic signs works to map the image of the Mongol body onto other, more familiar, icons of 'terrifying' alterity. The *Historia* paints the new Mongol threat with the same familiar face. As a result, the Mongol invaders become readily known to the text's audience while remaining curiously absent from the text itself.

The conjured Mongol body of the *Historia* materializes a conceptual understanding of Christian/Mongol difference. Thomas strengthens this understanding by similarly materializing Mongol sight as fundamentally different from rational, Christian sight. He does so through a remarkable narrative addition to the *Historia*: a scene that imagines Batu Khan speaking to his troops just before the Battle of Mohi. Batu's speech marks a dramatic shift in perspective within the *Historia* and is the only time the text not only grants the Mongols specific material presence but also a point of view. It is perhaps unsurprising then that Batu is introduced to the text via an act of looking. The *Historia* explains that just as the Hungarian troops were making camp, Batu, 'the elder of the two leaders of the Tatar host, ascended a hill to spy out carefully the disposition of the whole army' (263).[64] Emboldened by what he sees, Batu goes back to rouse his troops. 'We can be confident, comrades', he declares, 'for although there is a great host of this enemy, they have allowed themselves to take poor counsel, and will thus not be able to escape our hands. For I have seen them like sheep without a shepherd, enclosed within the narrowest of folds' (263).[65]

Overlooking the enemy camp, Batu sees the Hungarians as vulnerable to attack. In the language of his own analogy, he sees these 'sheep without a shepherd' through the eyes of a wolf. The sheep/wolf analogy is one that recurs throughout Thomas's chapters on the invasions. When a small Mongol host arrives at Split in search of Béla IV, Thomas describes how the Hungarian refugees became 'dazed' and 'wandered to and fro like sheep in a sheepfold trying to evade the jaws of the wolf' (267).[66] Once again, the Hungarians are likened to exposed sheep, the

64 'Tunc Bath, maior dux Tartarei exercitus, in quendam collem conscendens, speculatus est diligenter omnem dispositionem exercitus' (Thomas of Split, *Historia*, 262).
65 'Bono animo nos esse oportet, o sotii, quia licet magna sit multitudo gentis istius, tamen quia improvido reguntur consilio, non poterunt effugere manus nostras. Vidi enim eos quasi gregem sine pastore in quodam artissimo stabulo interclusos' (Thomas of Split, *Historia*, 262).
66 'sed tanto malo attoniti ibant circumquaque, velud oves in stabulo luporum morsus evadere perquirentes' (Thomas of Split, *Historia*, 266).

Mongols to a predatory wolf. Batu's speech is troublingly echoed by the behavior of the Hungarian refugees. Having been seen as sheep has made the Hungarians sheep-like, and therefore vulnerable to the 'wolf'. Thomas notes with some alarm that the Hungarians, 'seeing that they were surrounded on every side by bands of the enemy, lost all sense and reason' (267). Worse still, 'None would take counsel with his fellow, each one was concerned only for himself, and none could take thought for general salvation' (267). The Hungarians are entirely unmade by the reminder of having been already seen, losing their reason, their ethics, and ultimately their faith. Roger similarly describes the evacuative power of the Mongol gaze in the *Epistola*. In both accounts of the invasions, the experience of being beheld by the Mongols is transformative.

The *Historia* accounts for the transformative power of the Mongol gaze by representing sight as a zero-sum practice. This understanding of sight hinges upon the polysemy of the sheep/wolf analogy. Batu Khan's speech focuses on identifying how he sees the Hungarians in order to pose his wolfish sight as the correlate of rational sight. His speech, to put it another way, stages wolf-sight in opposition with rational (Christian) sight. The performance not only informs Thomas's audience that rational sight and wolf-sight are different but goes a step further to assert that the two modes of seeing are entirely incompatible. The *Historia* uses Batu to articulate Hungarian/Mongol difference. Although Batu addresses his 'comrades in-arms', the text makes no attempt to account for the reception of Batu's speech among his own people. This formal decision suggests that Thomas's audience is the actual intended audience of the speech – an impression strengthened by Batu's obvious (though improbable) references to Matthew 9:36 and Mark 6:34. In both passages, Christ, overlooking a crowd, likens the people he sees to sheep without a shepherd; but instead of having compassion for the sheep-like hordes, Batu sees the Hungarians as the wolf does: defenseless. By mirroring Christ's language, Batu's speech triggers an immediate moment of recognition for the text's presumed audience: 'sheep' are either protected by the shepherd or they are vulnerable to attack. The sight of sheep, in this case, functions as a heuristic for determining in/out groups within a Latin-Christian cultural framework. The viewer can either cognize sheep as objects for compassionate protection or as food for slaughter. To gaze upon sheep compassionately is to see as Christ does, and to gaze upon sheep greedily is to see in a manner opposed to Christ. Batu's material presence in the *Historia* dramatizes how the processes of sight ratify a Christ/anti-Christ binary. In other words, Batu performs a moment of *irrational* sight – sight motivated by the appetites of the sensitive soul,[67] not the will – within the text. The *Historia* uses Batu Khan to stage a moment of polarization. If rational sight is constitutive to the Latinate Umwelt (e.g., to see the 'sheep' as Christ does), then irrational sight is an oppositional – and potentially destructive – mode of looking (e.g., to see as the wolf does). The readily legible allusions to Matthew 9 and Mark 6 in Batu's speech encourage the audience to hold Christ (rational sight) and Batu (irrational sight) in direct contrast. We, the text's presumed Latin-Christian audience, are made aware of how Batu sees differently from *us* – how he sees 'sensitively' instead of rationally.

Throughout the *Historia*, Thomas repeatedly represents the Mongols in terms of the sensitive soul. Frequently he describes the Mongols as locusts, pestilent 'men without scruples who roamed the world fighting not to win a kingdom but simply from greed for plunder' (259).[68] Motivated 'simply' by the pursuit of material pleasure (plunder), the Mongols are depicted as moving through the world unthinkingly. Thomas ascribes them no strategy, no political aim. Indeed, he seems to position the Mongols as uniquely outside the realm of sociopolitical life. The *Historia* states that 'they do not adhere to the Christian, Saracen or Hebrew religion, and so no integrity is found in them, and they observe no faith of oaths. Against the custom of all peoples they neither receive nor send embassies either about war or about peace' (283).[69] Thomas defines the Mongols as a people who have rejected the constraints of human culture. United solely by a common greed, they are without faith and ethics, without law (the observance of oaths), and without custom. Having bucked the structures that, according to Thomas, make up rational life, the Mongols are only moved by the wants of the sensitive soul. They, like nonhuman animals, are governed by nature alone. Batu's wolfish gaze gives evidence to the idea that the Mongols are not

---

67 The Aristotelian tradition treats the sensitive soul as a system of innate abilities that coordinates an animate organism's vital functions with sense-perception (i.e., with the material world). Whereas humans alone possess the rational soul, all other animal life possesses the sensitive soul.

68 'qui non pro regnandi cupiditate sed pro predarum aviditate per mundum pugnando discurrunt' (Thomas of Split, *Historia*, 258).

69 'Preterea nec christiana, nec ebrea, nec saracenica se lege constringunt et ideo nulla veritas reperitur in ipsis, nullius iuramenti fidem observant. Et contra morem omnium gentium nec de bello nec de pace legationem recipiunt aut mittunt' (Thomas of Split, *Historia*, 282).

rational agents but are instead a kind of anti-cultural force. Considering again the transformative power of Batu's gaze, the Mongol threat is not limited to physical violence. After having been made into a sight (sheep-for-slaughter) by the Mongols, the Hungarian refugees that Thomas encounters all abandon their reason, their social responsibility, and their salvation when made aware of their ongoing status as 'sheep'.

By categorizing the Mongols as irrational viewers, the *Historia* limits Mongol agency to the pursuits and pleasures of the sensitive soul. Without the governing structures of politics, law, and religion – without, in other words, Thomas's markers for human culture – the text classes the Mongols as belonging to the natural world. Strikingly, the text builds upon this distinction to ultimately reframe the invasions as a kind of natural disaster. After Batu's speech, and after the Hungarians' devastating loss at Mohi, the *Historia* uses metaphorical expressions to recode the battle and its aftermath as natural events. The Mongol-as-natural-disaster calibration reaches a climax when the text narrates how Mongol troops pursued the Hungarian soldiers, even in retreat. Although Thomas notes how they 'cut down' the fleeing men, the attackers strangely disappear from the moment: 'The dead fell to the right and left; like leaves in winter, the slain bodies of these miserable men were strewn along the whole route; blood poured forth like torrents of rain. The miserable country, stained by the blood of its sons, was dyed red throughout its length and breadth.'[70] The passage notably deviates from Thomas's typical style, becoming uncharacteristically figurative as it describes the aftermath of the battle. Similarly observing that Thomas adopts 'great literary flourish' whenever describing specific Mongol military engagements, Sweeney argues that such narrative moments imagine the invaders as monstrous.[71] To push back on this reading slightly, I suggest that Thomas adopts this literary flourish to emphasize the Mongol invasions as a non-agential (at least on the human level) natural disaster. As in Roger's *Epistola*, Thomas represents Mongol violence as disembodied. The hands that fell the bodies, that caused the blood to pour forth, are once again rendered invisible. Instead, the vivid

---

70 As translated and quoted in Sweeney, who captures well the rhetorical flourish here, 'Thomas of Spalato and the Mongols', 163; 'Cadebant a dextris et a sinistris ybernalium foliorum instar, iacebant per totam viam miserorum prostrata cadavera, fluebat sanguis more torrentis fluvii' (Thomas of Split, *Historia*, 269).

71 Sweeney, 'Thomas of Spalato and the Mongols', 163.

imagery of the passage registers mass death as environmental change: bodies fall like leaves, blood like rain.

Thomas's poetics suppress the Mongols as causal agents at Mohi. Using *cadere* in the active voice, Thomas insinuates that the dead *fell* ('cadebant'), they are not felled; yet neither do they fall as agents of their own change. Notably, the *Historia* does not represent the slain as Christian martyrs, dying in defense of their faith. Instead, their bodies fall as leaves do: inanimate and without visible cause, marking little more than seasonal change. In reference to his work with Mark Turner on poetic metaphor, George Lakoff explains that overwhelmingly 'events (like death) are understood in terms of actions by some agent (like reaping)'.[72] Paul Binski makes a similar argument about the conventional ways in which death is represented in medieval visual culture. Underscoring how Christian doctrine makes death an unknowable experience (as opposed to a mortal process), Binski states that there is an 'odd cause and effect in medieval art which show[s] death in the world – in various forms of personification, usually as a corpse – literally as the cause of itself'.[73] Lakoff and Binski observe how personification works to represent death as an effect, the result of some cause (even if that cause is death itself). Conversely, Thomas's use of metaphor resists assigning an agent to the action of killing. Death, in this case, is still understood as an event (the effect of an action) – only, without a clear agent. Natural phenomena replace the momentarily absented bodies of the invaders, collapsing any clear distinction between the two. Just as the cause of falling leaves or flowing water is invisible and abstract, so too become the Mongols. The passage does, however, include a moment of personification. Thomas concludes his poetic passage on the Battle of Mohi by ascribing personhood to the blood-soaked landscape. Hungary, that 'unhappy country', is personified, 'stained with the blood of her sons' (269).[74]

[72] George Lakoff, 'The Contemporary Theory of Metaphor', in *Metaphor and Thought*, ed. Andrew Ortony, 2nd edn (Cambridge, UK, 1993), 202–51 (231–2). Chaucer, notably, bases the *Pardoner's Tale* on the Death-as-agent convention. When the Pardoner's three rioters vow to 'sleen this false traytour Deeth', they mistake conventional metaphor (Death as a personified agent) for factual statement (*The Riverside Chaucer*, ed. Larry D. Benson, 3rd edn (Oxford, 1988), line 699.
[73] Paul Binski, *Medieval Death: Ritual and Representation* (Ithaca, 1996), 70.
[74] 'infelix patria filiorum infecta cruore longe lateque rubebat' (Thomas of Split, *Historia*, 268).

The *Historia* de-emphasizes both the Mongols as agents and the Hungarians as Christian martyrs, suggesting that the 1241–2 invasions had no rational cause. By personifying Hungary (that 'unhappy country'), the text intimates that the kingdom itself – as opposed to 'her sons' – has caused its own destruction. As Thomas explains: 'Because the land of Hungary is fertile and abundant in all good things this presented her sons with the occasion to immoderately take pleasure in the many delights she supplied' (255).[75] The Christian sons of Hungary are not innately disposed to immoderate excess; rather, they have been seduced by their environment to abandon more wholesome pursuits for 'the enticements of the flesh' (255).[76] Thomas adds that these indolent men spent their days 'in elaborate banquets and effeminate frivolities', which had softened their minds to the point where they 'were unable to think of the sounds of war' (257).[77] Their later deaths would come to embody the ephemerality of worldly pleasure, for the green leaves of summer must inevitably fall by winter. Earthly delights had distracted the people of Hungary from attending to what is eternal, the realm of the divine.

Thus, Thomas attributes the slayings in Hungary as having divine, not human, cause. As the *Historia* explains, the Mongols' 'pestilential barbarity' was only one of three calamities that befell the Hungarians between the years 1241 and 1243 (304).[78] The sword, famine, and wild beasts – *ferrum, fame, fera* – each scourged the kingdom during this period, all with equal devastation so that 'the people of Hungary were no less afflicted' by any one event (305).[79] Motivated simply by the animal appetites of the sensitive soul, the Mongols' appearance within the *Historia* ('like locusts') is equated to other non-agential, natural disasters (265).[80] The sword, famine, and wild beasts each decimate the Hungarian population during a three-year span of time, descending upon the kingdom like plagues. Thus, in a counter-intuitive way, the

---

75 'Etenim terra Hungarica omnibus bonis locuplex et fecunda causam prestabat suis filiis ex rerum copia immoderatis delitiis delectari' (Thomas of Split, *Historia*, 254).
76 'carnalibus gaudentes illecebris' (Thomas of Split, *Historia*, 254).
77 'Tota dies exquisitis conviviis aut mollibus expendebatur iocis […] non de bellorum strepitu cogitare poterant' (Thomas of Split, *Historia*, 256).
78 'pestilens immanitas Tatarorum' (Thomas of Split, *Historia*, 303).
79 'ut non minus credatur hec acerba lues inedie gentem Ungaricam devastasse, quam pestilens immanitas Tatarorum' (Thomas of Split, *Historia*, 304).
80 'qui locustarum more paulatim ebulliebant de terra' (Thomas of Split, *Historia*, 264).

Mongols are cast by the *Historia* as a retributive force of God. Having already established the discrete kingdom of Hungary as worthy of indictment, Thomas concludes that 'by God's judgement [the people] paid no little price for the sins that they had committed' (305).[81] The Mongols pose no abstract threat to Christendom, they are merely avatars for God's judgement. By absenting the Mongols from its account of the 1241–2 invasions, the *Historia* makes visible the true threat to Christendom – loss of faith.

Illuminating Sight: English Visualizations of the Mongols

Despite their emphasis on ethnographic observation and experiential study, the eyewitness narratives of the 1241–2 Mongol invasions stop short at visualizing the Mongols. The Mongols are thus repeatedly represented as a sight that cannot be seen. However, if proximity is blinding then it stands to reason that distance can be illuminating. This is the position adopted by Matthew Paris, the English Benedictine monk and chronicler who wrote extensively about the Mongols in his monumental historiographic work, the *Chronica majora*. Matthew discusses the Mongols early, identifying the 1237–40 conquests of eastern Europe and the Caucasus as portending a future threat to Christendom. By 1250, the *Chronica* would come to name the Mongol invasions as the most significant event of the century. Matthew's close and sustained attention to the Mongols was unusual among European chroniclers. J.J. Saunders, for instance, has remarked with some surprise how 'the Englishman who never saw a Mongol in his life' offers a more robust account of the 1241–2 invasions than most of his Continental contemporaries.[82] I argue that it is precisely this distance – the space between Matthew and firsthand encounter, the space between England and central Europe – that informs how and why the *Chronica* narrates the invasions. In contrast with the eyewitness narratives of Roger of Torre Maggiore and Thomas of Split, Matthew repeatedly attempts to materialize the Mongols within the *Chronica*. Whereas proximity is blinding for both Roger and Thomas,

---

81 'flagellatum ex divino iudicio penam suorum expendit non mediocriter peccatorum' (Thomas of Split, *Historia*, 304).
82 J.J. Saunders, 'Matthew Paris and the Mongols', in *Essays in Medieval History Presented to Bertie Wilkinson*, ed. T.A. Sandquist and M.R. Powicke (Toronto, 1969), 116–32 (132).

Matthew strains to render the Mongols visible, to make them 'real' for an audience far removed from the conflict zone. Picturing the Mongols becomes an integral part of Matthew's historiographic project. The *Chronica* manifests the monstrous as an attestation of both Antichrist and, ultimately, divine order.

The *Chronica majora* represents the Mongols as monstrous from the very first. In an entry for the 1238 annal – three years before Batu Khan would lead his army across the Carpathians and into central Europe – Matthew introduces the Mongols as a people with 'very large heads, by no means proportionate to their bodies' that 'feed on raw flesh, and even on human beings'.[83] The *Chronica* immediately likens the disproportionate heads of the Mongols to the monstrous act of eating (raw) human flesh. As with Thomas's *Historia*, the *Chronica* conjures an image of the Mongol body to use as a heuristic device, a way to implicitly link appearance with behavior so that both appear innate.[84] After the fall of the major Kyivan Rus' principalities in 1240, Matthew quickly escalates this rhetorical framing. The 1240 annal includes a lengthy entry that addresses the Mongols campaigns as a decidedly millenarian event:

> That human joys might not long continue and that the delights of this world might not last long unmixed with lamentation, an immense horde of that detestable race of Satan, the Tartars, burst forth from their mountain-bound regions, and making their way through rocks apparently impenetrable, rushed forth, like demons loosed from Tartarus [...] The men are inhuman and of the nature of beasts, rather to be called monsters than men, thirsting after and drinking blood, and tearing and devouring the flesh of dogs and human beings. (1:312–13)[85]

83 *Matthew Paris's English History: From the Year 1235 to 1273*, trans. J.A. Giles, 3 vols (London, 1889–93), 1:131. All English citations come from this edition. Further references are given in-text.
84 Matthew's entirely false narrative around cannibalism draws from the Gog and Magog legend, which he later links directly to the Mongols.
85 The full passage in the Latin reads, 'Ne mortalium gaudia continuentur, ne sine lamentis mundana laetitia diu celebretur, eodem anno plebs Sathanae detestanda, Tartarorum scilicet exercitus infinitus, a regione sua montibus circumvallata prorupit; et saxorum immeabilium soliditate penetrata, exeuntes ad instar daemonum solutorum a tartaro, ut bene Tartari, quasi tartarei, nuncupentur, scatebant, et quasi locustae terrae superficiem cooperientes, Orientalium fines exterminio miserabili vastaverunt, incendio vacantes et stragibus. Peragratis Saracenorum finibus, civitates complanarunt, nemora succiderunt, castra subverterunt, vineas avulserunt, hortos destruxerunt, cives

Here the *Chronica* dramatically heightens the monstrosity of the Mongols. Matthew adds color to his previous description of the Mongol diet, now claiming that they thirst for blood and, seemingly, devour their victims whole. More notable, however, is his inclusion of more explicitly millenarian language. The Mongols issue forth from the mountains – an allusion to the Gog prophecy – as demons loosed upon the world to end human joy. Suzanne Lewis links Matthew's representation of the Mongols with an eschatological prediction that Antichrist would arrive in the year 1250.[86] As she explains, 'The impact of the Mongol invasion of Europe on the prophecy of Antichrist's advent in 1250 was so profound that Matthew decided, probably in the 1240s, to end his chronicle at midcentury, concluding his history with a dramatic summary of events portending the end of the sixth and last age that had begun with the Incarnation of Christ.'[87] According to his belief that Antichrist would soon materialize, Matthew contextualizes the Mongols as an apocalyptic sign.

Despite their firsthand exposure to Mongol warfare, neither Roger of Torre Maggiore nor Thomas of Split adopt such a view. Matthew, however, identifies the Mongols as harbingers of the apocalypse. This difference can partially be attributed to Matthew's approach to historical writing. The *Chronica majora* heavily revises and extends Roger of Wendover's *Flores historiarum*, adding entries from 1236 – when Roger died – to 1259, the year of Matthew's death. The original sections of the *Chronica* (1236–59) emphasize the events of Matthew's lifetime, so that 'the memory of modern events might not be destroyed by age or oblivion' (2:410).[88] As a universal history, the *Chronica* approaches these

---

et agricolas peremerunt. Et si forte aliquibus supplicantibus pepercerunt, ipsos, quasi ultimae conditionis servos, ante ipsos dimicare contra suos affines coegerunt. Qui si ficte pugnarent, vel forte clam munirent ut fugerent, ipsi Tartari a tergo insequentes eos trucidarunt; si strenue bellarentur et vincerent, nullas grates pro praemio reportarunt; et sic captivis suis quasi jumentis abutebantur. Viri enim sunt inhumani et bestiales, potius monstra dicendi quam homines, sanguinem sitientes et bibentes, carnes caninas et humanas laniantes et devorantes' (Matthew Paris, *Chronica majora*, ed. Henry Richards Luard, 7 vols, Rolls Series 57 (London, 1872–83), 4:76). All Latin citations come from Luard's edition.

86 Suzanne Lewis, *The Art of Matthew Paris in the* Chronica Majora (Berkeley, 1987), 103.
87 Lewis, *The Art of Matthew Paris*, 288.
88 'ne memoriam eventuum modernorum vetustas aut oblivio deleat, literis commendavit' (5:197).

modern events teleologically. Björn Weiler succinctly describes this teleological framework 'as a means of, on the one hand, offering moral counsel, and, on the other, of setting events within the broader context of human history and its place within a divine plan of creation'.[89] To that end, Matthew's discussion of the Mongols – particularly after the 1241-2 invasions – negotiates the growth of the unfamiliar empire in relation to a Christian cosmology. In contrast with how both Roger's *Epistola* and Thomas of Split's *Historia* present the 1241-2 Mongol invasions as indictments against the specific sins of the Hungarian people, the *Chronica* depicts the same events as having universal significance. Concerned with the broad implications of the invasions, the *Chronica* emphasizes the wide applicability of its Mongol narrative.

Although Matthew had no direct contact with the Mongols, as a monk of St Albans he did have privileged access to information about both Insular and Continental affairs.[90] In the 1257 annal, Matthew describes St Albans as an important repository for communications about the Mongols, declaring that 'if anyone is desirous of learning the impurities of these Tartars, and their mode of life and customs [...] he may obtain information by making diligent search at St Albans' (3:251).[91] For the *Chronica*, documentary evidence stands in lieu of a direct eyewitness, approximating firsthand experience. Four such documents are embedded within the *Chronica*: a letter from Henry, Count of Lorraine, to his father-in-law, the duke of Brabant, requesting immediate military assistance; a likely spurious letter from Frederick II to Henry III; a letter from Ivo of Narbonne to the archbishop of Bordeaux, written from the Austrian-Hungarian border; and a report from Peter, a Russian archbishop, who escaped to Italy after the Mongol conquests of the Kyivan Rus' principalities. Matthew would go on to add an additional seven testimonies to the chronicle's appendix. The letters that Matthew includes within the *Chronica*, particularly the seemingly invented letter from Frederick II, speak, in Michael Uebel's words, to the 'reality effects' of medieval Latin epistolography

---

89 Björn Weiler, 'Matthew Paris on the Writing of History', *Journal of Medieval History* 35 (2009), 254-78 (258).
90 The powerful Benedictine house frequently received communications from abbeys outside of England, in addition to regular visits from members of Henry III's court. See Saunders, 'Matthew Paris and the Mongols', 130-1.
91 'Ipsorum Tartarorum immunditias, vitam, et mores si quis audire desiderat [...] apud Sanctum Albanum diligens indagator poterit reperire' (Matthew Paris, *Chronica majora*, 5:655).

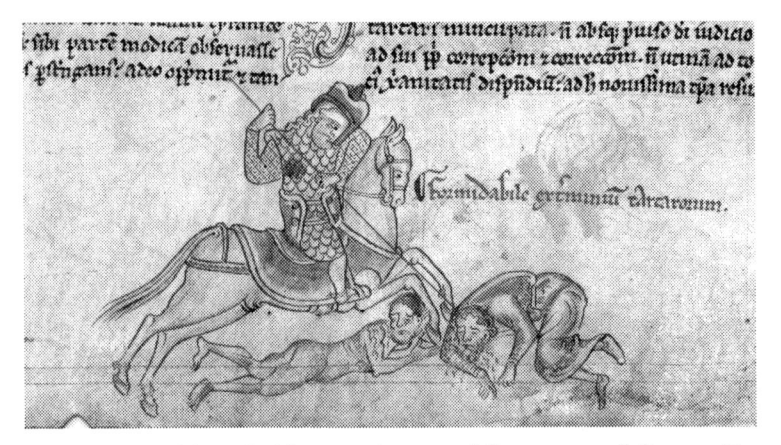

Figure 4.1 A Mongol rider spearing two fallen, unarmed figures. The Parker Library, Corpus Christi College, Cambridge, MS 16ii, fol. 145r, reproduced by kind permission.

that 'issue from a desire to bridge spatial as well as temporal gaps'.[92] The letters included within the *Chronica* not only give evidence to Matthew's conclusions but also make present these conclusions to an English audience, collapsing the space between St Albans and central Europe. The documents that Matthew includes within the *Chronica* point to a larger interest in creating an aesthetic experience for the reader. This effort to make the Mongols present in England – to make them tangible – is neatly exemplified by a curious detail included in the 1238 annal. In the 1238 entry on the Mongols, Matthew explains how 'the inhabitants of Gothland and Friesland, dreading [Mongol] attacks, did not, as was their custom, come to Yarmouth, in England, at the time of the herring fisheries'; as a result, the overabundance of herring – 'although very good' – caused a significant depreciation in price (1:131).[93] Even before the 1241–2 invasions, the *Chronica* correlates Mongol military advancements with English domestic issues

92 Michael Uebel, *Ecstatic Transformation: On the Uses of Alterity in the Middle Ages* (New York, 2005), 105.
93 'Unde Gothiam et Frisiam inhabitantes, impetus eorum pertimentes, in Angliam, ut moris est eorum, apud Gememue, tempore allecis capiendi, quo suas naves solebant onerare, non venerunt. Hinc erat quod allec eo anno in Anglia quasi pro nihilo prae abundantia habitum, sub quadragenario vel quinquagenario numero, licet optimum esset, pro uno argento in partibus a mari etiam longinquis, vendebantur' (Matthew Paris, *Chronica majora*, 3:489).

to demonstrate how the Mongols have a direct, negative material presence in England. As the real distance between the invasions and St Albans begins to narrow, Matthew begins to embellish his narrative with illustrations depicting the Mongols. Matthew, the scribe and illustrator of his own work, adds two such illustrations to his manuscript of the *Chronica majora*, Cambridge, Corpus Christi College, MS 16ii. Lewis has argued that Paris took an unorthodox approach to visual art, extending 'his recording of reality as he saw it into the realm of pictorial illustration'.[94] In the *Chronica*, text and illustration interplay so that narrative events 'are perceived concretely as visual images and sensory detail'.[95] Similar to the documentary evidence Matthew embeds within his written narrative, his stylistic 'realism' addresses the gaps between the viewer, representation, and represented object. Tellingly, the first of Matthew's two visual representations of the Mongols is a *bas-de-page* image that accompanies the fictive letter from Frederick II in the 1241 annal (see Fig. 4.1). The image is of a horsed figure, stockily drawn with – pulling from the 1238 reference – a large head. The lone horseman is shown wearing scaled armor (an approximation of Mongol plating) and a cap-like helm. Gazing beneath the rearing legs of his horse, the Mongol spears two unarmed victims that have fallen underfoot. The illustration is set below a letter that purports to hastily 'bring [the Mongols invasions] to your knowledge, although the true facts of the matter have but lately come to ours' (1:341).[96] The horsed figure gives sensory detail to the 'true facts' that Frederick narrates: for instance, his description of Mongol armor as 'pieces of iron stitched to them' (1:344).[97] Moreover, the image punctuates the letter's closing call to arms. Frederick's hope that 'every noble and renowned country lying under the royal star of the West, shall send forth their chosen ornaments preceded by the symbol of the life-giving cross' is paired with an image of Mongol brutality – emphasizing the need for Western authorities to set aside schismatic difference and band together in defense of Christendom.

94 Lewis, *The Art of Matthew Paris*, 428.
95 Lewis, *The Art of Matthew Paris*, 428.
96 'et quanquam ad nostram rei gestae Veritas sero pervenerit, quin ad vestram notitiam referamus, tacere non possumus' (Matthew Paris, *Chronica majora*, 4:112).
97 'insutis laminis feirreis pro armis muniuntur' (Matthew Paris, *Chronica majora*, 4:115).

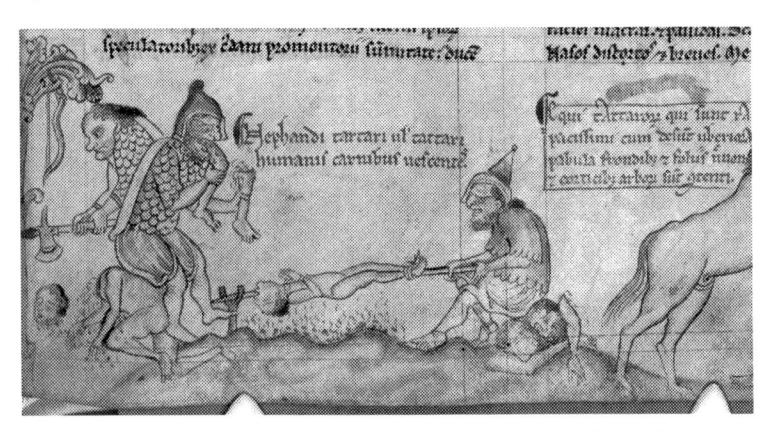

Figure 4.2 Mongol figures roasting and eating human flesh. The Parker Library, Corpus Christi College, Cambridge, MS 16ii, fol. 167r, reproduced by kind permission.

Frederick II's 1241 letter, whether authentic or not, marks a pivotal moment within the *Chronica*. Documentary evidence alone is no longer sufficient to make the Mongol threat known to a distant audience. Instead, Matthew must *show* his reader this threat. Matthew's second *bas-de-page* illustration (see Fig. 4.2) amplifies the monstrosity that he attributes to the Mongols. Appearing below the text of Ivo's letter, this second illustration captures, as Lewis observes, the 'sadistic and horrifying details' that Matthew adds to the letter.[98] The textual embellishments that Matthew adds all work to represent the Mongols as fantastically monstrous. One particularly gruesome vignette imagines how 'virgins were deflowered until they died of exhaustion; when their breasts were cut off to be kept as dainties for their chiefs, and their bodies furnished a jovial banquet to the savages' (1:470).[99] To complement this narrative of the 'demons loosed from Tartarus', Matthew exaggerates his earlier representation of Mongol violence. Inscribed 'Nephandi Tartari vel Tattari humanis carnibus uescentes', the second illustration depicts three Mongol warriors engaged in a cannibalistic feast. Grouped in a cluster toward the left of the image, the warriors are shown (in order from left to right): decapitating a captured man, eating two severed

98 Lewis, *The Art of Matthew Paris*, 285.
99 'Virgines quoque usque ad exanimationem opprimebant, et tandem abscisis earum papillis, quas magistratibus pro delieiis reservabant, ipsis virgineis corporibus lautius epulabantur' (Matthew Paris, *Chronica majora*, 4:273).

human feet, and roasting another human victim on a spit. To the right of the image (not visible in Fig. 2), a horse rears above the bound body of a female victim, gorging upon the leaves of a tree, in a position that evokes the letter's brutal account of rape. The illustration resonates with John Parker's consideration of the medieval aesthetic experience 'whereby false, unreal images are rightly taken to intimate via their unreality a form of truth'.[100] The *Chronica* embellishes Ivo's letter, both narratively and visually, to make the truth more real. As Parker goes on to explain, 'the miraculous aspect of aesthetic experience, whereby false, unreal images are rightly taken to intimate via their unreality a form of truth, contains the same typological conversion whereby historical events of dubious significance are sublimed into the stuff of faith, except that even the unconverted can accept the aesthetic version without contest'.[101] Through an aesthetic evocation of the senses – the representational sight of violence – the *Chronica* performs a kind of divine paradox that allows the Mongols to be 'seen' as they truly are: Antichrist.

*

This essay began with a consideration of 'darkness' as a useful heuristic device for approaching the epistemological resonances of the 1241–2 Mongol invasions in contemporary narrative accounts. To close, I return to the *Opus majus* where Bacon passionately proclaims that philosophy and 'the secret works of science' are 'absolutely necessary to the Church of God against the fury of Antichrist'.[102] Bacon interprets the sudden appearance of the Mongols as a sign that 'we are not far removed from the times of Antichrist'.[103] Under the looming 'darkness' of the Mongol threat, Bacon urges the pope to adopt natural science as a means of defense. Indeed, he attributes the unprecedented military success of the Mongols to their study of science (particularly astronomy); and further, he warns that by disavowing natural philosophy the Church 'will be

---

100 John Parker, *The Aesthetics of the Antichrist: From Christian Drama to Christopher Marlowe* (Ithaca, 2007), 84–5.
101 Parker, *The Aesthetics of the Antichrist*, 85.
102 Bacon, *Opus majus*, trans. Burke, 2:407; 'Et quia praecepistis ut scriberem de sapientia philosophiae, recitabo Vestrae Clementiae sententias sapientum, praecipue cum ecclesiae Dei sit omnino necessarium contra furiam Antichristi' (Bacon, *Opus majus*, 2:393).
103 Bacon, *Opus majus*, trans. Burke, 2:417; 'Et creditur ab omnibus sapientibus quod non sumus multum remoti a temporibus Antichristi' (Bacon, *Opus majus*, 2:402).

intolerably burdened by these scourges of Christian people'.[104] Whether followers of Antichrist or not, the Mongols – and other non-believers – are inherently anti-Christian for their use of science without faith. It is the providence of the Church to reunite natural and spiritual truths; and as Bacon makes clear in his discussion of vision, optical science can be weaponized. Indeed, he very explicitly frames optical science as a tool for conquest, citing Julius Caesar's use of mirrors to see the 'arrangement of the cities and camps' before invading England.[105] Through this anecdote, Bacon seems to collapse distinctions between non-believers and the political enemies of an empire-building state. In response to Mongol imperial expansion, Bacon, thus, begins to develop a logic of empire organized around *illumination*. Reversing, then, the 'darkening' effects of the 1241–2 Mongol invasions, Bacon's imagined form of Christian imperialism uses the tools of natural philosophy – the same tools used by the Mongols – to expose the enemy, to make visible the nonbelievers, and to inspire its own form of terror.

104 Bacon, *Opus majus*, trans. Burke, 2:417; 'aggravabitur intolerabiliter flagellis Christianorum' (Bacon, *Opus majus*, 2:402).
105 Bacon, *Opus majus*, trans. Burke, 2:581; 'Sic enim Julius Caesar, quando voluit Angliam expugnare, refertur maxima specula erexisse, ut a Gallicano littore dispositionem civitatum et castrorum Angliae praevideret' (Bacon, *Opus majus*, 2:165).

5

Richard de Bury's *Philobiblon*, *Translatio Studii et Imperii*, and the Anglo-French Cultural Politics of the Fourteenth Century[1]

EMMA-CATHERINE WILSON

The transfer of knowledge and martial power, *translatio studii et imperii*, was a celebrated theme in medieval Europe that was recurrently employed to legitimate regnal authority. According to the myth of *translatio*, intellectual and martial superiority were entwined and together moving ever-westwards, from Athens, to Rome, and on to Paris. In the late Middle Ages, the myth of *translatio* fueled the belief among French scholars and aristocrats that the renowned University of Paris symbolized France's cultural superiority over England. Despite the wealth of scholarship on French evocations of the *translatio* topos, medievalists have not yet given serious consideration to the possibility that late medieval English courtiers and intellectuals were similarly invested in the myth of *translatio studii et imperii*, the consonance between knowledge and power, and universities as sources of cultural capital. This essay examines a variety of texts composed or copied in fourteenth-century England that explicitly evoke the myth of *translatio* to claim that English learning at the University of Oxford had surpassed the French scholarship of Paris. Moving outward from literary analysis toward cultural history, I explore how these works functioned as textual agents shaping their age's linguistic and political worlds. Without reducing Anglo-French cultural politics to a single topos, this essay therefore aims to contribute to an understanding of how late medieval

---

1 I owe a debt of thanks to Dr Andrew Taylor for his supervision of my MA thesis, from which the present essay derives. I would also like to thank Professor Laura Ashe and my reviewers for their many useful comments.

English scholars and courtiers comprehended and legitimized their cultural competition with France.

In order to make sense of English evocations of *translatio* in the late Middle Ages, we must first understand the historiographical implications of this myth as well as the French tradition of *translatio* to which the English were responding. As Tullio Gregory, Enrico Fenzi, and Lorenzo DiTommaso, among others, have demonstrated, the myth of a succession of earthly empires was an ancient (if not primordial) conception of history that became Christianized in the Book of Daniel.[2] In this foundational Judaeo-Christian text, Daniel explains to King Nebuchadnezzar that his dream of the awesome statue with its head of fine gold, the chest and arms of silver, its belly and thighs of bronze, its legs of iron, and its feet partly of iron and partly of clay represents the degeneration of his kingdom.[3] This apocalyptic vision is extended to the rest of the world in Daniel's own dream, in which four great beasts come out of the sea and are successively destroyed to give way to God's everlasting kingdom.[4] Saint Jerome concluded that these beasts should be interpreted as the corrupted earthly empires of Babylonia, Persia, Greece, and Rome: the final and most gruesome of the monsters.[5] The myth of a succession of empires was thus woven into the very eschatological fabric of Christianity as the collapse of the fourth and final earthly kingdom – Rome – was to anticipate the apocalypse of Revelation.

However, in a medieval world that held the past as an unquestionable source of authority, this biblical version of the succession of empires myth could not be disentangled from other, secular variations that glorified the wisdom of ancient Athens and the martial glory of

---

2   For the ancient origins of the *translatio* myth, see Tullio Gregory, 'Translatio studiorum', in Translatio studiorum: *Ancient, Medieval, and Modern Bearers of Intellectual History*, ed. Marco Sgarbi (Leiden, 2012), 1–21; Enrico Fenzi, '"Translatio studii" e "translatio imperii": Appunti per un percorso', *Interfaces* 1 (2015), 170–208; and Lorenzo DiTommaso, 'The Four Kingdoms of Daniel in the Early Mediaeval Apocalyptic Tradition', in *Four Kingdom Motifs Before and Beyond the Book of Daniel*, ed. Andrew Perrin and Loren T. Stuckenbruck (Leiden, 2020), 205–50.

3   See Dan. 2:1–35 for Nebuchadnezzar's dream. The translation of the Bible used throughout is *The Project Gutenberg eBook of The Bible, Douay-Rheims Version, Challoner Revision The Old and New Testaments* (2011) <https://www.gutenberg.org/files/1581/1581-h/1581-h.htm>.

4   Dan. 7:1–28.

5   Fenzi, '"Translatio Studii"', 172.

pagan Rome. When medieval rulers such as Charlemagne legitimized their authority by figuring themselves as successors to the magnificence of Athens and Rome, they were thus hard pressed to fit themselves into the apocalyptic historical schema proclaimed in the Book of Daniel. Étienne Gilson and Serge Lusignan have shown how Carolingian thinkers tied themselves in theological knots or else patently re-wrote scripture in order to accommodate a fifth, French kingdom between that of Rome and of Christ.[6] Charlemagne's biographer, Notker of St Gall (c. 840–912), began his influential *Gesta Karoli magni* with the declaration that:

> Omnipotens rerum dispositor ordinatorque regnorum et temporum, cum illius admirandae statuae pedes ferreos vel testaceos comminuisset in Romanis, alterius non minus admirabilis statuae caput aureum per illustrem Karolum erexit in Francis.

(After the omnipotent ruler of the world, who orders alike the fate of kingdoms and the course of time, had broken the feet of iron and clay in one noble statue, to wit the Romans, he raised by the hands of the illustrious Charles the golden head of another, not less admirable, among the Franks.)[7]

In Notker's version of *translatio*, the succession of kingdoms thus continues past the fall of Rome on to Charlemagne's realm, which rose from the ashes of the ancient world as the golden pinnacle of human civilization. Notker's text also fixed in French historiography that the Holy Roman Emperor Charlemagne was a man of letters, a poet, and a philosopher and that it was under his guidance that knowledge had completed its journey from Athens, to Rome, and finally to Francia.[8]

---

6   See Étienne Gilson, *Les idées et les lettres* (Paris, 1955), esp. 171–96 and Serge Lusignan's many pieces on the *translatio* myth, notably, 'L'Université de Paris comme composante de l'identité du royaume de France: Étude sur le thème de la *translatio studii*', in *Identité régionale et conscience nationale en France et en Allemagne du Moyen Âge à l'époque moderne*, ed. Rainer Babel and Jean-Marie Moeglin (Sigmaringen, 1997), 59–72.
7   Notker of St Gall, *Monachi Sangallensis de gestis Karoli imperatoris*, ed. G.H. Pertz, Monumenta Germaniae Historica (Hanover, 1829), SS 2: 726–63 (731). English translation from 'The Monk of Saint Gall: The Life of Charlemagne, 883/4', in *Early Lives of Charlemagne by Eginhard and the Monk of St. Gall*, trans. A.J. Grant (London, 1926), 59–183 (59).
8   Fenzi, '"Translatio Studii"', 186.

The Carolingian developments of the *translatio* tradition long endured in the French discourse of royal power, though the apocalyptic tenor of the *translatio* myth increasingly gave way to a sense of intellectual optimism. Writing between 1180 and 1217 and inspired in part by the legacy of Charlemagne, the Cambro-Norman priest and royal clerk Gerald of Wales affirmed in his *De principis institutione*:

> Illud quoque dignum est nota, quod philosophie militieque se comitari semper studia solent, sicut in Grecia sub Macedone, sicut sub Cesaribus Rome, sicut et olim in Francia, sub Pipinis, Karolis et sub eorundem usque in hodiernum regia prole.

(It is also worth noting that the study of philosophy and warfare always go together, as in Greece under the Macedonian, Rome under the Caesars, and as formerly in France under the Pippinids and Carolingians and under their royal descendants until the present day.)[9]

In the thirteenth century, chroniclers such as Hélinand de Froidmont and William the Breton began to situate the University of Paris specifically as the locus of French wisdom.[10] In the *Gesta Philippi Augusti* (c. 1214–26), the later of these chroniclers praised King Philip II for having granted the University of Paris a royal charter in 1200 and claimed that Parisian learning had surpassed that of Athens and Egypt because of the protection and privileges granted to the scholars of Paris by King Philip and his father.[11] As Lusignan has amply traced, the close association between French royal power and the University of Paris gave

9   Gerald of Wales, *Instruction for a Ruler (De principis institutione)*, ed./trans. Robert Bartlett (Oxford, 2018), 40–1. See Lusignan's discussion of this passage in 'Les mythes de fondations des universités au Moyen Âge', *Mélanges de l'École française de Rome – Moyen-Âge* 115.1 (2003), 445–79 (451). For a text similarly optimistic about French superiority, see Alexander Murray's discussion of the 'Fountain of All Sciences' (c. 1243) in *Reason and Society in the Middle Ages* (Oxford, 2002), 252–3.
10   Lusignan, 'Les mythes', 153–4; Serge Lusignan, 'La topique de la *translatio studii* et les traductions françaises de textes savants au XIV siècle', in *Traduction et traducteurs au Moyen Age: Actes du colloque international du CNRS organisé à Paris, Institut de recherche et d'histoire des textes les 26–28 mai 1986*, ed. Geneviève Contamine (Paris, 1989), 303–15 (313). Another thirteenth-century text situating Paris specifically as the city having inherited the knowledge of Athens and Rome is the Boethian forgery *De disciplina scolarium* (discussed below).
11   Lusignan, 'Les mythes', 451.

fruition to the myth that Charlemagne himself had founded the great university.[12] This myth, first recorded in Vincent de Beauvais's *Speculum historiale* (c. 1235–64), was incorporated into the *Grandes chroniques de France* alongside Notker's earlier portrayal of Charlemagne as a scholar-ruler who had guided learning to France. The *Grandes chroniques* – the official vernacular history of France written and updated by the monks of Saint-Denis from 1250 until 1461 – constituted a powerful historiographical intervention by French monarchs and was far more sophisticated than any English propaganda effort of the period. The myth that Charlemagne had founded the University of Paris put forth in these chronicles confirmed for French scholars and princes that the good fortune and political power of France depended on the kingdom's continued cultivation of learning and benevolence towards its scholars.[13]

As it became increasingly expected for French monarchs to be patrons of learning, and as wisdom, with its implication of justice, became increasingly central to the exercise of royal authority in late medieval France, Latin texts were gradually translated into the vernacular for the education of princes and the wider nobility.[14] In the late thirteenth and early fourteenth centuries, both classical texts such as Vegetius's *De re militari* and Boethius's *De consolatione philosophiae* as well as more recent Latin compositions such as Vincent of Beauvais's *Speculum maius* and Giles of Rome's *De regimine principum* were translated into French for the benefit of the secular nobility.[15] This translation program would reach its apogee in the reign of King Charles V 'the Wise' (r. 1364–80), who famously founded an immense French royal library largely composed of vernacular translations.[16] It is perhaps in

12 Lusignan, 'Les mythes', 452–4.
13 Lusignan, 'L'Université de Paris', 62.
14 For the link between learning and power in late medieval France, see Bernard Guenée, *L'Occident aux XIVe et XVe siècles: les états* (Paris, 1993), 137–42; Jacques Krynen, *Idéal du prince et pouvoir royal en France à la fin du Moyen Âge (1380–1440): Étude de la littérature politique du temps* (Paris, 1981), 97–106; and Serge Lusignan, 'Université, savoir, et langue française: L'exercice du pouvoir sous Charles V', in *Traduire au XIVe siècle: Evrart de Conty et la vie intellectuelle à la cour de Charles V*, ed. Joëlle Ducos and Michèle Goyens (Paris, 2015), 59–72.
15 Lusignan, 'La topique de la *translatio studii*', 306. For further examples of French vernacular translation in this period, see Jacques Monfrin, 'Humanisme et traductions au Moyen Âge', *Journal des savants* 3.1 (1963), 161–90.
16 For Charles V's royal library, see Marie-Hélène Tesnière, 'La librairie de Charles V: Instructions, organisation et politique du livre', in *Traduire au XIVe*

this context, where royal power, learning, and linguistic translation coalesced, that the myth of *translatio studii et imperii* became most ideologically potent for French thinkers, especially those who sought to bolster the authority of the vernacular as a language of learning.[17] As Nicole Oresme proudly explained in the prologue to his translation of Aristotle's *Ethics and Politics* (c. 1371-7) commissioned by Charles V, the French king's translation project was the ultimate expression of *translatio studii* for, just as the Romans had translated Greek wisdom into Latin, so too Charles V now translated wisdom from Latin into French, a new language of learning.[18] For the French thinkers of Charles V's court, just as for courtiers writing in previous centuries, this perceived intellectual superiority equally implied France's military dominance.[19]

Across the Channel, the myth of *translatio* was equally well rooted in England. In the prose preface to his translation of Gregory the Great's *Regula pastoralis*, King Alfred the Great (848-99) famously figured the English as the inheritors of an intellectual and religious lineage that began with the Hebrews and continued through the Greeks and Romans. Lamenting the widespread decline of Latin learning that he witnessed in his kingdom, Alfred uses the myth of *translatio* to justify

---

siècle, ed. Ducos and Goyens, 363-78; Anne Dawson Hedeman's several studies on this subject, including 'History, Power, and Visual Memory in the Library of King Charles V', in *Le livre enluminé médiéval instrument politique*, ed. Vinni Lucherini and Cécile Voyer (Rome, 2021), 221-44; and Deborah McGrady, *The Writer's Gift or the Patron's Pleasure? The Literary Economy in Late Medieval France* (Toronto, 2019).

17 Serge Lusignan, *Parler vulgairement: Les intellectuels et la langue française aux XIIIe et XIVe siècles* (Montréal, 1987), 129-65. Rita Copeland further notes that 'the emergent power of the French language as a medium of *translatio studii* [...] authorizes itself through a material identification with royal power'; *Rhetoric, Hermeneutics, and Translation in the Middle Ages* (Cambridge, UK, 1991), 135.

18 Lusignan, 'La topique de la *translatio studii*', 310-11; Lusignan, *Parler vulgairement*, 154-65. For an edition of Oresme's prologue, see Nicole Oresme, *Maistre Nicole Oresme: Le livre de Ethiques d'Aristote*, ed. Albert Douglas Menut (New York, 1940). For further discussion of the politics of translators' prologues in the court of Charles V, see McGrady's excellent discussion in *The Writer's Gift*, esp. chapter 2, 'The Writer's Work: Translating Charles V's Literary Clientelism into Learned Terms', 54-87.

19 The theologian and translator Jean Golein went so far as to declare that France's victories against the English in the Hundred Years War were due to Charles V's unrivalled intelligence; see Lusignan, 'Université, savoir, et langue française', 33-4.

the translation of important books such as the *Regula pastoralis* into Old English, just as the Greeks, the Romans, and other Christians had successively translated Hebrew wisdom into their own vernaculars:

Ða gemunde ic hu sio æ wæs ærest on Ebreisc geðiode funden, & eft, þa [sic] hie Crecas geleornodon, þa wendon hi hie on hiora ægen geðiode ealle, & eac ealle oðre bec. And eft Lædenware swa same, siððan hi hie geleornodon, hi hie wendon ealla ðurh wise wealhstodas on hiora agen geðeode. & eac ealla oðra Cristena ðioda sumne dæl hiora on hiora agen geðiode wendon. Forðy me ðyncð betre, gif iow swa ðyncð, þæt we eac suma bec, ða þe nidbeðyrfesta sien eallum monnum to witanne, þæt we þa on ðæt geðeode wenden þe we ealle gecnawan mægen.

(Then I remembered how the law was first known in Hebrew, and again, when the Greeks had learned it, they translated the whole of it into their own language, and all other books besides. And again the Romans, when they had learned it, they translated the whole of it through learned interpreters into their own language. And also all other Christian nations translated a part of them into their own language. Therefore it seems better to me, if ye think so, for us also to translate some books that are most needful for all men to know into the language that we can all understand.)[20]

Imagining himself as a successor to Gregory the Great and Augustine of Canterbury, Alfred portrayed his act of translation as one of *translatio studii* that would revive English learning and prosperity.[21] As we shall see, the rhetoric of Alfred's prose preface long endured in English iterations of the *translatio* myth, especially those connected to the Wycliffite movement.

Another foundational text of the English *translatio* tradition was Geoffrey of Monmouth's *Historia regum Britanniae* (c. 1135–9). In this chronicle, Geoffrey recounts that Aeneas' great-grandson Brutus founded London as a 'Troia Nova' and posits the Britons as inheritors of

---

20   Alfred the Great, *King Alfred's West-Saxon Version of Gregory's* Pastoral Care, ed./trans. Henry Sweet (London, 1871; repr. 1934), 5–6. For further discussion, see Susan Irvine, 'The Alfredian Prefaces and Epilogues', in *A Companion to Alfred the Great*, ed. Nicole G. Discenza and Paul E. Szarmach (Leiden, 2014), 143–70 (153–60).
21   Alfred suggests this line of succession in the verse preface to his translation of *Regula pastoralis*, which Nicole G. Discenza has shown to reinforce the theme of *translatio studii* in the prose preface; see Nicole G. Discenza, 'Alfred's Verse Preface to the Pastoral Care and the Chain of Authority', *Neophilologus* 85 (2001), 625–33.

Trojan greatness and rivals of Rome.[22] This well-known legend inspired countless retellings in medieval and early modern England and pushed the myth of *translatio* to the forefront of Insular historiography.[23] Moreover, while Geoffrey's Trojan foundation myth initially implied a version of *translatio* centered on Trojan martial *imperium* rather than on *studium*, later authors who reworked and expanded his legends emphasized the efflorescence of learning in Britain.[24] Both Alexander Neckam's *De naturis rerum* (c. 1190) and Thomas of Ireland's *De tribus sensibus sacre scripture* (c. 1316–21) allude to a prophecy of Merlin that does not appear in either Geoffrey's *Historia* or *Prophetiae Merlini* (c. 1130–5) and that foretells that studies would flourish at Oxford.[25] For Thomas of Ireland especially, the twin threads of *translatio studii et imperii* animating this prophecy are inseparable: 'Militie enim victoria et philosophia et gloria quasi simul concurrerunt et merito, quia philosophia vera docet juste et recte regnare' (For in warfare, victory, philosophy, and glory coincide together as if at the same time, and appropriately so, because philosophy teaches us to rule justly and rightly).[26] Drawing on the ideal of the philosopher-king, Thomas therefore concluded that a state would only prosper 'quando philosophi regnabant et reges phylosophabantur' (when philosophers reigned and kings philosophized).[27]

22   Geoffrey of Monmouth, *The History of the Kings of Britain*, ed. Michael D. Reeve, trans. Neil Wright (Woodbridge, 2007), book 1, 4–30.
23   See Nicholas Birns, 'The Trojan Myth: Postmodern Reverberations', *Exemplaria* 5.1 (1993), 45–78; Sylvia Federico, *New Troy: Fantasies of Empire in the Late Middle Ages* (Minneapolis, 2003); Francis Ingledew, 'The Book of Troy and the Genealogical Construction of History: The Case of Geoffrey of Monmouth's *Historia regum Britanniae*', *Speculum* 69.3 (1994), 665–704; Lee Patterson, *Chaucer and the Subject of History* (Madison, 1991), esp. 84–98, 161–3; and Lee Patterson, *Negotiating the Past: The Historical Understanding of Medieval Literature* (Madison, 1987), esp. 157–62, 168–80. A Trojan foundation myth was equally influential in France and Burgundy, for which see Lusignan, 'Les mythes', 467, esp. n. 70.
24   See, for instance, the discussion of the Oxford *Historiola* below.
25   Lusignan, 'Université, savoir, et langue française', 71–2, n. 63. For Neckam, see also Ad Putter, 'King Arthur at Oxbridge: Nicholas Cantelupe, Geoffrey of Monmouth, and Cambridge's Arthurian Foundation Myth', *Medium Ævum* 72.1 (2003), 63–81 (68–9).
26   Thomas of Ireland, *De tribus sensibus sacre scripture* (Paris, Bibliothèque nationale de France, MS lat. 15966), transcribed in Lusignan, 'Université, savoir, et langue française', 71–2 (72). My translation.
27   Thomas of Ireland, *De tribus sensibus*, in Lusignan, 'Université, savoir, et langue française', 71–2 (72). My translation.

ANGLO-FRENCH CULTURAL POLITICS OF THE FOURTEENTH CENTURY 141

In turning to consider English evocations of *translatio studii et imperii* composed or copied in the fourteenth century, we may ask ourselves to what extent the contemporary French discourse of *translatio* encouraged the revival or modification of Insular versions of the myth. The English texts we now turn to explore strongly suggest that the English apprehended, at least in part, the rhetorical maneuvers of French *translatio*. For, in this period, English evocations of the myth appear designed precisely to respond to their French counterparts and to position the University of Oxford in direct rivalry with the University of Paris.

Richard de Bury's Philobiblon

The most elaborate treatment of *translatio* written in late medieval England was unquestionably the *Philobiblon*, or *The Love of Books*, composed by Richard de Bury, the Bishop of Durham, shortly before his death in 1345.[28] This Latin treatise demonstrates that Richard, one of King Edward III's mentors and most trusted advisors, conceived of the opening stages of the Hundred Years Wars not only as a martial conflict but also as an intellectual contest in which the scholars of Oxford were besting those of Paris.

Cast as an apologia for book collecting, the *Philobiblon* consists of twenty chapters that variously expound the importance of books, lament their ill-treatment, and explain how to properly manage a lending-library. The treatise is in many ways conventional, although the text's moralistic complaints and strict adherence to the rules of *dictamen* are livened by the author's exuberant confessions of bibliophilia, autobiographical anecdotes, and grotesque personification of

---

28 Although the *Philobiblon* is written in Richard de Bury's name and presents itself as an autobiographical treatise, doubts have been raised about the text's authorship, as in seven manuscripts it is attributed to the Dominican theologian Robert Holcot. Given the personal anecdotes corresponding to Bury's life interspersed throughout the *Philobiblon*, it is today generally agreed that the bishop was the author, even if it remains unclear how much he was assisted by the scholars he supported, including Holcot. For further discussion of the treatise's authorship see Beryl Smalley, *English Friars and Antiquity in the Early Fourteenth Century* (Oxford, 1960), 66–7; Noël Denholm-Young, 'Richard de Bury (1287–1345) and the *Liber epistolaris*', in *Collected Papers of N. Denholm-Young* (Cardiff, 1969), 1–41 (35); Michael Maclagan, Foreword to Richard de Bury, *Philobiblon*, trans. E.C. Thomas (New York, 1970), lxxiv–lxxxiii, esp. lxxv–lxxvi; and John Slotemaker and Jeffrey Witt, *Robert Holcot* (Oxford, 2016), 130–1.

books.[29] In a chapter titled 'Of the Numerous Opportunities We Have Had for Collecting a Store of Books', Bury boasts that he has rescued (that is, pilfered) manuscripts from the cabinets of the most famous monasteries, where they had lain attacked by moths 'in cinere et cilicio recubantes oblivioni traditi' (in sackcloth and ashes, given up to oblivion).[30] Elsewhere in the treatise, it is the books themselves that voice the horrors to which they are subjected by wars: 'Per bella namque ad patrias peregrinas distrahimur, obtruncamur, vulneramur et enormiter mutilamur, sub terra suffodimur, in mari submergimur, flammis exurimur et omni necis genere trucidamur' (For by wars we are scattered into foreign lands, are mutilated, wounded, and shamefully disfigured, are buried under the earth and overwhelmed in the sea, are devoured by the flames and destroyed by every kind of death).[31] They also lament their mistreatment by careless clergymen, possessioners, and mendicants: 'Morbis variis laboramus, dorsa dolentes et latera, et iacemus membratim paralysi dissoluti, nec est qui recogitet, nec est ullus qui malagma procuret' (We suffer from various diseases, enduring pains in our backs and sides; we lie with our limbs unstrung by palsy, and there is no man who layeth it to heart, and no man who provides a mollifying plaster).[32] As Emily Steiner and Michael Camille have shown, the personified manuscripts foreground the ways that books resemble bodies; they bewail their loose bindings as 'limbs unstrung by palsy' and their yellowed pages as flesh 'diseased with jaundice'.[33] The imaginative

29   See Smalley's discussion of Richard de Bury's sources in *English Friars*, 70–2 and Andrew Fleming West's careful enumeration of his allusions in Richard de Bury, *The* Philobiblon *of Richard de Bury*, ed./trans. Andrew Fleming West, 3 vols (New York, 1889), 3:102–52.
30   Richard de Bury, *Philobiblon*, ed./trans. E.C. Thomas, ed. with foreword by Michael Maclagan (New York, 1970), chapter VIII, 82–3. Hereafter cited as *Philobiblon*. All further quotations and translations from the text are from this facing-page edition.
31   *Philobiblon*, chapter VII, 76–7. The books' lament is not without irony, as Bury frequently identifies superiority in learning with military superiority; see below.
32   *Philobiblon*, chapter IV, 44–5.
33   Emily Steiner, 'Collecting, Violence, Literature: Richard de Bury's *Philobiblon* and the Forms of Literary History', in *The Medieval Literary: Beyond Form*, ed. Robert Meyer-Lee and Catherine Sanok (Cambridge, UK, 2018), 243–65; Michael Camille, 'The Book as Flesh and Fetish in de Bury's *Philobiblon*', in *The Book and the Body*, ed. Dolores Warwick Frese and Katherine O'Brien O'Keeffe (Notre Dame, 1997), 34–77.

force of Bury's treatise may well explain its popularity. The *Philobiblon* was widely circulated and survives in over thirty manuscripts as well as in a multitude of early printed editions.[34] Noël Denholm-Young tells us that the text 'was known at Oxford in 1358, and in the fifteenth century, if not earlier, [it] achieved a considerable reputation upon the Continent'.[35]

As a student at Oxford between 1302 and 1313 and again in 1313–16, Richard de Bury lived in a period of particularly bitter rivalry between his university and that of Paris. As is attested in an Oxford statute from the early fourteenth century (pre-1313), there were attempts at the University of Paris and other institutions to prevent Oxford degrees from being recognized.[36] In retaliation, Oxford declared that it would not receive graduates from these antagonizing universities.[37] However, despite the efforts of certain Parisian scholars to shut out Oxonians, by the first half of the fourteenth century, English philosophy had taken hold of Europe and 'the schools of Oxford attained a reputation throughout the academic world that they never quite equalled before or after'.[38] Despite this international prestige, Oxford had still not managed to obtain a licence of *ius ubique docendi* from the pope, a certification that permitted a university's graduates to teach at any institution in Christendom without further examination.[39] Oxfordians were all too aware that this privilege had already been granted to the University of Paris (along with that of Bologna) by the pope in 1291–2.[40] Indeed,

---

34 For a list and discussion of these manuscripts, see E.C. Thomas, 'Introduction: Bibliographical', in *Philobiblon*, xxxvii–lxxiii. The earliest extant manuscript is datable to c. 1370, about twenty-five years after Bury's death.
35 Denholm-Young, 'Richard de Bury', 33. The first printed edition of the *Philobiblon* was published in 1473 in Cologne, and the text was first printed in England in 1598.
36 J.M. Fletcher, 'The Faculty of Arts', in *The History of the University of Oxford, Volume One: The Early Oxford Schools*, ed. J.I. Catto with Ralph Evans (Oxford, 1984), 369–400 (398).
37 Fletcher, 'The Faculty of Arts', 398; George Haskins, 'The University of Oxford and the "Ius ubique docendi"', *The English Historical Review* 56.222 (1941), 281–92 (282, n. 2).
38 This is the slightly damning judgement of J.A. Weisheipl, 'Ockham and the Mertonians', in *The History of the University of Oxford*, ed. Catto with Evans, 607–58 (608).
39 Haskins, 'The University of Oxford', 283. Oxford unsuccessfully petitioned the pope for this prestigious licence multiple times (at least twice in 1296 and again in 1317) and apparently never received it.
40 Haskins, 'The University of Oxford', 283.

early in his career as a royal official, Richard de Bury had copied into his personal formulary a letter that Edward I (r. 1272–1307) had sent to the pope arguing that if the University of Paris had been granted *ius ubique docendi* then so should Oxford.[41] In an apparent allusion to Alcuin and other influential English scholars at Charlemagne's court, Edward pointedly reminded the pope that French scholarship originated from Englishmen, therefore undercutting the *translatio* myth that Frenchmen were responsible for the westwards transfer of knowledge and power to Paris.[42]

As the *Philobiblon* makes plain, Richard de Bury was familiar with the tradition that Paris had inherited the knowledge and power of the classical world, a commonplace that he likely encountered both as a student at Oxford in the early fourteenth century and later on his many diplomatic missions to France as an agent of Edward III.[43] Passages in his treatise equally reveal that his understanding of *translatio studii et imperii* was indebted to St Augustine's well-known passage on the despoiling of the Egyptians in *De doctrina Christiana*, where Augustine justifies early Christians' inheritance of older pagan wisdom.[44] Bury also recurrently alludes to the works and legacy of Boethius, who, as a great Roman translator responsible for the preservation of Plato and Aristotle in the West, became immensely influential for the medieval understanding of both the hermeneutics of linguistic translation and the myth of *translatio*.[45] As Brooke Hunter has shown, Boethius was

---

41 For a detailed study of Richard de Bury's personal formulary, known as the *Liber epistolaris*, see Denholm-Young, 'Richard de Bury' and the same author's introduction to Richard de Bury, *The* Liber epistolaris *of Richard de Bury*, ed. Noël Denholm-Young (Oxford, 1950). Edward I's letter to the pope is fully transcribed in Haskins, 'The University of Oxford', 290–1.
42 Lusignan, 'Les mythes', 466. Richard de Bury does not overtly draw on this rhetorical strategy in the *Philobiblon*, though it is employed in a foundation myth of the University of Cambridge (see Parker, *The Early History of Oxford*, 14) and in Ranulf Higden's *Polychronicon*, for which see Ranulf Higden, Polychronicon Ranulphi Higden monachi Cestrensis; Together with the English Translations of John Trevisa and of an Unknown Writer of the Fifteenth Century, ed. C. Babington and J.R. Lumby, 9 vols (London, 1865), 6:293.
43 For Richard de Bury's diplomatic missions, see below.
44 See further below.
45 Richard de Bury alludes to Boethius by name in the *Philobiblon* at 8, 18, 26, 76, 110, 128, and 130. For the bishop's numerous more subtle allusions and borrowings from Boethius, see West's 'Explanatory Notes to the Text' in his edition of *The* Philobiblon *of Richard de Bury*, 3:102–35. For Boethius's influence

keenly aware of the link between knowledge and authority and therefore 'depict[ed] his own projects of philosophical *transfero* – both linguistic translation and intellectual transfer – as culturally transformative and politically charged'.[46] Bury's familiarity with Boethius appears to have come in part via the thirteenth-century Boethian forgery *De disciplina scolarium* (c. 1230–40), a flagrantly anachronistic narrative of *translatio studii et imperii* that bolstered the authority of Parisian scholarship by recounting pseudo-Boethius's journey from Rome to Athens and finally to the new preeminent intellectual center of Paris.[47]

Informed both by the legitimating power of the *translatio* tradition as well as by a sense of intellectual rivalry with Paris, Bury employs the myth of *translatio* in the *Philobiblon* to distinctly nationalistic ends. In an especially charged passage, the bishop describes how Minerva, the goddess of strategic warfare, wisdom, and civilization, has left France and come to Britain:

> Minerva mirabilis nationes hominum circuire videtur, et a fine usque as finem attingit fortiter, ut se ipsam communicet universis. Indos, Babylonios, Aegyptios atque Graecos, Arabes et Latinos eam pertransisse iam cernimus. Iam Athenas deseruit, iam a Roma recessit, iam Parisius praeterivit, iam ad Britanniam, insularum insignissimam quin potius microcosmum, accessit feliciter, ut se Graecis et barbaris debitricem ostendat. Quo miraculo perfecto, conicitur a plerisque quod, sicut Galliae iam sophia tepescit, sic euisdem militia penitus evirata languescit.

> (Admirable Minerva seems to bend her course to all the nations of the earth, and reacheth from end to end mightily, that she may reveal herself to all mankind. We see that she has already visited the Indians, the Babylonians, the Egyptians and Greeks, the Arabs and the Romans.

---

on the hermeneutics of translation in the Middle Ages, see Copeland, *Rhetoric, Hermeneutics, and Translation*, esp. chapter 2, 'From Antiquity to the Middle Ages I: The Place of Translation and the Value of Hermeneutics', 37–62; for his cultural legacy, see Copeland's chapter on vernacular translations of Boethius's *De consolatione philosophiae* in the same volume (127–50) and Brooke Hunter, *Forging Boethius in Medieval Intellectual Fantasies* (New York, 2018).

46   Hunter, *Forging Boethius*, 63.
47   Richard de Bury appears to paraphrase *De disciplina scolarium* in at least two instances, for which see West's edition of *The Philobiblon of Richard de Bury*, 3:103, 116, 128. This Boethian forgery, which was early accepted at Oxford, is studied in detail in Hunter, *Forging Boethius*, and is edited in Pseudo-Boethius, *De disciplina scolarium*, ed. Olga Weijers (Leiden, 1976).

Already she has forsaken Athens, departed from Rome, passed by Paris, and now has happily come to Britain, the most noble of islands, nay, rather a microcosm in itself, that she may show herself a debtor both to the Greeks and to the Barbarians. At which wondrous sight it is conceived by most men, that as philosophy is now lukewarm in France, so her soldiery are unmanned and languishing.)[48]

Bury's portrait of Minerva travelling across the earth and dismissively passing by ('praeterivit') Paris before finally settling in Britain is the very personification of the *translatio* myth and is unmistakably nationalistically charged: the author is adamant that martial and intellectual power are entwined and that both have abandoned France for Britain.

Indeed, while Bury readily admits that Paris was once 'paradisum mundi' (the paradise of the world), home to Athenian wisdom and 'bibliothecae iocundae super cellas aromatum redolentes' (delightful libraries, more aromatic than stores of spicery), he insists that the impudence of young French scholars and their 'dispendioso compendio' (baneful haste) to earn their diplomas has sullied Parisian learning.[49] The subtleties, or refinements, of learning are now to be found in England:

> Isto, pro dolor! paroxysmo, quem plangimus, Parisiense palladium nostris maestis temporibus cernimus iam sublatum, ubi tepuit, immo fere friguit zelus scholae tam nobilis, cuius olim radii lucem dabant universis angulis orbis terrae. Quiescit ibidem iam calamus omnis scribae, nec librorum generatio propagator ulterius, nec est qui incipiat novus auctor haberi. Involvunt sententias sermonibus imperitis, et omnis logicae proprietate privantur; nisi quod Anglicanas subtilitates, quibus palam detrahunt, vigiliis furtivis addiscunt.

> (Alas! By the same disease that we are deploring, we see that the Palladium of Paris has been carried off in these sad times of ours, wherein the zeal of that noble university, whose rays once shed light into every corner of the world, has grown lukewarm, nay, is all but frozen. There the pen of every scribe is now at rest, generations of books no longer succeed each other, and there is none who begins to take place as a new author. They wrap

---

48 *Philobiblon*, chapter IX, 106–7 (Thomas has omitted to translate the clause, 'Iam Athenas deseruit, iam a Roma recessit', which I have supplied).

49 Bury adds that in the new-Athens of Paris there are 'Athenarum diverticula, Peripateticorum itinera, Parnasi promontoria et porticus Stoicorum' (the lounges of Athens; walks of the Peripatetics; peaks of Parnassus; and porches of the Stoics), *Philobiblon*, chapter VIII, 84–5; chapter IX, 104–5.

up their doctrines in unskilled discourse, and are losing all propriety of logic, except that our English subtleties, which they denounce in public, are the subject of their furtive vigils.)[50]

Bury here alludes to the rise of Oxford logic (for instance the theories of William of Ockham, Robert Holcot, and Thomas Bradwardine) and to Oxford's rivalry with Paris.[51] Despite his boasting at the pre-eminence of Insular thought, he cautions that it too is threatened by the increasing number of students 'praesumptionis pennas Icarias inexpertis lacertis fragiliter coaptantes' (slightly [or feebly] fastening to their untried arms the Icarian wings of presumption).[52] Still, the bishop hedges, English subtlety remains 'antiquis perfusa luminaribus' (illuminated by the lights of former times) and 'novos semper radios emittit veritatis' (is always sending forth fresh rays of truth).[53]

While his emphasis on the gradual accumulation of knowledge and the transfer of ancient scholarship from one master to another is reminiscent of Bernard of Chartres's (d. c. 1124) metaphor of dwarfs standing on the shoulders of giants, Bury adds to this scholastic vision the martial vision of a lineage of empires.[54] In his lengthy discussion of the violence committed against books, Bury emphasizes the manner in which empires forcibly reap the learning of their predecessors. The bishop's sense of history is vividly expressed in his conviction that the Romans plundered the achievements of the Greeks. Echoing St Augustine's *De doctrina Christiana*, Bury asks: 'Quid fecisset Vergilius, Latinorum poeta praecipuus, si Theocritum, Lucretium et Homerum minime spoliasset et in eorum vitula non arasset?' (What would Vergil, the chief poet among the Latins, have

---

50 *Philobiblon*, chapter IX, 104–7.
51 For the rise of Oxford logic, see Weisheipl, 'Ockham and the Mertonians'; and Gordon Leff, *Paris and Oxford in the Thirteenth and Fourteenth Centuries: An Institutional and Intellectual History* (New York, 1968), 294–309.
52 *Philobiblon*, chapter IX, 102–3.
53 *Philobiblon*, chapter VIII, 90–1.
54 John of Salisbury records Bernard of Chartres's metaphor thus: 'We are as dwarves seated on the shoulders of giants, that we may see more and further than they do, not because we are sharp-sighted or physically distinguished, but because the size of the giants raises us higher', quoted in Giancinta Spinosa, 'Translatio studiorum through Philosophical Terminology', in *Translatio studiorum: Ancient, Medieval, and Modern Bearers of Intellectual History*, ed. Marco Sgarbi (Leiden, 2012), 73–89 (76).

achieved, if he had not despoiled Theocritus, Lucretius, and Homer, and had not plowed with their heifer?).⁵⁵ Moreover, 'quid Sallustius, Tullius, Boetius, Macrobius, Lactantius, Martianus, immo tota cohors generaliter Latinorum, si Athenarum studia vel Graecorum voluminal non vidissent?' (what could Sallust, Tully, Boethius, Macrobius, Lactantius, Martianus, and in short the whole troop [or armed force] of Latin writers have done, if they had not seen the productions of Athens or the volumes of the Greeks?).⁵⁶ However, neither were the Greeks themselves the fountainhead of knowledge. For not even Aristotle, Bury continues, could have self-generated the entirety of his learning.⁵⁷ Rather, 'Hebraeorum, Babyloniorum, Aegyptiorum, Chaldaeorum, Persarum etiam et Medorum, quos omnes diserta Graecia in thesauros suos transtulerat, sacros libros oculis lynceis penetrando perviderat' (with lynx-eyed penetration, he had seen through the sacred books of the Hebrews, the Babylonians, the Egyptians, the Chaldæans, the Persians, and the Medes, all of which learned Greece had transferred into her treasuries).⁵⁸ Having learned the insights of this ancient lineage of *translatio studii*, Aristotle 'aspera complanavit, superflua resecavit, diminuta supplevit et errata delevit' (smoothed away their crudities, pruned their superfluities, supplied their deficiencies, and removed their errors).⁵⁹

At times, Bury's vision of progress develops into what might almost appear a sense of scientific advancement. In the chapter titled 'On the Gradual Perfecting of Books', the author confesses:

Sapientiam veterum exquirentes assidue [...] non in illam opinionem dignum duximus declinandum, ut primos artium fundatores omnem ruditatem elimasse dicamus, scientes adinventionem cuiusque fideli canonio ponderatam pusillam efficere scientiae portionem. Sed per pluriomorum investigationes sollicitas, quasi datis symbolis singillatim, scientiarum ingentia corpora ad immensas, quas cernimus quantitates successivis augmentationibus succrevereunt.

(While assiduously seeking out the wisdom of the men of old [...] we have not thought fit to be misled into the opinion that the first founders

55 *Philobiblon*, chapter X, 110–11. Compare Bury's rhetoric with St Augustine's account of the 'spoiling of the Egyptians' in *De doctrina Christiana*, trans. R.H. Greed (Oxford, 1995), book II, chapters 60–3, 124–31.
56 *Philobiblon*, chapter X, 110–11.
57 *Philobiblon*, chapter X, 108–9.
58 *Philobiblon*, chapter X, 108–11.
59 *Philobiblon*, chapter X, 108–11.

of the arts have purged away all crudeness, knowing that the discoveries of each of the faithful, when weighed in a faithful balance, makes a tiny portion of science, but that by the anxious investigations of a multitude of scholars, each as it were contributing his share, the mighty bodies of the sciences have grown by successive augmentations to the immense bulk that we now behold.)[60]

Bury continues that, when students continually reassess the doctrines of their masters, the product is 'aurum electum probatum terrae purgatum septuplum et perfecte, nullius erronei vel dubii admixtione fucatum' (refined gold tried in a furnace of earth, purified seven times to perfection, and stained by no admixture of error or doubt).[61] The bishop therefore articulates a vision of progress in which knowledge is gradually accumulated and received wisdom must continually be retested. On the whole, this perspective is congruent with the myth of *translatio* and Bury's argument that each nation in the lineage of worldly empires inherits, betters, and expands the wisdom of the empires that came before – and, by implication, that English learning has surpassed that of France.

According to the *Philobiblon*, the means for empires to accumulate, preserve, and flaunt their wisdom is through books. As we have seen in Bury's extended discussion of how the Greeks and Romans drew from the treasuries, or libraries, of the ancient world, manuscripts are considered priceless materializations of knowledge necessary for the transmission of learning through time and space. In other words, books are agents of *translatio studii*, for 'quiescentes quippe moventur, dum ipsis loca sua tenentibus, auditorum intellectibus circumquaque feruntur' (in truth, while resting they yet move, and while retaining their own places they are carried about every way to the minds of listeners).[62] In Bury's vision, where knowledge and power are inextricably entwined,

---

60 *Philobiblon*, chapter X, 108–9. When Bury notes that English subtlety is 'illuminated by the lights of former times [and] is always sending forth fresh rays of truth', he concomitantly declares that Paris 'plus antiquitati discendae quam veritati subtiliter producendae iam studet' (is now more zealous in the study of antiquity than in the subtle investigation of truth), chapter VIII, 90–1. One implication appears to be that the progress of Parisian learning has been stunted by an undue commitment to ancient wisdom and an inability to develop advancements or 'fresh rays of truth'. English learning, on the other hand, is rightly informed by ancient wisdom without being limited by it.
61 *Philobiblon*, chapter X, 108–9.
62 *Philobiblon*, chapter IV, 40–1.

books are therefore necessary for the ascendancy of England, and book-collecting is a virtuous endeavor that betters the whole nation.

Richard de Bury himself went to great lengths to preserve and increase his kingdom's store of books. Although no inventory survives of the bishop's library, he has often been considered the foremost English book-collector of his age. He is depicted in the *St Albans Chronicle and Register of Benefactors* (c. 1380) holding three volumes, and the fourteenth-century chronicler of the bishopric of Durham, William de Chambre, records that Bury had more books than any other bishop in England.[63] According to Chambre, he also had a library at every one of his residences, and his bedchamber was so strewn with books that one could hardly move without stepping on one.[64] In a frequently quoted passage, the chronicler Adam Murimuth further notes that Bury had more volumes than could be transported in 'five large carts'.[65] As Steiner wryly observes, Murimuth's comment does little to quantify Bury's collection unless we know the size of the carts in question and how many books each could carry.[66] Still, the sense remains that Bury's collection was exceptionally large. The *Philobiblon* divulges the many (often underhand) ways in which the bishop accumulated his collection and the great sums of money he has lavished on books, treasures that possessed his mind since boyhood.[67] Bury shamelessly admits that a number of his books were given to him as bribes while Chancellor and Treasurer, and we have already noted that others were stolen from

63 The illustration of Richard de Bury in the *St Albans Chronicle and Register of Benefactors* (BL, Cotton MS Nero D.vii, fol. 87r) is reproduced in Steiner, 'Collecting, Violence, Literature', 251. William de Chambre appears to have been writing twenty-odd years after Bury's death. For William's continuation of the *History of Durham*, including his account of Richard de Bury, see 'Continuatio historiae Dunelmensis', in *Historiae Dunelmensis scriptores tres*, ed. James Raine, Surtees Society Publications 9 (London, 1839), 124–56, esp. 125–30.
64 William de Chambre, 'Continuatio historiae Dunelmensis', 130.
65 Adam Murimuth, Continuatio chronicarum: *Robertus de Avesbury* de gestis mirabilibus regis Edwardi tertii, ed. Edward Maunde Thompson, Rolls Series 93 (London, 1889), 170.
66 Steiner, 'Collecting, Violence, Literature', 247–8.
67 Richard de Bury writes that 'mentem nostram librorum amor hereos possideret a puero, quorum zelo languere vice volumptatis accepimus' (the [o]vermastering love of books has possessed our mind from boyhood, and to rejoice in their delights has been our only pleasure), *Philobiblon*, chapter XI, 116–17.

England's finest monastic libraries.[68] On the whole, the *Philobiblon* reveals that Bury's book-collecting was nothing if not obsessive. However, the treatise tells us that the bishop's fanatical collecting stemmed not from greed but rather from the hope of bolstering English learning and glorifying the English crown. As Steiner affirms, the bishop 'regard[ed] [book] collecting as a distinctly nationalist endeavor [...] in the wake of the war with France'.[69] More specifically, Bury's bibliophilia was fuelled by his recognition of the cultural importance of English learning's pre-eminence over French scholarship and of the University of Oxford's pre-eminence over the University of Paris. Bury's ultimate plan for his immense library was to donate it to a college at Oxford that he hoped to found in honor of Edward III and Queen Philippa.[70] Despite his intentions, the bishop's immense debt – accrued in large part through book-collecting – prevented this project from coming to fruition. Bury's library was sold off piecemeal to settle his accounts upon his death, and today only a handful of volumes are known to have once belonged to him.[71] This is a sorry end to the library of a man who

68 The bishop readily admits: 'Librorum et maxime veterum ferebamur cupiditate languescere, posse vero quemlibet nostrum per quaternos facilius quam per pecuniam adipisci favorem' (We were reported to burn with such desire for books, and especially old ones, that it was more easy for any man to gain our favour by means of books than of money), *Philobiblon*, chapter VIII, 82–3.
69 Steiner, 'Collecting, Violence, Literature', 262.
70 Bury writes: 'In primis enim libros omnes et singulos, de quibus catalogum fecimus specialem, concedimus et donamus intuitu caritatis communitati scholarium in aula ·N· Oxoniensi degentium, in perpetuam eleemosynam pro anima nostra et parentum nostrorum necnon pro animabus illustrissimi regis Angliae Edwardi tertii post conquestum ac devotissimae dominae reginae Philippae consortis eiusdem, ut iidem libri omnibus et singulis universitatis dictae villae scholaribus et magistris tam regularibus quam saecularibus commodentur pro tempore ad profectum et usum studendi' (*Imprimis*, we give and grant all and singular the books, of which we have made a special catalogue, in consideration of affection, to the community of scholars living in [...] N [...] Hall at Oxford, as a perpetual gift, for our soul and the souls of our parents, and also for the soul of the most illustrious King Edward the Third from the Conquest, and of the most pious Queen Philippa, his consort to the intent that the same books may be lent from time to time to all and singular the scholars and masters of the said place, as well regular as secular, for the advancement and use of study), *Philobiblon*, chapter XIX, 168–9.
71 For these volumes, see Denholm-Young, 'Richard de Bury', 37, n. 4; Steiner, 'Collecting, Violence, Literature', 250, n. 26; and N.R. Ker, 'Richard de Bury's Books from the Library of St Albans', *Bodleian Library Record* 3 (1950–1), 177–9.

insisted that 'pretiosior est [...] cunctis opibus sapientiae libraria' (a library of wisdom [...] is more precious than all wealth).[72] The ruination of Richard de Bury's own library functions unintentionally to intensify the bishop's lament over the mistreatment, loss, and destruction of books and libraries throughout the ages. Bury was keenly aware of the fragile materiality of books, these agents of *translatio studii* that he saw as unavoidably implicated in the destruction of *translatio imperii*. Paradoxically, on the one hand, Bury deplores how books fall casualty to warring nations, and his sustained personification of manuscripts renders their destruction all the more horrific, for to burn a library is a 'infaustum holocaustum, ubi loco cruoris incaustum offertur' (hapless holocaust, where ink is offered up instead of blood) and where innocents are consumed by devouring flames.[73] Yet, on the other hand, the bishop is keen to signal books themselves as instruments of competition and conflict between empires, notably between England and France. While books were commonly understood as symbols of both wisdom and wealth in the late Middle Ages, Bury employs the topos of *translatio studii et imperii* to position books as emblems of national superiority and foretellers of martial victory, for, just as the scribes of Paris have stilled their quills and 'nec librorum generatio propagatur ulterius' (generations of books no longer succeed each other) in France, so it is provident that England should overmaster its rival both in study and in war.[74]

Bury's Cultural Legacy

Having witnessed Bury's nationalistic evocations of *translatio studii et imperii* in the *Philobiblon*, we still have the question of the popularity and political currency of the bishop's ideas. Given Bury's high standing in royal and intellectual circles, the chances of his ideas having broad cultural traction were very high. Mark Ormrod has persuasively demonstrated that Bury was one of Edward III's most trusted councilors and that, in his successive roles as the king's secretary, keeper of the privy

---

72 *Philobiblon*, chapter II, 28–9.
73 *Philobiblon*, chapter VII, 72–3. The bishop laments that much of ancient wisdom has been irretrievably lost because of such destruction. See, for example, his account of the burning of the library of Alexandria, chapter VII, 72–5.
74 *Philobiblon*, chapter IX, 106–7.

seal, and chancellor, he held considerable sway in multiple spheres, such as 'the general operation of domestic government, the management of the king's council and parliament, and the pursuit of international diplomacy'.[75] Steiner has even argued that 'in the 1330s and 1340s, Bury was perhaps the most powerful man in England'.[76]

Bury made multiple diplomatic trips to France in the lead up to the Hundred Years War. In 1325-6, he accompanied the future Edward III, then still prince, to France, and it is likely that as keeper of the privy seal he traveled again with Edward in 1331, when the king infamously visited Philip VI disguised as a pilgrim.[77] Bury also undertook the king's 'secret business' at the papal court of Avignon in 1331 and 1333, where he famously met Petrarch and discussed the location of the legendary 'Ultima Thule'.[78] Again in 1336, Bury was trusted to go to France with Bishop Orleton and others to negotiate pivotal matters such as the status of Aquitaine, the prospect of a joint Anglo-French crusade, and the proposals for Anglo-Scottish peace.[79] Later that year, realizing that the peace negotiations with France were at an impasse, Bury was involved in organizing the reconnaissance of Philip VI's suspected plans for a double assault of England, where one French armada would attack the south

---

75 Mark Ormrod, 'The King's Secrets: Richard de Bury and the Monarchy of Edward III', in *War, Government, and Aristocracy in the British Isles, c. 1150-1500: Essays in Honour of Michael Prestwich*, ed. Chris Given-Wilson, Ann Kettle, and Len Scales (Woodbridge, 2008), 163-78. For Bury's career, see also Denholm-Young, 'Richard de Bury', 24-32.

76 Steiner, 'Collecting, Violence, Literature', 244.

77 Ormrod, 'The King's Secrets', 175.

78 Ormrod, 'The King's Secrets', 175. Ultima Thule (lit. 'farthermost land') was believed in ancient and medieval times to be the most extreme northern island of the earth and was sometimes understood metaphorically as either a place beyond the known world or the utmost limit of discovery. According to Petrarch's letters, Bury told him that he could locate this legendary land once he returned home to his books and that he would write back to him. However, despite Petrarch's repeated letters, Bury seems to have never responded. Petrarch's papers also reveal that he found Bury a 'man with a sharp mind and considerable knowledge of letters' who 'since his youth was unbelievably curious about hidden things', quoted in Steiner, 'Collecting, Violence, Literature', 263 (Steiner also compares Petrarch's bibliophilia with Bury's throughout her chapter). Denholm-Young suggests that in fact Petrarch's praise of Bury seems to be 'qualified' as he calls the bishop '*literatus*, but only *sufficienter*'. See Denholm-Young, 'Richard de Bury', 27-8.

79 Ormrod, 'The King's Secrets', 175.

coast and another would head north to support the Scots.[80] In June 1338, Bury was commissioned to go to France for a final time, ostensibly for peace negotiations with King Philip, although Ormrod suspects that this diplomatic mission was intended as a cover both for Edward's war preparations with the Low Countries and to spy on the French.[81] After his return to England, the bishop was chiefly concerned with establishing and maintaining truces for the Anglo-Scottish border. From this overview of Bury's political career, it is clear that the bishop was 'closely involved in confidential diplomacy, the management and communication of royal government, and the organization of the opening stages of the Hundred Years War'.[82] What remains less certain is how Bury's firsthand participation in the high-stakes politics of the Hundred Years War may have been influenced by (or, conversely, may have influenced) his preoccupation with *translatio studii et imperii*.

We do know that, when on home soil, the bishop zealously promoted English learning and had 'a central role in the communication and confirmation of royal policy and patronage'.[83] We have already seen that Bury repeatedly invoked the glory of King Edward in the *Philobiblon*, and he also often acted on behalf of the king during royal inquires and visitations at Oxford and Cambridge.[84] As Beryl Smalley remarks, Bury enjoyed calling attention to his promotion of learning and seems to have consciously 'erect[ed] patronage into an ideal'.[85] It was under Bury's guidance, for instance, that Sir Philip de Somerville founded six theological fellowships at Balliol College in 1340.[86] Ormrod moreover suggests that the bishop may have been 'instrumental in setting up the recruitment stream that brought an increasing number of university men into clerical and diplomatic agencies of the state in the 1330s'.[87] Ormrod notes elsewhere that Edward III's own patronage as well as his 'understanding of the role of the universities' in royal administration

80 Ormrod, 'The King's Secrets', 176.
81 Ormrod, 'The King's Secrets', 176.
82 Ormrod, 'The King's Secrets', 176.
83 Ormrod, 'The King's Secrets', 168.
84 Denholm-Young, 'Richard de Bury', 27, 37.
85 Smalley, *English Friars*, 66.
86 Denholm-Young, 'Richard de Bury', 37. See also the discussion in T.H. Ashton and Rosamond Faith, 'The Endowments of the University and Colleges to *circa* 1348', in *The History of the University of Oxford*, ed. Catto with Evans, 265–310 (294).
87 Ormrod, 'The King's Secrets', 166.

and 'respect for the authority and value of higher learning' bespeak Bury's legacy.[88] The king bought at least one book from Bury's vast collection, and it is easily conceivable that he may have received more from the bishop as gifts.[89]

Scholars have often debated the degree of Bury's influence on the king and of his involvement in Edward's early education. The chronicler William de Chambre recorded that, before becoming bishop, Bury served as tutor to Prince Edward (then the earl of Chester).[90] While Denholm-Young is inclined to believe Chambre's history and that Bury was indeed in charge of Edward's education sometime between 1323 and 1326, most scholars tend to consider Bury less as the prince's official tutor and more as his intellectual and political mentor.[91] Bury remained exceptionally loyal to his pupil throughout his career and was even involved in Queen Isabella and Roger Mortimer's plot to depose Edward II and install the fourteen-year-old Edward III on the throne.[92] Afterwards Bury participated again in Edward's plot to overthrow his mother and her lover in 1330.[93] In short, Bury was indispensable to Edward and was granted a great many benefices in return for his constant service and mentorship.[94]

Beyond his royal offices, Bury was at the heart of England's most prestigious academic network and would have had no shortage of scholars with whom to discuss the combined transfer of intellectual and

---

88 W. Mark Ormrod, *Edward III* (New Haven, 2012), 309–10. In addition to his patronage of religious houses, Edward re-founded his father's King's Hall at Cambridge in 1337 and established two new colleges of secular canons at Winsor and Westminster in 1348. For Edward's patronage, see also J.R.L. Highfield, 'The Early Colleges', in *The History of the University of Oxford*, ed. Catto with Evans, 225–64 (239).

89 For the book purchased by Edward, see Ormrod, 'The King's Secrets', 165, n. 9.

90 Denholm-Young, 'Richard de Bury', 4. We do know with certainty that Bury began his career in royal service as a clerk in Prince Edward's household in October 1316.

91 Denholm-Young, 'Richard de Bury', 4. Denholm-Young adds that 'it may indeed be no chance that Edward was the first English king whom we know to have been able to write', 33.

92 Ormrod, 'The King's Secrets', 168.

93 Denholm-Young, 'Richard de Bury', 25.

94 Ormrod notes that in a letter to the exchequer in 1332 Edward III writes that Bury's outstanding accounts must be handled by proxy as 'the king cannot be without him' ('The King's Secrets', 169). A list of Bury's preferments is appended in Denholm-Young, 'Richard de Bury', 39–41.

martial superiority from France to England. The bishop housed a large group of chaplains and clerks 'who shared with him the daily readings at table, and the disputations after dinner'.[95] Many of these men would become some of the foremost minds of fourteenth-century England, including Robert Holcot; Thomas Bradwardine, later Archbishop of Canterbury; Walter Burley, the philosopher who reportedly tutored the Black Prince; Richard de Kilvington, later archdeacon of London; and three future bishops: Richard Bentworth, Walter Segrave, and Thomas Fitz-Ralph.[96] Most of these men were fellows of Oxford's Merton College, which was a preeminent center of philosophy and theology in Europe at this period.[97] Indeed, Denholm-Young argues that the bishop's patronage and encouragement of the remarkable group of scholars who gathered at Merton in the mid to late fourteenth century has too often gone unnoted.[98] It is not clear to what college Bury himself belonged when he earned his Master of Arts (and likely a Bachelor of Divinity) at Oxford in c. 1302–13, nor upon his unusual return to university as a canon in c. 1333–6.[99] However, financial accounts indicate that, as a royal commissioner on visitation to Oxford, Bury stayed at Merton at least once, further suggesting his attachment to the college.[100] Unfortunately, though we know that Bury was a mentor to his Merton fellows, as Smalley notes, 'we do not know what form his encouragements took'.[101] Thus, it is impossible to know with certainty to what extent Bury imparted his fascination with *translatio* to his protégés nor how much the topos bore on their later ideas. However, as J.A. Weisheipl affirms, it is without doubt that 'the camaraderie of colleges such as Merton and households such as Bishop Richard of Bury's at Durham tended to give English intellectuals of the period a sense of self-confidence hitherto unexpressed'.[102]

---

95 Denholm-Young, 'Richard de Bury', 36.
96 For a list of scholars associated with the bishop, see Denholm-Young, 'Richard de Bury', appendix II, 39.
97 See Weisheipl's discussion of Merton's dominance in the fourteenth century in 'Ockham and the Mertonians'.
98 Denholm-Young, 'Richard de Bury', 36.
99 Denholm-Young, 'Richard de Bury', 2, 28–9. Denholm-Young proposes that Bury returned to university (with special dispensation from the pope) to study theology as the bishop later confessed his dislike of law.
100 Denholm-Young, 'Richard de Bury', 29.
101 Smalley, 'English Friars', 67.
102 Weisheipl, 'Ockham and the Mertonians', 644.

In other words, Bury promoted a sense of English academic pride, one that the *Philobiblon* positions as explicitly nationalistic and anti-French. Everything considered, Bury was the most powerful and vocal proponent of *translatio* in fourteenth-century England, and he regularly performed symbolic acts to substantiate this nationalistic myth. Beyond the blatant statements of *translatio studii et imperii* in the *Philobiblon*, Bury mentored the foremost scholars of his generation, fostered English academic pride at Oxford, encouraged a sense of intellectual rivalry with Paris, and zealously collected books to physically manifest the transfer of learning to England. Given that the bishop also had the ear of the king and was directly involved in the royal preparations at the outset of England's war with France, further research considering Bury's political career alongside his cultural agenda may yet reveal additional insights on how the discourse of *translatio studii et imperii* shaped the opening stages of the Hundred Years War.

However, beyond Bury's patronage, the legacy of his *Philobiblon* at Oxford remains somewhat difficult to trace. E.C. Thomas notes that a passage from Bury's complaint against the mendicants appears in a somewhat altered form in the Oxford chancellor and proctor's book under the year 1358.[103] Despite the thirty-odd extant manuscripts of the *Philobiblon* and thus the text's apparent popularity, the next direct allusion to Bury's treatise by an Oxonian comes, to my knowledge, only in the sixteenth century, in Thomas Caius's *Assertio antiquitatis Oxoniensis academiae* (1566).[104] Caius's Latin tract proudly argues that the university at Oxford is more ancient than that at Cambridge, thus making it superior. Within two years, Caius's text was bitterly denounced in a tract written by his Cantabrigian counterpart, John Caius, who insisted that his university was the oldest and most renowned in Britain.[105] The two Caiuses were likely of no familial relation. Both, however, were curiously

---

103 Thomas' observation is absent from any modern edition of his translation, though it is cited in West's edition of *The* Philobiblon *of Richard de Bury*, 3:130, n. 79. See West's note for the passages concerned from the *Philobiblon* and the chancellor and proctor's book.
104 Andrew Fleming West, 'The Text of the *Philobiblon*', in *The* Philobiblon *of Richard de Bury*, 3:35–101 (61, n. 1). Caius was likely a Latinization of the name Kay, Key, or Keys.
105 There is no modern edition of either Thomas Caius's or John Caius's tracts. For an excellent discussion of these treatises, see James Parker, *The Early History of Oxford 727–1100: Preceded by a Sketch of the Mythical Origin of the City and University* (Oxford, 1885), 20–33.

eager to declare that they had read the *Philobiblon*. Thomas Caius claimed that 'he had read in the library of Durham College, Oxford, during the reign of Henry VIII (1509-47), the very copy of the *Philobiblon* which Richard de Bury gave in his lifetime to that library'.[106] Unfortunately, this copy of the *Philobiblon* was likely destroyed in 1550, when the libraries of all Oxford colleges except Lincoln were plundered by Edward VI's reformers and great piles of Catholic books were burned in the marketplace.[107] It may well be that more early Oxford copies of the *Philobiblon* were destroyed during this pillaging. As for John Caius, he claimed to have owned a manuscript of Bury's treatise (also since lost) that contained a copy of the foundation deed of Durham college.[108] Though Thomas Caius's and John Caius's tracts are most evidently concerned with the rivalry between Oxford and Cambridge, as we shall see, they are also implicated in the English universities' prolonged competition with French learning.

Other late medieval Oxford texts resonate remarkably with the *Philobiblon* even if they do not directly cite Bury's treatise. One such text is a poem known as the 'Planctus universitatis Oxoniensis' (c. 1356-7) concerning the St Scholastica Day riot of 1355. This Latin poem of nearly three hundred lines takes the form of a dialogue between a student and the University of Oxford, which 'speaks as the spirit of learning and civilization in general'.[109] Like Bury's admirable Minerva, this spirit of knowledge has traveled westwards across the globe. The spirit recounts that, during its westward progression, 'mihi consenciit semper milicia, / Et mecum transiit mundi potencia' (military prowess always bends to me, and with me comes worldly power).[110] The spirit continues that it has abandoned the great empires of the ancient world one after another because of their licentiousness, laziness, savagery, and hatred of priests.[111] Having passed by the Assyrians, the Medes, the Persians, the Greeks, the Romans, and thence the Gauls and the Germans, the spirit 'tandem Oxoniis diu reflorui' (at last reflourished in Oxford for a long

106 West, 'The Text of the *Philobiblon*', 92.
107 West, 'The Text of the *Philobiblon*', 92.
108 West, 'The Text of the *Philobiblon*', 61, n. 1. Durham College was the school that Bury wished to found and endow with his library. Ultimately, the college was established by his successor, Thomas Hatfield, Bishop of Durham, in 1381.
109 'Planctus universitatis Oxoniensis', ed. Henry Furneaux, in *Collectanea*, ed. Montagu Burrows, 4 vols (Oxford, 1896), 3:169-79 (177, n. 205).
110 'Planctus universitatis Oxoniensis', lines 219-20. Translations of this text are my own.
111 'Planctus universitatis Oxoniensis', lines 203-16.

time).¹¹² However, the spirit laments that 'gravissimis signis innotui / Quod in novissimis fiam despectui' (I learned by the most serious signs that I would be despised in these latest times) and that faults appear everywhere: the university's number of clerks dwindles; it is corrupted by fraud and bribery; and its students quarrel with the laity.¹¹³ Recalling Bury's warning that the subtleties of English thought may be ruined (like those of the French) by the impudence of young scholars, the spirit cautions that it could fly still further to the west and find a new, unspoiled race to distinguish.¹¹⁴ However – unsurprisingly – the spirit decides to stay in Oxford, for, of all the nations it has tried, the spirit of learning reverences this place and the English the most: 'Quamvis experior omnem progeniem, / Fili, plus vereor Anglorum speciem. / [...] Hic ergo capiam aeternam requiem' (Although I try all offspring, son, I most reverence the English type [...] Here, therefore, I will take my eternal rest).¹¹⁵

Another similar Oxford poem is 'Tryvytlam de laude universitatis Oxoniae', dated only to between the St Scholastica Day riot of 1355 and the first reign of Henry VI (1422–61).¹¹⁶ While the author, a Franciscan friar named Richard de Trevytlam, on the whole offers the university more censure than praise, he too employs the image of the wandering Minerva, who is here coupled with her Greek counterpart, Pallas. Addressing Oxford, the poet announces that 'perfeccius dotata diceris / Minervae munere, donoque Palladis' (you will be said to be most perfectly endowed by the favor of Minerva and the gift of Pallas) and that the time of Athens and Rome has passed.¹¹⁷ Oxford is now the

112 'Planctus universitatis Oxoniensis', line 221.
113 'Planctus universitatis Oxoniensis', lines 223–4, 225–44.
114 'Planctus universitatis Oxoniensis', lines 245–8: 'O si respiciam plagas occiduas / Et sic praeficiam gentes residuas; / Hae forsan salient in vires strenuas, / Ad tempus capient laudes praecipuas' (Oh if I would look upon the western quarters, I would place other nations in authority; These will perhaps jump into vigorous strength and receive temporary distinguished praises; my translation).
115 'Planctus universitatis Oxoniensis', lines 273–6.
116 Richard de Trevytlam, 'Tryvytlam *De laude universitatis Oxoniae*', ed. Henry Furneaux, in *Collectanea*, ed. Montagu Burrows, 4 vols (Oxford, 1896), 3:188–209 (189). Hereafter cited as Richard de Trevytlam, '*De laude universitatis Oxoniae*'.
117 Richard de Trevytlam, '*De laude universitatis Oxoniae*', lines 31–2. On Athens and Rome, Trevytlam writes: 'Athenas Cecropis fatebor sterilem, / Et Achademiam urbem inutilem, / Quae quondam dederat doctrinam uberem. / Pallebit livida domus Romulea, / Impar putabitur eius sciencia' (I will admit that Athens is barren, and the academy is a useless city, which once had given

'maximam Anglorum gloriam' (greatest glory of the English) and better informed than even Paris: 'Quicquit ediderit pulcra Parisius, / Ut verum fatear, informas melius' (Whatever beauties Paris might produce, to tell the truth, you [Oxford] form better).[118] Thus, the poet tells the University of Oxford: 'Toti seculo virtutem influis' (You bring virtue to the whole world).[119] By implication, it must purify itself of its recent evil doings, notably the university's persecution of its own students at the hands of the lay mob.

Whether the authors of either the 'Planctus universitatis Oxoniensis' or the 'Tryvytlam de laude universitatis Oxoniae' drew directly from Bury or rather from a broader discourse of *translatio studii et imperii* at Oxford is impossible to know. It is clear, however, that the *translatio* myth and the image of the wandering Minerva were familiar to a number of scholars at Oxford in the late Middle Ages, among them Bury, and that these tropes were employed to bolster a sense of English academic pride.

Translatio *in the University of Oxford's Foundation Myths*

In the remainder of this essay, I will explore other versions of the *translatio* myth that circulated at Oxford, notably those concerning the university's foundation.[120] Remarkably, all the origin stories discussed in the following pages appear to have formulated only in the fourteenth and fifteenth centuries, and the majority were composed specifically in the reign of Edward III (r. 1327–77). On the whole, these myths functioned to bolster Oxford's reputation in its period of bitter rivalry with the University of Paris. While Bury envisioned this *translatio* of learning as a linear succession (Minerva flew from France to England), the Oxford foundation myths promote an alternate version of *translatio studii et imperii* in which England supersedes France not by inheriting its rival's wisdom but by directly inheriting the wisdom of the ancient world. In

---

plentiful teaching. The spiteful house of Romulus will pale, its knowledge will be considered inferior; my translation), lines 42–6.

118 Richard de Trevytlam, '*De laude universitatis Oxoniae*', lines 7, 66–7. Translations of this text are my own.

119 Richard de Trevytlam, '*De laude universitatis Oxoniae*', line 91.

120 For the *translatio* myth's presence in the foundation myths of the University of Cambridge, see Parker, *The Early History of Oxford*, 25–38.

these retellings, English learning is the result of an early divergence from the well-known lineage of worldly empires and is thus independent from French scholarship. The first version of the Oxford foundation myth to which we turn is that promulgated by the university itself in the 'Chancellor's Book', which appears to have been compiled late in the reign of Edward III (c. 1375).[121] James Parker notes that the myth, commonly called the Oxford *Historiola*, also appears in two iterations of the university's 'Proctor's Book', one copied in 1407 and the other in 1477, as well as in BL, Cotton MS Claudius D.viii, which appears to have been copied directly from the Chancellor's Book sometime in the early fifteenth century.[122] The *Historiola* recounts:

> Contestantibus plerisque chronicis, multa loca per orbis climata variis temporibus variarum scientiarum studiis floruisse leguntur: omnium autem inter Latinos nunc extantium studiorum Universitas Oxoniensis fundatione prior, quadam scientiarum pluralitate generalior, in veritatis Catholicae professione firmior, ac privilegiorum multiplicitate praestantior invenitur. Prioritatem suae fundationis insinuant historiae Britannicae perantiquae: fertur enim inter bellicosos quondam Trojanos, qui, cum duce suo Bruto, insulam tunc Albion, postmodum Britanniam, ac demum dictam Angliam, triumphaliter occuparunt, quosdam philosophos adventantes locum habitationis sibi congruae in ipsa insula elegisse, cui et nomen videlicet *Grekelade*.

(By the concurrent testimony of several chronicles, many places throughout different parts of the world are said at various times to have gained repute in the promotion of the study of the various sciences. But the University of Oxford is found to be earlier as to foundation, more general in the number of sciences taught, firmer in the profession of Catholic Truth, and more distinguished for the multitude of its privileges, than all other *Studia* now existing amongst the Latins. Very ancient British Histories imply the priority of its foundation, for it is related that amongst the warlike Trojans, when with their leader Brutus they triumphantly seized upon the island, then called Albion, next Britain, and

---

121 A transcription of this origin myth is provided in 'Translatio universitatis de loco in locum', in *Munimenta academia, Or Documents Illustrative of Academical Life and Studies at Oxford*, ed. Henry Anstey, 2 vols, Rolls Series 50 (London, 1868), 2:367–9.
122 Parker, *The Early History of Oxford*, 307. Parker offers a useful discussion of the myth at 10–12.

lastly England, certain Philosophers came and chose a suitable place of habitation in this island, on which the Philosophers who had been Greek bestowed a name that they have left behind them as a record of their presence, and that exists to the present day, that is to say *Grekelade* [an ancient name for Oxford].)[123]

The *Historiola*'s myth patently builds on foundations provided by Geoffrey of Monmouth and is plainly a narrative of *translatio studii et imperii*; for, when Brutus colonized Britain, he brought with him 'warlike Trojans' as well as Greek philosophers who established the earliest and best university of the Latin-speaking world at Oxford. Notably, the *Historiola* implies a direct transfer of power and learning from the ancient world to England. France is entirely circumvented.

A second, more popular Oxford origin story is that which attributed the university's foundation to Alfred the Great. The earliest surviving account of Alfred's creation of the University of Oxford comes to us in Ranulf Higden's *Polychronicon*, written c. 1327–64 during the reign of Edward III. In the opening of book VI, Higden summarizes Alfred's life thus:

> Psalmos et orations in unum libellum compegit quem manuale appellans, i. e. *hand boc* secum jugiter tulit; grammaticam minus perfecte attigit, eo quod tunc temporis in toto regno suo nullus grammaticae doctor extiterit. Quamobrem ad consilium Neoti Abbatis quem crebro visitaverat, scholas publicas variarum atrium apud Oxoniam primus instituit; quam urbem in multis articulis privilegiari procuravit. Neminem illiteratum ad quamcunque dignitatem ecclesisticam ascendere permittens, optimas leges in linguam Angliam convertit.

> (He put together psalms and prayers into one little book that he called a manual, that is, *handbook*, and carried it carefully about with him. He attained but a very imperfect knowledge of grammar for the reason that at that time there did not exist throughout the whole kingdom a teacher of grammar. Wherefore by the counsel of S. Neot the Abbot, whom he frequently visited, he was the first to establish schools for the various arts in Oxford; to which city he granted privileges of many kinds. Allowing no illiterate person to be promoted to any ecclesiastical dignity, he translated the best laws into the language of England.)[124]

---

123 Ed./trans. Parker, *The Early History of Oxford*, 10, 307–8. For a possible explanation of the etymology of *Grekelade*, see 11–12.
124 Ed./trans. Parker, *The Early History of Oxford*, 47, 313–14.

Higden's account of Alfred's life is clearly indebted to Asser's *De rebus gestis Ælfredi*, or *Life of Alfred* (c. 893), in which the earlier chronicler recounts at length Alfred's literary talents, patronage, and promotion of vernacular culture. However, the assertion that Alfred established schools at Oxford is entirely absent in Asser's chronicle and appears to have been Higden's own addition to Alfred's legacy as a scholar-king.[125] Higden's account circulated widely in the late fourteenth and fifteenth centuries; the *Polychronicon* was exceptionally popular and survives in over 120 manuscripts.[126] In 1352, the chronicler was even called to court to present a copy of his text before the king.[127] As early as 1387, the text had been translated into English by John Trevisa for his patron Lord Berkeley.[128] Another anonymous translation was made in the fifteenth century, although it was Trevisa's text that was printed by both William Caxton and Wynkyn de Worde.[129]

Given the popularity of the *Polychronicon*, it is unsurprising that Higden's Alfred story quickly became part of the English canon of myths. The tale was early taken up and expanded by a host of late medieval chroniclers, for instance by John Rous in his *Historia regum Angliae* (c. 1480–6). Rous liberally embellishes the *Polychronicon*'s account and splices it with the Greek mytho-history of the Oxford *Historiola*.[130]

---

125 See Putter's discussion in 'King Arthur at Oxbridge', 66. For an early seventeenth-century edition of Asser's chronicle in which a passage was fraudulently added claiming that Alfred had founded the University of Oxford, see Parker, *The Early History of Oxford*, 39–47.
126 Antonia Gransden, *Historical Writing in England*, 2 vols (London, 1997), 2:43–4.
127 Ormrod, *Edward III*, 14.
128 For an analysis of Trevisa's translation in comparison with Higden's original Latin, see David Fowler, *The Life and Times of John Trevisa, Medieval Scholar* (Seattle, 1995), 176–89. For a discussion of Lord Berkeley's patronage and the context of Trevisa's translation, see Ralph Hanna III, 'Sir Thomas Berkeley and His Patronage', *Speculum* 64.4 (1989), 878–916 and Emily Steiner, 'Berkeley Castle', in *Europe: A Literary History, 1348–1418*, ed. David Wallace, 2 vols (Oxford, 2016), 1:227–39.
129 Gransden, *Historical Writing*, 52. For a facing-page edition of all three versions of the *Polychronicon*, see Babington and Lumby's edition cited above at n. 42. In addition to the narrative of *translatio* animating Higden's account of Alfred, the chronicler at one point curiously notes that Roman *imperium* passed from the French to the Germans, *Polychronicon*, 6:241.
130 See Parker's discussion of Rous's chronicle in *The Early History of Oxford*, 5–17, 50–2.

Higden's myth appears again in Thomas Rudborn's *Historia major* (c. 1440), and it is repeated almost verbatim in the late fourteenth-century *Brampton Chronicle*, also known as the *Chronicon journallense*.[131] Parker adds that the same story is alluded to in a number of the University of Oxford's legal proceedings in the late fourteenth century, usually as a bid to remind the king that the university had been founded by his predecessor and thus deserves royal protection.[132] In the sixteenth century, the accounts that Alfred had founded the University of Oxford were picked up once again by Thomas and John Caius in their infamous feud, in which the Cantabrigian John Caius bitterly argued that these stories were 'certainly nothing else but mere figments, composed for the sake of glorifying the University of Oxford'.[133]

Of course, John Caius was correct. The Alfred legend is completely historically implausible.[134] Still, it was disseminated as fact by generations of late medieval English chroniclers no doubt eager to put Oxford on par with 'Charlemagne's' University of Paris. As we have seen, the myth that Charlemagne had founded the University of Paris was a powerful historiographical intervention by French monarchs. In addition to bolstering Charlemagne's legacy as a scholar-king who guided learning from Athens to France, the myth encouraged the ideological link between the power of French rulers and the learning of Parisian scholars. When the English belatedly claimed that Alfred had founded the University of Oxford, they were taking part in the same cultural phenomena linking knowledge with power as well as positioning their ascendant university in direct rivalry with the famed University of Paris.

The Alfredian foundation myth moreover implied for Oxonians a distinctly English inheritance. Indeed, Antonia Gransden notes that Higden's embellishment of Alfred's legacy reflects the chronicler's patriotic tendency to 'glorify the Anglo-Saxon past'.[135] King Alfred's Englishness and his role as an agent of English vernacular *translatio studii* were particularly accentuated by fourteenth-century Insular

---

131 Parker, *The Early History of Oxford*, 48–9.
132 Parker, *The Early History of Oxford*, 52–7.
133 John Caius quoted in Parker, *The Early History of Oxford*, 32.
134 Parker, *The Early History of Oxford*, 3.
135 Gransden, *Historical Writing*, 52. For Higden's patriotic tendencies and construction of a sense of national community, see also Kathy Lavezzo, *Angels on the Edge of the World: Geography, Literature, and English Community, 1000–1534* (Ithaca, 2006), 71–92 and Andrew Galloway, 'Latin England', in *Imagining a Medieval English Nation*, ed. Kathy Lavezzo (Minneapolis, 2003), 41–95 (45–73).

authors concerned with contemporary debates about the translation of the Bible into English, among them Trevisa. In the preface to his translation of the *Polychronicon*, known as the 'Dialogue between a Lord and a Clerk upon Translation', Trevisa emphasized that Alfred's *translatio* of knowledge to England involved the linguistic translation of religious and secular knowledge into the English vernacular:[136]

> Aristoteles bokes and oþere bokes also of logyk and of philosofy were translated out of Gru [Greek] into Latyn. Also atte prayng of Kyng Charles, Iohn Scot translated seint Denys hys bokes out of Gru ynto Latyn. Also holy wryt was translated out of Hebrew ynto Gru and out of Gru into Latyn and þanne out of Latyn ynto Frensch. Þanne what haþ Englysch trespased þat hyt myȝt noȝt be translated into Englysch? Also Kyng Alured [Alfred], þat foundede þe vnyuersite of Oxenford, translated þe beste lawes into Englysch tonge and gret del of þe Sauter out of Latyn into Englysch, and made Wyrefryth, byschop of Wyrcetre, translate Seint Gregore hys bokes Dialoges out of Latyn ynto Saxon.[137]

Therefore, just as Carolingian kings (here Charles the Bald) had Greek and Latin texts translated into French, so too King Alfred rightfully had ancient wisdom, even the Bible, translated into English. Trevisa's insistence on Alfred's translation of the Psalter has often been read as a signal of his Wycliffite sympathies and even of his potential participation in the translation of the Bible into English.[138] David Fowler notes that the passage quoted above from Trevisa's 'Dialogue between a Lord and a Clerk' occurs 'in almost the same words […] in the preface to the later

---

136 Ronald Waldron notes that there is at present 'no evidence that Trevisa was directly acquainted with King Alfred's Preface to the *Pastoral Care*, the Worcester copy of which we now know as MS Hatton 20. Everything that he cites of the Old English tradition of translation from Latin he could have learned from Higden'; see Ronald Waldron, 'John Trevisa and the Use of English', *Proceedings of the British Academy* 74 (1988), 171–202 (176–7).

137 John Trevisa, 'Trevisa's Original Prefaces on Translation: A Critical Edition', ed. Ronald Waldron, in *Medieval English Studies Presented to George Kane*, ed. Edward Donald Kennedy, Ronald Waldron, and Joseph Wittig (Cambridge, UK, 1988), 285–99 (292); Waldron's critical notations have been omitted.

138 See Anne Hudson, *The Premature Reformation: Wycliffite Texts and Lollard History* (Oxford, 1988), 395–6; Waldron, 'John Trevisa and the Use of English', esp. 176–7; David Fowler, *The Life and Times of John Trevisa*, esp. chapter 5 'The English Bible', 213–34; and Emily Steiner, *John Trevisa's Information Age: Knowledge and the Pursuit of Literature, c. 1400* (Oxford, 2021), esp. chapter 3 'Radical Historiography: Langland, Trevisa, and the Polychronicon', 66–105.

version of the Wycliffite Bible itself'.[139] Like the French translators of the court of Charles V, English authors of the late fourteenth century put the myth of *translatio* to use to justify the viability of their vernacular as a language capable of expressing both religious and secular truths.[140] In England, this myth was anchored by the figure of Alfred the Great, who was proudly remembered as the Anglo-Saxon scholar-king who had transferred knowledge to England both through his translation of texts into the English vernacular and his foundation of the preeminent center of English learning at Oxford.

Conclusion

The English evocations of *translatio studii et imperii* we have witnessed in this essay bear testimony to the cultural competition between England and France in the late Middle Ages. In England, as in France, the well-rooted repertoire of *translatio* myths was reinvigorated and expanded in this period marked by the bitter rivalry between the universities of Oxford and Paris and later by the military conflict of the Hundred Years War. Between two 'familiar enemies' that were culturally extremely similar at the highest echelons, the myth of *translatio* functioned to infuse learning itself with a sense of national pride.[141] Books, libraries,

139 David Fowler, 'John Trevisa', in *Authors of the Middle Ages*, ed. David Fowler, J.A. Burrow, and Michael C. Seymour, 4 vols (London, 1994), 1:69–99 (86). The passage in the preface to the Wycliffite Bible reads 'and not oneli Bede, but also king Alured, that foundide Oxenford, translatide in hise laste daies the bigynnyng of the Sauter into Saxon, and wolde more, if he hadde lyued lengere. Also Frenshe men, Beemers [people of Bohemia], and Britons han the bible, and othere bokis of deuocioun and of exposicioun, translatid in here modir langage, whi shulden not English men haue the same in here modir langage', *The Holy Bible, Containing the Old and New Testaments with the Apocryphal Books, in the Earliest English Versions Made from the Latin Vulgate by John Wycliffe and His Followers*, ed. Josiah Forshall and Frederic Madden, 4 vols (Oxford, 1801), 1:59.
140 See Steiner's discussion of the inspiration Trevisa and Berkeley drew from Charles V's translation program in *John Trevisa's Information Age*, chapter 2, 'Paris in Gloucestershire', 1–28.
141 For the intertwined linguistic, literary, and cultural identities of England and France within the context of the Hundred Years War, see Ardis Butterfield, *The Familiar Enemy: Chaucer, Language, and Nation in the Hundred Years War* (Oxford, 2009); Elizaveta Strakhov, *Continental England: Form, Translation, and*

and universities therefore became nationalistically charged weapons in a competition for cultural superiority.[142]

Chaucer in the Hundred Years' War (Columbus, 2022); and Joanna Bellis, *The Hundred Years War in Literature, 1337–1600* (Woodbridge, 2016).

142 In 1425, this competition took a direct and practical turn when John, Duke of Bedford underhandedly acquired Charles V's monumental French royal library while acting as Regent of France, thereby enacting the literal transfer of learning from Paris to England. A portion of these French royal books may afterwards have passed via Bedford's brother – the well-known literary patron Humphrey, Duke of Gloucester – to the University of Oxford. For Bedford's acquisition of the French royal library, see Jenny Stratford, *The Bedford Inventories: The Worldly Goods of John, Duke of Bedford Regent of France* (London, 1993), 95–6, 125, and *passim*. For Duke Humphrey's ownership of French royal books and patronage of Oxford, see David Rundle, 'Habits of Manuscript-Collecting: The Dispersal of the Library of Humfrey, Duke of Gloucester', in *Lost Libraries: The Destruction of Great Book Collections since Antiquity*, ed. James Raven (London, 2004), 106–24 and Alessandra Petrina, *Cultural Politics in Fifteenth-Century England: The Case of Humphrey, Duke of Gloucester* (Turnhout, 2004), esp. 164–6.

6

Margery Kempe's Penitential Credit[1]

NANCY HAIJING JIANG

Near the end of *The Book of Margery Kempe* is an episode that highlights how this famous mystic and prophet of Christ depends on commercial credit. The episode recounts Margery Kempe's arrival in London after a whirlwind pilgrimage to Germany has utterly depleted her resources, leaving her with nothing in her purse and dressed only in a 'cloth of canvas' (line 8179).[2] In such dire straits, Kempe turns to credit to make ends meet, believing that in the city she might borrow money. Until such a loan is arranged, however, Kempe decides to hide her identity so that others in the city might not discover her impoverished state: 'Sche, desiryng to a gon unknowyn into the tyme that sche myth a made sum *chefsyawns*, bar a kerche befor hir face' (She, wanting to pass unknown until the time that she might have borrowed money, bore a kerchief before her face, lines 8183–4, italics mine).[3] She does not have to hide for long. Soon enough, her credit endeavors are successful and, more adequately attired, Kempe visits a 'worschepful wedows hows' (line 8216). There, before the widow and her friends, including some who had previously mocked her eccentric spirituality, she proclaims a message of repentance, rebukes some of their ungodly behaviors, and openly defends herself against her mockers, doing so with such apparent success that they all repent and acknowledge her special status in Christ.[4]

---

1   I would like to thank Katharine Breen, Barbara Newman, Susie Phillips, Annie Sutherland, and Lily Stewart for their care and insights, as well as Laura Ashe, Phil Knox, Wendy Scase, and the anonymous reviewers of this journal.
2   All quotations from *The Book of Margery Kempe* are taken from *The Book of Margery Kempe*, ed. Barry Windeatt (Harlow, 2000). Citations are by the line numbering in the edition.
3   *MED*, s.v. *chevisaunce*, n. 6a: 'The borrowing of money, esp. on security and/or at interest.'
4   At this social gathering, Kempe's slanderers mock her supposed religious

The latter half of this episode has unsurprisingly garnered scholarly interest through the years, with its emphasis on Kempe's upper-class engagement, sensitivities about dress, and public self-defense acting as key examples of the social and worldly dimensions of her mysticism – dimensions that have long marked her as a radical and controversial religious figure within late medieval England.[5] Yet the details of her credit practice that begin this episode are also important, unveiling crucial aspects of Kempe's spirituality. For her successful *chevisaunce* in London reveals not only her ongoing credit knowledge and creditworthiness long after her departure from trade but also, perhaps more surprisingly, how her access to credit ensures the success of her spiritual mission, opening opportunities for her to enter certain social spaces and assert her message of God's salvation and her own religious authority. Rather than simply a throwaway narrative detail, this episode presents her engagement with commercial credit as a necessary part of her spiritual life – one that ultimately helps her to solidify her position as a holy woman of God.

For many years, scholars of Margery Kempe have discussed the ways in which this mystic leverages her pre-conversion trades and commercial practices to shape and advance her unique spiritual agenda. Nicholas Watson, for instance, has examined Kempe's financial entanglements with her confessors-cum-scribes to highlight how their transactional partnerships helped produce her *Book*; Sheila Delaney explores Kempe's agile bargaining strategies to gain sexual independence and negotiate for a mystical union with Christ; and Kate Crassons argues that even

---

hypocrisy, claiming that despite her show of pious fasting, she actually desires the best fish at table (lines 8188–265). Kempe apparently defends herself so well that 'thei wer rebukyd of her owyn honeste, obeyng hem to aseeth makyng [...] [h]ir spekyng profityd rith mech in many personys' (they were rebuked by her decency, humbling themselves to make recompense [...] her speaking greatly profited many persons, lines 8246–52).

5   For a recent discussion of this scene and Kempe's social identity, see Laura Kalas and Laura Varnam, 'Introduction', in *Encountering* The Book of Margery Kempe, ed. Laura Kalas and Laura Varnam (Manchester, 2021), 1–20 (1–2). On this scene and medieval defamation, see Edwin Craun, '*Fama* and the Pastoral Constraints on Rebuking Sin: *The Book of Margery Kempe*', in *Fama: The Politics of Talk and Reputation in Medieval Europe*, ed. Thelma Fenster and Daniel Lord Smail (Ithaca, 2003), 187–209. On this scene and Kempe's worldly ambitions, see Kate Crassons, *The Claims of Poverty: Literature, Culture, and Ideology in Late Medieval England* (Notre Dame, 2010), 214–15.

presentations of Kempe's saintly poverty are imbued with the ideologies of personal profit, ironically transforming it into a means for her to maintain financial security.[6] Yet within this fertile conversation about Kempe's mercantile spirituality, her credit practice is typically glossed over, read not as an important component of her mysticism but rather as residue from her mercantile past that merely filters through to her mysticism. Crassons, for instance, interprets Kempe's *chevisaunce* as one example of the many commercial comforts that her version of poverty 'accommodates' – comforts that reveal Kempe's continued mercantile ethos despite her outward rejection of it at the start of the *Book*.[7] Yet I suggest that Kempe's credit activity, as the London episode indicates, is more than just a practice she 'accommodates' in her spirituality but is, in fact, uniquely integral to it, deserving of the same scholarly attention as the other, perhaps more overt, aspects of her mercantilism.

This essay illuminates the crucial and multifaceted role credit plays in the formation and consolidation of Kempe's sanctity. I argue that in Kempe's *Book*, credit is far more than an economic practice Kempe maintains throughout her spiritual life; I show that it also becomes one of her strategies for conceptualizing and legitimizing her spiritual life and special status. To do so, I focus on three distinct ways that credit

---

[6] Nicholas Watson, 'The Making of *The Book of Margery Kempe*', in *Voices in Dialogue: Reading Women in the Middle Ages*, ed. Kathryn Kerby-Fulton and Linda Olson (Notre Dame, 2005), 407-10; Sheila Delaney, 'Sexual Economics, Chaucer's Wife of Bath, and *The Book of Margery Kempe*', *Minnesota Review* 5 (1975), 104-15; and Crassons, *Claims of Poverty*, 177-220. For more scholarship on Kempe's mercantilism, see David Aers's chapter on Kempe in his book, *Community, Gender, and Individual Identity: English Writing 1340-1430* (London, 1988), 73-116; Roger Ladd, 'Margery Kempe and Her Mercantile Mysticism', *Fifteenth-Century Studies* 26 (2001), 121-41; Brian Gastle, 'Breaking the Stained-Glass Ceiling: Mercantile Authority, Margaret Paston, and Margery Kempe', *Studies in the Literary Imagination* 36 (2003), 123-73; and Christine Cooper-Rompato, *Spiritual Calculations: Number and Numeracy in Late Medieval English Sermons* (University Park, PA, 2022), 115-28.

[7] Crassons discusses the London *chevisance* episode and Kempe's surprising tolerance towards borrowing on interest, especially in light of the medieval church's stance against usury; see Crassons, *Claims of Poverty*, 204, 214-15. To my knowledge, the only other scholar apart from Crassons to discuss Kempe's credit activity is Anthony Goodman, who mentions in passing that her ability to borrow money 'suggests that her credit was good'; see Goodman, *Margery Kempe and Her World* (Harlow, 2002), 71. Goodman does not explore her credit further apart from to speculate that John Kempe may have left her a substantial bequest after his death.

culture bolsters her spirituality. First, I examine how Kempe uses credit to shape and reinterpret her relationship with the penitential system as she progresses from a lay penitent to a holy saint.[8] As scholars have noted, Kempe, echoing hagiographical tropes, depicts penance as a force for sanctification that elevates her to a level of spiritual perfection.[9] In that state, her acts of penance transform into 'supererogatory acts' (acts beyond God's requirement), which, like those of other medieval saints, are deposited in a heavenly 'treasury of merit' that Christians can draw from to advance their own penance.[10] Yet unlike other saints, Kempe signals her participation in saintly supererogation by imbricating her acts with secular credit culture, depicting them as a sort of 'penitential credit' that circulates to people in whom she chooses to invest, and all the while enlarges her own spiritual estate. Second, I suggest that apart from borrowing the framework and imagery of real-world lending practice to conceptualize penance, Kempe also depicts her penitential credit as converging with and sustaining actual credit arrangements, in ways that eventually garner her a level of financial creditworthiness within her community. As this happens, I argue, the *Book* not only rehabilitates some of the economic reputation and security Kempe lost after her business failures and departure from trade but also accentuates

8 On Kempe's relationship with penance, and her progression in sanctity, see Sarah Salih, 'Margery's Bodies: Piety, Work, and Penance', in *A Companion to the Book of Margery Kempe*, ed. John H. Arnold and Katherine Lewis (Cambridge, UK, 2004), 161–76.
9 On Kempe's use of hagiographic tropes in general, see Clarissa Atkinson, *Mystic and Pilgrim: The Book and the World of Margery Kempe* (Ithaca, 1983); Gail McMurray Gibson, *The Theatre of Devotion: East Anglian Drama and Society in the Late Middle Ages* (Chicago, 1989), 47–65; Lynn Staley, *Margery Kempe's Dissenting Fictions* (University Park, 1994), 39–82; Catherine Sanok, *Her Life Historical: Exemplarity and Female Saints' Lives in Late Medieval England* (Philadelphia, 2007), 116–44; and Karen A. Winstead, *Fifteenth-Century Lives: Writing Sainthood in England* (Notre Dame, 2020), 101–12.
10 On Kempe as mediator for others, see Gastle, 'Breaking the Stained-Glass Ceiling', 104; and Katherine J. Lewis, 'Margery Kempe and Saint-Making in Later Medieval England', in *A Companion to the Book of Margery Kempe*, ed. Arnold and Lewis, 202–3. On the 'treasury of merit', indulgences, and the saints, see Robert Shaffern, 'Indulgences and Saintly Devotionalisms in the Middle Ages', *The Catholic Historical Review* 84 (1998), 643–61; Robert Swanson, 'The Medieval Theology of Indulgences', in *Promissory Notes on the Treasury of Merits: Indulgences in Late Medieval Europe*, ed. Robert Swanson (Leiden, 2006), 11–36; and Swanson, *Indulgences in Late Medieval England: Passports to Paradise?* (Cambridge, UK, 2007).

this creditworthiness as evidence of her credibility as God's witness and saint. Finally, I highlight that as Kempe integrates credit into her spirituality, her *Book* also exposes some of the issues in medieval credit culture. In part, she does so to reveal real precarities within contemporary economic life. But more than that, she also uses this exposure to teach her readers about trusting in the face of uncertainty, enabling them to better believe her spiritual authority and handle doubt. Of course, despite my emphasis in this essay on the trust and creditworthiness Kempe acquires through her credit work, I acknowledge the mistrust she often suffers for her eccentric spirituality, and the tensions this causes within her community.[11] I do, however, demonstrate that her text uses credit to evidence her credibility against her detractors' doubts and, in that process, to critique their misjudgment while affirming her followers who chose to have faith in her. In doing so, I draw our attention to a novel way that the *Book* constructs, reinforces, and ultimately defends the validity of Kempe's saintly status.

To make legible Kempe's spiritual uses of credit, I begin by situating her in the history of women's credit work, placing her alongside case studies of other creditworthy women in the late medieval period who used their credit access to affect their position within the community. This section shows that while the medieval credit market was dominated by male participants, many women did have significant roles in their credit network that established them as valuable, creditworthy contributors in their commercial circle – a position that Kempe herself occupied as an independent businesswoman in her hometown of Lynn. Constructing a rich credit context through which to understand Kempe's mercantile background, I turn to her dramatic conversion as she leaves a life of trade and enters into one of penitential fervor. I then examine how her

11 On Kempe's social ostracism, see Staley, *Dissenting Fictions*, 47–51. Despite the critical tendency to focus on Kempe's detractors, there is a current trend in Kempe scholarship, which this essay builds on, to foreground the importance of community within her *Book*. For instance, Rebecca Krug has focused on the affective spiritual community Kempe generates with her readers (*Margery Kempe and the Lonely Reader* (Ithaca, 2017)); Anthony Bale and Daniela Giosuè have explored Kempe's female network ('A Women's Network in Fifteenth-century Rome: Margery Kempe Encounters "Margaret Florentyne"', in *Encountering* The Book of Margery Kempe, ed. Kalas and Varnam, 185–204); and Susan Maddock investigates the support Kempe had from her friends from Lynn ('Margery Kempe's Hometown and Worthy Kin', in *Encountering* The Book of Margery Kempe, ed. Kalas and Varnam, 163–84).

previous credit knowledge helped her remake her acts of penance into transferrable assets for others while also affording her greater spiritual, economic, and even textual authority. In this way, I show that credit in *The Book of Margery Kempe* is not simply a commercial habit from Kempe's past that seeps into her new life in Christ; it actually functions as one of her key tools for establishing the legitimacy of that life, crucially enabling her self-fashioning into one of God's holy saints.

Creditworthy Women

As economic life in late medieval England grew evermore reliant on financial credit, establishing oneself as a creditworthy person became a concern for all medieval subjects.[12] In an era with no formal credit ratings, this task not only involved proving one's financial solvency and repayment capacity but also included a wide constellation of social metrics, from communal standing, generosity to neighbors, moral reputation, religious piety, physical attire, and even caliber of friends.[13] Indeed, as a number of scholars have posited, nearly all aspects of a person's life during this period – whether it be their household name or their religious virtue – could be commodified as 'currency' for the circulation of credit.[14] Yet apart from simply depending on numerous arenas, pre-modern creditworthiness also informed and affected those same arenas, such that

12   Scholars have long shown the ubiquity of credit in both urban and rural contexts in the medieval period. See, for example, Christopher Briggs, *Credit and Village Society in Fourteenth-Century England* (Oxford, 2009); Richard Goddard, *Credit and Trade in Later Medieval England, 1353–1532* (London, 2016); and Daniel Lord Smail, *Legal Plunder: Households and Debt Collection in Late Medieval Europe* (Cambridge, MA, 2016), 90.
13   Craig Muldrew's seminal study on the social history of credit in early modern England pioneered research into how pre-modern creditworthiness depended on reputation in community; see Muldrew, *Economy of Obligation: The Culture of Credit and Social Relations in Early Modern England* (New York, 1998). For similar arguments about medieval credit, see Martha Howell, *Commerce before Capitalism: 1300–1600* (Cambridge, UK, 2010), 143–207; Emily Kadens, 'Pre-Modern Credit Networks and the Limits of Reputation', *Iowa Law Review* 100 (2015), 2430–55; Smail, *Legal Plunder*; and Hannah Robb, 'Reputation in the Fifteenth-Century Credit Market: Some Tales from the Ecclesiastical Courts of York', *Cultural and Social History* 15 (2018), 297–313.
14   Muldrew, *Economy of Obligation*, 3; Howell, *Commerce before Capitalism*, 29; and Robb, 'Reputation in the Fifteenth-Century Credit Market', 298.

establishing this attribute could greatly influence a person's position in spheres far beyond the marketplace. Alexandra Shepard, for instance, illuminates how pre-modern subjects invoked their ability to ascertain credit to prove their general reliability as witnesses in court, while Ian Forrest, in his innovative study on trust in the late medieval church, has demonstrated that men who garnered trust in the market also had opportunities to shape ecclesial governance.[15] In other words, creditworthiness in the late medieval period not only had economic value but also social, communal, and even religious significance.

Despite largely agreeing that creditworthiness was an invaluable attribute for pre-modern subjects, many scholars have traditionally questioned whether it could be associated with women in that period, with some like Martha Howell suggesting that the gendered obstacles women faced in the credit market made creditworthiness itself 'an exclusively male virtue'.[16] Yet, as more recent scholarship has made clear, while it was harder for women to compete with men in the credit market (especially in more profitable levels of high finance investment), at the local level, many played vital roles in credit networks as trusted and often independent lenders, borrowers, and guarantors – roles that would have required them to establish creditworthiness in their own right.[17]

15 See especially Forrest's example of Hugh Writhel of Dorset who was inducted into a group of elite 'trustworthy men' of the church but also acted as a creditworthy debt guarantor in a property transaction (Ian Forrest, *Trustworthy Men: How Inequality and Faith Made the Medieval Church* (Princeton, 2018), 189). On the language of creditworthiness in the early modern court, see Alexandra Shepard, *Meanings of Manhood in Early Modern England* (Oxford, 2003), 193; and Shepard, *Accounting for Oneself: Worth, Status, and the Social Order in Early Modern England* (Oxford, 2015), 36–81.

16 Howell, *Commerce before Capitalism*, 196. See also Christopher Briggs, 'Empowered or Marginalized? Rural Women and Credit in Later Thirteenth- and Fourteenth-Century England', *Continuity and Change* 19 (2004), 13–43. A crucial account of the gendered inequalities of the pre-modern marketplace is Judith Bennett, 'Theoretical Issues: Confronting Continuity', *Journal of Women's History* 9 (1997), 73–93.

17 See, for example, Marjorie McIntosh, *Working Women in English Society: 1300–1600* (Cambridge, UK, 2005), 85–114; McIntosh, 'Women, Credit, and Family Relationships in England, 1300–1620', *Journal of Family History* 30 (2005), 143–63; Richard Goddard, 'High Finance: Women and Staple Credit in England, 1353–1532', in *Women and Credit in Pre-industrial Europe*, ed. Elise M. Dermineur (Turnhout, 2018); Teresa Phipps, 'Creditworthy Women and Town Courts in Late Medieval England', in *Women and Credit*, ed. Dermineur, 73–94; and Teresa

This section draws out specific case studies of creditworthy women at varying life stages (single, married, and widowed) to reveal the power of their creditworthiness as well as the various avenues and strategies they leveraged to help them acquire that all-important status. While Forrest's work highlights specific examples of late medieval men who benefited from credit culture to influence ecclesial governance, I show the versatile influence of creditworthy women as crucial background to demonstrate how Kempe might have harnessed credit to grant herself trustworthiness and agency in the church.

One primary way women gained creditworthiness in their local lending networks was through working in the market economy. While most women were not recognized as having distinct occupational identities, many of them, of all marital statuses, did work to generate an income.[18] Indeed, there were some women – most commonly wealthier single women unhampered by coverture (laws that denied married women independent legal identity) – who independently ran respected and established commercial enterprises, dealing single-handedly with supplier negotiations, legal contracts, and, crucially, credit relationships that garnered them trust and respect in their credit networks.

Some independent working women not only had the means to establish their own creditworthiness but could also help others gain access to credit. One such woman was Joan Brailsford, who lived in late fourteenth-century Nottingham and worked as a professional potter and occasional ale seller.[19] Brailsford was a frequent participant in her

---

Phipps, *Medieval Women and Urban Justice: Commerce, Crime, and Community in England, 1300–1500* (Manchester, 2020). On early modern women's credit activity, see Alexandra Shepard, 'Crediting Women in the Early Modern English Economy', *History Workshop Journal* 79 (2015), 1–24; Cathryn Spence, *Women, Credit, and Debt in Early Modern Scotland* (Manchester, 2016); and Amy Froide, *Silent Partners: Women as Public Investors during Britain's Financial Revolution, 1690–1750* (Oxford, 2017).

18 On the history of women's work in the medieval market economy, see Judith Bennett, *Ale, Beer, and Brewsters in England: Women's Work in a Changing World, 1300–1600* (Oxford, 1996); and McIntosh, *Working Women*.

19 Brailsford is frequently described as a 'potter' in the Nottinghamshire borough court rolls, CA 1296/I (1396-7) 67, 149, 158, held in the Nottinghamshire Archives Office. It is clear that she also sold ale, see CA 1294 (1394-5) 199. Nottinghamshire borough court rolls from 1303 to 1475 are transcribed and translated by Trevor Foulds and J.B. Hughes for the University of Nottingham's 'Urban Culture Network' at <https://www.nottingham.ac.uk/research/groups/ucn/online-sources/online-sources.aspx>.

local credit market because of the assets gained from her trade.[20] For example, in 1395, Brailsford sued Richard Brasse to recover 3s. 11d. that she had loaned him in cash, which demonstrates that she had enough personal capital to lend to others.[21] Aside from lending, Brailsford was also a trusted borrower, as shown by her debt cases, which highlight the number of times varying people in her community saw fit to give her a loan, with some traders (like John de Etwall) lending to her repeatedly.[22] Her considerable creditworthiness meant that Brailsford was also trusted by traders to help secure the loans of others. In 1394–5, John de Etwall not only lent money to Brailsford but also agreed to use her as guarantor for Richard Brasse over a loan of 20d.[23] Perhaps Etwall trusted Brailsford because of her capital, or perhaps Brailsford had established a good reputation with Etwall through trading relations over the years, or maybe it was because Etwall saw Brailsford as Brasse's close business partner who would keep him accountable (she did, after all, loan him almost 4s.). Either way, both Etwall and Brasse evidently recognized Brailsford's status in the local credit market as one of significant value, treating her as someone with substantial creditworthiness who could maintain her own economic obligations and bolster the credit relationships of others.

Just as independent working women became creditworthy through the assets and status gained from business, so too did many widows

20 Most of Brailsford's credit activity can be traced through her debt lawsuits where she appears as a lone litigant in nineteen cases between the years of 1394 and 1398. Out of her nineteen disputes, she was defendant ten times and plaintiff nine times. The rest of Joan's cases are primarily detinue suits (the unlawful detainment of goods). See various incidents in rolls CA 1294 (1394–5), 1295/I (1395–9), and 1296/I (1396–7). A large portion of Brailsford's cases involved the Etwall family, with whom she clearly conducted regular business. Phipps briefly discusses the case of Joan Brailsford in *Medieval Women*, 57 and 'Creditworthy Women', 94; however, most of the information supplied here – from her occupation to her later role as a guarantor – is my own.
21 CA 1294 (1394–5) 611.
22 Since formal litigation was often the normal, final stage of many credit transactions in fourteenth-century England, high debt litigation levels did not necessarily signal someone's financial crisis but rather their commercial integration and creditworthiness, highlighting just how many people trusted them with financial credit. For more on this argument, see Briggs, *Credit and Village*, 152; and Phipps, 'Creditworthy Women', 84.
23 CA 1294 (1394–5) 610.

from wealthy families acquire creditworthiness because of the newfound freedom and resources they received upon their husband's death. Having the same rights to contract as men, wealthy widows wishing to enlarge their estate often turned to independent moneylending and venturing as a source of income.[24] Even without participating in credit work directly, a widow's role as executrix of her husband's estate could also embroil her in numerous credit relationships. Since a significant portion of most people's estates at this time was tied up in the debts owed to them or that they owed, widows involved in these varying credit transactions often became visible credit participants in their commercial circles.[25]

Endowed with the financial means and opportunity, certain wealthy, creditworthy widows sometimes had even more negotiatory sway than the men in their lending circle. Such was the case of Margery Mautby: the widowed mother of the famous Margaret Paston, whose letters detail the lives of a rich mercantile family in fifteenth-century England.[26] When a debt dispute arose between Margaret's husband, John Paston, and their neighbor Lady Morley, to whom he owed a large sum of money, it was ultimately Mautby who helped settle the case.[27] According to Lady Morley, John had reneged on his debt too many times to warrant any more concessions, and she was ready to 'sew þer-fore as law wyl' (sue as the law allows), despite pleas from him and his wife to the contrary. After hearing of her son-in-law's plight from Margaret, Mautby visited Morley to remind her of the Mautby family's creditworthiness and the good relationship between their two households.[28] In doing so, Mautby obtains a debt cessation from Morley – 'a grawnt of

---

24 Goddard, 'High-Finance', 31; Elise Dermineur, 'Introduction', in *Women and Credit*, ed. Dermineur, 5; and Caroline Barron, 'Introduction', in *Medieval London Widows, 1300–1500*, ed. Caroline Barron and Anne Sutton (London, 1994), xiii. On widows' economic position in general, see B.A. Holderness, 'Widows in Pre-industrial Society: An Essay upon their Economic Functions', in *Land, Kinship, and Lifecycle*, ed. Richard Smith (Cambridge, UK, 1985), 423–42.
25 McIntosh, 'Women, Credit, and Family Relationships', 153.
26 On the Pastons, see Barron, 'Who Were the Pastons', *Journal of the Society of Archivists* 4 (1972), 530–5; and Gastle, 'Breaking the Stained-Glass Ceiling', 130–5.
27 This story is found in *Paston Letters and Papers of the Fifteenth-Century*, ed. Norman Davis, 2 vols (Oxford, 1971, 1976), 1:221–2.
28 Margaret recalls that Morley, despite John's tardiness, had always held the Mautby family to high esteem, especially their good debt-repayment record: 'Sche hath wrytyng þer-of hw Syre Robert of Mawthby and Ser Jon my grawnsyre, and dyverse oþer of myn awncetorys payd jt and seyd nevyre nay þer-to', *Paston Letters*, ed. Davis, 1:222.

seyd lady þat xuld nowth ben don a3ens [John] þer-jn' (a grant from the said lady that nothing would be done against John) – overriding John's tardiness and untrustworthiness with her own reputation. Mautby's case reveals a creditworthy widow who knows how to leverage that status as a powerful bargaining chip and is able to smooth over financial and relational issues in order to ensure the success of her daughter's family.

Depending on regional interpretations of coverture restrictions, some wives from richer mercantile families might also play an integral role in their household's credit responsibilities and even exercise their own lending interests.[29] Almost all wives had to manage household resources, which integrated them within the credit relations entangled in those assets, and many were co-partners with husbands in the family business, ensuring that they were equally implicated in many of the same credit networks as their husbands.[30] Furthermore, aside from partnering in their husband's business, some wives also had their own enterprises for which they handled credit negotiations independently, as demonstrated by the spousal debt cases that still identify the wife as the loan's primary recipient. Those cases often issued separate essoins (excuses for non-appearance) for the spouses if they did not show up, further indicating that the wife was still responsible for her loan, and was seen not as an inferior extension of her husband's business but as someone accountable for her financial obligations.[31]

That wives could also have individual creditworthiness can be seen in the case of Alice de Ellehale, a female merchant from fourteenth-century Chester. In 1318, William le Rous sued Alice and her husband William de Ellehale for a sum of 42s. that he had lent specifically to Alice.[32] Rous produced a tally stick to prove the debt, and while both spouses denied its validity, it was Alice who had to swear an oath affirming the tally's

29 On variations in coverture law according to region, see Cordelia Beattie, 'Married Women, Contracts, and Coverture in Late Medieval England', in *Married Women and the Law in Premodern Northwest Europe*, ed. Cordelia Beattie and Frank Stevens (Woodbridge, 2013), 133–54. Wives might also contract under the legal status of *femme sole* that granted them 'sole' responsibility over economic matters, but this was fairly rare outside of London; see Marjorie McIntosh, 'The Benefits and Drawbacks of *Femme Sole* Status in England, 1300–1500', *Journal of British Studies* 44 (2005), 410–38.
30 Goddard, 'High Finance', 27. On the economic enterprises of wives, see Hanawalt, *The Wealth of Wives: Women, Law, and Economy in Late Medieval London* (Oxford, 2007).
31 Phipps, 'Creditworthy Women', 89.
32 Cited in Phipps, 'Creditworthy Women', 86.

falsity.[33] Alice's individual creditworthiness can be traced in several aspects of this case. Recognized as a *mercatrix* by the court (and not just as someone's wife), Alice had acquired the loan without her husband as co-signer, indicating that Rous entrusted her with a high-value loan as an individual debtor and implying that she held high social and financial status in her credit network in her own right.[34] What is more, that the judge requested her oath over others in court, evidently recognizing the loan as sealed under her name, suggests that it was her word and witness that mattered to the judge and counsel, more than her husband's. Alice's position in court is thus indicative of a wife whose creditworthiness was distinguishable from her husband's, revealing the levels of personal agency she had within both the marketplace and a court of law.

Tracing the credit activities of late medieval women through letters and court records reveals not only their rich and varied roles within lending networks but also their ability to assert themselves as trusted and valuable participants in those networks. While creditworthy women were undoubtedly fewer than creditworthy men, the type of credit work they engaged in shows that they became reliable guarantors, privileged borrowers, and wealthy creditors. Working with men and women alike, they carefully navigated the gendered obstacles of the marketplace to cultivate their reputations and assets so as to make themselves creditworthy contributors in their commercial community. Indeed, their creditworthiness granted them certain levels of access and mobility in numerous arenas in that community – from the marketplace to the courtroom. It was this economic attribute that Margery Kempe also acquired in her pre-conversion trade and that, as I will show, she uses to dramatically shape her later spiritual endeavors.

'An ernest-peny of hevyn': From Financial to Penitential Credit

Before she publicly renounced her worldly ways to embark on a radical life of penance, Kempe appears to have been a woman of considerable credit. Married to John Kempe, a wealthy merchant-class burgess (an elected town official typically from elite mercantile families), Kempe is shown to have a crucial role in managing her household's resources and

---

33 Phipps, *Medieval Women*, 71.
34 Alice is identified as *mercatrix*, her husband as *mercator*. Notably, Alice is not referred to as a *femme sole*. For more details on this case, see Phipps, *Medieval Women*, 71.

expenditures – a task that would have situated her within the various credit networks that enabled large households like hers to obtain goods and increase their wealth.[35] Furthermore, if Kempe, as many scholars have posited, was the daughter of John Brunham (one of the most eminent and active merchant burgesses of fourteenth-century Lynn), then she would have brought into the marriage considerable assets, which, along with the significant social clout attached to her name, likely positioned her as a reputable and invaluable stakeholder in all of John Kempe's financial affairs.[36] Most important of all, like Alice de Ellehale and Joan Brailsford, Kempe is presented as someone who ran business enterprises independently (her brewery and her mill), which implies navigating numerous credit negotiations. While these enterprises ultimately fail, it is also important to remember that her text also highlights her initial success as 'on of the grettest brewers in the town' (line 276). As Judith Bennett has shown, notable female brewers in late medieval England – a position Kempe apparently held – were often well trusted in their commercial circles and established within a large credit network of traders and clientele.[37] Kempe, then, in the years leading up to her religious conversion, is easily comparable to the other creditworthy women discussed in this essay – a highly visible and valuable contributor to the credit market who maneuvered around its gendered obstacles to acquire relative economic independence and market mobility within her commercial sphere.

Of course, as her *Book* recounts, the infamous commercial failures that eventually pave the way for her religious life do damage her creditworthiness. Especially after the failure of her horseman and horses

---

35 Apart from a time of about eight months after Kempe's pregnancy when she suffered a trauma-induced breakdown, she is described as having the keys to the buttery: '[She] preyd hir husband as so soon as he cam to hir, that sche mygth have the keys of the botery to takyn hir mete and drynke as sche had don beforn' (lines 238–9). This illustrates her considerable involvement in managing and procuring household goods.
36 In fact, as Kempe constantly reminds John, her family's social and economic status was much higher than his. When he reprimands her for buying clothes, for instance, she mocks him, saying 'that sche was comyn of worthy kenred – hym semyd nevyr for to a weddyd hir – for hir fadyr was sumtyme meyr of the town N. and sythen he was alderman of the hey Gylde' (lines 264–7). On Kempe's relationship with the Brunham (or Burnham) family, see Goodman, *Margery Kempe*, 48–55; and Bale, *Margery Kempe: A Mixed Life* (London, 2021), 25–31.
37 Bennett, *Ale*, 35.

at her mill, word of her cursed enterprise spreads all over Lynn that 'neythyr man ne best don servyse to the seyd creatur' (line 312). But, as demonstrated by numerous instances in her text, the substantial capital she possesses near the start of her spiritual career, along with her mercantile expertise, means that Kempe continues to participate regularly in credit activity. In one striking episode before her pilgrimage to Jerusalem, Kempe barters with her husband for a chaste marriage by promising to take responsibility for his many debts: 'Grawntyth me that ye schal not komyn in my bed, and I grawnt yow to qwyte yowr dettys' (lines 779-80). In an instance that demonstrates both her bargaining prowess and significant finances, her text depicts her as a powerful debt negotiator who leverages considerable personal assets to settle her conjugal debts by paying off her husband's financial ones.[38] Later in her spiritual career, even without the financial resources she had near the beginning, Kempe still borrows from others on her pilgrimages and back home, often for the purpose of buying clothes or making ends meet between her many spiritual endeavors. Apart from the London *chevissaunce* episode discussed at the beginning of this essay, her text also details how Kempe, upon returning to England after her pilgrimage to Jerusalem, wants to 'fyndyn a good man whech wolde lendyn [her] ii nobelys tyl [she] myth payn hym ageyn to byen [her] clothys wyth' (lines 3435-6). A persistent refrain throughout her text, these instances of credit activity depict a woman both familiar with the mechanisms of financial credit and constantly involved in the credit system long after her departure from the trading world.

Yet more than just maintaining her credit involvement for practical, economic reasons, Kempe also harnesses this mechanism to envision her spiritual mission – in particular her relationship with penance as she transforms from an abject sinner into a bride of Christ. In many ways, Kempe's penitential trajectory follows that of other contemporary female saints who inspired her narrative. Like the conversions of Marie d'Oignies and St Bridget of Sweden, Kempe's dramatic conversion is accompanied by repentance and 'gret bodyly penawns' (line 41) – she prayerfully weeps for her sins, fasts, wears a hairshirt and so on – all of which eventually qualify her for a superior, and more intimate, spiritual

---

38   Kempe's debt barter with her husband has fascinated scholars for decades, and numerous studies have addressed it. For some examples, see Delaney, 'Sexual Economics', 104-15; Staley, *Dissenting Fictions*, 62-3; and Gastle, 'Breaking the Stained-Glass Ceiling', 138-9.

union with Christ.[39] In chapter 5, for example, after years of rigorous penance, Kempe receives a vision from Christ who commends her penitential efforts, assures her that her sins are completely forgiven ('I [...] foryefe the thi synnes to the utterest [uttermost] poynt', line 498), and promises her an unending alliance: 'For I am thi love and schal be thi love wythowtyn ende' (line 505).[40] But even as her progression in penance follows the typical hagiographical pattern, it is also uniquely consolidated by notions of financial credit. For immediately after this vision, Kempe's union with Christ is not only confirmed as true but also reframed as a sort of credit contract. Following Christ's instructions, Kempe reveals her vision to her confessor (an unnamed anchorite at Lynn's Dominican priory) in order to gain clerical recognition for her special grace.[41] Upon hearing of her visionary encounter, the confessor confirms Kempe's spiritual exceptionalism by assuring her that she now 'han an *ernest-peny* of hevyn' (lines 535–6, italics mine).[42] Using a term that connotes a small sum typically passed from debtors to creditors as a pledge for loans, the confessor legitimizes Christ's union with Kempe by describing it as a credit contract between her and her savior, and representing himself as their witness.[43] What is more, by figuring Christ as the earnest-penny's giver, the confessor implies that Christ is now answerable

39 On the penance of holy women, especially their 'bodyly' or physical penance, see Caroline Walker Bynum, *Holy Feast and Holy Fast: The Religious Significance of Food to Medieval Women* (Berkeley, 1987), 238–43; Barbara Newman, *From Virile Woman to WomanChrist* (Philadelphia, 1995), 108–36; and Anke Bernau, 'Gender and Sexuality', in *A Companion to Middle English Hagiography*, ed. Sarah Salih (Cambridge, UK, 2006), 104–21 (112).

40 Progression into a state of penitential perfection is witnessed in the lives of numerous medieval saints. For example, Elizabeth of Hungary is divinely assured three times that her sins are completely forgiven after penance; see, *The Two Middle English Translations of St. Elizabeth of Hungary*, ed. Sarah McNamer (Heidelberg, 1996), 92, 96, and 98.

41 On confessors' authenticating their female penitents' visions, see Janette Dillon, 'Holy Women and Their Confessors or Confessors and Their Holy Women? Margery Kempe and Continental Tradition', in *Prophets Abroad: The Reception of Continental Holy Women in Late Medieval England*, ed. Rosalynn Voaden (Cambridge, UK, 1996), 115-40.

42 *MED*, s.v. ernes, n. 3, 'ernes-peni [...] a small advance payment or fee'.

43 On the use of the 'earnest penny' in lending and borrowing, see James Davis, *Medieval Market Morality, Law, Life, and Ethics in the English Marketplace 1200–1500* (Cambridge, UK, 2012), 201; and Howell, *Commerce before Capitalism*, 26.

to Kempe in their new spiritual union, held accountable for his promise to grant grace and love to her even as she continues to commit her life to him. In other words, Kempe is now redirected by her confessor to act as Christ's creditor, with the right to expect pledged returns from Christ in the foreseeable future. Validating her special grace and divine union in this way, the confessor thus invites Kempe to engage with Christ not only in a spiritual union but also in a credit partnership. In doing so, he endows the skills and customs from her previous trading relationships with distinct spiritual worth, transforming them into strategies that she can apply within her new alliance with the Son of God.

Conceiving of Christ as her credit partner allows Kempe to recast her spiritual endeavors in a distinctively credit-centric light, especially her previous acts of penance. With her sins forgiven to the 'uttermost', Kempe transforms her penitential practices from repayments for her own sins into investable assets that Christ, acting on her behalf, can extend to others for their benefit while simultaneously advancing her own spiritual agency – a sort of 'penitential credit' as it were.[44] Perhaps the best place to witness this is chapter 8, that famous account of her appointing Christ as the 'executor' (line 634) of her spiritual deeds. In this chapter, Kempe begins by recognizing how much she owes her confessor, the 'gostly fadyr Maystyr N',[45] for listening to her confessions: 'I may nevyr qwyte hym the goodnesse that he hath don to me and the gracyows labowyrs that he hath had abowt me in heryng of my confessyon' (lines 625, 628–30).[46] Seeing his priestly duties as 'labowyrs' that she cannot pay for herself ('I may nevyr qwyte hym'), Kempe asks

---

44 That Kempe has transcended the need for traditional penances has been acknowledged by other scholars. Salih, for instance, argues that 'with her sins forgiven and her salvation assured, she has finally no need of "penawns"' ('Margery's Bodies', 176). For a recent discussion of Kempe's penances and their progression, see Winstead, *Fifteenth-Century Lives*, 114–15.

45 Spearing has identified 'Maystyr N' as Robert Spryngolde, the parish priest of St Margaret's Church, Lynn; see A.C. Spearing, 'Margery Kempe', in *A Companion to Middle English Prose*, ed. A.S.G. Edwards (Cambridge, UK, 2004), 83–97.

46 In this passage, 'qwyte' meaning 'to pay' fits most appropriately as Kempe speaks of the priest's work as 'labor'; see *MED*, s.v. *quiten*, v. 1a, 'to pay for (sth.)'. Yet since Kempe sees herself as being behind on her payment, she also places herself in a position of indebtedness to the priest in a way that can evoke the second meaning of 'qwyte' as an act of debt repayment; see *MED*, s.v. *quiten*, v. 1b, 'to repay a debt [...] discharge (a debt)'.

Christ to remunerate the priest by allocating him a seat in heaven. Yet still unsatisfied, Kempe goes on to request that merits from the 'god werkys that [Christ] werkys in [her]', 'in prayng, in thynkyng, in wepyng, in pilgrimage goyng, in fastyng' (lines 635–6) might also extend to Master N, transferring them to the confessor as if he had completed it himself: 'It is fully my wyl that thow yeve Maystyr N. halfyndel to encres of hys meryte, as yf he dede hem hys owyn self' (lines 636–8). What had been staples in Kempe's penitential regime are now presented as supererogatory works that, like those of the saints before her, can extend to others for their salvation. But here, more than just mirroring this tradition, Kempe also sees them as quantifiable assets, obtained with her Christ-executor ('god werkys that thow werkys in me'), which he can now distribute to her confessor to make up what she previously could not pay on her own. Materializing her acts of penance as calculatable, creditable goods, this episode showcases both Kempe's progression in sanctity and, most crucially, her transactional power. For in directing Christ to extend penitential credit to her confessor in this way, Kempe transforms confession itself into a reciprocal engagement, elevating herself from a passive penitent into a collaborative spiritual business partner – someone who has enough spiritual capital both to pay the confessor for his labor and to further invest in his heavenly estate should he continue to hear her confessions.

Not only does Kempe extend her penitential credit to her confessor to empower herself within confession, she also extends it to her friends, family, and enemies so that she might engender a broad penitential credit network, spreading her spiritual works even further afield while affording herself certain spiritual returns. After Christ assures her that he will do for her confessor what she has requested, Kempe then asks him, as her 'executor', to give the 'other halvendel on [his] frendys and [his] enmys and on [her] frendys and [her] enmys' (lines 638–9). Pleased with her request, Christ promises to be 'a trew executor to [her] and fulfyllen all [her] wylle', and even tells her that for her 'gret charyte [she ...] schalt have dubbyl reward in hevyn' (lines 642–3), guaranteeing a quantifiable heavenly return for the spiritual expenditures he extends on her behalf. Depicting vast amounts of spiritual wealth flowing to those in need, the scene reflects contemporary discourses on the treasury of merit and Kempe's role as one of its supererogatory contributors. But Kempe's particular vision for how her personal supererogatory acts will be distributed also departs from that model somewhat, shifting its focus away from a *treasury* of merits that any Christian can access towards a *circulation* of merits within a web of interpersonal obligations, favors, and even investments that her Christ-executor will navigate for her – a distribution model that mirrors more closely the credit-laden world of medieval testamentary law than that of ecclesial indulgences.[47] Rather than just guarding and dispensing her merits to all sinners, Kempe envisions Christ paying back her advisors, allocating merits to her friends, crediting merits for pardoning her enemies, and even receiving promises that such allocations will 'dubbyl' her spiritual capital in heaven. Indeed, since Kempe does not actually die at this point in her narrative, these testamentary plans are also figured as ongoing endeavors, outlining a continuous collaboration between her and Christ to circulate and even invest her merits in a way that enlarges others' spiritual capital as well as her own. In doing so, Kempe does more than place herself in the tradition of the saints, joining them in contributing to the penitential system after transcending into a superior spiritual union with Christ. She also carves out a unique position for herself within that tradition – one that allows her to carry out her own personal spiritual agenda.

'I trust ryth wel': Creditworthiness and Spiritual Credibility

As the *Book* goes on to present Kempe's later spiritual life and pilgrimages abroad, her penitential credit and the world of financial credit begin to share more than just a conceptual framework, with the former becoming increasingly implicated in her actual monetary affairs. This is most noticeable in the years during and immediately after her pilgrimages in Rome and Jerusalem when the *Book* depicts Kempe as giving away money as part of her penitential devotion and, most importantly, expecting Christ to provide her with tangible, monetary returns – as if repaying her for the 'goods' that she entrusts into his care. Giving their spiritual credit partnership a striking economic aspect, these moments in the text thus transform Kempe's penitential credit into a sort of

---

47 As mentioned earlier in this essay, a significant portion of most people's estates in the late medieval period was tied up in the debts owed to them or what they owed. This meant that executors were often embroiled in local credit networks. For more on the intersections between executorship and credit, see Paul Brand, 'Aspects of the Law of Debt, 1187–1307', in *Credit and Debt in Medieval England, c. 1180–c. 1350*, ed. Phillipp R. Schofield and Nicholas J. Mayhew (Oxford, 2002), 19–41 (32).

monetary investment and Christ himself into a creditworthy business partner. Yet apart from demonstrating Christ's creditworthiness, Kempe also uses these opportunities to bolster her own status as a creditworthy woman. In part, she does this to rebuild some of the financial reputation she lost during and after her previous trading failures, countering the many doubters and dissenters who mock her apparent lack of economic sense. But perhaps more importantly, Kempe also deploys her distinct form of Christ-given creditworthiness as evidence for her saintly credibility as she attempts to combat the persistent derision she suffers as an outspoken, eccentric, and often divisive, female mystic. Pitting her creditworthiness against the varying forms of mistrust she experiences, the *Book* not only provides an example of a medieval woman appropriating credit culture for her own advancement but also a crucial commentary on the importance of pre-modern creditworthiness itself, illuminating its versatile potential in varying arenas of medieval life, including as a strategy to counter disbelief.

From the first instance that Christ commands her to hand out her goods in alms and endure saintly poverty, Kempe trusts that he will materially remunerate her for what she gives up on his behalf. After her confessor asks her, as part of her penance, to serve a poor woman and join her in poverty (lines 2800–9), Kempe soon receives a parallel summons from Christ to 'yevyn awey al hir good and makyn hir bar for hys lofe' (lines 3012–13). Such material deprivation is fairly standard penitential practice within hagiographical writing, especially in the *vita* of St Francis of Assisi.[48] Yet unlike St Francis, who gladly endured this poverty for many years, Kempe anticipates from the outset that she will soon be elevated from her destitution through divine provisions. In chapter 37, when she gives away all her money, as well as that which she borrowed from her travel companion Richard the Hunchback, she is so confident that Christ will give her money back that she guarantees Richard a repayment for his loan: 'Ye schal come to me in Brystowe in the Whitsunwoke, and ther schal I pay yow ryth wel and trewly be the grace of God, for I trust ryth wel that he that bad me yevyn it awey for hys lofe

---

48 On the parallels between the life of St Francis and Kempe, see Roy Eriksen, 'An Arena for the Holy: The *Imitatio Francisci* of Margery Kempe', in *Sacred Text, Sacred Space: Architectural, Spiritual, and Literary Convergences in England and Wales*, ed. Joseph Sterrett and Peter Thomas (Leiden, 2011), 77–96. On Kempe and Franciscanism more generally, see Karma Lochrie, *Margery Kempe and Translations of the Flesh* (Philadelphia, 1991), 158–60; and Crassons, *Claims of Poverty*, 178–91.

wil help me to payn it ageyn' (lines 3021–4). Stipulating the specific time and place for the return of the loan, Kempe invokes the conventions and expectations of contemporary debt and credit agreements to assure Richard of the validity of her promise.[49] However, instead of simply swearing on Christ's name to seal the debt agreement as most medieval traders would, Kempe actually figures him as primarily responsible for the debt itself, as someone whom she can fully 'trust' to return the money he took for his kingdom.[50] In other words, after following his commands to give away her goods, Kempe contracts Christ as a debtor by writing him into a specific repayment schedule according to her terms, aligning her penitential poverty with the monetary investments she engaged in throughout her previous mercantile experiences.[51]

In fact, in the very next chapter, Christ begins to fulfil those repayment expectations by sending Kempe a veritable barrage of financial and material aid, proving himself to be an unerringly creditworthy partner. First, he confirms in a vision that her act of penitential devotion will not

---

49 On stipulating time and place in medieval credit agreements, especially in formal debt bonds that stand in court (also known as a *recognizance, obligation,* or *bill*), see M.M. Postan, 'Private Financial Instruments in Medieval England', *Vierteljahrschrift für Sozial-und Wirtschaftsgeschichte* 23 (1930), 26–75 (28–9). Of course, Kempe does not actually enter into a legal debt bond with Richard at this point, merely an informal agreement. But her discussion of time and place suggests her familiarity with debt bond procedure.
50 On the practice of swearing on God's name when issuing an oath or a loan, see Davis, *Medieval Market Morality*, 72.
51 My reading of this scene challenges the majority of scholars who read Kempe's extreme submission to Christ's call for poverty as a sign that she, at this point in her text, completely abandons her past mercantile principles. Ladd, for instance, suggests that Kempe's radical almsgiving signals 'a thorough rejection of her former estate and its materialism' (Ladd, 'Mercantile Mysticism', 129), and Staley suggests that here Kempe's actions 'pose a direct threat to a society that identifies its good with its goods' (*Dissenting Fictions*, 71). Crassons is one of the few scholars to read this scene as a reflection of Kempe's mercantile past rather than a rejection of it. She argues that Kempe's disregard for Richard's wellbeing and entitlement to his possessions actually reinforces the materialistic tendencies she had developed during her trading years, see Crassons, *Claims of Poverty*, 200–2. While I agree that this scene has more connections to her mercantile affiliations than previously supposed, I do not think she actually feels entitled to Richard's money, considering how clearly her text describes the money as borrowed, for example: 'And anon sche […] yaf awey swech good as she had and sweche as sche had *borwyd* also of the broke-bakkyd man that went wyth hir' (lines 3013–6, emphasis mine).

only generate merit for others, nor simply garner her spiritual rewards in heaven, but also secure her financial assets on earth, assuaging her potential fears for 'wher sche schuld han hir levyng' by telling her, 'drede the not, dowtyr, for ther is gold to-the-ward […] I have frendys in every cuntre and schal make my frendys to comfort the' (lines 3034–9). Indeed, Christ's pledge, 'ther is gold to-the-ward', reflects late medieval money or property transfer documents, wherein the preposition *toward* is often used to describe the dispatch of goods from one party to another.[52] Christ even maps out the various avenues through which Kempe will receive her gold, specifying that his 'freyndys in every cuntre' will provide for her, effectively drawing on a large network of contacts who will ensure that she is repaid. Having 'good trost it schuld be as he seyd' (lines 3041–2), Kempe then sees instant returns. On the same day as her vision, she meets a man in the streets who, having heard of her 'talys […] yaf hir mony, be the whech sche was wel relevyd and comfortyd' (lines 3045–8). A short time later, Kempe reconnects with Dame Margarete Florentyn, who decides to feed her every Sunday and gives her 'viii bolendinys [coins used in fifteenth-century Rome] therto' (line 3070). And later still, an English priest supplies her with 'gold sufficiently to come hom' (line 3183). In light of such detailed accounts, it is little wonder that Clarissa Atkinson has argued that Kempe's *Book* presents Christ as 'a great banker or merchant prince'.[53] But placed in the context of the debt Christ owes to Kempe, these carefully documented provisions prove not simply Christ's wealth or generosity but also, most importantly, his creditworthiness, demonstrating his infallible track-record of repaying Kempe for the 'good' (line 3013) she gives away at his command. In this way, then, Kempe frames Christ with the metrics of creditworthiness that a late medieval audience would recognize – from his wide circle of faithful associates to his continual repayments – presenting him as her trustworthy business partner who can transform her penitential devotion into a secure economic venture.

To a certain extent, Kempe's presentation of Christ's creditworthiness reflects contemporary discourses on charity propagated by the church.

52 *MED*, s.v. *toward*, prep. 9, 'in descriptions of the transfer of money or property: to (sb.); from (sb.)'. See the associated quotation from Oseney Reg. 123, 'A marke […] for all seruice, save the seruice of iij s. that þe saide chanons schall acquite towarde the Chefe lordes, that is to say […] towarde Richard flitz Odo, xvi d.'
53 Atkinson, *Mystic and Pilgrim*, 60. On Kempe's divine provisions, see also Crassons, *Claims of Poverty*, 192–4.

Late medieval pastoral instruction on the principle of charity abounds with stories that feature God faithfully providing for those who give goods away at his command.[54] Emphasizing that God will remember all who relinquish their comforts for the sake of others, clerical writers sold charity as a sure way of gaining rewards in heaven, spiritual peace on earth, and even, on certain occasions, material goods. A most striking exemplum that details the material rewards of charity is found in the late fourteenth-century penitential handbook *The Book of Vices and Virtues* (c. 1370), which recounts a tale of how God gives money to a man who donates his cow to a priest.[55] A poor man, who hears a priest say that God will 'ȝelde an hundred [a hundredfold] so moche as men ȝeueþ for hym', gives his cow to the priest in the hope that such fortune will come true. When nothing happens, the man decides to kill the priest for his supposed trickery, but on the way to commit the crime, he finds a 'grete heep of gold', leading him to relinquish his initial murderous intent since 'God hadde ȝolde hym þat he bihiȝth hym' (God had given to him what he had promised him).[56] Presenting the act of charity here as a form of *quid pro quo* with which God must comply, the narrative positions God himself as a debtor obligated to return to Christians what he promises them in advance, or else face disastrous consequences if he loses his creditworthiness.

Kempe's emphasis on Christ's creditworthiness, however, is far more than just a reiteration of pastoral discourse on charity. For after Christ gives Kempe material provisions during her pilgrimage, her focus shifts from his ability to pay her back towards her ability to pay back others, enhancing her own creditworthiness so that people might trust in her. Such is her agenda upon her return to England in chapter 44, where tales of her eccentric behavior, which cause her much 'schamys and reprevys' (reproofs, line 3462), lead many to distrust her. Mocking her excessive tears and consistent wearing of white clothes, residents of Lynn question her display of spirituality, concluding that 'sche had a devyl wythinne hir' (lines 3469–70), with the result that some who had previously supported her begin to 'put hir awey and bodyn hir that sche schulde not come' (lines 3482–3). Other former supporters, hearing

---

54 For a discussion of medieval charity and its benefits, material and spiritual, see Adam Davis, *The Medieval Economy of Salvation: Charity, Commerce, and the Rise of the Hospital* (Ithaca, 2019).
55 *The Book of Vices and Virtues*, ed. W. Francis, EETS, o.s. 69 (London, 1942), 198.
56 There are multiple versions of this story within late medieval penitential tradition, see #4089, in Frederic Tubach, *Index Exemplorum* (Helsinki, 1969).

of her radical penitential almsgiving, start to mistrust her economic reasoning and refuse to fund her next pilgrimage to St James's shrine at Santiago de Compostela. Instead, they ask her to explain her treatment of Richard's money, lack of financial sense, and how she might remain solvent: 'Why have ye yovyn awey yowr good and other mennys also? Wher schal ye now have so meche good as ye owe?' (Why have you given away your own money and that of others? Where shall you now get as much money as you owe?, lines 3490–1). To counter the plethora of doubts directed at her from all sides, Kempe, rather than addressing all of them at once, chooses to focus on and establish her financial creditworthiness, presenting it as tangible evidence of her trustworthiness not only with material resources but also, perhaps more surprisingly, as a holy woman of God.

With care and precision not unlike that of a medieval merchant recording credit and debt in an account book, Kempe documents how she gains money to repay Richard on time, elaborating the return in a way that visibly testifies to her honesty and trustworthiness. Kempe begins by telling her friends about Christ's unerring reputation, drawing on his unbeatable repayment record abroad as evidence that she will soon have enough to return what she owes: 'Owr Lord schal helpyn ryth wel, for he fayld me nevyr in no cuntre, and therfor I trust hym ryth wel' (lines 3492–4). Then, similar to her pilgrimage in Rome, she starts to receive a supply of miraculous monetary provisions, only this time she notes that they arrive not only steadily but also increasingly exponentially. The *Book* describes the first provision as coming almost directly after she has spoken to her friends: '*and sodeynly* cam a good man and yaf hir fowrty pens' (lines 3495, italics mine) – a moment of emphasized immediacy that showcases the certainty of Christ's provision as well as the credibility of her word. Next, she gains money from a female friend of Lynn who 'yaf hyr vii marke for sche schulde prey for hir whan that sche come to Seynt Jamys' (lines 3502–3), detailing with exactitude how this sum enlarges the capital of the first instance (40d., about 3s.) more than thirty times (7 marks, about 93s. or almost £5).[57] After that, noting precisely that 'sche forth and cam to Brystowe on the Wednysday in Whitson-weke' (line 3511), the same time and place she had stipulated

---

57 One mark was equivalent to two-thirds of a pound, or 13s. 4d. For medieval money conversion, see Margaret E. Bowman, *Romance in Arithmetic: A History of Our Currency, Weights, and Measures and Calendars*, 4th edn (London, 1969), 2–14.

for Richard's loan return, Kempe depicts a literal fortune that comes her way, allowing her to return all the borrowed money on time: 'Ther was yoyvn hir so meche mony that sche myth wel payn the forseyd man [Richard] al that sche awt hym' (lines 3521–2). Calling attention to her timely repayment of debt, her ability to keep her word to Richard, as well as the substantial amount of money she received in excess of what was needed ('so meche mony'), Kempe proves herself financially solvent and trustworthy – arguably more successfully than she did during some of her secular business pursuits. Harnessing Christ's reputation and his monetary provision, Kempe thus elevates herself and her own work as creditworthy, rebutting the doubting naysayers who disparage her economic sense by showing her penitential devotion to be a secure, perhaps even profitable, endeavor.

Yet more than simply demonstrating her financial solvency, Kempe's creditworthiness also establishes her authenticity as a holy woman and, thereby, the hagiographic tropes of her *Book*. For her creditworthiness also illuminates the numerous ways Christ miraculously 'ordeyned for hir' (provided for her, line 3520), confirming to her community and her readers that she is truly singled out by him to receive special grace and is, therefore, worthy of support and adoration. Indeed, after Kempe returns Richard's loan in Bristol, she meets a man in that city – named Thomas Marchale – who is so drawn in by God's grace enacted through her that he funds her next mission and becomes her spiritual disciple. Moved deeply by Kempe's stories about God, his love and provisions, Marchale decides to give her the most exorbitant sum yet for her pilgrimage to Santiago de Compostela, 'x marke [… to help her travel] to Seynt Jamys' (lines 3575–6), and even offers to follow her on pilgrimage, where he will join in her radical almsgiving according to her direction, 'what that ye byd me yevyn to any powr man er woman I wyl do yowr byddyng – alwey o peny for yow, another for myselfe' (lines 3577–8). Clearly persuaded that Kempe is a conduit for God's grace through her tales, Marchale adopts her as a spiritual instructor, mirroring her own penitential practice so that he might save himself from sin. What is more, his faith moves him to materially support her religious endeavors, using his money not only to aid Kempe's work financially but also to multiply its spiritual output as he gives out alms on her behalf ('alwey o peny for yow'). Trusting in her spiritual authority so much that he willingly offers himself and his resources for her service, Marchale thus fashions himself into her fervent follower and devotee, acting as a crucial foil against the voices questioning her spiritual validity. Seen from this encounter, Kempe's creditworthiness not only works to overturn the economic doubts of her friends in Lynn but also acts as a unique token of her sanctity, providing a tangible, material signpost that encourages the discerning, like Marchale, to believe in her saintly authority and invest in her spiritual mission.

To 'Prevyn felyngys' and Manage Credit Precarity

In tracing the numerous ways Kempe uses credit and creditworthiness to bolster her own spiritual authority, it is important to note how she simultaneously highlights certain issues in contemporary credit culture. For while Kempe exploits the versatile potential of this economic attribute, her creditworthiness also subverts many factors associated with credit access, such as persistent displays of wealth, physical attire, communal standing, and prudent economic behavior, none of which are typically ascribed to Kempe herself. She is creditworthy primarily because of her unique alliance with Christ – an alliance invisible to others until he performs miracles. What is more, her seemingly reckless treatment of Richard's money appears, under normal circumstances, neither trustworthy nor wise and certainly not conducive to showing financial integrity before others. In light of such behavior, it is not unreasonable of Kempe's friends in Lynn to regard her as uncreditworthy and question her ability to repay her debts. Yet by paying Richard's loan on time, Kempe ultimately overturns their initial judgement, showcasing the power of Christ's hand in her life while demonstrating that the typical standards for creditworthiness can be unstable. In this way, then, Kempe's unique brand of creditworthiness at once depends on *and* problematizes the ways people judged each other in the credit market. For mercantile readers of Kempe's text, such a problematization would have likely struck a poignant chord because it does, in fact, reflect a pervasive anxiety about credit culture that modern scholars and medieval merchant sources have likewise highlighted: that in an era when credit was gained not by credit ratings but by cultivating perceptions, creditworthiness, despite its growing value in society, was indeed slippery and easily misjudged.[58] For medieval credit participants,

---

58 For example, Florentine merchant Giovanni Morelli, in his fourteenth-century merchant manual, stressed the need to 'transact business with trustworthy persons who enjoy good reputation' but follows that up by saying

dealing with this precarity involved developing an increasing number of loan security measures, from lending collaterals to formal debt bonds.[59] Yet for Kempe, as I will show, credit precarity is not just an issue to be exposed and managed but also an opportunity to train her audience in reading and trusting her tokens of divine authenticity in the face of uncertainty – an opportunity, in other words, to further advance proofs of her own sanctity.

This striking duality in Kempe's uses of credit culture (she both exploits and problematizes it) is especially evident once she returns from Santiago de Compostela. In an episode that focuses on how her priest authenticates her visionary insights, or tries to 'prevyn this creaturys felyngys' (line 1760), before she writes the *Book*, Kempe depicts her power of prophecy as manifesting in a series of commercial credit transactions that saves her priest from bad investments.[60] While many medieval female saints, such as St Bridget and St Catherine of Siena, underwent clerical testing to validate their revelations, the validity of Kempe's visions is demonstrated in distinctively mercantile terms. Taking credit as a central theme, the episode draws on this economic practice to emphasize Kempe's credibility.[61] Rather than simply emphasizing Kempe's own creditworthiness, the episode also works to uncover those who are uncreditworthy, in a way that exposes the precarities of determining and establishing creditworthiness itself.

Whereas the clerical tests of St Bridget rested on her ability to differentiate between divine and demonic spirits, Kempe's test involves her

---

'and if you ever get cheated by them, do not fall again into their clutches', insinuating that the best of reputations may turn out to be false. This example is cited in Kadens, 'Pre-Modern Credit Networks', 2442. For more on the precarity of credit and creditworthiness in this time, see Muldrew, *Economy of Obligation*, 157; and Howell, *Commerce before Capitalism*, 25.

59 On the increase in the use of credit security measures during this time, see Kadens, 'Pre-Modern Credit Networks', 2449.

60 While located earlier in her book in chapter 24, this episode likely took place in the latter half of Kempe's spiritual career in 1430, after her pilgrimage to Santiago de Compostela. Watson argues convincingly that this later episode was grouped with chapters 23 and 25 because they all deal with the priest's testing of Kempe; see Watson, 'Making of *The Book*', 405–6.

61 St Catherine of Siena was tested by the Dominican order while St Bridget was examined by her priest-scribe Alfonso de Jaén; see Dillon, 'Holy Women', 124–6; and John Coakley, *Women, Men, and Spiritual Power: Female Saints and Their Male Collaborators* (New York, 2006), 25–44.

identifying bad debtors.[62] The first is a young man who asks the priest for a loan to make ends meet while on the run after an accidental murder. The priest is inclined to help, drawn in by the man's 'fayr fetury[s]' (fair features, line 1788), 'gestur and vestur' (line 1790), and promise of many 'good frendys in other placys' (line 1820) who will repay the debt. But when the priest asks Kempe and a reputable burgess in Lynn to give extra aid, Kempe is 'sor mevyd in hir spiryt ageyns that yong man' (line 1799) and tells the priest to give his money instead to those 'thei knewyn wel for wel dysposyd folke and hir owyn neybowrys than other strawngerys' (lines 1802–4). Despite the burgess's support for Kempe's advice, the priest refuses to listen and lends the man silver anyway, at which point Kempe has a 'felyng in hir sowle as owyr Lord wold schewyn' (line 1832) that the man will never return with the money again. Highlighting that her prophecy does come true, much to the priest's chagrin, the scene not only demonstrates the efficacy of Kempe's revelations but also problematizes the language and metrics of creditworthiness. For despite his eventual unreliability, the young man's appearance, attire, and supposed friendship network, are, in fact, factors typically associated with a creditworthy person. His failure to return the money and his deception of the priest, then, call into question how securely these factors correlate with creditworthiness. In comparison with Kempe's timely return of Richard's loan, the man's default on his loan throws her own creditworthiness into even sharper relief. Kempe might have none of the young man's outward fineries or his initial displays of trustworthiness, yet she is undeniably creditworthy through Christ's grace. Subverting expectations within credit culture, the contrast between Kempe and the young man challenges the reliability of external appearances for determining a person's value or trustworthiness. In doing so, it not only enhances the validity of Kempe's unique, Christ-given creditworthiness; it also underscores the risky nature of lending itself during a time when credit decisions were often based on outward appearances that could easily deceive rather than on formal credit ratings.

Yet even as this episode illustrates the precarious nature of credit, it is not dismissive of credit itself nor does it take credit precarity as a sign to abandon this market altogether. In fact, the episode also critiques those like the priest who do not take the problem of credit precarity seriously and enter loan agreements without due caution. At several moments in

---

62 *The Revelations of St. Birgitta of Sweden Volume I: Liber Caelestis, Books I–III*, introduction and notes by Bridget Morris, trans. Denis Searby (Oxford, 2006), 58.

this scene, the priest's foolishness and gullibility are judged just as much as the young man's deception. The text emphasizes the priest's lack of knowledge about the young man's history, 'whech yong man the preste nevyr sey beforn' (lines 1776–7), his prideful belief in the young man's 'flateryng hym' (line 1819), and ultimately his rashness in lending money 'in schort tyme [...] he lent hym sylver' (lines 1821–4) – actions that were continually warned against in contemporary credit discourse.[63] Aware that creditworthiness could be misread, medieval borrowers and investors stressed prolonged caution before entering credit arrangements, which meant taking time to know a person and test their creditworthiness, and gathering evidence of their uprightness through protracted personal interaction, or finding trusted people who could vouch for them.[64] For instance, an ordinance for Northampton in 1260 stresses that anyone giving credit at a fair should not agree hastily but first 'find out how the borrower left his last creditor'.[65] Indeed, Kempe herself practically spells this advice out to the priest when he comes to her in support of the young man, informing him, alongside her divine promptings against the young man, that this person is a 'strawnger', and there are others whom 'thei *knewyn wel* for wel dysposyd folke' (lines 1802–3, italics mine). According to several scholars, this interjection indicates Kempe's conservative stance on charity, revealing at once her concerns about the underserving poor and her somewhat bourgeois attitude towards alms.[66] Yet Kempe's words also align closely with the pre-modern credit advice to know the debtor first.[67] The priest's

63 On how the episode emphasizes the priest's gullibility, see Staley, *Dissenting Fictions*, 73.
64 The emphasis placed on finding someone to vouch for a borrower before lending can be seen in the case of Mathys Verge, a Venetian merchant, who arrived in Antwerp in 1542 but could not obtain a loan until a prominent local merchant gave assurance of his viability; for this case, see Donald Harreld, 'Foreign Merchants and International Trade Networks in the Sixteenth-Century Low Countries', *Journal of European Economic History* 39 (2010), 11–31 (22); and more generally Smail, *Legal Plunder*, 124–8.
65 Cited in Davis, *Medieval Market Morality*, 206.
66 P.H. Cullum, '"Yf lak of charyte be not ower hynderawce": Margery Kempe, Lynn, and the Practice of the Spiritual and Bodily Works of Mercy', in *A Companion to the Book of Margery Kempe*, ed. Arnold and Lewis, 188; Ladd, 'Mercantile Mysticism', 128; and Crassons, *Claims of Poverty*, 198.
67 The phrase 'sor mevyd in hir spiryt' (line 1799) that precedes this advice about giving money to known borrowers contrasts with the line 'as owyr Lord wold schewyn' (line 1832) that precedes her prophecy. The former phrase

dismissal of Kempe's advice and the ensuing consequences, then, not only expose the precarity in medieval credit culture but also show that trust must be founded on knowing or obtaining sufficient evidence about a borrower first.

Of course, in an episode that centers on testing Kempe's own authenticity, this piece of credit procedure becomes far more than just a lesson about taking credit precautions; it also works to reinforce her own credibility as a saint. On one level, juxtaposing her visionary insight with practical credit advice enables Kempe to make her revelation itself more convincing for a pre-modern audience steeped in the culture of credit. Perhaps this is why the burgess of Lynn, a mercantile man likely well versed in credit matters, believes her revelatory word while the priest does not. But on another level, the credit convention of proving the debtor first also highlights a key contrast between her and the bad debtor that argues for her credibility further – a contrast between those who cannot prove their trustworthiness and those who, like Kempe, have the means to do so. Her text makes this comparison especially clear in the next credit arrangement the priest encounters, this time with a book-salesman who asks the priest for a down-payment on a book before delivering it to him.[68] After Kempe prays and receives a warning not to trust this seller, the priest, learning his previous lesson, listens to Kempe and refuses the initial offer. He even adopts her previous credit precautions and sets about questioning the seller's history, his origin, home life, and whether he can bring the book first, none of which the seller can answer sufficiently.[69] The seller eventually leaves, promising to come back with the book, only to be never seen again, at which point the priest writes that he '*knew wel* that the forseyd creaturys felyng was trewe' (line 1877, italics mine). Ostensibly, Kempe's revelations are legitimized

---

suggests that her advice is based on intuition drawn from her experiences while the latter implies that the prophecy comes directly from God.

68   I define credit arrangement here in its broadest financial sense: a mechanism by which people postpone the payment or delivery of money, goods, or any other economic obligations. According to this definition, the seller here would have been a debtor, owing the priest a book for which he (the priest) has already paid. I take this broad definition from McIntosh, 'Women, Credit, and Family Relationships', 144.

69   'The preste askyd wher was hys dwellyng. "Ser", he seyde, "but fyve myle fro this place in Penteney Abbey". "Ther have I ben", seyd the prest, "and I have not sey yow" [...] the preste preyd hym that he mygth have a sygth of the boke' (lines 1865–71).

in this striking ending by the continued accuracy of her prophecies, which convinces the priest to write her *Book*. Yet his concluding words heighten her authenticity even more by invoking a clear disparity between the untrustworthy seller with no verifiable history despite his probing and Kempe whom he 'knows' to be 'true' because he has tested her revelations. Learning from the precarious world of credit to trust only when sufficient proof can be found, the priest thus encourages Kempe's audience to take this credit maxim as a crucial case for her legitimacy. Unlike the two men who appear reputable but cannot prove their trustworthiness to him, Kempe *is* known by the priest who has proven her authenticity and will testify about her before others. Indeed, he is even willing to write the narrative of her life so that it might be perused, understood, and presented as evidence to defend her spiritual status against all who doubt her based on outward appearances, which, as this episode has shown, carry far less weight than Christ's approval.

*

This essay has illuminated the pervasive presence of credit in *The Book of Margery Kempe*. In doing so, it has shown that credit is far more than an economic habit Kempe maintains out of practical necessity. The mechanisms of credit contracts are her source of spiritual inspiration, allowing her to conceptualize and reimagine her role in the penitential system and with Christ himself: the language and notions of creditworthiness are her stratagems for accrediting her own spiritual legitimacy, helping her counter mistrust and doubts from her dissenters, and the precarities of the credit market are her lessons in close-reading evidence, providing her the opportunity to further validate her saintly authenticity. Of course, Kempe is by no means a simple model of credit practice. She establishes creditworthiness despite appearing reckless with resources and initially untrustworthy with others' money, overturning credit expectations to demonstrate the power of Christ's miracles in her life. In this way, Kempe subverts aspects of credit culture even as she exploits them, manipulating those features in numerous ways in order to solidify her divinely chosen status. Presenting such a multifaceted engagement with the late medieval credit market, the *Book* thus reveals Kempe to be not only deeply knowledgeable about all facets of credit but also highly invested in harnessing that knowledge for her own agenda, transforming it into a crucial tool for constructing and consolidating her spiritual authority. It is another example of how her text, as Sarah Beckwith has emphasized, cannot be 'reducible' to either a spiritual or business domain but instead closely amalgamates the two.[70]

By unveiling Kempe's ability to leverage credit to grant herself spiritual agency, this essay has also accentuated the power of late medieval creditworthy women. Placing Kempe in conversation with the other wealthy merchant widows, wives, and working women discussed in this essay shows that while Kempe might be exceptional in her creative appropriation of credit as a spiritual tool, her exceptionalism has its foundation in the sort of credit agency that many other women in her economic position also possessed. She belongs to a rank of late medieval women who asserted themselves as creditworthy and who used this status to affect their position in their commercial and community networks. In emphasizing the significance of credit culture for Kempe's own spiritual advancement, then, her *Book* also invites inquiry into the position of other creditworthy women and their role in all areas of late medieval experience, including those where their authority was typically undermined or erased.

---

70 Sarah Beckwith, *Christ's Body: Identity, Culture, and Society in Late Medieval Writings* (London, 1996), 102.

7

Books, Translation, and Multilingualism in Late Medieval Calais[1]

J.R. Mattison

In one Middle English version of the *Secretum secretorum*, the translator begins his work by layering and concealing the languages, translations, and individuals who have transmitted book and text: he acknowledges part of the textual tradition of this 'booke of good and vertuous condicions to the gouernaunce of his royal persoon. whiche was made by the prince of philisophers [*sic*] Aristotle'.[2] He incorporates not only Aristotle's opening letters to Alexander, but also the prologue of Philip of Tripoli, who translated the original Arabic *Sirr al-asrār* into Latin. Philip's own narrating voice intrudes to explain that he encountered a hermit who gave him the treatise and that 'I translated this booke out of Greeke in to latyn*ne*' for an unnamed 'moost noble kinge', in the same way that Aristotle compiled the text for his king Alexander.[3] This story of the *Secretum*'s translation elides both Philip's use of the Arabic original – instead claiming an imaginary Greek source – and the further passage of the *Secretum* into French and finally into Middle English, the language in which the reader receives this textual history. Indeed, the translation of Philip's prologue in the later translator's work almost seems to claim that 'this booke' is in Latin, not English. In this way, the

1 My thanks to Maggie Crosland, Anne Salamon, Misty Schieberle, Elizaveta Strakhov, the anonymous reviewers, and the attendees of the Multilingual Dynamics of Medieval Literature in Western Europe conference at Utrecht University, 21–3 September 2022 for their feedback and suggestions. I am grateful to Yasmin Ibrahim for her assistance with the records at The National Archives.
2 Oxford, University College, MS 85, p. 70. The text also appears in Secreta secretorum: *Nine English Versions*, ed. M.A. Manzalaoui, EETS, o.s. 276 (Oxford, 1977). The manuscript is paginated rather than foliated.
3 University College 85, p. 73. In other versions, it is clear that the king is Frederick II, but he is here left unnamed.

English of the English translation is rendered less visible. The opening of the *Secretum* creates an edited narrative about its own languages, sources, and movements. In its particular manuscript context, this *Secretum* translation only further complicates the relationships among language, translation, and individuals. A motto and insignia at the start of the *Secretum* indicate that it was destined for a family in Calais. However, the manuscript's illuminations and borders indicate that it was made in London, not on the Continent, despite its Continental-looking bastard secretary script (see Fig. 7.1). Moving between languages, decorative styles, individuals, and physical locations, this *Secretum* reflects larger trends of translation and exchange across Europe in the later Middle Ages. Beyond this single manuscript, books and book owners in Calais were similarly embedded in such movement across borders, what we might call transnational exchange.

England and Middle English participated in a European literary culture: like this *Secretum*, many Middle English texts were translations from French, Latin, and other languages, while English book owners had a taste for works from abroad. English authors, too, entered into literary exchanges with Continental writers.[4] Recent scholarship has elucidated how French was not tied to any notion of France and instead stretched across borders, connecting English readers to those in the Latin kingdoms of Jerusalem.[5] Translation, rather than representing English monolingualism and inward attention, has been reimagined as evidence of multilingualism and outward connections.[6] Both the circulation of individual manuscripts and the transmission of texts in translation

---

4   E.g., Ardis Butterfield, *The Familiar Enemy: Chaucer, Language, and Nation in the Hundred Years War* (Oxford, 2009); Elizaveta Strakhov, *Continental England: Form, Translation, and Chaucer in the Hundred Years' War* (Columbus, 2022); and David Rundle, *The Renaissance Reform of the Book and Britain: The English Quattrocento* (Cambridge, UK, 2019).

5   See the project Medieval Francophone Literary Culture Outside France <https://medievalfrancophone.ac.uk>; Jane Gilbert, Simon Gaunt, and William Burgwinkle, *Medieval French Literary Culture Abroad* (Oxford, 2020); Dirk Schoenaers and Alisa van de Haar, 'Een bouc in walsche, a Book Written in French: Francophone Literature in the Low Countries', *Queeste* 28 (2021), 1–29; *Medieval Francophone Literary Culture outside France: Studies in the Moving Word*, ed. Nicola Morato and Dirk Schoenaers (Turnhout, 2019).

6   Michelle Warren, 'Translation', in *Middle English: Oxford Twenty-First Century Approaches to Literature*, ed. Paul Strohm (Oxford, 2007), 51–67; Catherine Batt, 'Translation and Society', in *A Companion to Medieval English Literature and Culture, c. 1350–c. 1500*, ed. Peter Brown (Malden, MA, 2008), 123–39.

Figure 7.1 The opening page of a Middle English *Secretum secretorum* with a rebus for the Whetehill family of Calais. Oxford, University College, MS 85, p. 70. Reproduced by kind permission of The Master and Fellows of University College Oxford.

across borders demonstrate various aspects of England's transnational relationships. Like the Middle English *Secretum*, which transmits Greek and Arabic knowledge derived from a more immediate French source, such connections layer languages from across centuries.[7] Attending to England's transnational networks – whether material or literary connections between England and places beyond its borders – transforms our understanding of what constitutes English literature. As Jonathan Hsy has argued, the multilingual, transnational 'orbits' of writers and texts can reimagine the Middle Ages 'not as a fixed point of origin for nation- or language-based literary histories [...] but rather as a dynamic world that is already in perpetual motion'.[8] Such interpretations of literature that situate English within broader geographic scales reside alongside those that explore forms of local reading, which are different but no less important. Particular manuscripts, like the so-called Findern manuscript and the so-called Thornton manuscript, or types of manuscripts, like common profit books, might circulate among a specific set of readers.[9] These studies, while not the opposite of transnational ones, more often focus on a locality's internal culture. We can imagine England's literature at different geographic scales.

These broad-stroke transnational connections are made up of smaller moments of transmission, whether certain soldiers returning from the Continent with humanist books in tow, or English poets adopting and adapting French poetic forms. Specific places like Calais, home to the *Secretum* manuscript, facilitate these moments. The town has been a point of scholarly interest as a military and cultural centre located between England and the Continent. This essay examines the role of Calais in connecting England to a European literary culture in the second half of

---

7   On the *Secretum* in England, see Elizaveta Strakhov, "'Travel' of the Mind via Study: *Translatio studii et imperii*', in *The Routledge Companion to Medieval English Literature, 1100–1500*, ed. Sif Ríkharðsdóttir and Raluca Radulescu (New York, 2022), 125–35.
8   Jonathan Hsy, *Trading Tongues: Merchants, Multilingualism, and Medieval Literature* (Columbus, 2013), 7.
9   CUL, MS Ff.1.6; Lincoln, Lincoln Cathedral, MS 91; BL, Add. MS 31042. On Findern, see Richard Beadle and A.E.B. Owen, *The Findern Manuscript, Cambridge University Library MS Ff.1.6* (London, 1977). On Thornton, see *Robert Thornton and His Books: Essays on the Lincoln and London Thornton Manuscripts*, ed. Susanna Fein and Michael Johnston (York, 2014); on common profit books, Wendy Scase, 'Reginald Pecock, John Carpenter and John Colop's "Common-Profit" Books: Aspects of Book Ownership and Circulation in Fifteenth-Century London', *Medium Aevum* 61 (1992), 261–74.

the fifteenth century to elucidate how such a culture both crosses borders and is centred on a particular group of men in administrative positions. I argue that in Calais, transnational reading results not from large-scale geographic movement, but rather localised links. First, I re-examine the evidence for books in Calais, building a picture of the Pale as a centre for literary activity and easy exchange with Continental neighbours. Then, I turn to the family that owned the copy of the *Secretum secretorum*: the Whetehills of Calais. I demonstrate that the Whetehills owned a larger, unrecognised book collection. Situating the manuscript containing the *Secretum* within this collection reveals a multilingual household with specific access to Continental sources. I argue that the apparent patterns of broad, pan-European textual circulation can be traced to localised instances of exchange, providing new insight into the people, places, and circumstances that contributed to English literary culture's Continental links. Further, different patterns of circulation and connection emerge when we examine specific texts as well as their larger genres, particular translations as well as their textual traditions. Focusing on these differences reveals local, personal networks of circulation that form part of the broader, shared tastes for certain kinds of literature. The literary culture of book owners in Calais might draw from a wealth of sources. These local instances of transmission configure the relationships among nations, their citizens, and languages, producing new connections that look across borders rather than within them.

As a location for making translations and buying books from European sources, Calais often represents the overlapping spheres of English, French, and Flemish literary cultures. It is both connected to England and to European centres of book production. Excavating the specific circulation of certain texts, translations, and books within its seemingly pan-European culture contributes to an understanding of the transmission of literature across borders.

Books in Calais

French but not part of France, English but not in England, Calais was, as Marion Turner describes it, 'a borderland, an occupied territory, and a trading hub'.[10] From 1347 until 1558, the town remained in English hands and became a crucial trading post as the home of the wool staple.

---

10 Marion Turner, *Chaucer: A European Life* (Princeton, 2019), 71.

Even after the official end of the Hundred Years War in 1453, the region remained a site of political tension. The surrounding counties were controlled not by the Valois kings but by the dukes of Burgundy and then their heirs, the Habsburgs. In addition to its military and political importance, Calais triggered the literary imagination: scholars have noted that it was a hub of literary activity.[11] Laurence Minot, Guillaume de Machaut, Geoffrey Chaucer, Jean Froissart, Eustache Deschamps, and others turned their pens to Calais and its fate.[12] Not only was the region the site of composition of works like *Knyghthode and Bataille*, written by a 'person of Caleys', but it also 'seems fraught with imaginative potential', for authors writing both in French and in English.[13] Richard Caudrey's *Libelle of Englyshe Polycye*, for example, is intimately concerned with the Siege of Calais in 1436, while Eustache Deschamps refers to the city in several ballades as a symbol of English incursions into France.[14] In Calais, French, Anglo-French, English, Latin, and even Dutch were used in life and in literature, making the Pale a multilingual meeting point rather than a boundary.[15] For the French, the English, and the Dutch, the town proved a fertile ground for thinking about their complicated, interconnected identities.

In addition to its literary potential, Calais was home to a number of men interested in reading. In the second half of the fifteenth century, a small 'Calais group', a name Livia Visser-Fuchs and Anne Sutton tentatively suggest, included men such as William Hastings, Baron Hastings and lieutenant of Calais; Sir John Donne, also lieutenant of Calais and

11 Julia Boffey, 'Books and Readers in Calais: Some Notes', *The Ricardian* 13 (2003), 67–74; Livia Visser-Fuchs and Anne Sutton, 'Choosing a Book in Late Fifteenth-Century England and Burgundy', in *England and the Low Countries in the Late Middle Ages*, ed. Caroline Barron and Nigel Saul (Stroud, 1998), 61–98; David Wallace, *Premodern Places: Calais to Surinam, Chaucer to Aphra Behn* (Oxford, 2004); David Wallace, 'Calais', in *Europe: A Literary History, 1348–1418*, ed. David Wallace (Oxford, 2016), 180–90.
12 See esp. Wallace, 'Calais'; and Wallace, *Premodern Places*, 22–90.
13 Wallace, *Premodern Places*, 45. On *Knyghthode and Bataile*, see Daniel Wakelin, 'The Occasion, Author, and Readers of *Knyghthode and Bataile*', *Medium Aevum* 73 (2004), 260–72.
14 Sebastian Sobecki, *Last Words: The Public Self and the Social Author in Late Medieval England* (Oxford, 2019), 101–26; Wallace, 'Calais', 186–7; Wallace, *Premodern Places*, 48–61.
15 See Butterfield, *Familiar Enemy*, 139–43, 170–2; Ad Putter, 'The Dutch Connection in Middle English Poetry, Chaucer and After', conference presentation, New Chaucer Society, Durham, UK, 13 July 2022.

Hastings' brother-in-law; Sir James Tyrell, lieutenant of Guînes in the Pale; and Thomas Thwaytes, treasurer of Calais.[16] The number of books linked to Calais is relatively large, and I add several more here. These men owned everything from books of hours to chronicles of England and France, sourcing their books from England, France, and the Low Countries.[17] Based on surviving books and records, the material tends towards the historical and the didactic, but is relatively diverse.[18] Certain texts, like Vegetius' *De re militari* and its translations, were particularly popular.[19] Advice to princes, reflections on good governance, and histories tracing Europe's changing borders may have felt like apt reading for England's last remaining Continental foothold.[20] Yet such genres also had pan-European appeal and were owned by English people not associated with Calais. Advice to princes and universal histories, for example, were widespread in Latin and vernacular languages across Francophone Europe.

In addition to the extant books of men working in Calais, other documentary evidence reaffirms these trends, while also hinting at the greater availability of French for those stationed on the Continent. One book list, perhaps providing a sense of literary taste, survives in the household books of John Howard, first Duke of Norfolk. Howard was appointed deputy lieutenant of Calais in 1470 and reappointed after Edward IV's re-accession when Hastings took the post of lieutenant.[21]

16   On these figures in Calais, see David Grummitt, "'For the Surety of the Towne and Marches": Early Tudor Policy towards Calais, 1485-1509', *Nottingham Medieval Studies* 44 (2000), 184-203.
17   Visser-Fuchs and Sutton, 'Choosing a Book', 61-98; Janet Backhouse, 'Founders of the Royal Library: Edward IV and Henry VIII as Collectors of Illuminated Manuscripts', in *England and the Fifteenth Century: Proceedings of the 1986 Harlaxton Symposium*, ed. David Williams (Woodbridge, 1987), 23-42; Backhouse, 'Sir John Donne's Flemish Manuscripts', in *Medieval Codicology, Iconography, Literature, and Translation: Studies for Keith Val Sinclair*, ed. Peter Rolfe Monks and D.D.R. Owen (Leiden, 1994), 48-57.
18   Visser-Fuchs and Sutton, 'Choosing a Book', 80, point out that Edward IV's books, counting both those made in Flanders and those made in England, represent an eclectic collection.
19   Catherine Nall, *Reading and War in Fifteenth-Century England, from Lydgate to Malory* (Cambridge, UK, 2012), 33-4.
20   Cf. Boffey, 'Books and Readers', 67; Nall, *Reading and War*, 33-4.
21   Anne Crawford, 'Howard, John, First Duke of Norfolk (d. 1485)', *Oxford Dictionary of National Biography* (Oxford, 2004-) <https://www.oxforddnb.com/>.

Howard's list survives as an addition in one of his household books, along with the names of ships, without any clear indication of where the books came from or why the list was made. The editors of Howard's household books propose that Howard took them with him to Scotland in the 1480s.[22] Importantly, all twelve titles, as well as two added at a later date, are of books in French and are likely from either France or the Low Countries.[23] These include Honoré Bovet's *Arbre des batailles*, Alain Chartier's *Belle dame sans mercy*, the *Ditz moraulx des philosophes*, and 'Pontius', a copy of *Ponthus et Sidoine*.[24] It is possible that Howard's time in Calais facilitated his ownership of these books in French. This list spans prose and verse, fourteenth-century translations from Latin and fifteenth-century French debates, romance and history writing, and probably manuscripts and printed books. Even though the relationship of Howard to these books is unclear, the list nevertheless reflects the kinds of surviving books owned by men in Calais. As a pan-European vernacular used beyond the borders of the kingdom of France, French held cultural value for English readers.[25] People in Dutch-speaking areas to the east of Calais also copied, read, and translated works in French. Living and working in Calais would have also required good knowledge of French, and any books made on the Continent would have been far

22 *The Household Books of John Duke of Norfolk and Thomas Earl Surrey*, ed. J. Payne Collier (London, 1844), xxvii, 277; *The Household Books of John Howard, Duke of Norfolk, 1462–1471, 1481–1483*, ed. Anne Crawford (Wolfeboro Falls, NH, 1992), xix.
23 In the fifteenth century, England imported most of its printed books from Italy, Germany, and the Low Countries. Imports of printed books from France increased in the sixteenth century. However, not all of Howard's French titles existed in editions printed in the Low Countries. See Margaret Lane Ford, 'Importation of Printed Books into England and Scotland', in *The Cambridge History of the Book in Britain, Volume 3: 1400–1557*, ed. Lotte Hellinga and J.B. Trapp (Cambridge, UK, 1999), 179–202.
24 The list reads: 'La destructiō de troye / la recuel des histoires troianes / labre [sic] des bataìles / Pontius / Sir Baudin cōte de Flandres / La belle d. s. mercy / les acusasions de la d. / le myror delamort/ Le Jeu des Eches / Le Jeu des Des / Le debat de la demoiselle et bō freres / Lamant rendu Cordelier / Les d dessages / Paris et Vienne.' See Collier, *Household Books*, 277. The fifteenth-century prose *Ditz moraulx des philosophes* by Guillaume de Tignonville seems a more likely identification for 'les d dessages' than the thirteenth-century verse *Dits et proverbs des sages*.
25 Cf. Gilbert, Gaunt, and Burgwinkle, *Medieval French Literary Culture Abroad*.

more likely to be in French than in English. The popularity of French-language books in Calais, therefore, might arise from geography and from linguistic facility as well as from literary taste. In this sense, owning French would be easier and more practical for those who spent their time in Francophone areas.

In appearance, many of Calais's surviving books resemble the large, illuminated manuscripts in French that Edward IV ordered from Flanders in the 1470s and '80s. Calais was geographically close to Flemish book-producing centres like Bruges, closer than other centres like Rouen, Paris, or London. Flanders developed its own artistic style, characterised by lavish and realistic borders around miniatures and vernacular texts copied in elaborate *lettre bâtarde*.[26] Janet Backhouse argues that 'it is not unlikely that the distinctive style of script seen in our group of English-owned but Flemish-decorated manuscripts reflects the work of professional scribes employed by the English community at Calais'.[27] Given the number of male book owners associated with the city, Calais seems to have been something of a textual nexus, whether as a centre of writing itself or as a convenient location from which English people could access books from other nearby places. John Donne, for instance, received a copy of the *Faiz du grant Alexandre* from Margaret of York and her stepdaughter Marie de Bourgogne that had been produced in Flanders in the third quarter of the fifteenth century.[28] Richard Neville, earl of Warwick and captain of Calais, can only be associated with one surviving book, made in Bruges in 1464.[29] In comparison to other Englishmen, both Donne and Neville may have had easier access to Flemish books because of their positions in Calais. Importantly, Neville's book predates Edward IV's extensive commissioning of Flemish

26 Hanno Wijsman, *Luxury Bound: Illustrated Manuscript Production and Noble and Princely Book Ownership in the Burgundian Netherlands (1400–1550)* (Turnhout, 2010), 38–79; Thomas Kren and Scot McKendrick, *Illuminating the Renaissance: The Triumph of Flemish Manuscript Painting in Europe* (Los Angeles, 2003). See especially the introduction and essay by McKendrick in this volume.
27 Backhouse, 'Sir John Donne's Flemish Manuscripts', 53.
28 BL, Royal MS 15 D.iv. On Margaret's and Marie's books, see Wijsman, *Luxury Bound*, 190–200.
29 Livia Visser-Fuchs, 'The Manuscript of the *Enseignement de vraie noblesse* Made for Richard Neville, Earl of Warwick, in 1464', in *Medieval Manuscripts in Transition: Tradition and Creative Recycling*, ed. Geert H.M. Claassens and Werner Verbeke (Leuven, 2006), 337–62.

manuscripts. Even though many of the men in the so-called Calais group were closely linked to Edward IV, the taste for Flemish books was not necessarily an imitation of royal interests.[30] Indeed, English book owners since at least the beginning of the fifteenth century had a longstanding interest in books from the Low Countries in all languages, especially books of hours.[31] Yet, not all books associated with Calais owners were contemporary Flemish productions: James Tyrell, for example, added his name to a Parisian *Bible historiale* that had been produced in the second quarter of the fourteenth century.[32] Tyrell's interests mirror the wider interests of fifteenth-century book owners in England, many of whom also owned fourteenth-century manuscripts from Paris.[33] While books owned by Hastings, Thwaytes, and others might reflect a broader interest in certain types of Flemish decoration – corresponding with Edward IV's collection of Flemish books found at Eltham palace – Calais allowed space for access to more than one type of book.

Yet the coherence of Calais as a bookish centre is less straightforward than it seems. It is not clear whether Calais engendered bookishness, or whether men with courtly connections and disposable incomes landed positions there. Because the force at Calais was England's only standing army in the second half of the fifteenth century, a large number of English men of a certain level of importance were connected to the city. For instance, Anthony Woodville briefly held the position of lieutenant of Calais in 1471, but his bookish interests are likely unrelated to his time there.[34] David Grummitt argues that administrative positions in Calais,

30 Cf. Backhouse, 'Founders', 31.
31 Wijsman, *Luxury Bound*, 138–9.
32 BL, Royal MS 18 D.viii. Tyrell's name appears on fol. 178v, 'Pertene a Sire Jakes Tyrell.' Visser-Fuchs and Sutton, 'Choosing a Book', 82, attribute two surviving manuscripts to Tyrell but do not give references. I have been unable to discover the second, apparently surviving manuscript, or if Royal MS 18 D.viii is one of the manuscripts they had in mind.
33 See J.R. Mattison, '"Cest livre est a moy": French Books and Fifteenth-Century England' (unpublished PhD thesis, University of Toronto, 2021).
34 Woodville translated *The Dictes and Sayings of the Philosophers* (1477), *The Morale Prouerbs of Cristyne* (1478), and *The Book Named Cordyal* (1479), and owned manuscripts including BL, Harley MS 4431; BodL, MS Bodley 264; and London, Westminster Abbey, MS 21. See Elizaveta Strakhov and Sarah Wilma Watson, 'Behind Every Man(uscript) Is a Woman: Social Networks, Christine de Pizan, and Westminster Abbey Library, MS 21', *Studies in the Age of Chaucer* 43 (2021), 151–80 (166, 168–70).

especially after 1471, represented direct relationships with Edward IV.[35] Positions in Calais, then, were rewards for loyalty among men who might already be interested in books. Additionally, as the site of England's wool staple, the town had an unusual concentration of economically and politically important merchants, sometimes with vast fortunes and social positions to raise with cultural purchases.[36] While books new and old might have found owners in Calais, it was also a home for the kinds of people who were more disposed to book ownership.

A closer examination of surviving manuscripts reveals too that such English book owners looked both to the Continent and England; they were not exclusively focused on sourcing 'the perfection of Low Countries art'.[37] For instance, Sir Humphrey Talbot, high marshal of Calais and a son of Sir John Talbot (d. 1453), owned an *Anciennes chroniques de Flandres*, produced in Flanders in the third quarter of the fifteenth century.[38] (Space for a coat of arms in the manuscript has been overpainted by Robert Cotton, so it is not possible to determine whether Talbot was the original commissioner of the book.)[39] Yet, Talbot also owned a copy of Lydgate's Middle English *Troy Book*.[40] His interest in a French chronicle from Flanders did not preclude his ownership of an English book from England. Among less prominent members of Calais society, the same pattern is repeated: William Sonnyng, a Calais merchant alderman, owned at least two surviving manuscripts and one printed book.[41] The printed book, Richard Pynson's c. 1492

35 David Grummitt, 'William, Lord Hastings, the Calais Garrison and the Politics of Yorkist England', *The Ricardian* 12 (2001), 262–74 (265).
36 On the wool staple, see Alison Hanham, *The Celys and Their World: An English Merchant Family of the Fifteenth Century* (Cambridge, UK, 1985), 224–51; and Susan Rose, *The Wealth of England: The Medieval Wood Trade and Its Political Importance, 1100–1600* (Oxford, 2018), 72–80, 100–7.
37 Visser-Fuchs and Sutton, 'Choosing', 97 n. 141.
38 BL, Cotton MS Nero E.iii. The name 'humfrey talbot' appears on a square of parchment that has been pasted on to fol. 305v, perhaps drawn from a former flyleaf. The name is followed by 'Dorensavent Bukyngham' – the name and motto of the Stafford family – and a Middle English stanza in this second hand, not Talbot's. See Boffey, 'Calais', 73.
39 Cotton Nero E.iii, fol. 15r.
40 Manchester, John Rylands Library, MS Eng. 1. See W.G. Clark-Maxwell, 'An Inventory of the Contents of Markheaton Hall: Made by Vincent Mundy esq. in the Year 1545', *Journal of the Derbyshire Archaeological and Natural History Society* 51 (1930), 117–40 (137–9).
41 For a brief biography of Sonnyng, see Boffey, 'Calais', 72. These are New York, Morgan Library and Museum, MS M.122 (*De regimine principum* in

edition of the *Canterbury Tales*, indicates not only Sonnyng's Chaucerian interests but also confirms that books were imported from London to the Continent.[42] In this *Canterbury Tales*, Sonnyng added his name in the middle of the *Merchant's Tale* while he was 'demourant a Tournay' (staying at Tournai), beyond the borders of the Pale.[43] Such a placement, within the tale told by the pilgrim most closely aligned with Sonnyng's own profession, seems suggestive. Sonnyng apparently took the book with him as he travelled; if he was still alive at the time, he may even have been in Tournai when it was under English control, 1513-18.

Sonnyng's manuscripts expand his literary interests: one contains a copy of *De regimine principum* in French, one of the most popular European works of the later Middle Ages, and the other includes Bovet's *Arbre des batailles*, another extremely popular French prose work also owned by John Howard.[44] In this latter manuscript, the *Arbre* has been combined with Middle English texts including Lydgate's *Churl and the Bird* and the *Libelle of Englysh Polycye*. Neither the Lydgate text nor the *Libelle* seems to have circulated beyond England, and indeed the latter text adopts a steadfastly anti-French sentiment.[45] Beyond these individual

---

French); Boston, Boston Public Library, MS f Med 92 (*Arbre des batailles* and other texts); and Glasgow, University Library, Sp. Coll. Hunterian Bv.2.1 (Richard Pynson's 1492 print of the *Canterbury Tales*). On the Morgan manuscript, see Mattison, 'Cest livre', 115-18, 190-1, 263; J.R. Mattison and Alexandra Gillespie, 'Books and Materiality', in *The Routledge Companion to Medieval English Literature, 1100-1500*, ed. Ríkharðsdóttir and Radulescu, 39-56 (49).

42 Sp. Coll. Hunterian Bv.2.1, STC 5084. For the provenance of this copy, see the University of Glasgow Library Record at <https://eleanor.lib.gla.ac.uk/record=b3088508>.

43 Sp. Coll. Hunterian Bv.2.1, sig. m7r.

44 On *De regimine principum*, see Charles Briggs, *Giles of Rome's De regimine principum: Reading and Writing Politics at Court and University, c. 1225-c. 1525* (Cambridge, UK, 1999). There are at least eighty-four surviving copies of the *Arbre des batailles* in French, and six whose locations are now unknown. See Honoré Bovet, *L'Arbre des batailles*, ed. Reinhilt Richter-Bergmeier (Geneva, 2017), 765-72. Five manuscripts of the *Arbre*, including Sonnyng's, can definitely be associated with England, and two further manuscripts might have circulated there. On copies of the *Arbre des batailles* and the French translations of *De regimine principum* from England, see Mattison, 'Cest livre', 268-9, esp. n. 996. A Middle English translation of the *Arbre*, translated by Gilbert of Haye, survives in Edinburgh, National Library of Scotland, Acq. MS 9253.

45 On the lack of English texts' circulation in Europe, see Aisling Byrne, 'From Hólar to Lisbon: Middle English Literature in Medieval Translation, c. 1286-c. 1550', *Review of English Studies* 71 (2019), 433-59. For some examples of Middle

book owners, Middle English works such as *Knyghthode and Bataille*, as Daniel Wakelin suggests, might have circulated among Calais society.[46] Despite their access to Continental manuscripts, Calais book owners maintained an interest in Middle English. Calais was not only a conduit for English readers to buy books from European book producers but also a location for reading – and composing – Middle English. More than has been previously recognised, Calais readers were multilingual and sourced their books from various locations.

Further still, there may have been slight changes in the taste for books over the course of the fifteenth century that reflect political circumstances. After 1453 and into the sixteenth century, internal English conflicts, fluctuating trade agreements, and power struggles among the Flemish cities, Burgundian dukes, French kings, French duchies, and the English meant that loyalties and alliances changed frequently.[47] Humfrey Talbot's *Chroniques* demonstrates the shifting geographies of books sourced from the Continent. Talbot's own father had commissioned a manuscript for Margaret of Anjou in Rouen, a popular source of books for English people in the mid-fifteenth century, especially while Normandy was controlled by England.[48] Edward IV's appointees in Calais, by contrast, seem to have turned to the Burgundian Netherlands as their source for books. The king's Burgundian alliances – not least the marriage of his sister to Charles the Bold and his own exile in Flanders in 1470–1 alongside Hasting and Woodville – may have shifted the attention of his administrators towards the Low Countries, despite existing English interest in books from Normandy and Paris.[49] On the other hand, Henry VII's subsequent interest in manuscripts from France may have influenced Calais dwellers during his reign.[50]

English texts in Europe, see Mattison and Gillespie, 'Books and Materiality', 44–5.
46 Wakelin, 'The Occasion, Author, and Readers', 268.
47 David Nicholas, *Medieval Flanders* (New York, 1992), 392–400; Bernard Chevalier, 'The Recovery of France, 1450–1520', in *The New Cambridge Medieval History, c. 1415–c. 1500*, ed. Christopher Allmand, 7 vols (Cambridge, UK, 1998), 7:408–30 (408–11).
48 BL, Royal MS 15 E.vi.
49 For a summary of the complications of Yorkist and Tudor foreign policy, see Rosemary Horrox, 'Yorkist and Early Tudor England', in *The New Cambridge Medieval History, c. 1415–c. 1500*, ed. Allmand, 7:477–95 (478–83).
50 Janet Backhouse, 'The Royal Library from Edward IV to Henry VII', in *The Cambridge History of the Book in Britain, Volume 3: 1400–1557*, ed. Hellinga and Trapp, 267–73 (272–3). Cf. Kathleen Scott, 'Manuscripts for Henry VII, His

Henry had spent his own exile in Brittany under the protection of its duke, François II, where he might have acquired some early fifteenth-century French manuscripts. Although the relationship between Henry VII and Charles VIII had periods of tension as Henry protected his Breton alliances, his taste in manuscript styles shifted slightly westward from his predecessor.[51] For instance, Thomas Thwaytes' *Chroniques de Saint Denis* made in 1487 was illuminated by French and English artists, while his two earlier manuscripts given to Edward IV have been associated with Flanders.[52] Highlighting these possible politicised trends disrupts any vision of Calais as a static locus; it was influenced by both domestic and international relations. Close to the Burgundian Netherlands and French royal domains, Calais had the potential to facilitate English access to multiple book-producing areas, while allowing those on the southern side of the Channel to maintain their access to Middle English literature.

In addition to accessing books from beyond the Pale, Englishmen in the town may have turned to the professional scribes who found homes there. Although Calais was perhaps not thought of as a centre for book production, those with the skills to produce books were no doubt to be found there. Trained scribes must have participated in the administration of the garrisons and the wool staple. Evidence from England and the Continent demonstrates that such documentary scribes could also produce literature.[53] However, it is difficult to trace Calais's scribes because many of the documents relating to Calais and to the wool staple were destroyed when the town was retaken by the French in 1558.[54]

Household and Family', in *The Cambridge Illuminations: The Conference Papers*, ed. Stella Panayotova (London, 2007), 279–86.

51 Janet Backhouse, 'Illuminated Manuscripts Associated with Henry VII and Members of His Immediate Family', in *The Reign of Henry VII: Proceedings of the 1993 Harlaxton Symposium*, ed. Benjamin Thompson (Stamford, 1995), 175–87 (179).

52 BL, Royal MS 20 E.i-vi; BL, Royal MS 14 D.ii-vi; BL, Royal MS 17 E.v. Backhouse, 'Founders', 34–5.

53 E.g., Sebastian Sobecki, 'The Handwriting of Fifteenth-Century Privy Seal and Council Clerks', *Review of English Studies* 21 (2021), 1–27; Misty Schieberle, 'A New Hoccleve Literary Manuscript: The Trilingual Miscellany in London, British Library, MS Harley 219', *Review of English Studies* 70 (2019), 1–24; and Lawrence Warner, *Chaucer's Scribes: London Textual Production, 1384–1432* (Cambridge, UK, 2018).

54 Documents kept in England survive. See Rose, *Wealth*, 76.

Nonetheless, Sonnyng's *Arbre des batailles* is signed by the scribe, who describes himself: 'Nomen scriptoris V.C. congnomine moris / calesie natus sit sanctis consociatus' (The name of the scribe V.C., last name Moris, born in Calais, may he be united with the saints).[55] Here, Moris plays on a wider scribal formula found in manuscripts from across Europe from the thirteenth-century onwards.[56] It takes the general form 'Nomen scriptorius […] plenus amoris', where the scribe's first name, usually of three syllables, fills out the rhyme. For example, in an unrelated manuscript of English verse, one scribe ends Chaucer's *Legend of Good Women* with '*et nomen scriptoris nicholaus plenus amoris*'.[57] Moris creates a particularly Calaisian form of a wider European signature, adapting his own name and hometown to the rhyme. Moris writes in a practised but rapid cursive; the same script was used for both documents and books in fifteenth-century Europe. We might speculate that Moris found other employment copying documents. Other professionals came to Calais from further afield: one of Thomas Thwaytes' books also contains a scribal colophon, which comments that it was made:

> Par le commandement de noble homme messier Thomas Thwaytes cheuallier engloys conseiller de […] prince Henry le vij[e] […] et tresorier de ses ville et marches de Calays. Et fut ce present et premier volume desdictes cronicques paracheue et fine de la main de Hugues de Lembourg natif de Paris poure clerc et humble seruiteur domestique du dessus nomme tresorier.[58]

(By the order of the noble sir Thomas Thwaytes, English knight, counselor to […] Prince Henry VII […] and treasurer of his city and marches of Calais. And this first volume of the chronicle was made and finished by the hand of Hugues of Limbourg, native of Paris, poor clerk and humble domestic servant of the said treasurer.)

---

55 Boston f Med 92, fol. 143r.
56 John Friedman, *Northern English Books, Owners, and Makers in the Late Middle Ages* (Syracuse, NY, 1995), 67–72; Lucien Reynhout, *Formules latines de colophons*, 2 vols (Turnhout, 2006), 1:186–94; M.B. Parkes, 'Richard Frampton: A Commercial Scribe, c. 1390–c. 1420', in *Pages from the Page: Medieval Writing Skills and Manuscript Books* (Farnham, 2012), II, 113–24 (123). Some earlier scholars misinterpreted 'plenus amoris' as the surname *Fullalove*, when it is almost certainly not.
57 CUL, Ff.1.6, fol. 67v.
58 BL, Royal MS 20 E.iii, fol. 94v. Translations, unless otherwise noted, my own.

Here, Hugues could have been working in Calais itself, or somewhere else in the region. The toponymic 'de Lembourg' might indicate an association – perhaps familial, perhaps professional – with Limbourg in the Burgundian Netherlands, even though he makes it clear that he is a 'native of Paris'. This Parisian nevertheless worked in an English knight's household. In contrast to Moris, Hugues uses a more formal *lettre bâtarde* full of flourishes, strapwork, and careful letterforms. While such hands also appear in documents and letters, his work demonstrates the grades of bookhands available to scribes in Calais itself.[59] Further, Hugues' career demonstrates the porous borders between the Pale, surrounding duchies, and French royal domains. Book producers as well as books moved between England and the Continent through Calais. While Calais was a home base from which interested readers sourced books from further afield, it was also the location of book creation itself.

One manuscript of *Ponthus et Sidoine*, which has not previously been linked to Calais, highlights the overlapping geographies of books and book producers in the town (see Fig. 7.2). The same romance is also mentioned in Howard's list of books. In this manuscript, a series of names fill the flyleaves, including the name and motto, 'a que fortune Mongomery T', which appears twice, once in dry point. This signature belongs to Sir Thomas Montgomery, deputy lieutenant of Guînes, Essex knight, and colleague of several of the men mentioned above.[60] Montgomery owned property in Essex and was a knight of the body from 1461 to 1483. In this capacity, he participated in various ambassadorial missions, such as escorting Margaret of York to Flanders in 1468 and conveying Margaret of Anjou to Rouen in 1475, working alongside Thwaytes.[61] During such travels, Montgomery could have picked up this French-language manuscript written on paper that was made in Angers in the duchy of Anjou, which was controlled by Margaret's father René.[62] However, the paperstock could have been transported

---

59 Sebastian Sobecki, 'The Handwriting of Fifteenth-Century Signet Clerks', in *Scribal Cultures in Late Medieval England: Essay in Honour of Linne R. Mooney*, ed. Margaret Connolly, Holly James-Maddocks, and Derek Pearsall (York, 2022), 82–124 (83–6). Technically, the smaller *lettre courante* was used in documents, but it is modelled on *lettre bâtarde*.
60 CUL, MS Ff.3.31, fols 136v, iii r.
61 A. Compton Reeves, 'The Foppish Eleven of 1483', *Medieval Prosopography* 16 (1995), 111–34 (120–1).
62 Paul Binski and Patrick Zutshi, *Western Illuminated Manuscripts: A Catalogue of the Collection in Cambridge University Library* (Cambridge, UK,

Figure 7.2 An unusual full-page initial with an aphoristic saying in a manuscript of *Ponthus et Sidoine*. Cambridge, University Library, MS Ff.3.31, fol. 88r. Reproduced by kind permission of the Syndics of Cambridge University Library.

across Europe to be turned into a book elsewhere. The manuscript contains unique decorative initials with unusual, elaborate strapwork, unlike the strapwork found in many French- and Flemish-made books. The large initial letters – which sometimes stretch the whole length of the text block – contain tight, fine, pen curlicues and cross hatching that contrast with the broad, parallel pen strokes often found in such strapwork. While Paul Meyer claimed that the manuscript 'a été exécuté en Angleterre' (was executed in England), Paul Binski and Patrick Zutshi class the manuscript as 'French (?)'.[63] It is written in a bastard cursive hand, similar to hands found across the Low Countries, France, and even England in the fifteenth century.[64] This particular scribe has taken further liberties, incorporating a possibly unique verse introduction to the prose romance and adding aphoristic and moralistic mottos within the initial letters that reflect a chapter's events. For example, in the section where Ponthus and a group of children survive a storm at sea, the initial reads, 'bonne fortune auint' (good fortune arrives).[65] Written on paper and containing only the strapwork initials with a yellow wash, the manuscript bears little resemblance to the ornate Flemish manuscripts on parchment favoured by Hastings, Donne, and Thwaytes, even though the script is similar. Montgomery's missions to Flanders, France, and Calais would have enabled his access to such books in French, but it is not impossible that he could have bought the book in England, or that it was made there. Foreign scribes and artists are known to have worked in England, and almost all paper used in England was imported.[66] This manuscript's unlocalisability illustrates the muddiness of manuscript geographies: even though Calais book owners seemed to

---

2011), cat. 343; *Le Roman de Ponthus et Sidoine*, ed. Marie-Claude de Crécy (Geneva, 1997), ix–x.

63 Paul Meyer, 'Les Manuscrits français de Cambridge', *Romania* 15 (1886), 236–357 (276); Binski and Zutshi, *Western Illuminated Manuscripts*, cat. 343. Meyer does not explain why he attributes the manuscript to England, and some of his attributions have proved specious. I have not found a second manuscript with similar initials, but this does not preclude the possibility that they exist.

64 Such cursive would have been familiar to the English through the King's French secretaries. See Sobecki, 'Signet Clerks', 82–124. On Ricardus Franciscus, who writes in such a hand, see below.

65 CUL, Ff.3.31, fol. 9v.

66 Mattison and Gillespie, 'Books and Materiality', 42–4, 46; Orietta da Rold, *Paper in Medieval England: From Pulp to Fictions* (Cambridge, UK, 2020), 10–15.

gravitate towards certain types of books from certain places, they nevertheless participated in a wider European book trade.

Montgomery's manuscript adds one further disruption: while many discussions of Calais book owners have focused on men in positions of power and their homosocial, military connections, the manuscript of *Ponthus et Sidoine* indicates that women also participated in Calais's textual world. Montgomery's is far from the only name in the manuscript: his is accompanied by that of 'Ysabell euer to B', 'Elyzabeth', 'Jane b', and 'Gresylde', and the note 'I ves[...] kateryn heranys'.[67] These common women's names could be various family members, but I have not been able to match them to specific people.[68] Importantly, these names demonstrate that the 'Calais group' might hide an array of women readers. The John Teye and Robert Tyrell who also wrote their names might be relations of the Thomas Tyrell and the Henry Tey who witnessed Montgomery's will.[69] Thomas Tyrell is also likely related to James Tyrell, the owner of the *Bible historiale* and Montgomery's successor as lieutenant of Guînes. The names of unrelated men, alongside the five women's names, might indicate that this manuscript circulated beyond a familial network, perhaps among those living at Guînes.[70]

These owners and their books develop a picture of the multilingual, transnational nature of reading in Calais. There emerges a community at once connected to England and to broader European textual networks. Predominantly Francophone with an interest in Europe's leading medieval genres, these Calais book owners were mobile, moving not only back and forth across the Channel but among various Continental regions. They create an impression of Calais as a

---

67 CUL, Ff.3.31, front pastedown. Other names appear on fols 136v, iii r–v, iv r.
68 Montgomery's first wife was Philippa Helion, by whom he had one daughter, name unknown. His second wife was Lora Berkeley, widow of Montgomery's commander John Blount, with whom he had no children. After Montgomery's death, Lora married Sir Thomas Butler and had a daughter Elizabeth, who might or might not be the Elizabeth who wrote her name in the book.
69 TNA, PRO 11/30/327, fol. 22v; CUL, Ff.3.31, fol. iv r. 'Tyrell R' is likely Robert Tyrell, owner of another manuscript, CUL, MS Add. 4089, a copy of the *Secretum secretorum* in French, but likely produced in England. Binski and Zutshi, *Western Illuminated Manuscripts*, cat. 272 ascribe the provenance to England and I agree based on the style of the opening initial. However, it seems likely to me that the scribe would have been French or French trained.
70 On women in book networks, see Strakhov and Watson, 'Behind Every Man(uscript)', 151–80.

crossroads, an access point for popular literature and fashionable books for both men and women.

The Whetehills of Calais

The books of one further family – the Whetehills of Calais – clarify the mechanisms behind the pan-European bookish movement that emerges from the above argumentation. This family's books are not only multilingual but also develop out of transnational textual and manuscript production. However, rather than representing the broad movement of books between England and the Continent, the Whetehills' books show how such movement occurs through specific, individual connections. While the texts owned by the Whetehills participate in those same genres with pan-European appeal read by others in Calais, these texts' particular translations derive from more geographically localised sources. Further, because these manuscripts are in French, English, and Latin, they not only reflect the tastes of a multilingual household but also indicate attitudes towards language. Careful study of the Whetehills' manuscripts and their texts, which have not previously been considered together, reveal localised patterns of circulation, the building blocks of a wider literary culture. Excavating these connections demonstrates the development of transnational reading in Calais, at both a familial and community level. The Whetehill household's reading material brings out a layered interplay of languages, texts, and manuscripts as they are transmitted across borders.

The Whetehills have been linked to University College MS 85, the manuscript containing the Middle English *Secretum secretorum* discussed at the start of this essay, which accompanies two other texts: an English version of Alain Chartier's *Quadrilogue invectif* and a text called *The III Consideracions Right Necesserye to the Good Governaunce of a Prince*. Unlike most books associated with Calais, University College MS 85 was produced around 1470 in London, not France, Flanders, or the town itself.[71] It predates, by some eight to fifteen years, the elaborate, large format, Flemish-made manuscripts owned by Edward

---

71 Kathleen Scott, *Later Gothic Manuscripts, 1390–1490* (London, 1996), cat. 118; *Fifteenth-Century English Translations of Alain Chartier's* Le traité de l'esperance *and* Le quadrilogue invectif, ed. Margaret S. Blayney, 2 vols, EETS, o.s. 270 and 281 (London, 1974–80), 2:39.

IV, Hastings, Thwaytes, and the others mentioned above. It is closer in date to that of Richard Neville, earl of Warwick and Captain of Calais, and to the French books from Normandy that were popular with English soldiers in the mid-fifteenth century.[72] Two folios contain a curious design of a green hill with a pair of blue arms that protrude from it holding a sheaf of wheat aloft. The motto 'Oublier ne doy' also appears on the first folio, repeated twelve times. This design has most often been interpreted a rebus for Whetehill (wheat hill, see Fig. 7.3).[73] Originally a merchant family, the Whetehills were well connected and sufficiently wealthy to afford such a manuscript.[74] Certainly, three texts translated from French that deal with good governance would seem appropriate reading material for a family in Calais.[75] However, further details about the Whetehill family strengthen their claim to the manuscript.

72   E.g., BL, Royal 15 E.vi; on Norman books and English owners, see Catherine Reynolds, 'English Patrons and French Artists in Fifteenth-Century Normandy', in *England and Normandy in the Middle Ages*, ed. D. Bates and Anne Curry (London, 1994), 299–313.

73   Kathleen Scott also points to the Wheatley family of Echingfield, Sussex, whose arms contained a sheaf of wheat, and to Christopher Garneys of Calais whose motto might have been 'Oublie ne doy'. See Scott, *Later Gothic Manuscripts*, cat. 118; Blayney, *Fifteenth-Century English Translations*, 2:40–1; Christopher Garneys likely knew the Whetehills; Elizabeth Whetehill, wife of Sir Richard, appears alongside 'Lady Garnysche' in a letter from one John Worth to Honor, Lady Lisle. See G.W. Davis, 'Whetehill of Calais, Part 2', *The New England Historical and Genealogical Register* 103 (1949), 5–19 (13). Charles the Bold's motto was 'oublier ne puis'.

74   The Whetehills were eventually granted arms. These arms are described as 'per fesse, *azure* and *or*, a pale counterchanged, three lions rampant *or*', with no Whetehill rebus. See G.W. Davis, 'Whetehill of Calais Part 1', *The New England Historical and Genealogical Register* 102 (1948), 241–53 (245). Davis does not comment on when the Whetehills received their arms. Interestingly, Janet Backhouse connects BL, Royal MS 14 D.i to Edward IV's manuscripts, noting its similarities to those owned by Thwaytes and Donne. Its unidentified owner's arms are '*azure* a lion rampant *or* armed and langued *gules*' (Backhouse, 'Founders', 29), which might have a connection to the Whetehill arms with its '*azure* a lion rampant'.

75   In the sixteenth century, the manuscript was apparently in the possession of Michel Otteu, who describes himself as surgeon to Maximilian II, Holy Roman Emperor. He penned verses in Latin and French on four folios for Anne, Duchess of Somerset in 1565. See Blayney, *Fifteenth-Century English Translations*, 2:40–1; University College 85, pp. 2, 18, 180, 185. Otteu reports his own name and occupation on p. 180, but I have been unable to find a physician of this name

Figure 7.3 The opening page of a Middle English translation of Alain Chartier's *Quadrilogue invectif* with the wheat hill design and the motto 'oublier ne doy'. Oxford, University College, MS 85, p. 1. Reproduced by kind permission of The Master and Fellows of University College Oxford.

The family member most likely connected to University College MS 85 is Richard Whetehill, who was born in Northamptonshire around 1410, and who was first a merchant in London and then of the Staple in Calais. He rose to become controller of the town, then its mayor in the 1450s, and by 1461, lieutenant of the castle at Guînes.[76] On the Continent, Whetehill undertook important ambassadorial duties as he negotiated northern Europe's complex and shifting territorial boundaries in Normandy, Picardy, Artois, Paris, and the Burgundian Netherlands. He worked particularly on behalf of Richard Neville, earl of Warwick, facilitating communication between Neville and Louis XI. He also channelled letters directly between the French and English kings, as well as Neville.[77] In one of his letters, 'escript de ma main au chastel de Guisnes' (written in my hand at the Castle of Guînes), Whetehill promises Louis that he will forward the king's messages to Neville right away.[78] The anonymous writer of the 'Abbeville Letter' (a letter from an unnamed official to Louis XI reporting on diplomatic talks with the English in the early months of 1464) comments to Louis that news of the nobleman Jean de Lannoy would appear in 'une lettre que Mr de Warvich luy [Lannoy] a rescriptes que vous envoie, ensemble la copie d'icelles translatés d'anglois en franchois de la main dudit Richart Witel' (a letter in which Warwick has replied to him [Lannoy] that [I] send to you, together with the copy of the same, translated from English to French in the hand of the said Richard Whetehill).[79] This aside demonstrates that Whetehill had a high linguistic facility in order to translate diplomatic correspondence, and

---

in Maximilian's court. Otteu's ownership might indicate that the manuscript remained on the Continent until the mid-sixteenth century. Maximilian II was the great-grandson of Marie de Bourgogne, and thus a descendant of the dukes of Burgundy who controlled the areas around Calais in Whetehill's lifetime. The manuscript was possibly given to University College by Obadiah Walker, master of the college, in the seventeenth century.

76   Davis, 'Whetehill of Calais, Part 1', 241–3.
77   Edward Meek, 'The Practice of English Diplomacy in France 1461–71', in *The English Experience in France, c. 1450–1558*, ed. David Grummitt (London, 2017), 63–84 (68–9). See also Cora L. Scofield, *The Life and Reign of Edward the Fourth: King of England and of France and Lord of Ireland*, 2 vols (London, 1967), 1:322–3; and J. Calmette and G. Périnelle, *Louis XI et l'Angleterre, 1461–1483* (Paris, 1930), 42–54. BnF, MS fr. 2811, fols 53r, 64r contains Jean de Tenremonde's letters to Louis IX. There, Tenremonde spells Whetehill's name as 'VVitel'.
78   Scofield, *Life and Reign*, 2: appendix III, printed from BnF, MS fr. 6971, fol. 388.
79   Meek, 'Diplomacy', 69; Jean de Waurin, *Anchiennes croniques d'Engleterre*, ed. E. Dupont, 3 vols (Paris, 1858–63), 3:182.

enough scribal training to write letters to the French king. Whetehill did not confine his missions to French royalty, for in 1465 he joined none other than William Caxton to negotiate a new trade treaty with the Duke of Burgundy, Charles the Bold.[80] At the time, Caxton was governor of the English nation in Bruges, and it would be seven years before he turned to printing. Whetehill's brief connection with Caxton might hint at his access to similar networks of texts that Caxton later printed. In both his ambassadorial and military duties, Whetehill was well rewarded: Louis XI, for instance, gifted him 'belle vaisselle' in 1464, and Neville paid Whetehill £20 for the same mission, on top of Whetehill's yearly income received from Edward IV.[81] Despite his allegiance to Neville, who was killed by Edward's forces at the Battle of Barnet, he received a pardon in 1471 from Edward that allowed him to keep his French lands and his position at Guînes.[82] By 1473, Whetehill had left Calais and settled in Boughton, Northamptonshire, where he died c. 1484–5.[83]

Alongside his diplomatic duties, Whetehill's connections to wealthy families with literary interests were expanded by his family. His five daughters married important men in Calais and England, including John Pympe, friend to the Paston family, who married his daughter Elizabeth.[84] His only son Adrian continued living in Calais, where he was also controller and held various lands. Adrian's daughter Anne married John Radcliffe, Lord Fitzwalter, another Paston friend. Adrian's son Richard achieved a knighthood in 1513 after the English took Tournai. John Paston III considered a marriage with one of Adrian's daughters in 1476, but the marriage did not take place.[85] Just after Anne's

80 N.F. Blake, 'Caxton, William', *Oxford Dictionary of National Biography* (Oxford: 2004–) <https://www.oxforddnb.com/>; Scofield, *Life and Reign*, 1:356–7; Thomas Rymer, *Foedera, Conventiones, literae et cujuscumque generis acta publica*, 20 vols (London, 1710), 11:536.
81 Scofield, *Life and Reign*, 1:346 n. 4.
82 David Grummitt, 'William, Lord Hastings, the Calais Garrison and the Politics of Yorkist England', *The Ricardian* 12 (2001), 262–74 (263–5).
83 This is the date given by Davis, 'Whetehill of Calais, Part 1', 245, with supporting documentary evidence that Whetehilll was still alive in 1483; Grummit, 'Calais Garrison', 266, indicates that Whetehill died in 1478.
84 Pympe composed rhyme royal stanzas for John Paston II while Paston was in Calais in 1477. *The Paston Letters and Papers of the Fifteenth Century*, ed. Norman Davis, 3 vols, EETS, s.s. 20–2 (Oxford, 2004), 2:417–18.
85 Davis, 'Whetehill of Calais, Part 1', 252, writes that Anne, Adrian's daughter, married Radcliffe, while Colin Richmond, *The Paston Family in the Fifteenth Century: Endings* (Manchester, 2000), 158–9, writes that Margaret, Adrian's

marriage in that year, John Paston II wrote to Hastings praising Anne's servant Richard Stratton. Stratton, Paston noted, had previously been employed by Richard Whetehill at Guînes and spoke English, French, and Dutch.[86] That Stratton's linguistic abilities were a recommendation for Hastings' employment might speak to the nature of Whetehill's multilingual household: it might not only have been Richard Whetehill, in his duties as an ambassador, who used French and maybe Dutch in daily life. Through marriages to Pympe, Radcliffe, and others, the Whetehills were loosely connected to the bookish families of East Anglia.

This brief history of the Whetehills makes them likely candidates for owning University College MS 85. They had the wealth, connections, linguistic ability, geographic mobility, and possible interest in the kinds of texts contained therein. Their history reveals the contexts of this manuscript: they were established in Calais society and administration. Further still, they can be linked to France, Flanders, and England, and they travelled frequently in the region. Their administrative, diplomatic, and social ties may have brought them into the orbit of other book owners and reveal the potential overlap between diplomatic and literary connections.

Whetehill's Oxford, University College, MS 85

Although all the texts in Oxford, University College 85 are in English, the manuscript is deeply embedded in an Anglo-French context, from its scribe to its texts. Most scholarly attention has focused on studying the manuscript's texts individually rather than collectively. Although all three texts have been edited, the translation of the *Quadrilogue invectif* in particular has garnered the most attention as evidence for interest in Alain Chartier's work in England. In other studies, the manuscript's scribe has been identified as Ricardus Franciscus, who is known for his trilingual copying for English patrons.[87] Analysing the three texts and the

---

sister, married Radcliffe. Both refer to the *Complete Peerage*. The confusion may arise from the fact that Anne was sister to *Sir* Richard Whetehill, grandson of Richard Whetehill. Margaret married Thomas Walden of Calais around 1460 and had had two children with him by the time that he died in 1474.
86 *Paston Letters and Papers*, ed. Davis, 1:600.
87 For an overview of Ricardus Franciscus, see Martha Driver, "'Me fault faire": French Makers of Manuscripts for English Patrons', in *Language and Culture in Medieval Britain: The French of England, c. 1100–c. 1500*, ed. Jocelyn

manuscript's scribe together reveals patterns of circulation that provide a new perspective on Anglo-French literary culture. Richard Whetehill, and possibly his wife Joan, about whom nothing is known including her surname, seem the most likely commissioners of the manuscript.[88] Situating University College 85 within Whetehill's household and book collection, which has not previously been attempted, yields new insight into the local nature of European reading in Calais. I discuss these geographic resonances first through its scribe, and then in its texts.

The identification of the scribe of University College MS 85 as Ricardus Franciscus orients the manuscript toward an English and Continental perspective. As Kathleen Scott has commented, the manuscript, with its 'flamboyant, spiky script [...] [gives] the impression of a Continental book', with its *lettre bâtarde* script that attests to the influence of French scripts in England.[89] Using the same script as that employed by Thwaytes's Hugues de Limbourg, Ricardus was either French or trained in France and adept at penning manuscripts in Latin, French, and English: his distinctive, slashing bastard secretary, with abundant hairlines and hairline vertical otiose strokes on *t* in the final position, is frequently ornamented with elaborate strapwork and banderoles containing mottos.[90] In script, the manuscript conforms to the kinds of books available to Englishmen in Calais from France and Flanders.

However, contextualising University College MS 85 among Ricardus's other manuscripts reveals its particular English connections. Only

---

Wogan-Browne with Carolyn Collette, Maryanne Kowaleski, Linne Mooney, Ad Putter, and David Trotter (York, 2009), 420–43 (420–38). For a list of manuscripts assigned to Ricardus, see Deborah Thorpe, 'British Library, MS Arundel 249: Another Manuscript in the Hand of Ricardus Franciscus', *Notes and Queries* 61 (2014), 189–96. On Ricardus Franciscus in University College 85, see Martha Dana Rust, *Imaginary Worlds in Medieval Books: Exploring the Manuscript Matrix* (New York, 2007), 171–3.

88 Adrian was only in his twenties in the late 1460s or early 1470s. Whetehill could have ordered the manuscript while reporting to Edward IV in London. In 1467, Edward excused him from travelling to London to make his reports, which implies that Whetehill was in London at other times. It is not out the realm of possibility, however, that someone ordered the book for Whetehill.

89 Scott, *Later Gothic Manuscripts*, cat. 118.

90 For a description of Ricardus's hand, see M.B. Parkes, *Their Hands before Our Eyes: A Closer Look at Scribes; The Lyell Lectures Delivered at the University of Oxford* (Aldershot, 2008), 118–19. Parkes does not note the vertical hairlines, but they are apparent in manuscripts across the scribe's attributed corpus, from San Marino, CA, Huntington Library, MS HM 932 to BodL, MS Ashmole 764.

four manuscripts attributed to Ricardus Franciscus contain his name or initials. The letterforms in University College 85 match exactly those in one of those signed manuscripts, New York, Morgan Library and Museum, MS M.126, a copy of Gower's *Confessio Amantis*.[91] For instance, all letters are formed with the same angle of the pen and decorated with hairlines and other flourishes. Ascenders, especially on *d*, have an exaggerated curve, with a looping stroke connecting the top of the ascender to the bowl. The top of the upper compartment on *g* is formed with a straight, horizontal line. The right stroke of the bowl on *h* curves to the left below the baseline. Long *s* has a bulge in the middle. Both manuscripts have the same mottos in their decorative banderoles, including 'vive la belle', 'ave maria gracia plena', and 'prenez en gre'.[92] While there is some doubt that certain manuscripts assigned to Ricardus were actually penned by him, the similarities between MS 85 and the signed Morgan Library, MS M.126 situate the former more firmly in his corpus.[93] Importantly, the banderoles may narrow the date. Scholars have argued that Ricardus's *Confessio* was produced for Elizabeth Woodville for her marriage to Edward IV, drawing particular attention to the significance of 'vive la belle' in this context.[94] Using the same phrase in both manuscripts, Ricardus might have created them around the same time, c. 1470.

91 Morgan M.126 has several banderoles with Ricardus Franciscus's first name. The signatures include 'ma vie endure qd R' (fol. 39v), 'Rychard' (fol. 65v), and 'a mon plesir qd R' (fol. 101r). The presence of other mottos, detailed below, connect this manuscript to others also signed with the name Richard/Ricardus.
92 E.g., Morgan M.126, fols 50v, 65v, 67v, 95r; University College 85, pp. 18, 28, 32, 177, 178. Scott, *Later Gothic Manuscripts*, cat. 118, misreads the motto, reading backwards, as 'Belle la vigne', reading *u* as *n* and supplying *g*. These mottos also appear in other manuscripts attributed to Ricardus, e.g., Ashmole 764, fols 26v, 95r. This manuscript was also produced around 1470. In BodL, MS Laud Misc. 570, made 1450, the banderoles only contain John Fastolf's motto 'me fault faire'. On Ricardus Franciscus's mottos, see Rust, *Imaginary Worlds*, 166–76. On the use of 'prenez en gre' in a variety of contexts, see Kathleen Scott, '*Prenes en gre* All Over Again', *Journal of the Early Book Society* 19 (2016), 249–66.
93 E.g., Sonja Drimmer, 'Failure before Print (The Case of Stephen Scrope)', *Viator* 46 (2015), 343–72 (352 n. 42). I am preparing other work that questions the attribution of another manuscript assigned to Ricardus Franciscus, CUL, MS Add. 7870.
94 Martha Driver, 'Women Readers and Pierpont Morgan MS M.126', in *John Gower, Manuscripts, Readers, Contexts*, ed. Malte Urban (Turnhout, 2009), 71–107.

As noted above, Richard Whetehill had access to the king's circle, and possibly the same craftspeople. Additionally, Whetehill's ownership of a manuscript penned by Ricardus not only connects him to his king but a particular group of powerful men: Ricardus made manuscripts for heralds, members of the Order of the Garter, and London guilds, all groups that Whetehill encountered during his time as a merchant, ambassador, and administrator. In particular, Whetehill worked with various members of the Garter, including Richard Neville, John Baron Wenlock, William Hastings, Thomas Montgomery, and Charles the Bold. While Whetehill did not work with John Fastolf, who owned a manuscript copied by Ricardus Franciscus, he knew Fastolf's neighbours, the Pastons. His choice of Ricardus as a scribe illustrates both his English *and* his Continental ties. Ricardus's work reflects both Continental books and books owned by some of Whetehill's colleagues, acquaintances, and superiors. While Ricardus's hand connects University College MS 85 to a broader interest in *lettre bâtarde* manuscripts, it also indicates a more specific moment in time and connection to a particular circle of patrons.

Other aspects of the manuscript's production situate it within a particularly English context, despite its visual allusions to Continental books and its Continental owners. The artists in University College MS 85 contributed to a handful of other manuscripts produced in London in the 1460s and 1470s. Scott links the border artists to thirteen other manuscripts, many of which are associated with London and date to the period of c. 1465-75.[95] One of the border artists in MS 85 appears in three other Middle English manuscripts attributed to Ricardus: the copy of Gower's *Confessio Amantis*, a Middle English *Golden Legend*, and Lydgate's *Fall of Princes*.[96] The artist of the two miniatures in MS 85, the so-called *Quadrilogue* Master, may also have completed the first initial in Ricardus-copied *Fall of Princes*. This evidence connects MS 85 to an English production context, one located particularly in London. At the same time, the inclusion of the Whetehill rebus and 'oublier ne doy' in the borders and miniatures mark this manuscript as a commissioned object: made specifically for the Whetehills, it was always destined to travel across the Channel to Calais. Even in the interconnectedness of its producers, the manuscript nonetheless looks to an

---

95 Scott, *Later Gothic Manuscripts*, cat. 118.
96 Scott, *Later Gothic Manuscripts*, cats 118-20. Morgan M.126; BL, Harley MS 4775; Philadelphia, Rosenbach Museum, MS 439/16.

audience beyond London. It is perhaps just a coincidence – indicative of the overlapping nature of families of a certain rank and an interest in books – that Sir Richard Whetehill's daughter Elizabeth, Richard Whetehill's great-granddaughter, married John St John, a relation of the St Johns of Bletsoe who owned BL Harley 4775, the *Golden Legend* penned by Ricardus and decorated by the same border artist as Oxford, University College, MS 85.[97]

In addition to these aspects of production, the manuscript's texts offer further evidence of its relationship to both a broader literary culture and to a more localised situation. At first glance, the contents of MS 85 – Middle English versions of the *Quadrilogue invectif*, the *Secretum secretorum*, and the *III Consideracions of Princes* – seem typical of an English and Calaisian fifteenth-century reader. Translations from French and advice to princes were usual reading material. Additionally, Chartier's poetry and prose, in French and in English translation, were popular in England and Calais, despite the anti-English sentiment in some poems.[98] Howard's booklist, for example, contains the *Belle dame sans mercy*. More importantly for Whetehill's book, the *Quadrilogue* was translated twice. The other translation survives in four manuscripts, while the version in MS 85 is unique.[99] (Margaret Blayney compares the translations and finds that in University College 85 to be more literal and better versed in French.)[100] The *Secretum secretorum* also had many English readers for its Latin, French, and English versions. In addition to the verse translation attributed to Lydgate and Benedict Burgh, there are at least fifteen different English prose translations.[101] M.A. Manzalaoui

---

97 Davis, 'Whetehill Family of Calais, Part 2', 14; and see the *British Library Catalogue: Archives and Manuscripts* entry for Harley 4775.
98 On Chartier in England, see Julia Boffey, 'The Early Reception of Chartier's Work in England and Scotland', in *Chartier in Europe*, ed. Emma Cayley and Ashby Kinch (Cambridge, UK, 2008), 105–16; Catherine Nall, 'William Worcester Reads Alain Chartier: *Le Quadrilogue invectif* and Its English Readers', in *Chartier in Europe*, ed. Cayley and Kinch, 135–47; and Ashby Kinch, 'Chartier's European Influence', in *A Companion to Alain Chartier: Father of French Eloquence*, ed. Daisy Delogu, Joan E. McRae, and Emma Cayley (Leiden, 2015), 279–302. On the *Belle dame sans mercy* in England, see Olivia Robinson, *Contest, Translation, and the Chaucerian Text* (Turnhout, 2020), 133–74.
99 Blayney, *Fifteenth-Century English Translations*, 2:4–31.
100 Blayney, *Fifteenth-Century English Translations*, 2:46.
101 Manzalaoui, *Nine English Versions*, xlvii, charts the relationship between the English versions and edits nine of them.

links the translation in University College 85 to the abbreviated French text, called 'Version C', the version that Middle English poet Thomas Hoccleve corrected and that English scribe John Shirley used as the base text for his translation.[102] 'Version C' was the most popular of the French versions. However, like the University College 85 translation of the *Quadrilogue*, this Middle English *Secretum* is unique. The *Secretum* translator provides no identifying clues as to their identity, including if they are the same person who translated the *Quadrilogue*. Finally, the *III Consideracions*, which could be the work of a third translator, draws on two popular texts discussed above: Giles of Rome's *De regimine principum* and Vegetius's *De re militari*, both of which circulated in England and Calais in Latin, French, and English. This treatise's didactic content is familiar, representing the kinds of texts popular not just in England and Calais but across Europe in their many translations.

Despite the pan-European aspects of these texts when understood through their genres and textual traditions, their specific instantiations in this manuscript can also be interpreted as separate from this broader literary culture. The translations of the *Quadrilogue* and the *Secretum*, while versions of popular texts, are specifically unique. Further, the textual tradition of the *III Consideracions* makes clear these localised contexts. While it is related to *De regimine principum* and *De re militari*, it translates a lesser-known fourteenth-century tract, made in 1347 either for Valois king Jean II, while he was duke of Normandy, or for Charles de Navarre before he assumed the title; the author reports only that 'un prince de royal noblesse / qui en aage de joennesse' (a royal prince of a young age) requested to learn 'de moy gouverner sagement' (to rule myself wisely).[103] The French version, which includes

102 John Offord copied the version (in French) corrected by Hoccleve. See Schieberle, 'Hoccleve Literary Manuscript', 4, 13–4; Sebastian Sobecki, 'Communities of Practice: Thomas Hoccleve, London Clerks, and Literary Production', *Journal of the Early Book Society* 24 (2021), 51–106 (78).
103 *Four English Political Tracts of the Later Middle Ages*, ed. Jean-Philippe Genet (London, 1977), 210, cf. 177. Both Jean and Charles had literary interests. Jean was aged twenty-eight and quelling rebellious Norman nobles at the time. Charles was just fifteen, but his father had died in 1343, making his future role as king of Navarre more imminent. Either situation could prompt such a tract, although Charles might be better described as 'en aage de joennesse'. Michel-André Bossy, 'Charles d'Orléans and the Wars of the Roses: Yorkist and Tudor Implications of British Library MS Royal 16 F.ii', in *Shaping Courtliness in Medieval France: Essays in Honor of Matilda Tomaryn Bruckner*, ed. Daniel O'Sullivan and

a verse introduction and conclusion omitted in the English, names itself *Grace entière*.[104] The contents of MS 85 reveal a tension between texts understood broadly and in their specific instantiations: while the *Quadrilogue*, the *Secretum*, and the *III Consideracions* all derive from popular genres and traditions, well known to readers across Europe in many languages, their appearances and combination in this manuscript represent a unique slice of reading in Calais. While manuscript survival does not necessarily reflect medieval dissemination, the history of the works places MS 85 both in a European network and a single household's individual experience. Interpreting them from the perspective of their manuscript instantiations, rather than their wider genre, yields a different relationship between MS 85 and books in Calais. Although it fits within the literary interests of Calais, Whetehill's book is nevertheless set apart in the uniqueness of its translations.

The circulation of *Grace entière* in particular hints that the manuscript may have emerged from a narrower context than its general contents suggest. The title appears in the inventories of Charles V and Charles VI, where, despite its short length, it is listed as a separate item covered in yellow silk with silver clasps.[105] It seems possible that this yellow book would have been purchased by John of Lancaster, Duke of Bedford, in 1425 and sent to Rouen in 1429, along with the rest of Charles' library. After Bedford's death in 1435, some of those books crossed the Channel, but others remained on the Continent.[106] Indeed, one of the few books Bedford is known to have given away in his lifetime was an eleven-volume Bible, which he gave to Richard Sellyng as surety for payment

---

Laurie Shepard (Cambridge, UK, 2013), 61–80 (76), assumes that Jean II is the dedicatee. Timothy Hobbs, 'Prosimetrum in *Le livre dit grace entière sur le fait du gouvernement d'un prince*: The *Governance of a Prince* Treatise in British Library MS Royal 16 F.ii', in *Littera et sensus: Essays on Form and Meaning in Medieval French Literature Presented to John Fox*, ed. D.A. Trotter (Exeter, 1989), 49–62, did not know either of the earliest French manuscripts. As far as I am aware, *Grace entière* has not been edited.

104 Genet, *Four English Political Tracts*, 211, 219.
105 *Recherches sur la librairie de Charles V*, ed. Léopold Delisle, 2 vols (Paris, 1907), 2:90, item 528. Delisle finds the book in five of Charles's inventories.
106 *The Bedford Inventories: The Worldly Goods of John, Duke of Bedford, Regent of France*, ed. Jenny Stratford (London, 1993), 96.

of the soldiers' wages in Calais in 1434.[107] Coincidentally, Sellyng's son married a Whetehill daughter, Anne.[108]

The text of *Grace entière* survives in three manuscripts, two of which predate University College 85.[109] Each of these combines the tract with other texts. It is possible that *Grace entière* remained in the region and did not stray far. One of the surviving manuscripts, Rouen, Bib. municipale 1233, seems to have been owned in the region around Rouen from the sixteenth century, if not before. It combines *Grace entière* with particularly Norman contents, including a *Chronique de Normandie*.[110] If the tract was composed for Jean II, rather than Charles de Navarre, it was while he was Duke of Normandy and facing rebellious Norman nobles, perhaps lending the text a Norman context. The most recent manuscript of the French *Grace entière*, BL, Royal MS 16 F.ii, comes from near Calais, but in the areas controlled by the dukes of Burgundy: it was initially designed with Yorkist iconography, possibly for Edward IV, at the instigation of Thomas Thwaytes in the early 1480s. Later, Tudor royal librarian Quentin Poulet, who was Flemish, altered it for Henry VII, employing Flemish artists. Thwaytes's commission links this copy to Edward's bookish administrators in Calais, while Poulet's changes add a Flemish touch.[111] Thwaytes's *Grace entière* and Whetehill's

107 *Bedford Inventories*, ed. Stratford, 93. Stratford assumes that the Bible was destroyed when Balinghem Castle was captured by the Burgundians in 1436.
108 Davis, 'Whetehill of Calais, Part 1', 248–9. It is unclear who Anne's parents were. In Sir Richard Whetehill's will, she is referred to as 'myne Aunt'. John Sellyng was Anne's first husband. Her second was William Muston of Calais.
109 BnF, MS fr. 15352; Rouen, Bib. municipale, MS 1233; and BL, Royal MS 16 F.ii.
110 I have not seen Rouen, Bib. municipale 1233, nor is it digitised, but from Genet's description, the *Chronique*, *Grace entière*, and the *Arbre des batailles* seem to be late fourteenth-century, while two further poems on Normandy have been inserted between the *Chronique* and *Grace entière* (see Genet, *Four English Political Tracts*, 176). The earliest surviving copy of the text, in BnF fr. 15352, where it is combined with the *Établissement de saint Louis* written by a different scribe, dates from the mid-fourteenth century. It was part of the library of Charles de Montchal (1586–1651), archbishop of Toulouse.
111 Janet Backhouse, 'Charles d'Orléans Illuminated', in *Charles of Orléans in England (1415–1440)*, ed. Mary-Jo Arn (Cambridge, UK, 2000), 157–63 (158); Backhouse, 'Henry VII', 176; Bossy, 'Charles d'Orléans', 76. The opening verses read 'lan de septante et trante / tenans quatorze cens de sente' (the year of seventy and thirty following fourteen hundred, i.e., 1500) instead of 'l'an de dix sept et trente / tenans de treize cens la sente' (the year of seventeen and thirty following thirteen hundred, i.e., 1347); Royal 16 F.ii, fol. 210v. On Charles

III Consideracions might have arisen from a shared source. *Grace entière* and its English translation circulated across borders in northern France, Calais, and Flanders. Although the contents of *Grace entière* would have been familiar to readers of *De regimine prinicipum* and *De re militari*, its circulation appears to have followed a particular, and circumscribed, geographic route.

Two other manuscripts contain the *III Consideracions*, although University College 85 is the earliest and best text. While the other two copies of the *III Consideracions* lack certain provenance, their textual combinations also hint at possible connections to the families already associated with Calais. One, Cambridge, Trinity College MS O.5.6, combines the *III Consideracions* with Stephen Scrope's text of the *Dicts and Sayings of the Philosophers* (with William Worcester's corrections), as well as the verse translation of *Sydrac and Boctus*.[112] Although Trinity College O.5.6 is one of several copies of Scrope's *Dicts*, Scrope and Worcester had possible connections to the Whetehills.[113] As part of Fastolf's household, they knew the Pastons, as the Whetehills did, and they would have been familiar with the work of Ricardus Franciscus.[114] These are at least suggestive connections between the *III Consideracions* and Scrope's text. In the other manuscript of the *III Consideracions*, Cambridge, Harvard University, Houghton Library, MS Eng. 530, a single scribe copied the text and Lydgate's *Serpent of Division*. This booklet was then added to a manuscript of texts derived from one of John Shirley's manuscripts.[115] The second scribe in Houghton Eng. 530 copied Lydgate's *Guy of Warwick*, along with the Shirleyan introduction that claims it was made for Margaret, Countess of Shrewsbury.

---

d'Orléans' poems in the manuscript, see Elizaveta Strakhov, 'Opening Pandora's Box: Charles d'Orléans's Reception and the Work of Critical Bibliography', *Papers of the Bibliographical Society of America* 116 (2022), 499–535 (532–5).
112 The beginning of the *III Consideracions* is lacking in this manuscript.
113 On manuscripts of the *Dicts and Sayings*, see The Dicts and Sayings of the Philosophers: *The Translations Made by Stephen Scrope, William Worcester, and an Anonymous Translator*, ed. Curt F. Bühler, EETS, o.s. 211 (London, 1941), xx–xxxii.
114 Scrope's *Epistre Othea* in Cambridge, St John's College, MS H.5 is often said to be in Ricardus's hand, but the hand there bears little resemblance to his other work and is unlikely to be his. However, Scrope would have known BodL Laud Misc. 570, which *is* in Franciscus's hand and is signed with his name.
115 Linne R. Mooney, 'John Shirley's Heirs', *The Yearbook of English Studies* 33 (2003), 182–98 (194–6).

Such Warwick connections are again suggestive in light of Whetehill's service to Richard Neville: Shirley worked for Richard Beauchamp, Richard Neville's father-in-law and the predecessor to his title of earl of Warwick. *Guy of Warwick*, which narrates his ancestor's deeds and was made for Neville's wife's half-sister, would seem not unrelated. While the other two copies of the *III Consideracions* lack direct connections to Whetehill's book, they nevertheless demonstrate certain textual connections that could imply possible connections to Whetehill's friends and superior. The only text in Whetehill's manuscript to survive in more than one copy, the *III Consideracions* demonstrates a narrow circulation, just like its French source.

We have seen that the circulation of the texts in University College MS 85 and their sources point to possible localised distribution patterns. Further attention to MS 85's texts reveals that, although these works would have been known in England, these copies might have been tailored to their audience. All three translations downplay the political valence of their French sources. In the *Quadrilogue*, the Middle English omits many references to France. The personification of France is renamed 'The Land'. The Hundred Years War becomes a general conflict: 'Agincourt', for example, is translated as the 'vnhappy bataill'.[116] Such a translation could allow Chartier's lessons to apply to England as well as France, as Blayney suggests.[117] However, the success of unedited versions of the *Quadrilogue* in England demonstrates that English readers found no hurdle in 'France'.[118] Alternatively, editing out references to France and its fraught relationship with England would also befit an ambassador who frequently wrote to the French king. In fact, MS 85 maintains Chartier's name and employment as 'secretarie somtyme to the Kynge of Fraunce', as well as the prologue's references to the King of England as the 'auncien aduersarie'.[119] The opening illumination, too, features 'The Land' wearing a cloak with fleur-de-lys, obviously marking her as France. While references to France are muted, the manuscript preserves a sheen of its French origins. By contrast, the *Secretum* has fewer comments on

---

116 Blayney, *Fifteenth-Century English Translations*, 1:191, line 30; Blayney, *Fifteenth-Century English Translations*, 1:141, line 6. Here and elsewhere, I have used the edited texts for brief references. For longer quotations, I have turned to the manuscript.
117 Blayney, *Fifteenth-Century English Translations*, 2:47.
118 See Nall, 'Worcester'.
119 University College 85, p. 5.

contemporary politics to be similarly edited. The translator preserves the French prose text's comments on 'the destruccion of the reame of Ingland'.[120] In the *III Consideracions*, the translator removes the opening and closing verses, which date the poem to 1347 and counsel the 'prince de royal noblesse'.[121] Removing the dedicatory poems, the English translator opens up the audience of the *III Consideracions* beyond its singular, royal audience. In general, the *III Consideracions* does not refer to England, but it does praise 'holy kinge Lowes, sometime of Fraunce' and urges princes to 'reede and write frenshe, latyn and othir langage'.[122] In these references, the text, at the very least, nods to France rather than England. As in the *Quadrilogue*, such references preserve a sense of a world beyond England and English without overt reference to a specific political or temporal situation. All the works in the volume conjure a sense of the Continent while maintaining a more neutral tone.

The coherence of this perspective across the manuscript, as well as the shared scribe, importantly raises the question whether all three texts share a translator, and therefore a singular, localised source. Further, if all three were translated together, they might elucidate Whetehill's textual networks. Blayney, Manzalaoui, and Genet do not look across the texts. Reading them together reveals a number of similarities: each translates a French source with a heavily Frenchified vocabulary. French cognates like *puissance*, *sapience*, *semblable*, and *esperance* resonate through each of the translations.[123] Each translation renders its French source in a literal manner. Blayney in particular notes that the translator of the English *Quadrilogue invectif*, 'in his literal renderings [...] frequently did violence to English idiom and sometimes [...] created great awkwardness'.[124] One passage renders Chartier's 'Et ceulx qui le bien de vertu et le salut publique, mesmement aux entreprinses [sic] de guerre, ne veulent plus que le gaing n'y feront ja au paraller oeuvre salvable' (And those who do not wish for the good of virtue and public safety, especially in war, more than gain, will never achieve wholesome work in the end) with the English, 'And they that the well of vertu and the publique saluacion

---

120 Manzalaoui, *Nine English Versions*, 286, line 14. In Shirley's translation of the same French prose version, he extends this passage on England.
121 Genet, *Four English Political Tracts*, 210.
122 Genet, *Four English Political Tracts*, 203–4, 205.
123 E.g., Blayney, *Fifteenth-Century English Translations*, 1:135, lines 14, 19; Genet, *Four English Political Tracts*, 181.
124 Blayney, *Fifteenth-Century English Translations*, 2:46.

namelye in thenterprises of werre, desire nothinge ellys sauf the gettinge of goddes [sic], they shall neuer doo at the longe wey no soluable ne actuell deede.'[125] Here, the English translates 'le bien de vertu' as 'the well of vertu', and 'ja au paraller' as 'at the long wey'. It renders each word but misses the sense of the French. Such literal translations also take place in the other two texts. For example, in the French *Secretum*, Alexander writes to Aristotle that, 'Dotteur de justice et tres noble recteur, nous segnifions a ta grant saigesse que nous auons trouué ou royaume de Persesse plusiers homs lesquelz habondent tres grandement en raison et entendement soubtil et penestratif.' The University College 85 translator renders the same sentence as 'Doctoure of justice and moost noble rectoure, we certifie to thy grete wysdome that we haue founde in the reame of Perse diuers men which ben of habundant wysdome and reson, and of grete and subtile vndirstandinge.'[126] The translator not only follows the sentence structure almost exactly but also turns the French verb 'habondent' into the English adjective 'habundant', thereby maintaining the phonic resonance. Similarly, in the *III Consideracions*, further awkward translations occur. The earliest French manuscript of *Grace entière* reads 'La terce partie dez rentes et reuenues dessus dittes appartenans au roy et au prince doit estre ordonnee a estre mise en garde et en tresor. Car ainsi comme de sens est neccessaire au prince est neccessaire aly auoir habu*n*dance de richesse et de pecune. Et cedit le saige ou liure de ecclesiastes en la bible.'[127] In the *III Consideracions*, this sentence becomes, 'The thrydde partye of the rentys and reuenwes aboue seide appe*r*tenauntes to akinge or prince shulde be ordeyned to be putt in sauf garde and in treaserye of the prince for like as habundaunce of wytte and wisdome is necessarye vnto aprince soo it is necessarye in maner to haue richesse and treasure as wittnessith the wise man in the boke of ecclesiastique.'[128] Once more, the translator follows the French almost word for word at the opening of the chapter, so that the English grammar suffers. The translator too chooses English words – for example, *appertenauntes* and *habundaunce* – that echo the sound of the

---

125 Both the French and the English are from Blayney, *Fifteenth-Century English Translations*, 2:53.
126 Both the French and the English are taken from Manzalaoui, *Nine English Versions*, 260.
127 BnF fr. 15352, fol. 167rv. Cf. Royal 16 F.ii, fols 220v–21r.
128 University College 85, p. 146. I have opted to follow the manuscript here, including the word division, and omitting Genet's clarifying punctuation.

French as closely as possible. In each text in the manuscript, the French original guides English word choice and syntax. Just as the contents of the works create a general sense of referring to France, so too does the approach (or approaches) to translation produce a sense of the French within the Middle English.

Further common features in the translations might stem from their shared scribe, a possible shared exemplar, or even a single translator. Even though translators' prologues were frequent additions to Middle English versions of French texts, none of the texts in University College MS 85 highlight their status as translations, nor make any reference to their translators.[129] This shared lack of interest in marking the translations as translations could be a compiler's decision. Additionally, both Richard Hamer and Martha Driver agree that Ricardus Franciscus was an accurate copyist, who followed his exemplars faithfully.[130] Features of orthography, therefore, might reflect the habits of the translator or translators, rather than scribal idiolect. Hamer analyses the *Quadrilogue* and the *Secretum* and concludes that 'the spellings of these texts are so similar that they may well have been copied from the same exemplar'.[131] Adding the *III Consideracions* to this comparison reveals that all three texts share the same spellings of various words, for example *peas, enmyes, sugite, ceason, peeple, habundance,* and *habundant*.[132] However, there are certain differences in spelling and vocabulary: the *Quadrilogue* and the *Secretum* both favour third-person singular *be* and plural *ben*, while the *III Consideracions* seems to use *is* more frequently. Both the *Quadrilogue* and the *III Consideracions* most often use the French loanword *sage*, while the *Secretum* favours Germanic *wyse*. Blayney notes that there are a handful of Northern forms in the *Quadrilogue*,

129 On translators' prologues, see Elizabeth Dearnley, *Translators and Their Prologues in Medieval England* (Cambridge, UK, 2016).
130 Martha Driver, 'More Light on Ricardus Franciscus: Looking Again at Morgan M. 126', *South Atlantic Review* 79 (2014), 20–35 (23–9); Richard Hamer, 'Spellings of the Fifteenth-Century Scribe Ricardus Franciscus', in *Five Hundred Years of Words and Sounds: A Festschrift for Eric Dobson*, ed. E.G. Stanley and Douglas Gray (Cambridge, UK, 1983), 63–73.
131 Hamer, 'Spellings', 72.
132 E.g., Blayney, *Fifteenth-Century English Translations*, 1:143, lines 13, 18, 22; 177, line 8; 195, line 31; 197, line 21; Manzalaoui, *Nine English Versions*, 252, line 6; 260, line 4; 304, line 6; 322, line 12; 328, line 4; 344, line 25; Genet, *Four English Political Tracts*, 184, 185, 186, 187, 190.

but these are not evident in the other two texts.[133] Additionally, despite Ricardus's reputation for accuracy, all three texts contain obvious errors, such as 'tkinke' for 'thinke', 'diease' for 'disease', 'bubgit' for 'subgit', and 'rowe' for 'growe'.[134] Sometimes a word such as *and* is copied twice, or word order is confused.[135] These errors could point to a shared, sloppy exemplar. While it is possible that the three texts stem from a common exemplar, or even a common translator, they also demonstrate certain differences that are not currently explainable. At the very least, their similar vocabulary and literal translation habits provide a coherence that might at least indicate a shared translation milieu. Circumstances, too, seem suggestive. Because Calais was a centre a text making, someone in Calais could have translated the texts, perhaps even Whetehill himself.

Examining the copying, circulation, content, and language of the texts and sources of University College MS 85 demonstrates a sense of specificity and tailoring. As well as connecting Whetehill to a broad, pan-European literary culture, MS 85 also indicates Whetehill's links to regional networks. The manuscript and its texts situate its reader (or readers) within an international yet localised textual community.

Reading between Languages

The language of University College MS 85 raises further questions about this manuscript's place in the idea of a pan-European literary culture. Whetehill must have been at least bilingual because he worked in French and English in his daily life. Given the popularity, legibility, and availability of French texts in Calais, why would Whetehill order a collection of Middle English texts? These translations take few liberties, maintaining a feeling of the French language, even as they are in Middle English. Significantly, as mentioned above, none of the texts notes its status a translation: any acknowledgement of the transmission from one language to another occurs implicitly and is deemphasised through decorative, linguistic, and textual choices. Here, translation feels superfluous: it is necessary neither to comprehension, nor to present reformed

---

133 Blayney, *Fifteenth-Century English Translations*, 2:34–5. Neither Manzalaoui nor Genet comment on dialect. If there are Northern forms in these texts, I have not recognised them.
134 University College 85, pp. 24, 25, 76, 144.
135 University College 85, pp. 85, 143.

texts with particularly English perspectives. Indeed, the manuscript gestures at French and at Continental books, even within its Middle English text and English production connections. The pervasive mottos and scribal sayings throughout add hints of multilingualism that disrupt any monolingual fabric. In its layered languages, translations, producers, and authors, MS 85 prompts the question of how English fits into the Whetehill household.

The Whetehills' other books – not considered in previous discussions of University College MS 85 – illuminate their multilingual textual world. Richard's will does not survive, and Adrian's does not mention any books. However, the will of Adrian's wife Margaret (d. 1505) mentions a primer and the 'book that was Richard Gurneys'.[136] Her daughter-in-law Elizabeth (d. 1542), wife of Sir Richard, bequeathed two primers and the 'boke […] that Lee gave me'.[137] These unnamed, gifted books could have been in several languages. Instead of content and language, these descriptions emphasise the Whetehills' connections to a Calais reading circle beyond their family. Even as the gifted books are passed on to new owners, they maintain their connection to the original giver. They suggest the local, personal exchange of books. Additionally, Richard and Adrian left behind at least fifteen account books for Calais and Guînes, covering the period from September 1460 to August 1492.[138] These would eventually have been sent back to England to the Exchequer, but were accumulated as booklets over a number of years, possibly in Calais. While not personal items, nor literary material, the account books nonetheless contributed to the Whetehills' life in words. These accounts – ranging from a single folio to a collection of booklets of nearly one hundred folios – are almost entirely in Latin and written in a variety of hands in several scripts. These documents provide evidence for the Whetehills' facility with Latin and the possibility that they could have read their *Secretum secretorum* or the *III Consideracions*' sources in yet another language. In the accounts from the 1460s and 1470s, openings that use decorated headings in bastard secretary hands, sometimes with elaborate strapwork, recall Ricardus's work in University College MS 85. The appearance of this script in

---

136 TNA, PROB 11/14/883.
137 TNA, PROB 11/29/449.
138 TNA, E 101/195/13, E 101/196/2, E 101/196/8, E 101/196/9, E 101/196/20, E 101/198/1, E 101/198/10, E 101/198/15, E 101/199/1, E 101/199/7, E 101/199/8, E 101/199/12, E 101/199/14, E 101/200/1, E 101/200/18.

the Whetehills' working lives might indicate that MS 85's script would have felt quotidian and familiar, rather than foreign or unusual. MS 85 might have looked like a Continental book *and* like the kind of English business item that the Whetehills used regularly. Further, the account from March 1461 to March 1463 contains an *ex libris* that notes that it is 'infrascriptus Ric*ard*us Whetehill p*er* manus suas'.[139] Whetehill writes in a legible secretary hand, demonstrating his own knowledge of both writing and the process of compiling folios. This account is bound in a limp parchment skin held together by simple parchment tackets, the kind of binding that would be done at home. Other books are penned by different scribes: for example, John Warderoper, who copied part of the accounts from 1472 to 1474, writes in anglicana and furnishes his initials with strapwork.[140] Other accounts contain trained secretary hands.[141] While University College 85 is in the hand of a London-based scribe, the Whetehills apparently also had trained multilingual scribes at their disposal closer to home and were themselves capable of producing books, judging from the account books.

In addition to these documents and references to books in wills, a second surviving literary manuscript belonged to the Whetehills. This manuscript, BnF, MS fr. 328, has not previously been linked to the Whetehills, or even to an English owner. It contains the same emblem of a hill holding a sheaf of wheat that is found in University College MS 85. If we accept that these hills are a rebus for Whetehill, then this second book should be considered as coming from the same family. It contains a copy of a universal chronicle called the *Livre des histoires du miroer du monde* (not to be confused with any of the other different medieval texts of similar names) and has space for at least seventy-one wheat hills in its border decoration, almost one on every other folio.[142]

---

139 TNA, E 101/196/2, fol. 36v. The *ex libris* is written in anglicana, in a hand that is different from the hand that writes secretary script throughout the manuscript; it is not Richard's hand if the secretary hand is indeed Richard's, as I have assumed; 'infrascriptus' would translate as 'written below', but here probably refers to 'further on' in the manuscript.
140 TNA, E 101/196/1. Warderoper is named in the *ex libris* on fol. 35v. This book has more than one hand at work.
141 TNA, E 101/195/13, E 101/196/9.
142 This counts the wheat hills that are complete, that are sketched, and that are outlined by a border. The border artist stopped sketching at BnF, MS fr. 328, fol. 64r, so there could have been even more spaces for wheat hills between fol. 64 and the manuscript's end at fol. 100v.

BOOKS, TRANSLATION, AND MULTILINGUALISM

When complete, the *Miroer* should run from Adam and Eve to the birth of Christ, but this copy ends with the life of the Roman emperor Cincinnatus. The manuscript is only half decorated, but even in its unfinished state, it represents a more lavish expenditure than its Middle English companion. There are fifty-two extant miniatures with full page borders, and 121 unfinished grounds or blank spaces.[143] The artists enacted at least one time-saving – and therefore cost-saving – measure: they traced the same border design through each folio, creating mirror images on recto and verso. In so doing, they maintained a high level of decoration without inventing new designs for each of the many borders. The manuscript could have been ordered by the Whetehills themselves or produced for them as a gift.

The design of the borders not only indicates the prospective owner but also provides a possible date. On at least four folios, the main artist has incorporated a ragged staff into the border design to the right of the wheat hill (see Fig. 7.4).[144] These folios depict the stories of Abraham and Isaac, Jason and Hercules, and the Trojan War. A ragged staff, held by a bear, was normally associated with the earls of Warwick. Notably, Philippe de Commynes, the memoirist and diplomat, commented that during his visit to Calais in 1471, he was surprised to find the men in the garrison wearing ragged staffs on their hats along with Neville's livery.[145] Neville's own manuscript of the *Enseignment de vraie noblesse* includes a bear and ragged staff on the first folio.[146] The use of the ragged staff, without the bear, in the border decoration might reflect Whetehill's close affiliation with the earl. After Neville's death in 1471 at the Battle of Barnet, where he fought against Edward IV's army, Whetehill's former alliance with Edward's opponent would not have been something to celebrate in the wake of his defeat. Whetehill himself maintained his command of Guînes despite his former loyalty. It is likely, then, that the

---

143 It seems that the figures in the border and the vine designs are the work of different artists, as some grotesques have been left blank even on folios where the vines and flowers are fully painted.
144 BnF fr. 328, fols 8r, 19r, 40rv.
145 Philippe de Commynes, *Mémoires*, ed. Émilie Dupont, 3 vols (Paris, 1840–7), 1:253–4, 'et [Wanelock, i.e., John Wanlock, Neville's deputy] avoit le ravestre d'or sur son bonnet [...] et tous les aultres semblablement; et qui ne le povoit avoir d'or, l'avoit de drap'. Commynes also narrates Wanlock's disloyalty towards Neville; when Neville sought refuge at Calais also in 1471, Wanlock refused him entry. Commynes, *Mémoires*, 1:236–7.
146 Geneva, Bib. Publique et universitaire, MS fr. 166, fol. 3r.

Figure 7.4 A page from *Le Livre des histoires du miroer du monde* with wheat hill design accompanied by a ragged staff. Paris, BnF, MS fr. 328, fol. 8r. Source: <gallica.bnf.fr>/BnF. Reproduced with permission from the Bibliothèque nationale de France.

Miroer predates Neville's death, which occurred about the same date as that given to University College MS 85. The events of the War of the Roses and Whetehill's potentially precarious position might explain the *Miroer*'s unfinished state. In its decoration, the manuscript indicates personal loyalties and a particular period.

Unlike University College MS 85, this *Miroer* manuscript was made on the Continent. Its exact origin, however, is unclear: François Avril attributes the illumination in the manuscript to Paris, while Christiane Raynaud counts it among Burgundian manuscripts of Alexander the Great whose owners are unknown.[147] Its decorative styles are similar to those found in northern French and Flemish manuscripts, and it seems more likely to have been produced close to the Whetehills' home than in Paris.[148] The manuscript was owned in the sixteenth or seventeenth century by Philippe de Béthune (1565–1649), a French diplomat who spent much of his life in Normandy not far from Calais.[149] Philippe's arms are stamped in gold on the current binding. After the death of Charles the Bold in 1477 and into the sixteenth century, France, the Holy Roman Empire, and then Habsburg Spain jockeyed for control of the areas around Calais – and then Calais itself.[150] This later Norman provenance suggests that the book reached the Whetehills' hands, and

---

147 François Avril, *Fichier des manuscrits enluminés du département des manuscrits*, BnF, MS NAF 28635 (4), p. 221, sourced from <https://gallica.bnf.fr/ark:/12148/btv1b10000507p/f360> but currently unavailable; Christiane Raynaud, 'Alexandre dans les bibliothèques bourguignonnes', in *Alexandre le Grand dans les littératures occidentales et proche-orientales: Actes du Colloque de Paris, 27–29 novembre 1997*, ed. Laurence Harf-Lancner, Claire Kappler, and François Suard (Nanterre, 1999), 187–214 (192 n. 20).

148 The manuscript is similar in design to BodL, MS Douce 336–7, which was produced in Normandy, and contains similar initials painted in a highly realistic style. Similar decorated initials appear in some of Edward IV's manuscripts from Flanders, such as BL, Royal MS 17 E V and BL, Royal MS 18 E V. Similar borders appear in Geneva, Bibliothèque de Genève, MS fr. 85, although the miniatures there, by Simon Marmion, are of higher quality. I am grateful to Maggie Crosland for discussing the manuscript's illuminations with me.

149 Béthune is a mere seventy-five miles from Guînes, and seventy-eight miles from Calais.

150 For overviews of this history, see Chevalier, 'Recovery of France', 408–30 and Bertrand Schnerb, 'Burgundy', in *The New Cambridge Medieval History, c. 1415–c. 1500*, ed. Allmand, 7:431–56; Robert Stein, *Magnanimous Dukes and Rising States: The Unification of the Burgundian Netherlands, 1380–1480* (Oxford, 2017), 262–4.

that even after Richard and Adrian returned to England with their spouses in their old age, the book remained on the southern side of the Channel even as that region experienced shifting political control. Henry II's eventual reconquest of Calais may have caused the book to fall into French hands. No books in any of the surviving Whetehill wills match the *Miroer* manuscript's content and appearance.

While the general content of the *Miroer* is relatively familiar, this particular text – like Whetehill's three Middle English texts – had a relatively limited circulation. Six extant manuscripts and seven surviving incunables printed in Lyon in 1479 transmit the *Miroer*.[151] Of the manuscript witnesses, most can be linked to people in northern France and the Loire from a patchwork of duchies: for example, Anne Salamon has argued that the earliest manuscript of the *Miroer*, BodL, MS Douce 336–7, was made for Jeanne Paynel and Louis d'Estouteville in the 1450s. D'Estouteville (d. 1464) was a Norman noble and commander of Mont Saint-Michel, who sometimes engaged in diplomatic negotiations. [152] Piotr Tylus argues that the *Miroer* in BnF fr. 328 is textually closest to BnF, MS fr. 9686, which contains no original arms but belonged to the translator and ambassador Jacques Gohory in the sixteenth century, and to Kraków, Staatsbibliothek zu Berlin, Preussischer Kulturbesitz, Biblioteka Jagiellonska, Gall. F° 0129, which contains the arms of Charlotte de Beauvau, wife of the fifteenth-century diplomat Yves de Scépeaux.[153] Two other *Miroer* manuscripts have connections to the Loire: one contains an explicit that dates its copying to 1482 in Angers,

---

151 Almost all the following information is taken from *H(istoires) U(niverselles) en français au XVe siècle*, ed. Anne Salamon et al., Conseil de Recherches en Sciences Humaines du Canada, 2014–23 <http://hu15.github.io/histoires-universelles-xv/index.html>. I am grateful to Anne Salamon for discussing these manuscripts with me. See also Anne Salamon, 'Writing University History in the Fifteenth Century: Introducing H(istoires) U(niverselles) 15', *The Values of French*, 10 March 2021 <https://tvof.ac.uk/blog/writing-universal-history-in-the-fifteenth-century-introducing-histoires-universelles-15>.
152 The manuscript source for the printed editions is unclear, but since they postdate Whetehill's copy, they are less important here.
153 Piotr Tylus, 'Un nouveau manuscrit d'un *Miroir du monde*', *Romance Philology* 58 (2004), 99–107 (104–6); Raphaëlle Décloître and Anne Salamon, 'Description: Berlin en dépôt à Krakow, Staatsbibliothek zu Berlin – Preussischer Kulturbesitz, Biblioteka Jagiellonska (Bibliothèque Jagellone), Gall. f° 0129', *H(istoires) U(niverselles) en français au XVe siècle* <http://hu15.github.io/histoires-universelles-xv/content/miroir-du-monde/BJ-gall-f-0129/fiche-jag-gall-129.html>.

while the other was owned by Marguerite de Rohan, wife of Jean d'Angoulême, brother of Charles d'Orléans and former English prisoner of war.[154] Collectively, these manuscripts demonstrate a geographically localised circulation in northern and western France in the second half of the fifteenth century, even though a series of dukes, counts, and kings variously controlled these regions. That several of these people had diplomatic connections might have facilitated the movement of the text across France's internal borders. The *Miroer* was also a text particularly owned by noblewomen, and perhaps transmitted through their marriages. It is possible that the Whetehill rebus refers to any of the Whetehill women, rather than to Richard or Adrian. Like *Grace entière*, the *Miroer* had a localised audience to which the Whetehills had political and geographic proximity. There is no further evidence of English interest in the *Miroer*, even though English readers sought out other universal and local chronicles in French from Normandy and Flanders.[155] That an English bureaucratic family tapped into an interconnected, local, French textual culture demonstrates a close link between such multilingual administrators and their Continental neighbours. Further, BnF MS fr. 328 suggests that the Whetehills may have looked to France rather than England in developing their distinct, literary tastes.

This French manuscript owned by the Whetehills reflects not the broad exchange of books between England and the Continent but the circulation of a single text among readers in one region. The Whetehills participated in a local form of transnational exchange, conditioned by geographic proximity or diplomatic duties such as Richard's translation of diplomatic letters discussed above. Further, MS fr. 382's French language confirms that Richard Whetehill not only owned and read French literature but also that he had links to Francophone literary networks. Taken together, the Whetehills' two main manuscripts connect distinct networks of circulation that move across languages and borders. The Middle English texts of University College MS 85, then, are unlikely to represent a need to access popular texts in English. Rather,

154 Chantilly, Bib. du Château Musée Condé, MS 0723; BnF, MS fr. 684.
155 E.g., Edward IV's *Fleur des histoires*, BL, Royal MS 18 E.vi. Various manuscripts of the chronicles of Normandy had English owners, e.g., BL, Harley MS 1717, a *Chroniques de Normandie* with fifteenth-century Latin and Middle English additions, or Cotton Nero E.iii, the *Anciennes chroniques de Flandres* owned by the Talbots and Staffords, or the chronicle 'Sir Baudin côte de Flandres' in Howard's booklist, both mentioned above. England had its own tradition of universal chronicles, such as Nicholas Trevet's *Les cronicles*.

the Middle English may reveal a desire for particular interpretations offered through each of the translations. Translating offers an opportunity for adaptation, one that more clearly situates originally French texts within an Anglo-French milieu. It creates connections, too, among three texts that might otherwise seem only loosely related as advice for princes: Middle English becomes the compiler's affirmation that the three separate texts fit with each other and that they are aimed at an English audience. While each of the Middle English texts participates in a larger textual tradition popular among Calais inhabitants, Englishmen and Europeans alike, they are also unique productions that deviate in their particularities. English as English, as a language different from French, both does and does not matter. Other critics have interpreted translation as a method for textual adaptation, one that promotes intertextual and multilingual reading.[156] This manuscript, which does not hide its French affiliations, nests English within a multilingual context, implying connection, closeness, and exchange rather than cultural hierarchy, replacement, or antagonism. Translation in these manuscript contexts is not a mode of asserting English monolingualism but rather a form of celebrating English multilingualism. The Whetehills' book collection incorporates English into a Francophone sphere; here, English and French are not just adjacent, but overlapping. The new light on the historical and cultural context of University College MS 85 reveals English's role in the Whetehill household. Read within this multilingual context, the manuscript's monolingualism loses its strict boundaries. The manuscript's texts, appearance, and movements mimic Whetehill's own positions as translator, scribe, and diplomat.

Taken collectively, Oxford, University College MS 85, BnF MS fr. 328, the Whetehill account books, and the references to books in the Whetehill women's wills paint a picture of a multilingual, dynamic household involved in literary and documentary culture. However, the Whetehills' texts point to personal connections, whether with individuals who gifted unnamed books, or with diplomatic colleagues who might provide access to lesser-known texts. Even from the small number of extant items, it is clear that the Whetehills were connected to a larger culture of the written word. While it would be easy to describe their books in terms of pan-European tastes for popular titles, closer attention reveals the mechanisms and networks that underpin such taste. I began

---

156 Warren, 'Translation', 51–67; Nall, *Reading and War*, 5–7; Batt, 'Translation and Society', 123–39.

by narrating how the translator of the *Secretum secretorum* presents an edited version of the text's languages and history: such complex textual histories are reflected in the histories of extant manuscripts.

Attending to the varying circulation of genres, texts, textual traditions, and languages yields shifting patterns of connection and alliance. From one perspective, University College MS 85 might look unremarkable, even shabby, taken alongside the illuminated, Flemish manuscripts of French texts owned by Whetehill's superiors. Its English might even seem like a poor imitation of an inaccessible French culture. Yet, focusing on the Whetehills, the sources of their texts, their scribes, and their decorators reveals a different interpretation, one that connects the Whetehills both to the familiar names associated with book ownership in Calais and to previously unrecognised French sources. Shifting between connections in France and England and French and English sources, the Whetehills participated in a pan-European literary culture, but one that was shaped by their location and personal connections.

Printed in the United States
by Baker & Taylor Publisher Services